TOM CARROLL

COLT'S CRISIS

Book one of the COLT GARRETT series

FoR MARIA,
I hope you enjoyed
Reading This copy of "crisis"
as much as I did writing it.

Tom Carroll

ISBN: 978-1-947863-10-1 (Paperback edition)
ISBN: 978-1-947863-11-8 (Kindle edition)

Library of Congress Control Number: 2020949629

This is a work of fiction. Names, characters, dialogue, places, incidents and opinions expressed are the product of the author's imagination or are used fictitiously, and any resemblance to actual persons, living or dead, business establishments, events, or locales is entirely coincidental, and not to be construed as real. Nothing is intended or should be interpreted as expressing the views of the U.S. Navy or any other department or agency of any government body.

Cover art and design by bookcoverart.com

The appearance of U.S. Department of Defense (DoD) visual information does not imply or constitute DoD endorsement. The United States Department of Defense's Prepublication & Security Review cleared this manuscript for public release on Oct. 26, 2020.

Printed and bound in the United States of America.
First printing November 2020.

Published by Kirby Publishing, LLC
Lacey, WA 98503

Visit www.tomcarrollbooks.com for more information

For Laurie, Amanda and Sean,
and for all the men and women
who have stood watch on a ship at sea

Why is America lucky enough to have such men? They leave this tiny ship and fly against the enemy. Then they must seek the ship, lost somewhere on the sea. And when they find it, they have to land upon its pitching deck. Where did we get such men?

James Michener, The Bridges of Toko-Ri

Day One

Arlington National Cemetery, Arlington, Virginia

Large, shapeless patches of snow lingered on the grass and headstones as the sun cast its light over the sacred ground. The combination of a brisk wind and freezing temperatures that had kept the tourists away now gave the cemetery a haunting yet solemn air.

The old man's knees cracked as he slowly rose after setting down a bouquet of flowers at the base of the Space Shuttle *Challenger* Memorial. Marking the commingled and partial remains of the seven astronauts who had died aboard the *Challenger* in January of 1986, the memorial honored Captain Michael Smith of the U.S. Navy, Lieutenant Colonel Francis Scobee and Lieutenant Colonel Ellison Onizuka of the U.S. Air Force, astronaut and electrical engineer Dr. Judith Resnik, payload specialist Gregory Jarvis, physicist Dr. Ronald McNair, and high school social studies teacher Sharon Christa McAuliffe.

The weathered and white-haired man looked at the seven faces depicted on the memorial and wondered how many years would pass before they were as forgotten as the over 400,000 other heroes interred at Arlington. He raised his right arm and saluted the seven victims as he had been taught to do so many years before at Annapolis. He paused to read the poem by Royal Canadian Air Force fighter pilot John Gillespie Magee, Jr. engraved on the back of the memorial.

It read:

High Flight

Oh! I have slipped the surly bonds of Earth
And danced the skies on laughter-silvered wings;
Sunward I've climbed, and joined the tumbling mirth
Of sun-split clouds, — and done a hundred things

You have not dreamed of — wheeled and soared and swung
High in the sunlit silence. Hov'ring there,
I've chased the shouting wind along, and flung
My eager craft through footless halls of air...

Up, up the long, delirious burning blue
I've topped the wind-swept heights with easy grace
Where never lark, or ever eagle flew —
And, while with silent, lifting mind I've trod

The high untrespassed sanctity of space,
Put out my hand, and touched the face of God.

As he turned from the *Challenger* memorial, the man reflected back on his own career, from naval aviator to test pilot and eventually, NASA astronaut. Most people would have considered that a sufficient level of achievement in one life, but ambition, ego, and a hunger to do more had led him to the U.S. House of Representatives, the U.S. Senate, and finally, to his appointment as the twenty-eighth U.S. secretary of defense, or more commonly, SECDEF. His predecessors were some of the most recognized names in government, starting with James Forrestal in 1947 and including

Robert McNamara, Melvin Laird, James Schlesinger, Donald
Rumsfeld, Caspar Weinberger, Dick Cheney, Robert Gates, Leon
Panetta, Ash Carter, and James Mattis. It's a fairly impressive and
exclusive club which now included him, Patrick O'Kane.

Yet over the last few years, his accomplishments had begun to
seem more like just a list of jobs, and Pat found that his memories
were focused more on departed family and friends than on medals,
honors, and accolades. His wife had died more than ten years ago
from a form of cancer that most people had never heard of and
doctors were unable to treat. He missed his wife deeply, and now, as
he approached eighty years of age, he wondered when his own time
would come. At last, he arrived at her gravestone. It had been a day
as cold as this when she was laid to rest, and tears soon formed in his
eyes as he knelt to place the flowers he had so carefully cut from the
garden she herself had artfully planted in their greenhouse more than
a decade ago.

Chief Warrant Officer and Supervisory Special Agent Glenn
Carpenter watched O'Kane from a respectful distance. Carpenter
was an experienced officer of the U.S. Army Protective Services
Battalion, the unit within the Army's Criminal Investigation Division
which was responsible for the protection of SECDEF, the Army
Chief of Staff, and other senior civilian and military officials of
the DOD. He and his detail of five special agents were tasked with
the 24/7 protection of the defense secretary, and they took their jobs
seriously. Dressed in dark business suits and sporting the stereotypical
sunglasses and earphone radios, most people assumed they were
agents of the U.S. Secret Service.

Carpenter saw O'Kane kneel at his wife's grave, first with concern
as the frail-looking man touched his chest and cried out audibly,
but then with horror as O'Kane suddenly fell to the snow-covered
earth. Carpenter drew his Sig Sauer 9mm pistol as he sprinted to
reach the secretary. After checking for a pulse, he shouted into his

radio microphone, "This is WHISKEY ONE. LEATHERNECK is down! I say again, LEATHERNECK is down!"

Delta Airlines Flight 167 - Seattle to Tokyo

Another flight.

Another long, crowded, intercontinental flight.

The Airbus A350 didn't seem to be moving at all, even as it soared 36,000 feet above the earth. After decades of flying, Colt Garrett still marveled at the convergence of forces and technology that enabled an object this large to defy gravity and deliver hundreds of people across an ocean. And meanwhile, Colt figured, most passengers were probably more concerned with the movie selection than with the mysterious wonders of powered flight.

Colt switched on the entertainment screen in his business class enclosure to track the flight as it cruised along the great circle route, from Seattle heading northwest across the Gulf of Alaska near Kodiak, continuing west and then southwest along the Aleutians and Russia's Kamchatka Peninsula, then further southwest along the Kuril Islands and finally over the Japanese Islands. He found it interesting that a straight line between two points on the earth's surface was depicted as a curve on some types of charts — one of his many idiosyncrasies as a retired naval officer was his insistence on not calling them maps. In a little more than ten hours, he'd be in Tokyo.

Flying had been part of Colt's work-life since graduating from college. First, he served as an officer in the U.S. Navy, then worked for a big six technology consulting firm, then ran his own management consulting practice for several years. He used to enjoy travel, particularly air travel. But since 9/11 and

5

the resulting enhancements to air travel security, he no longer enjoyed the airline experience, which now seemed to be more similar to taking a long-distance bus ride. Now he was serving as undersecretary for policy at the U.S. Department of Defense, developing defense strategies which eventually were distilled down into policy recommendations for the secretary of defense and ultimately, the president of the United States. Although the job had its challenges, including long hours, lofty demands from legislative oversight committees, the relentless press, the job matched his skills, and he excelled at it. He was at his best when trying to sift through vast amounts of mundane information to find the true essence of a problem, a skill that had brought him success no matter his position in an organization.

This flight from Seattle to Tokyo was the last leg in a long journey from the Pentagon in D.C. to the operating forces of the U.S. 7th Fleet, homeported in Yokosuka, Japan. Colt was on a fact-finding mission to observe the Navy's level of capability in the Sea of Japan, as tensions between North Korea and the U.S. continued to escalate. He wanted to see first-hand how DOD policy was being carried out by U.S. naval and air forces in the Pacific theater.

This trip was also allowing him to deal with some personal issues. His wife, Linda, was still living in their home in Olympia, the Washington state capitol, so Colt added a two-day layover so he could visit her and attempt to repair their marriage.

Thirty years ago, locals would have said that Olympia was an hour south of Seattle, but today, with increasing traffic and the growth of Joint Base Lewis McChord near Tacoma, the halfway mark, the Seattle-to-Olympia commute could sometimes take up to three hours. Olympia was nestled at the southernmost end of Puget Sound, the second largest estuary in the U.S. Formerly the home of the famed Olympia Brewing Company

("It's the Water"), state government agencies and a handful of colleges and hospitals now provided most of the employment opportunities in the surrounding areas of Thurston county.

Colt had been a geographic bachelor ever since accepting the president's appointment as defense undersecretary, more than three years ago. Although it meant relocating to the other Washington, Linda had declined to move with him. She didn't think it was fair of Colt to ask her to leave her home, close friends, and family, all so he could chase his dream of "making a difference," and their relationship had suffered ever since. Now, on the short side trip to Olympia, Colt had reconnected with Linda, and they had rekindled the deep affection they had cultivated from more than thirty years of marriage. Sadly, when it came time for Linda to drive Colt to the Seattle airport, their old frustrations managed to surface, and their goodbyes were emotional yet guarded.

Their son, Dan, had sided with his mother, of course. The two had always been close, but even more so after Dan was commissioned as an ensign in the Navy and then, later, earned his Wings of Gold as a naval aviator, proudly following in the footsteps of Linda's father. Afterward, wanting to be based close to home, Dan had asked to fly the EA-18G Growler electronic warfare aircraft in a squadron based at Naval Air Station Whidbey Island in Washington State. The squadron was currently embarked on USS *Ronald Reagan*, a *Nimitz*-class supercarrier, forward-deployed to the western Pacific. Colt hoped this trip would also allow him to visit the *Reagan* and see his son.

When the flight attendant began handing out dinner menus, Colt glanced quickly at the interesting looking woman seated next to him. Actually, near him was more accurate. The Airbus 350-900 business class section was laid out in a 1-2-1 configuration in a herringbone pattern. Colt was seated in the left-hand seat of the two center seats. Leaning over to offer a menu, the flight attendant introduced herself as Ashley, making Colt wonder if that was her real name or her "flight" name. Some of his airline pilot friends had shared with him the growing practice of flight attendants using made-up names to protect themselves from the unwanted advances of inebriated passengers.

"Mr. Garrett?" Ashley asked. "Would you like something to drink?"

"Yes," Colt replied. "I'll have a Heritage BSB, neat. And the sirloin tip dinner if you have any left."

After taking Colt's order, Ashley turned to the passenger near him.

"And Commander, what would you like this evening?"

During the boarding process, Colt had noticed that the confident-looking woman had a black, satchel-type Pelican case, about five inches thick, with two padlocks, shackled to her seat support. He momentarily flashed back to an experience many years ago involving a shackled briefcase, a memory he preferred to forget.

After the flight attendant moved on to the next aisle, Colt turned to his neighbor and offered his hand.

"Hmm, a navy commander with a courier case. You must be pretty important!"

The woman looked back at him, squarely in the eye. "You're looking pretty important yourself!" she teased, and they both laughed. Now, Colt had the opportunity to look closely at the woman for the first time. She appeared to be about forty years old, which made sense for a navy commander. She was casually dressed in dark jeans and a royal blue silk blouse, with a striking-looking solitaire diamond necklace, but no wedding ring. "I'm

Jennifer Abrams," she said. "But people call me Jen."

"I'm Colton Garrett, but people call me Colt."

"So, Colt, what do you do when you're not flying across the Pacific?"

"Well, I'm what most people call a policy wonk."

"How does one become a policy wonk?" she asked with a grin. "Is there a school for that?"

"Kind of," he replied. "I studied at the Jackson School at the University of Washington. Based my doctoral dissertation on Hobson's Choice and how that concept is so often reflected in international relations."

Jen's eyes narrowed in playful focus. "I think I've heard of that. Doesn't it have something to do with the illusion of choice, being forced to pick between two bad options?"

"Almost. What you just described is technically a dilemma. The concept of Hobson's Choice is deciding between something and nothing at all. It's supposedly based on a story about Thomas Hobson, who owned a horse stable in Cambridge. Students at Cambridge University would rent his horses, often selecting his best horses and then mistreating them. To prevent his best animals from constantly being abused, he created a rule that students could take any horse they wanted, as long as it was the horse next to the stable door. Take it or leave it."

"And you received a Ph.D. for that?" Jen kidded.

Colt noticed and liked how her eyes seemed to sparkle when she spoke.

"Not exactly," he replied. "My research focused on negotiations between nations when one side holds all the cards, leaving the other party with only two options: accept the offer or walk away. No further negotiation; take it or leave it."

Jen thought for a moment, then asked, "So the concept of unconditional surrender used during World War II is an example of Hobson's Choice?"

"Exactly, although in war it typically means both sides still agree to abide by international law. Ulysses S. Grant was the first to use the unconditional surrender concept during the confederate surrender of Fort Donaldson in the Civil War."

Jen nodded, and Colt watched as she put on her noise-canceling headphones and picked up her paperback — the international signs that a conversation is over. Colt had lots of experience with this particular type of non-verbal communication. *Such is the burden of a policy wonk,* he thought.

After dinner was served and eaten, the flight attendants began the evening ritual of morphing the business class section into a flying Pullman sleeping car, helping passengers push the correct buttons to convert their upright seats into flat beds. Colt and Jen both used the bathrooms to change into sleeping clothes, and then the cabin lights were dimmed to allow passengers the luxury of sleeping their way across the Pacific.

Six hours later, Colt abruptly woke from an old recurring dream involving a shackled courier case. His heart was racing, and his pajama top was wet with perspiration. He hadn't had the dream for quite some time, and he thought he was through with them. But seeing Jen's courier case must have brought back memories of that terrible day many years earlier. Colt was concerned he might have cried out during the dream, as his wife told him he had done frequently. He decided to use the restroom to freshen up and then get a cup of herbal tea before attempting to return to sleep. He was standing by the mid-cabin galley when flight attendant Ashley noticed him leaning against the plane's bulkhead.

"Trouble sleeping?" she asked sympathetically.

"Yep, it's one of the benefits of getting old. You can't possibly sleep your life away!"

"Who says you're getting old?" she argued.

Ashley had first noticed the nice-looking man seated in 12G when he boarded the flight in Seattle, and she had been waiting for a chance to initiate a conversation with him. She would often select a male passenger on transoceanic flights to engage in harmless flirting, safe in the knowledge she would never see the person again after the flight's end. And this guy was appealing: medium height, slender build, and about sixty years old with dark brown hair and greying temples. He was conservatively and tastefully dressed in a classic Brooks Brothers Fitzgerald gray pinstripe suit, white oxford button-down shirt, and navy rep tie. He now wore black pajamas and the slippers provided in Delta's business class amenities kit.

"Well, sometimes I sure feel old. I'm Colt Garrett," he said, offering his hand.

"Nice to meet you, Colt. Ashley Walters. How did you get the name Colt?"

"It's short for Colton, an old family name, and I've been ribbed about it since I was a kid. How long have you been flying with Delta, Ashley?"

"Ever since graduating from Western Washington. A bachelors in sociology didn't leave me with many options, so I joined my roommate and applied to Delta."

"You were lucky to be based in Seattle from the start."

"Well, it wasn't from the start. I was originally based in Salt Lake City, and I was climbing the seniority ladder when Delta established a major hub in Seattle. I jumped at the chance to transfer, and as a bonus, I get to be closer to my parents in Bellingham."

"Do you like the life? Has to be tough on a relationship," said Colt.

"You're right about that. But fourteen years and a disastrous divorce later, I'm still flying. Delta has been good to me. The benefits are great, and I love the stand-by travel. Life's actually pretty good."

"Any kids from the marriage?" asked Colt.

"No. My ex was a pharmaceutical sales rep and constantly on the road, and my career was equally as unpredictable. I guess we were both just too into our careers, and that didn't leave time for babies. Do you have a family?"

Colt replied, "My daughter Alexandra's 29, married, and living near my wife in Olympia. She's CEO of a network management firm I started many years ago. My son Dan is 26 and is a Navy pilot based on a carrier in the western Pacific. I hope to get a chance to see him on this trip."

Ashley started brewing another pot of coffee. "You live in Olympia?"

"Not for the past three years, but my wife lives there. I work at the Pentagon and live nearby."

Ashley wondered about a marriage separated by a continent and three time zones. At least she and her former husband had lived in the same house. Colt was quiet as another passenger entered the galley and poured a cup of coffee.

Colt placed his empty teacup on the counter. "Well, I think I'll try to get some sleep before it's time for breakfast."

As he squeezed by Ashley to go back to his seat, she pressed against him and whispered, "I think Colt's a cool name."

Colt worked his way back to his seat and eased into his bed. He felt a little uncomfortable from the flirtation with the flight attendant, something he hadn't experienced in a very long time. She was much too young for him, and besides, he was still married and hoped to remain so. He reached up, turned off the reading lamp, and closed his eyes. Not that he had any hope of getting back to sleep. Colt envied those who could sleep on a plane, a skill he couldn't master. He wasn't sure if it was the plane's motion or the strange noises, but he knew from experience this was going to be another long night. He decided to think about the fact that he would get to see his son in a few days, and if he did, what would they say to one another?

Day Two

Delta Airlines Flight 167 – Final Descent into Narita Airport, Tokyo

The plane's cabin was back to normal: window screens raised, lights on, beds turned back into airline seats, passengers once again in their street attire. As Colt gathered his personal items and prepared for landing, flight attendants came down the aisles in unison, offering Delta credit card applications to passengers while the lead flight attendant read the benefits of card ownership into the microphone. Colt declined the card application when Ashley approached, but she smiled and handed him one anyway. "I do recommend you look this over carefully!" she teased.

Glancing up from her book as Colt opened the credit card application, Jennifer Abrams could see that a hand-written note had been tucked inside. "If you're ever in Seattle and need a distraction," it read, "give me a call!" Ten digits concluded the message.

"You seem to have had an eventful evening," Jen commented. "I must be a pretty sound sleeper."

Embarrassed a little by her comment, Colt quickly recovered and feigned smugness in his best Agent 007 style. "I tried to be discrete," he replied.

They both laughed as the plane touched down. Colt noticed that the pilot had immediately applied reverse thrust, probably so he could take the high-speed runway exit and make the scheduled arrival time.

Colt exited the plane with the other business class passengers and waited at the jetway exit for his executive assistant, who had been flying in coach. A good-sized fellow, Lenny Wilson, had been Colt's EA since accepting the president's appointment. A native Bostonian and proud graduate of the U.S. Merchant Marine Academy, Lenny's quick wit and irreverent sense of humor made him a perfect confidant and traveling companion. Colt trusted him implicitly, and Lenny had grown equally fond of his scholarly and insightful boss. If there were two things Lenny would change about Colt, they would be his lack of political awareness and his unshakable belief in always speaking the truth. The beltway was no place for people of integrity, he reasoned.

"Well, boss, how was your flight? Hope you got a good night's rest. I know I sure did. Twenty-two inches of seat room is perfect for a man of my size! Plus, I had twin babies ten feet away who must've decided to cut some teeth during the night."

Colt was prepared for Lenny's complaints, which happened after every long flight. DOD policy permitted senior appointed officials to upgrade their tickets, allowing Colt to switch to first or business class, while poor Lenny was left to fly with the masses.

Colt's mind wandered briefly as he remembered flying with his wife and kids to Disneyland many years earlier. Seven-year-old Dan, seated next to him in first class, had noticed and commented, "One of the coach people is using *our* bathroom." Colt later agreed with his wife that it was time the family flew coach.

"Well, Lenny, next time we fly, I recommend you use those well-placed connections you're always talking about to get yourself an upgrade and a bed! But for now, how about focusing on finding our luggage and getting us through customs?"

"Roger that, sir!"

Headquarters, Republic of Korea Marine Corps (ROKMC), Hwaseong, South Korea

Lieutenant General Cho Yeong-su had served his nation throughout his entire adult life, his constant adversary being the Korean People's Army (KPA), the military forces of North Korea. For more than 30 years, he had been preparing for war with North Korea to ensure that the marines under his command would emerge victoriously. He considered it a sacred duty, one that required all of his attention, conviction, and commitment. The son of a rice farmer, he had been raised in South Korea on a small farm near the port city of Busan. He had done well in school and attracted the attention of local government officials, eventually attending the prestigious Korea Military Academy, South Korea's equivalent to the U.S. Military Academy at West Point. He excelled in the school's four-year course of study, graduating at the top of his class. But rather than pursue a traditional career with the esteemed South Korean Army, he opted for the glamour and *esprit de corps* of the Republic of Korea Marine Corps, a world-class fighting force closely modeled after the U.S. Marines. Although technically a branch of the Korean Navy, most of his countrymen perceived the South Korean Marines as an independent service, a perspective still encouraged and actively promoted today by General Cho. As its commandant, he led an elite and highly motivated force of over 29,000 troops specializing in amphibious warfare and rapid reaction missions. The small yet highly trained force was organized into two divisions, two brigades, and a number of smaller, more specialized units.

For several years, North Korea had pointed to the accumulation of American weapons in South Korea as justification for not ratifying an arms reduction agreement with the United States. Then, in the mid-1990s, the U.S. had announced its plan to remove chemical and biological weapons from all overseas locations, including 110 biological warheads, which had been stored for many years in South Korea. A removal operation had soon begun worldwide, and U.S. officials, working with host South Korean forces, had started processing the weapons for shipment from South Korea back to the States. These particular biological warheads contained Anthrax 455, a genetically-altered version of Anthrax with spores significantly decreased in size to facilitate enhanced airborne dispersal, and could be delivered to a target population via gravity bombs or cruise missiles. Bacillus anthracis, the bacteria that causes anthrax, had been used for over 100 years to sicken or kill livestock, crops or people.

As the 110 biological warheads were being prepared for trans-Pacific transport, then-Major Cho Yeong-su had been responsible for physical security inside his country. As such, he was appointed to oversee the entire shipment process. Before loading the assembled weapons onto the train bound for Busan, Major Cho had reviewed the printed shipment manifest, not noticing that the document erroneously listed the quantity as 101, a potentially confusing error made by the simple inversion of the second and third digits.

After Cho's security detail completed the loading, they had begun their rail journey to the port city. During the trip, Cho decided to check on the weapons again to be sure they were safe. This time, with little else to do on the train, he opted to personally count them, and something didn't fit. After double- and triple-checking his count, he realized what had happened: He had signed a shipping manifest for 101 warheads, but actually had 110 of them in his custody, nine more than were documented. Immediately, a plan had begun to form in his mind.

Back in the 90s, most South Koreans had not been concerned

with their government obtaining weapons of mass destruction. But now, with the recent rhetoric coming from the North, public sentiment was shifting toward an internal force structure that didn't depend upon the U.S. for defense. Cho knew his secret cache of nine small warheads could theoretically replace some of the warheads in the Hyunmoo family of cruise missiles used by the ROK forces. This would allow South Korea to threaten the North in the event of invasion. For many years, Cho had been secretly storing the nine warheads in scattered locations throughout South Korea. Now held on a remote island in the Sea of Japan, the warheads needed to be moved again to an even more secure location. And they could only be moved by someone Cho trusted. The Spartans would be perfect for the task.

Formed in 2016, the Spartan 3000 Regiment was Cho's brainchild, and as such, reflected his personal warrior ethos. More than 3,000 of the most motivated and capable ROK marines had been selected, tested, and forged into this elite fighting force. Although the Spartan Regiment's primary mission was to destroy an enemy's key military facilities, it had also been trained to assist with domestic natural disasters. Able to deploy anywhere within 24 hours, the Spartan Regiment was Korea's A-Team.

Serving as the first Spartan commander, Colonel Chang Min-su had been personally selected for the job by General Cho. The two marine officers had known one another for more than 20 years, and Chang worshiped General Cho as if Cho were his father.

The commandant always knew he could trust Colonel Chang with his most critical secrets. Now, sitting at his desk, Cho pressed a button on his phone. "Mrs. Han," he said. "Please send in

Colonel Chang."

Hours later, Colonel Chang emerged from Cho's office, feeling pleased and honored to have been selected for such a vital task by the commandant. He found it almost unbelievable how General Cho had the bravery and audacity to steal the Americans' weapons. Even more astounding was the fact that he had kept their existence a secret from the entire South Korean military, including its commander in chief. Chang finished a few administrative tasks and then told his aide he was leaving for the day.

As he climbed the last steps to his apartment, Chang was delighted at the prospect of seeing his girlfriend. He had met Kang Ji-woo six months earlier while on vacation in Hawaii, and she had just recently moved into his apartment. The stunning 32-year-old, who worked as a respiratory therapist at nearby Sacred Heart Hospital, seemed to turn heads whenever they went out on the town. At 46, Chang suspected that his wealth and position actually had more than a little to do with her interest in him, but he didn't care. Plus, she was the only woman he had ever spent time with who showed an interest in his work.

Ji-woo gasped with joyful surprise as Chang unlocked the door and entered into their apartment. She was an exceptionally beautiful woman with large, dark, mesmerizing eyes and shimmery black hair that flowed over her shoulders. She wore an exquisitely embroidered silk kimono Chang had bought for her on a recent trip to Tokyo, and he could see now that it was all she had on. "Now, tell me all about your day," she purred softly as she untied the kimono's belt and let the garment drop to the ground.

Later, after Chang was deep asleep, Ji-woo gathered up their clothes from the floor and added them to the black dry cleaning bag that hung on the back of the bedroom door. She had been using Mr. Yi's Alterations and Dry Cleaning Service exclusively since moving in with Chang, dropping the couple's clothes off at the shop every Friday like clockwork. Ji-woo selected a clean, blue-striped Ralph Lauren shirt from her closet and carefully buttoned the left cuff while making sure the right cuff was unbuttoned. She placed the shirt in the dry cleaning bag and returned to their bed, excited at the prospect of another covert rendezvous as well as the chance to impress her superiors in Pyongyang, North Korea.

Naval Criminal Investigative Service (NCIS) Field Office, Yokosuka, Japan

Special Agent in Charge Tim Brannigan had a big job, and it had just gotten bigger. He was already responsible for all NCIS operations and investigations taking place in northeast Asia, and he managed satellite offices in Okinawa, Sasebo, Seoul, Yokosuka, Misawa, Chinhae, and Busan. This morning he had learned that he also would be providing a personal protection detail for the U.S. undersecretary of defense for policy, Colton Garrett. Garrett was scheduled to arrive that morning at Narita International Airport, and would then be driven to U.S. Fleet Activities Yokosuka to visit the Commander, U.S. 7th Fleet on board his flagship, USS *Blue Ridge*. The undersecretary would be remaining in theater for several weeks, visiting a variety of U.S. bases and ships. He would need to be assigned an NCIS special agent for his protection. Senior Field Agent Anna DeSantis was the obvious choice. She was one of Brannigan's most capable agents and had recently completed the DOD executive protection course. Probably more important, she was currently unassigned. DeSantis was well known for her legendary sense of fairness, and Brannigan did not look forward to hearing her argue why she shouldn't be assigned this "babysitting" duty. Nevertheless, he yelled to his assistant through the closed door, "Jerry! Find DeSantis and send her in here!"

USS Blue Ridge (LCC 19), Alpha Pier, Yokosuka, Japan

USS *Blue Ridge* was the lead ship of the *Blue Ridge*-class amphibious command ships of the U.S. Navy, and the flagship of the U.S. 7th Fleet. Forward-deployed to Yokosuka, Japan, it was the third U.S. Navy ship to be named for the Blue Ridge mountain range in the Appalachian Mountains. Its mission was to support the commander and staff of the U.S. 7th Fleet with state-of-the-art command, control, communications, computers, and intelligence services. Launched in 1969, *Blue Ridge* was the navy's oldest active commissioned ship and had the distinction of flying the First Navy Jack at its bow. Displacing more than 19,000 tons, *Blue Ridge* was more than 630 feet long and had a beam of 110 feet. It was steam-powered and could sustain more than 20 knots over 10,000 nautical miles.

Vice Admiral Kurt Shaffer — callsign TEDDY — sat in the *Blue Ridge's* flag cabin reflecting on his decades-long friendship with Colt Garrett. It had started years earlier when they were both stationed in Air Wing Seven onboard USS *Dwight D. Eisenhower* during a Mediterranean Sea deployment. Colt, a lieutenant then, was serving as an air intelligence officer for the Scorpions of

VAQ-132, an EA-6B Prowler electronic warfare squadron. Kurt was a lieutenant junior grade aviator flying the Voight A-7D Corsair II for Attack Squadron 45. After getting to know one another, the two junior officers became fast friends, but not until after "the incident."

Once, during battle group workups in the Caribbean Sea, Kurt had been flying back to the *Eisenhower* after a practice bombing run on a remote island range. He had spotted the aircraft carrier, joined the recovery pattern, and successfully landed. After climbing down the plane's ladder, he was surprised to be abruptly escorted up several decks to meet with the carrier group's admiral, a man who Kurt didn't recognize. Had there been a change of command since he had launched only a few hours earlier? The "new admiral" wasted no time in letting Kurt know that he had just made an egregious error in judgment and ship recognition. Instead of landing on the *Eisenhower,* Kurt had unwittingly landed on her sister ship, USS *Theodore Roosevelt.* Kurt still remembered the taunting chorus of jeers as he made his way back to his Corsair. Thinking things couldn't get worse, he was horrified to see *Roosevelt* Sailors had repainted his jet with the *Roosevelt's* insignia. Wonderful.

Upon his return to the *Eisenhower,* he immediately headed to the intel center for a mission debriefing session. Opening the door, Kurt found his skipper, Commander John Dickenson, and a handful of his fellow squadron pilots waiting for him, seated around the debriefing table. Since all the other aircraft that had flown that day had already debriefed, the room was uncharacteristically empty. Kurt sat down in front of air intelligence officer Colt Garrett, who asked, "Okay, Mr. Shaffer, what do you have for me?"

"I was a sole aircraft mission to Vieques, dropped four GBU-12 bombs, all safely on range."

"Take any gas from the tanker?" asked Colt.

"Yep, I took 2.2 from Texaco," Navy slang for a fuel tanker.

"Dump any gas?"

"Nope."

"Okay," Colt paused. "Anything, well, unusual to report?"

Kurt looked around the silent room to find everybody eagerly anticipating what he would say next. He thought for a long and uncomfortable ten seconds, and then finally uttered, "I decided to do a touch-and-go on the *Teddy Roosevelt* since it was on my way back to the *Eisenhower*."

The room erupted into unbridled laughter, as a couple of pilots actually fell to the deck. Skipper Dickenson ordered, "Okay, knock it off, gentlemen. Lieutenant Garrett, please continue."

Colt couldn't resist. "Let me get this straight," he said. "You landed on the wrong boat, and now you're giving me some B.S. story about a planned touch-and-go?"

Skipper Dickerson interrupted again. "Alright, I think we're done here. Anything else, Mr. Garrett?"

"That's it, Skipper. Oh, one more thing. I need your pilot to sign the report form."

Kurt grabbed the form, signed it, and threw his pen at Colt's chest, mumbling, "Intel puke!" as he stood and headed for the door.

As Kurt stormed out, Colt called after him, "Hope you enjoy your new callsign, *TEDDY!*" Again, the room erupted into laughter as Kurt disappeared from view, and the door slammed. From that day forward, Kurt Shaffer's callsign was *TEDDY*, his momentary error in ship identification was immortalized, and

Colt and Kurt later became best friends.

Kurt Shaffer's career as a naval aviator had moved forward after what both friends came to refer to as "the incident," as did Colt's as an intelligence officer. Colt's next duty station was Fleet Ocean Surveillance Information Facility (FOSIF), Rota, Spain. During the 1980s, Rota was considered the choice assignment for hard-chargers in the intel community, those destined for eagles or stars on their collars.

Kurt lost contact with Colt for a few years until he heard that Colt had suddenly resigned his commission despite having been deep selected for promotion to lieutenant commander and receiving the Navy Cross for heroism during a top-secret mission in Europe. The Navy Cross was the U.S. military's second-highest decoration awarded for valor in combat. *Who resigns after getting deep selected for promotion and receiving the Navy Cross?* the admiral had wondered.

Shaffer maintained sporadic contact with Colt through the years that followed. He knew Colt had joined the Naval Reserve after leaving active duty and had returned as a surface warfare officer, completely separating himself from the intelligence community. Colt completed 30 years of active and reserve service and retired as a captain while simultaneously pursuing his civilian consulting career. Then, about three years ago, Shaffer learned that Colt had been appointed by the Harrison administration as undersecretary of defense for policy. He had watched with interest some of Colt's confirmation testimony with the Senate Armed Services Committee. He admired his friend's intelligent yet candid responses to senators' questions and wasn't surprised when Colt received unanimous approval.

And now he's come for a visit to the 7th Fleet, Kurt thought.

Regardless of the purpose of the visit, the three-star admiral was determined his friend would be greeted with full military honors.

Colt briskly walked up *Blue Ridge's* aft gangway with Lenny in tow. He smiled to himself as he heard the ship's topside loudspeaker sound eight bells in four sets of two, and then announce, "DEFENSE POLICY, ARRIVING!" As he crossed the ship's quarterdeck, Colt passed through two rows of eight Sailors wearing their pressed service dress blues, who saluted to the notes of a boatswain's pipe as he received formal side honors. At precisely the same moment, another Sailor quickly hoisted the flag of the undersecretary of defense up the signal mast. Vice Admiral Kurt Shaffer, Commander, U.S. 7th Fleet, saluted and offered his hand. "Welcome aboard, Mr. Undersecretary!"

Later, in the admiral's cabin, the two friends caught up on the life and career events that had taken place since their last meeting. "Well, Colt," Kurt asked, "what brings you to my neck of the woods?"

Sitting back in his chair, Colt placed the heavy ceramic Navy coffee cup down on the end table and replied, "Officially, Kurt, I'm here to observe 7th Fleet operations and any interactions with the North Koreans and the Chinese. POTUS and SECDEF are concerned that the region has been heating up, and they want to be assured that the Navy's getting everything it needs in order to handle any eventual contingency."

"*Any* contingency?" the admiral questioned.

"Look, we both know the Chinese have been flexing their naval muscles out here recently, and on top of that, the president is very focused on moving the North Koreans toward reunification. One of his highest priorities is to get some sort of meaningful and verifiable force reduction before he eases trade restrictions. A strong and visible fleet presence is essential to both initiatives. Besides, the South Korean government is keen to normalize relations with the North, and to see that we formally and finally end the Korean War."

"Okay, I understand. By the way, your young assistant, Mr. Wilson, mentioned you'd like to visit the *Reagan* Battle Force while you're here. I think we can arrange that. Why the *Reagan*?"

"To be honest, Kurt, I thought I'd take the opportunity to see Dan and maybe patch things up a bit. He isn't too pleased that his mom and I are living apart, and I'm getting the lion's share of the blame." Colt looked down at the blue carpet and waited for Kurt's reply. He was uncomfortable sharing his personal reasons for the trip and hoped that Kurt wouldn't think less of him. The admiral purposely let his friend suffer a bit longer, and then broke into a hearty laugh. "Got you, you old SOB! Of course, you can visit Dan! You must be very proud of him! I just wanted to see you squirm since I haven't forgiven you yet for christening me TEDDY! And do say hello to young Dan for me. I haven't seen him since his commissioning. But before you visit the *Reagan*, I need to brief you on the current CTF 70 commander, Rear Admiral Joseph Carlisle."

"You don't mean the son of *Senator* Emmett Carlisle?"

Emmett Carlisle was a senior member of the U.S. Senate, representing the state of Alabama. With only 100 members and regarded by many to be the world's most exclusive club, the Senate was considered the pinnacle of most aspiring politicians' careers.

"That's the one. And it's my understanding that Rear Admiral

Carlisle hopes to inherit his father's seat in the not too distant future."

"He doesn't want to stay in the Navy? He seems to have had a great career, and getting the 7th Fleet carrier group command sets him up nicely for a second star."

"I truthfully don't think another star is in Joe Carlisle's future, Colt. He seems to have slipped through the cracks. He became infamous as an A-6 Intruder bombadier/navigator. The story goes that when his pilot put the plane into an uncontrolled flat spin, Joe Carlisle was supposed to tell the pilot which direction the aircraft was spinning so he could input the correct stick and rudder. Instead, Carlisle shrieked, 'Do some pilot shit!' into the intercom. Carlisle and his pilot safely ejected, and the plane crashed into the Mediterranean. Carlisle somehow also survived the resulting mishap investigation, probably because of his influential father. He continued to get choice assignments and has now clearly risen to his own level of incompetence. He's scheduled to be relieved in a few months, and I'm crossing my fingers he keeps his act together long enough for his relief to assume command."

Colt hated the fact that capable officers were occasionally overlooked because some other "fortunate son" had the good luck to have a senator as a father. When Colt was initially appointed to serve as undersecretary, he made it what he hoped was crystal clear to his son, Dan, that he should not expect favoritism from his father.

"I still don't get why he doesn't just clean up his act and get that second star," said Colt.

"The Navy's not for everyone. I guess I don't have to tell you that."

Kurt was still mystified why someone with Colt's service record would resign so early and restart his career. And he still wanted to know about that Navy Cross.

Colt quietly said, "I had my reasons, Admiral," and stood to leave the cabin. Kurt bounded out of his chair and replied, "Oh, come on Colt. If I can't say that to you, who can?"

After a momentary pause, the conversation continued. "Hey, I have something for you!" The three-star admiral stepped across the cabin and handed Colt a package he had hidden behind the chair. Colt open the box and found a 1911 semiautomatic pistol inside.

"I know you still like going to the gun range, and I thought I'd get you a pistol from your past."

When Colt attended Navy Officer Candidate School in Newport, Rhode Island, the standard military sidearm was the model 1911 in .45 caliber. The beautiful stainless-steel weapon in Colt's hand was a much more modern version with a 4½ inch barrel to allow concealed carry.

"I got you the 9mm version because the ammo is easier to find, and the felt recoil is less. There's a leather holster there for you, too! You can take it with you to the *Reagan* and practice with the security team. That should really piss-off Joe Carlisle! I'd give a month's pay to see the look on his face when he learns the undersecretary for policy is shooting a 1911 off his fantail!"

This was an exceptional gift, and Colt immediately felt humbled by his friend's thoughtfulness.

"Thanks, Kurt, really. But how did you get it to Japan?"

The admiral smiled. "Old buddy," he teased, "some things are best left unexplained. You'll have no trouble getting it to the *Reagan* because I'm flying you out there on an Osprey. Getting it

29

back stateside will be your problem!"

The Hyatt Regency, Tokyo

Colt paced his room at the Hyatt, unable to sleep. He wasn't sure if it was jet lag, the unfamiliar surroundings, or the prospect of seeing his son the next day. Most likely, it was all of the above. An hour later, he finally relented, putting on a pair of jeans, a collared shirt, and a sport coat and headed for the hotel's lounge. Hotel lounges were the same the world over, filled with patrons wishing they were home but trying to have a good time. He sauntered over to the bar and had just sat on a stool when he heard a woman's familiar voice shout, "Hey, Colt! Come join us!"

Colt turned and saw Ashley, the Delta flight attendant, waving from a booth near the window. She was sitting across from a couple he guessed were also flight attendants, and as he approached their table, Ashley scooted over to make room for him on her side of the booth.

"Hi, I'm Carol, and this is Steven. You already know Ashley."

"Careful you two, Colt is a Fed," teased Ashley.

"That's just great," Steven said. All we need is an FAA dude hanging with us as we party the night before a flight!"

It was clear the party had been going on for some time, based on the number of empty glasses on the table.

Colt smiled. "Actually," he said, "I don't work for the FAA — I work at the Pentagon."

The two other flight attendants weren't paying attention. Steven was listening to Carol describe her Bahama vacation plans and what she was planning to wear once she hit the beach.

"What do you do at the Pentagon?" Ashley inquired, as she leaned closer to him.

Colt considered all the ways he had answered that question in the past, and he just didn't feel like telling another lie. He simply said, "I'm the undersecretary of defense for policy. I'm the principal adviser to the secretary of defense for matters concerning the formation of national security and defense policy for our nation. I was appointed by President Harrison with the consent of the Senate, and I serve at the pleasure of the president." Ashley didn't try hiding how impressed she was. "Well, I'll be damned!" she gushed and grabbed his arm.

After an hour of flight attendants' tales of various obnoxious passengers, Colt was ready to call it a night. He paid the table's bill and headed for the elevators, with Ashley, Carol, and Steven not far behind. He pressed the "up" button, the doors opened, and all four walked in. Steven pressed the button for the 32nd floor, the concierge level. All four exited, and Colt opened his room door while the others passed behind him on the way to their rooms.

Once inside, Colt removed his jacket and shirt and sat down to remove his shoes when he heard a knock at the door. He opened it to find Ashley looking up at him with a smirk on her face. "Carol and Steven are hooking up tonight," she said. "I thought I might hang out here with you?"

Ashley saw the concerned look on Colt's face. "Come on, just one little drink?"

Ashley walked in past Colt and over to the window to admire the view, while Colt poured two glasses of wine from the complimentary bottle provided by the hotel. She took a sip from her glass. "I need to visit the restroom," she explained. "I'll be back to you in just a sec," and with that, she gave Colt a kiss on his cheek and stepped into the restroom.

Seriously tempted by Ashley, Colt had made this mistake before. But this time, he really wanted to see if he could make his marriage work. A time comes in every man's life when he's faced with a decision that challenges his values and his self-control; this was one of those times. When Ashley came back into the room, Colt looked into her hopeful eyes and knew what he had to do.

"I'm pretty tired, Ashley, and I have a long day ahead of me tomorrow. I really like you, but I think it's best for both of us to end the evening." He steered Ashley in the direction of the door, and they exchanged polite good nights.

Back in her room, Ashley leaned against the closed door and thought, *Great, I finally meet a nice guy who's actually somebody, and it turns out he's too nice.* She walked across the room and climbed into her bed. As she drifted off to sleep, she reminded herself, *Well, there is always tomorrow's flight.*

Day Three

Russian Military Intelligence HQ, Khodinka Airfield, Moscow, the Russian Federation

So, the old man died before we could kill him, Colonel General Igor Korobov thought to himself as he read the headline in the American newspaper. The Chief of the Main Intelligence Directorate of the General Staff, Armed Forces of the Russian Federation (GRU), found it ironic that his best and most reliable source of intelligence was the American news media. If either the Federation Council politicians or the ruthless bureaucrats running the Foreign Intelligence Service (SVR) ever discovered this fact, he was confident his agency's budget would be decimated. He also was resentful that while most of the world was familiar with the SVR and its infamous predecessor, the KGB, the larger and much more powerful GRU was still practically unknown. After all, the GRU survived the transition from the former Soviet Union to the new Russian Federation — unlike the old KGB and its ruthless history.

The GRU had, for decades, been operating a program to place illegal intelligence officers, those without the protection of diplomatic status, in countries around the world. These operatives provided a cornacopia of western intelligence to GRU headquarters, covering a wide variety of military, economic, political, and cyber topics of interest. The GRU headquarters were located at Khodinka Airfield, which also included a range of other military and aerospace facilities. Korobov's office was located in a building known as "the aquarium" because of the large amount of glass used in its design. Only a Russian bureaucracy would decide to house its major intelligence agency in a transparent, glass-enclosed structure.

But the world was finally paying attention to the GRU. In a 2018 *Washington Post* article, a former KGB officer was quoted as saying that GRU officers refer to themselves as the "badass guys who act." The KGB officer continued quoting his GRU associates: "Need us to whack someone? We'll whack him! Need us to grab Crimea? We'll grab Crimea!" Then in early 2019, Britain's *The Guardian* ran an article claiming that a suspect linked to the 2018 poisoning and attempted murder of the former Russian double-agent Sergei Skripal and his daughter in Salisbury, England, had been identified as a high-ranking officer in the GRU. Although Korobov's superiors on the Russian General Staff were horrified with the publicity, Korobov was privately pleased that the GRU was finally getting the attention it deserved, and as a result, GRU morale was reaching an all-time high. In fact, recruitment was improving, and Korobov was enjoying increased prestige and influence within the halls of the General Staff. Apparently, he wasn't the only one who read western newspapers. *Perhaps a fourth star* was *in his future!*

The natural death of the American secretary of defense was timely, if not convenient. A GRU operation had been in the final planning stages to eliminate the prominent cabinet member and former astronaut because of what many referred to as the *O'Kane Doctrine* — a complete set of American policies and actions solely aimed at reducing Russia's global prestige and influence. Although the undersecretary of defense for policy, Colton Garrett, was the doctrine's principal author and advocate, his mentor, Secretary

O'Kane, had claimed it as his own. Garrett had coordinated with the U.S. State Department in a combined program of military and diplomatic initiatives that were successfully limiting Russian expansion, both geographically and in its relations with central European nations.

GRU analysts estimated that O'Kane's death would now mean the deputy secretary of defense, Travis Webb, would soon be appointed as acting secretary and eventually be scheduled for Senate confirmation hearings. Webb, an electrical engineer and Vanderbilt University graduate had vast experience in defense procurement and design — skills that had initially brought him to the department of defense. He had come to the attention of the GRU many years earlier and a special relationship had been cultivated with the rising star along the way. Webb had expensive tastes that his government salary didn't fully cover, and his resulting personal debt had created classic intelligence leverage for the GRU. Additionally, the GRU had discovered photos of Webb taken during his time at Vanderbilt that would be embarrassing at the least, should they become public. Webb could be depended on to be much more supportive of Russian interests than his recently departed superior. His new position of leadership at the DOD would mean a return to the normalcy that had existed between America and Russia before O'Kane had become secretary. And there was an added bonus: Webb would be directed to ask for undersecretary Colton Garrett's resignation. The *O'Kane Doctrine* would simply melt away.

The White House, Washington D.C.

"So, the old man finally died. I thought it would never

happen." President William Charles Harrison was reading the Army CID report detailing Secretary O'Kane's death, as he sat in the Oval Office at the *Resolute* desk. A gift from Queen Victoria to President Rutherford Hayes, the desk had been built in 1880 from the oak timbers of the British navy ship HMS *Resolute*. Every U.S. president since Hayes — except Johnson, Nixon, and Ford — had used the *Resolute* desk. Perhaps the most famous photograph of the desk was taken of President Kennedy's son, John John, peering out from under the desk just a year before his father was assassinated on a sunny day in Dallas. This was a historic piece of furniture, and the sitting American president was a man who loved history.

A life-long politician and native Floridian, Bill Harrison had held almost every public office in his state, from port commissioner to governor. He didn't believe in policies or initiatives nearly as much as he believed in himself, and this trait allowed him to successfully avoid being on the wrong side of an issue when political winds invariably changed. Harrison was a politician's politician, famous for his ability to meet a stranger at a rally or fundraiser and instantly make that individual feel as if he or she was the most important person in the room.

Harrison's chief of staff, Eric Painter, stood near the famous desk and nodded. "Yes, sir, he's dead alright. I personally saw the body at the morgue." Painter had been a reliable constant at the president's side since their first campaign to get Harrison elected as Florida's attorney general, and there were very few secrets between the two men. Every time Bill Harrison moved up, so did his sidekick. Eric Painter very much enjoyed being the number one adviser to the most powerful person in the world. The key to his success in that role was being prepared with an answer before a question was asked.

"Of course," said Harrison, thinking aloud, "the simplest thing would be to immediately appoint O'Kane's deputy Webb as acting secretary to give us time to find someone more capable. But how the hell can I do that with yesterday's blog posting old photos of Webb in blackface while he was at Vanderbilt? Am I the only one who doesn't have one of these ridiculous photos of themselves looking like a jerk? I mean really, Eric, can't we vet these people better before they make our shortlist? Makes us look like fools for appointing them!"

Harrison was referring to the recent series of political disasters caused by the surfacing of racially charged photos involving some of the Washington's most notable elected officials. The resulting public outcry had reached a crescendo, and pictures of Webb posing as a black minstrel were now saturating the cable news channels.

"You're right, sir. Webb is done. We need to stick a fork in him and distance the administration immediately. I already have his signed resignation letter, and the communications team is drafting a statement as we speak for today's press briefing."

"Thanks, Eric. I knew you would move quickly. But where does that leave us in appointing an acting SECDEF? It probably should be someone who's already been confirmed, who wouldn't be seen as controversial. I don't want another media show to distract attention from getting my budget passed."

"I've given this some thought, sir," Painter quickly responded, "and I think it should be one of the current undersecretaries of defense. They've all been confirmed by the Senate, and they all understand defense policy and current issues. It also helps that they've all been cleared for top-secret and sensitive compartmented access. Would you like to look at the list?"

The president's chief of staff deftly moved behind the president's chair and set down a typed, double-spaced list.

"Six undersecretaries of defense, sir, all Senate confirmed. Acquisition, research, finance, personnel, intel and policy."

"Who do we have in Policy and Intel?" asked the president. Policy and Intelligence were considered the principal DOD functions.

"Garrett has Policy, and Holmes has Intel, sir. Here are their files." Eric set the two files on the desk. The well-prepared chief of staff had been at his own desk since 3:00 am working the problem. He had come to the conclusion the two men whose files were now before the president were the best choices for the nomination.

Harrison carefully read over both files, and then, setting them down, paused, and asked, "Okay, Eric. Which one?"

Painter had prepared for this question as well and was ready with his well-reasoned answer.

"I like them both. They have the right background, experience, intelligence, and loyalty for the job. Neither had an issue during the confirmation process, and they both have good reputations with the service chiefs. But if forced to choose, I'd go with Garrett."

"Why Garrett?"

"Two reasons, sir. First, he was the author of the *O'Kane Doctrine*. Pat O'Kane pushed it as his own, but it was Garrett's concept from the beginning. He was the one who worked with the state department to implement a comprehensive strategy to make it work. He doesn't trust the Russians, probably because he spent time as a Navy intelligence officer during the Cold War, and he is a Navy Cross recipient. In fact, if you have time, I strongly recommend you read the unredacted version of his award citation. Reads like something out of an epic spy novel. Guy's a hero."

"Interesting," mused the president. "I've met him a few times and heard him brief in the situation room. Frankly, he didn't strike me as anything special. What's your second reason?"

Painter smiled. "He probably didn't appear special because he's not a politician. Not a political bone in his body. He has no political aspirations, and both sides of the aisle like and respect him. He's the safer choice of the two, which is the second reason I like him for this appointment. He won't be in front of the cameras espousing any policies that differ from yours."

"I like that," the president said, hiding the fact that Painter's slight against politicians had not been lost on him. "Anything else?"

"Just a couple more things. First, Garrett's in the western Pacific, flying out to the *Reagan* today for a force review. He most likely won't be back for a while. But it works out perfectly because we can make the announcement today and the press can't get at him for a few weeks. That would allow the Webb resignation to be old news by the time Garrett gets back to Washington. Second, I think you should temporarily appoint Undersecretary Steve Holmes as deputy secretary. That would give us some options, should Garrett not work out. In other words, we can delay the decision to select O'Kane's permanent replacement until we see how Garrett performs."

The president scooted his chair up to the famous desk, picked up a silver pen, and started drafting a note. Handing it to Painter, he ordered, "Have this sent immediately to Garrett onboard

Reagan as a personal-for-his-eyes-only message and follow it up with an all-forces message announcing the appointment. I'll let the press know tomorrow when I board Marine One for the flight to Andrews."

A moment later, the experienced chief of staff emerged from the Oval Office, thinking to himself, *And that's how things get done!*

Flag Cabin, USS Ronald Reagan (CVN 74)

Rear Admiral Lower Half Joseph Carlisle took several moments to contemplate his reflection in the mirror secured to the cabin's bulkhead. He liked what he saw: a trim, six-foot two-inch man dressed in the summer khaki uniform of a U.S. Naval officer.

His short-sleeved khaki shirt was unadorned except for the gold Naval Flight Officer wings pinned over his left chest pocket and a white nametag pinned over his right. And the only things indicating his rank as a rear admiral were the single silver metal stars pinned on each collar. He disliked having to include the words "lower half" following his rank, but they were required. Only a two-star admiral was considered a *real* rear admiral. *Not to worry,* he reassured himself, *because I'm just a few months away from completing this tour as Commander, Task Force 70. The only thing now that could keep me from that second star would be — God forbid — a major aircraft mishap or severe damage to one of my ships.*

Regardless of his direct involvement in — or even awareness of — a mishap, he knew the Navy would hold him accountable for any major incident. He also knew that would be the end of his Naval career. Despite its obvious risks, he had enjoyed this command tour with its broad range of responsibilities. The 7th Fleet's website had proclaimed, "CTF 70 has tactical control of carrier strike groups, cruisers, and destroyers that deploy or transit through the U.S. 7th Fleet area of operations. The CTF 70 commander also serves as Commander, Strike Group 5, the Navy's forward-deployed strike group centered around *Ronald Reagan* and the embarked air wing, Carrier Air Wing 5." But truth be told, Admiral Carlisle preferred the more appealing title of Commander, Battle Force 7th Fleet.

Carlisle's chief of staff, Captain Gary Winters, stood quietly as the admiral preened and primped himself in front of the mirror. Captain Winters had begun his career as an F-14 pilot, eventually transitioning to the F/A-18 as the Hornets replaced the Tomcats. Generally speaking, he had little respect for Admiral Carlisle and had disapproved of his constant need to self-promote while covering his ass. Naval officers were trained to assess risks and make the hard decisions to ensure that assigned forces were in top combat readiness, and sometimes that meant taking chances. Unfortunately, Carlisle was not that type of officer, and Winters personally looked forward to when Rear Admiral Joe Carlisle would be relieved of his duties by a more capable officer. Suddenly, Carlisle interrupted Winters' private musings.

"Gary, tell me again about this guy, Jarrett, and why he's coming to the *Reagan*?"

"It's Garrett — with a G. Colton Garrett. He's been O'Kane's policy undersecretary, and the message said he's coming here to observe our operations, with a particular interest in our interactions with the Chinese and the North Koreans. Also, his son is a Growler driver in VAQ-132 so he'll be visiting with him as well."

Finally stepping away from the mirror, the admiral walked across the room and sank into one of the plush, overstuffed chairs in his spacious cabin.

"You're telling me I have to put up with this civilian so he can go see his kid? Sounds like a candidate for the waste, fraud, and abuse hotline."

"Yes, sir. But his file indicates he actually did serve. Graduated from OCS in '81, then did a tour as a surface guy in a minesweeper before a change of designator to Special Intel. Two Mediterranean deployments in a Prowler squadron and then a tour at Rota." He took a breath. "That's when it gets a bit strange."

"Strange, how?" asked the admiral.

"The guy was doing some sort of secret squirrel stuff, got a Navy Cross, and then was early selected for promotion to lieutenant commander. Then poof, all of a sudden, he resigns his commission and gets out of the Navy. I heard he joined the Reserves but then asked to be re-designated as a surface warfare officer. He eventually retired as a captain after doing 30 years. Like I said, strange."

"Well, you don't see many guys with a Cross. I wonder what he did to get it."

"No idea, Admiral. But I took a look at the awards manual, and it says it requires combat heroism at great risk to one's life." He used air quotes to emphasize his last five words. "His award citation is heavily redacted for national security reasons, and the scuttlebutt is that Garrett doesn't like to talk about it."

Admiral Carlisle thought to himself, *If I won a Navy Cross, I'd sure as hell talk about it!*

"It doesn't matter, Gary, and neither does he. He's just an

opportunistic Pentagon civilian visiting his kid on the taxpayer's nickel. Just keep him out of my way, and away from the news interview team. I don't want him distracting them from doing what they came to do."

What the news team had come to do, three days ago, was an in-depth profile of Rear Admiral Joe Carlisle, highlighting his successful Naval career and how it might transition into a political future. His father, Senator Emmett Carlisle, had recently begun hinting about it, and it was no secret the senator hoped his son would take his seat. To that end, Admiral Carlisle wanted some slick and polished media to clearly demonstrate his fitness and worthiness to follow in his father's footsteps. Garrett needed to stay clear.

"What about Garrett's berthing arrangements, Admiral? Shouldn't we be putting him in your cabin? He does rank above a four-star," the ever-tactful chief of staff pointed out. Navy protocol required the significantly senior DOD official to be berthed in the Flag cabin.

"Have you lost your mind, Gary? I'm not giving up my cabin for some jumped-up reserve captain. Put Garrett and his assistant in Commander Simpson's cabin. When Simpson gets back from leave, we can move Mr. Undersecretary somewhere else — if he's still on board. He might not like it, but I bet he won't have the balls to say anything to me about it."

Captain Winters thought to himself that anybody who had earned a Navy Cross probably wouldn't shy away from dressing down a one-star admiral if he wanted to, but with Carlisle's current surly mood, he decided to let things be.

"What about full honors when he lands? I could ask Captain Solari to have a boatswain's mate and side boys pipe the side as Garrett exits the Osprey. That's how the *Lincoln* handled it when George Bush flew aboard in an S-3. Garrett did do 30 years in the Navy and has a command at sea pin; he'll know the honors he's due."

Admiral Carlisle had moved back to the mirror and was focused on getting his hair part just right when he finally answered his chief of staff, "No formal side honors, Gary. Fuck him!"

Neptune's Grounds Café, Bremerton, Washington

Sara Olson thought back to her very first day at Neptune's and her first meeting with Derwin Young, Neptune's assistant manager, and Sara's direct boss. Derwin was an optimistic, overly happy person, definitely a glass-half-full type of guy. He was a recent graduate of U.C. Santa Cruz, where he had earned a bachelor's degree in psychology, which no doubt explained his present employment at Neptune's. Derwin lived in his parents' basement apartment in downtown Bremerton. When not working, he passed the time interacting online with fellow believers of flat earth theory and a host of other far-fetched conspiracy ideas. But Derwin's major claim to fame was his former role as assistant to the mascot while he attended college. The Santa Cruz mascot was Sammy the Slug, eloquently described by students as "what it would look like if you made your snot into a mascot." Derwin Young hoped and waited four long years to "put on the slime." Each time there was a vacancy, he wasn't selected.

Sara disliked her job at Neptune's. She disliked dealing with customers, she disliked taking their orders, she disliked making their pretentious coffee drinks, and she barely tolerated her co-workers, most of whom were only looking to find a way out of the small Navy town and start their lives anew.

But most of all, Sara disliked Derwin Young. His cheery disposition masked his passive-aggressive nature, and he seemed to take every opportunity to personally counsel her on her negative attitude. It was during one of these "mentoring" sessions that Sara found herself exploring ways to end Derwin's life. *What about the red plastic coffee stir stick he used to pick his teeth? Could the espresso machine be altered to electrocute him? Perhaps he could simply slip on the wet floor and accidentally crack his skull?* she wondered. Sara often asked herself what she had done to deserve this punishment, and when it would end? She had excelled at her studies in university and was quite proud of her master's degree in applied mathematics. She had dreamed of pursuing a doctorate and securing a teaching position at a renowned university. But fate and a lack of options had dealt her a cruel hand, and she knew there was nothing she could do about it.

Today was pretty typical. Sara was working the register and taking coffee orders from the Sailors and civilians who worked at the Naval shipyard two blocks away. Young Sailors would often flirt with her. She knew young men found her attractive, and that probably was one of the reasons she got this job. The civilian shipyard workers tended to ignore her, preferring to just get their coffee ordered with as little human interaction as possible. For her own amusement, Sara would sometimes write the wrong name on someone's coffee cup, only to enjoy the resulting commotion when customers complained about getting an incorrect order. Hilarious.

There was another set of customers Sara found much more interesting: the homeless. *If America was the wealthiest country in the world,* she wondered, *how could so many people be living on the street?* It was the most surprising part of her relocation experience, and she never got over her disbelief. Some of these sad-looking people she would only see once or twice, but there were also some regulars who hung out at Neptune's, sitting at the same tables every day. Occasionally she'd see them outside the restaurant on street corners holding cardboard signs that seemed to change with the seasons.

One man whom Sara had nicknamed Mr. Trench because of his torn wool overcoat always sat in the corner at the table across from the cash register. He would order a mint tea and read *Captain Horatio Hornblower* as he nursed his cup throughout the morning, only putting down his novel to come to the counter and request more hot water for his one teabag. He never spoke much, except for the time Sara asked him why he read the same book, over and over. "Are you ever surprised by the ending?" she kidded him one day. "No, young lady," he replied. "I just enjoy a story where the good guys win . . and get the girl!" Several weeks ago, she had watched him pick up the book after a customer had left it on a table, and now she suspected he reread the book over and over, not for the reason he gave, but because it was the only one he possessed.

The "Cat Lady" usually sat down toward the other end of the counter, where customers lined up while waiting for their orders. She earned her nickname because of the mangy orange cat that never left her side, primarily because it was wearing one of those red "Emotional Support Animal" vests with a leash looped around the woman's wrist. The Cat Lady spent most days quietly working crossword puzzles she had found in discarded newspapers.

Derwin hated having the homeless people in his restaurant, but the owner insisted on giving them a warm place to take shelter from the cold wind blowing off Puget Sound. Sara didn't mind the homeless people being there. She knew from personal experience that they were just trying to get by. And besides, anybody that Derwin disliked was okay with her.

Onboard a CMV-22B Osprey to USS Ronald Reagan

The Osprey was the newest aircraft in the fleet, and easily the most unique. The Navy's first tilt-rotor aircraft, the CMV-22B Osprey, was the maritime version of the Boeing aircraft which was already in service with the Marines and Air Force. The Navy's version had several enhancements, including improved range and long-distance communications capabilities. Ospreys combined the vertical take-off and landing ability of a conventional helicopter with the high speed and long-range capability of fixed-wing aircraft. The features making all this possible were the engines mounted on each wingtip. After the aircraft launched vertically into the air, the engine/transmission nacelles rotated forward through 90 degrees for level flight. Powered by two Rolls Royce Liberty engines, an Osprey could cruise at almost 300 knots with a ceiling of more than 25,000 feet. The Navy was replacing its aging fleet of C-2A Greyhounds with the Osprey, delivering mail, people, and spare parts to aircraft carriers and other ships stationed around the world. The Osprey's vertical take-off and landing capability also dramatically reduced the carrier manpower needed to launch and recover the aircraft. The C-2A Greyhound required nearly 100 crew to man the various stations required for traditional catapult launch and arrested gear landings.

In contrast, the Osprey required just the same minimal carrier crew required by traditional helicopter operations. Also, the Osprey could load a spare engine for the F-35C Lighting II while the C-2A could not. The F-35's large Pratt & Whiney engine power module weighed more than 9,500 pounds in its shipping container, and although the gigantic MH-53 helicopter could lift one, its range was limited to about 50 nautical miles versus 1,000 or more miles for the Osprey. It was an easy decision for the Navy.

Colt was thrilled to be flying in the Osprey. He had wanted to experience the plane since it had become operational a few years earlier. He sat back in one of the marginally comfortable seats that lined the sides of the cargo bay. A thinly padded fold-down seat with a canvas back, it was a far cry from the nicely upholstered business class seat of the Airbus A350 he had occupied on yesterday's long flight from Seattle.

And the in-flight customer service was also just a bit different. After all 10 passengers had boarded and were buckled in their seats, Naval Aircrewman 1st Class Marcus Barkis turned around to face them. "Good morning," he announced. "I'm Petty Officer Marcus Barkis, and I'm your crew chief. Lieutenant Commander Jennings and Lieutenant Foley are your pilot and co-pilot, and Petty Officer Fry is our flight engineer. In the event of an in-flight emergency, if you notice a large green object, I recommend that you immediately get up and follow it as it will be me, running for the ramp exit, because nobody's ever survived an Osprey crash! Also, this aircraft has no restrooms," he said with a wink. "I hope you all took care of business before you left flight operations. There also are no reading lights, air vents, or attendant call buttons near your seat. If you need to get my attention, simply release your safety belt. Your unrestrained and wildly flailing body careening around the aircraft *might* cause me to look up from my novel." And with that, he concluded, "Have a nice flight!"

Up in the cockpit, Lieutenant Commander Sandra Jennings pressed the aircrew-only intercom button. "Very funny, Barkis. You do remember I told you the passenger in the grey suit is the undersecretary of defense? Congratulations! You just joined the *Petty Officer for Life* club."

Colt was excited to be visiting a carrier group again. His last experience had been when he deployed onboard USS *Forrestal* (CV 59) in the Mediterranean Sea during the mid-1980s. The *Forrestal* was named for James Forrestal, America's first secretary of defense. Nicknamed the FID for "first in defense," the carrier was more widely known as "the forest fire" after a horrific fire killed 134 men in the Gulf of Tonkin during the Vietnam War. Future U.S. Senator John McCain was on board *Forrestal* during the fire, which was so disastrous the Navy completely reworked its firefighting techniques and training syllabus.

In addition to the *Reagan*, Task Force 70 also included three *Ticonderoga*-class guided-missile cruisers and eight *Arleigh Burke*-class guided-missile destroyers. Carrier Air Wing 5, the airwing commander, was also embarked on *Reagan*, along with over 90 aircraft, including four F/A-18 Super Hornet fighter squadrons, an EA-18G Growler electronic attack squadron, an E-2D Hawkeye early warning squadron, a CMV-22B Osprey squadron and two MH-60 Seahawk helicopter squadrons. Various support and logistics ships were also attached, as well as an unseen but ever-present *Los Angeles*-class attack submarine, dedicated to protecting the surface ships from subsurface and surface threats. All in all, a potent and impressive force, capable of projecting overwhelming power in support of U.S. interests and those of its allies.

Ever since the first carrier, USS *Langley* (CV 1) launched an airplane in 1920, politicians have periodically considered removing them from the fleet, citing fiscal concerns, and evolving war-at-sea tactics and strategies. But when the threat of a crisis surfaces anywhere in the world, it's no accident that the first question that has come to the lips of every U.S president since Franklin Roosevelt has been, "Where are the carriers?"

Seated directly across from Colt inside the Osprey was Commander Jen Abrams, Reagan's intelligence officer and who was Colt's seatmate during his Delta flight from Seattle to Tokyo. Both Jen and Colt were caught off guard when they were introduced to one another in flight operations prior to boarding the aircraft. Jen was more than a little annoyed that Colt hadn't fully identified himself on the long flight that night. She felt she might have said something wrong or acted too familiar. *Policy wonk, my eye,* she thought. *He IS policy!*

"Sir," she said, "I wish you had told me who you were during that flight from Seattle. I could have used the time to brief you on *Reagan's* operations and general capabilities."

"Thank you, Commander," Colt replied, "but no worries. I've

found it's better not to talk shop when traveling. I'd rather read books and watch old movies to pass the time. I'm sure we'll have more than enough time to talk about the ship and its capabilities when we get there."

In fact, Colt hadn't immediately recognized Jen when he first saw her inside the military terminal. The starched khaki uniform and black jacket she had on now were dramatically different from the more casual jeans and silky blouse she had been wearing on the flight from Seattle. The only item he did recognize from the night before was the black satchel Pelican case still cuffed to her wrist. Colt had another brief flash of the same stressful memories that had robbed him of sleep on the transpacific flight.

Seated next to Commander Abrams was NCIS Special Agent Anna DeSantis. Wearing dark slacks, a crisp white shirt, and a navy blue NCIS windbreaker, she had an efficient look one would expect from a senior field agent.

How long am I going to have to stay on that "bird farm" and babysit Mr. Policy? she wondered. *Personal protection detail? Protection from what?* Nearly 5,000 people were on board the *Reagan*, all with security clearances. Anti-air, anti-surface, and anti-subsurface ships and aircraft created an impenetrable fortress of protection all around them. *What more could a 120-pound woman with a .40 caliber pistol do?* DeSantis thought to herself. She knew spending time on this detail wasn't going to do her career any good, not while other special agents were out there conducting counterintelligence operations or arresting felons.

She had to admit that Colton Garrett seemed like a decent enough guy, not pompous like some of the others she had guarded. His EA, Lenny Wilson, had already briefed her on Garrett's background and personal habits. Nothing strange or out of the ordinary. Evidently, Garrett's codename was "PATRIOT." While most people assumed senior government officials' codenames were assigned by the Secret Service, they were, in fact, assigned by the White House Communications Agency. Lenny Wilson had confided to Anna, "Garrett thinks his codename refers to his commendable Navy service. Truth is, I suggested the codename to the guys at the White House because he's a huge fan of the Seattle Seahawks, and he hates my New England Patriots because of our Super Bowl win in 2015," Lenny chuckled. "He'll kill me if he ever finds out!" Now, the more she thought about it, Anna realized Garrett wasn't a bad guy at all. She decided to accept her fate and see the protection assignment as an all-expense paid three-week pleasure cruise.

Unbuckling his seat belt, Colt got up, stretched his back, and walked forward to the cockpit to talk with the pilots. He accepted the communications headset offered him.

"Morning, sir! What can we do for you? Everything okay back there?"

Lieutenant Commander Sandra Jennings had been working out some fuel consumption calculations on the aircraft's system computer while co-pilot Lieutenant Steve Foley "had the airplane." Now Jennings turned around to greet the VIP.

"The ride's just fine, Commander, thanks," Colt said. "I just wanted to find out what you two aviators think about this machine. It's a new concept for the Navy."

"We love it, sir!" she exclaimed. "A year ago, Steve and I were flying Sierras out of Naval Station Norfolk. Now, we're flying the coolest aircraft in the fleet." The MH-60S helicopters were conventional helicopters and affectionally known as "Sierras" by the men and women who flew them.

"Any issues with the plane at all? We need to make certain you're all getting everything you need to make this program work!"

Sandra Jennings was a graduate of the Naval Academy, where she had majored in aeronautical engineering. She held a master's degree in systems analysis from the Naval Postgraduate School in Monterey, California. She was sharp and confident, and she knew how to answer a question from a man who was more than eight miles above her pay grade.

"It's an outstanding program, sir, and I'm proud to have been selected for it. We're just experiencing some of the typical bugs one finds with new airframes."

Colt realized he had put the pilot in an awkward position. He smiled at her and replied, "I read you, Commander. And if you ever consider a tour as a defense attaché, just get in touch. We can always use smart people with finely-tuned diplomatic skills." He disconnected his headset, handed it back to the pilot, and returned to his seat.

"Nice work, Ma'am!" smirked Lieutenant Foley, as he sharply banked the Osprey and began the setup for vertical flight. He loved this part of the approach best when the Osprey became the world's largest, most advanced, and most expensive toy transformer.

Commanding Officer's Stateroom, VAQ-132 Scorpions, the Reagan

Commander Thomas Robinson commanded Electronic Attack Squadron 132, home-based at Naval Air Station Whidbey Island.

He was responsible for the squadron's five EA-18G Growlers and the more than 200 men and women it took to fly and support those aircraft. A Naval Flight Officer, his job when flying was to operate the aircraft's complex electronic warfare systems which protected the battle group when underway and air wing aircraft during strike missions. On the bulkhead above the desk in his stateroom was a framed quotation from his favorite book, *The Bridges of Toko-Ri* by James Michener:

> *Why is America lucky enough to have such men?" it read. "They leave this tiny ship and fly against the enemy. Then they must seek the ship, lost somewhere on the sea. And when they find it, they have to land upon its pitching deck. Where did we get such men?*

Tom Robinson thought the book, and that quote in particular, perfectly described the challenges faced by naval aviators. This morning, Tom (callsign ARROW, as in straight as an arrow) was having a chat with Lieutenant Dan Garrett, one of the most capable and promising young pilots in his squadron. During the squadron's previous deployment to the Mediterranean, Dan had been awarded the Distinguished Flying Cross for downing a Syrian SU-22 jet that was bombing U.S.-supported Kurdish Militia ground forces.

Although the DFC plus two Air Medals made him the most decorated pilot in the squadron, Dan was struggling with his decision regarding his next assignment. One of the most important jobs of commanding officers was to lead and mentor their junior officers, so Tom Robinson had scheduled time to help the young pilot work through his options. And he liked this kid.

"So, what are you thinking, Dan?" asked the commander.

"Well, Skipper, I really like driving the Growler. I like the mission — you know, protecting others — and I like our ready room. The problem is that this tour is coming to an end, and my next tour is an unassociated shore rotation. I don't think I'm cut out to leave the cockpit for a desk job just yet."

Tom thought for a minute. This was not his first conversation with a pilot making a career decision. "We all have to spend time out of the cockpit, Dan. But we know eventually, we'll make it back." He saw the let-down look on Dan's face and kept talking. "But I can see that's not the answer you were looking for."

The young pilot knew he was putting his skipper on the spot. He held him in high regard and had learned much from him about being a leader; he didn't want to let him down.

"I'll probably just request an NROTC instructor billet and use the opportunity to build up some pilot-in-command hours so I can get my Air Transport Pilot rating. I have about three years left on my commitment to the Navy, and the airlines are going to be hiring lots of pilots to replace the guys hitting 65."

It was true: The impending pilot shortage was taking a toll on the ranks of military pilots, and none of the branches had thus far solved the problem. Changes to flight pay and assorted other attempts to reverse the trend weren't working.

Tom asked, "Isn't there anything at all you want to do in the Navy?"

"Yes, sir. I'd like to be a test pilot, but I don't have the required technical degree."

The U.S. Naval Test Pilot School was located at Naval Air Station Patuxent River, Maryland, and was considered the very top rung of the aviator profession. "Pax River" was where the best of the best tested every airframe the Navy fielded. Pilots pushed aircraft beyond their designed capabilities, purposely making the aircraft fail. And when they were successful, test pilots earned their pay by recovering the aircraft from disaster and landing them safely. Based on these flights, detailed procedures were developed so that fleet pilots could avoid catastrophic incidents and successfully complete combat missions. Test Pilot School alumni included a who's who of naval aviation, with graduates including Alan Sheppard, Scott Carpenter, Jim Lovell, Wally Schirra, John Glenn, Pete Conrad, Mark Kelly, Bill McCool, and Jim Stockdale.

A selection board met every six months to identify up and coming officers to whom they would offer admission to the school. The application announcement message also listed minimum qualifications, which included a hard science undergraduate degree, waivable only under special or extreme circumstances. Dan was an outstanding pilot with rare skills, but he knew it would take something more than skills to get a tech degree waiver.

"Isn't your dad a big wheel in the Pentagon?" Tom asked. "Maybe he could pull a few strings for you. Don't be too proud to ask for his help."

Dan laughed. "I don't think that dog will hunt, sir. Back when he first went to work there, my dad made it very clear he wouldn't be helping me with my career. He's kind of a hard-ass about those things."

The television monitor mounted on the skipper's cabin bulkhead suddenly showed a camera's view of an approaching aircraft. Both men paused to watch the strange airplane transform itself into a helicopter and then gently set down on the flight deck directly opposite the carrier's superstructure. Neither man was accustomed to seeing the unique airplane operate, so in silence, they continued to watch, captivated, as its two large, black turboprops stopped spinning and the flight deck crew quickly secured the plane with tie-down chains.

"That is one strange bird!" said Tom as they watched a group of officers approach the Osprey and wait by the tail ramp. "Isn't that the ship's C.O., Captain Solari? Why would she be meeting the mail plane?"

"Beats me, sir," Dan replied. They watched Captain Solari come to the position of attention and salute a distinguished-looking man in a grey suit who came walking down the Osprey's cargo ramp.

"I wonder who the hell that is," remarked Tom.

The young pilot blinked his eyes as he suddenly realized who he was looking at on the monitor.

"That, Commander Robinson, is my father!"

The USS Ronald Reagan, the South China Sea

Anyone who has been aboard a *Nimitz*-class aircraft carrier invariably describes the ship as a floating city. At more than 1,000 feet in length, three NFL football games could be played simultaneously on its massive flight deck. The nuclear-powered *Reagan* could cruise at over 30 knots for several years without refueling its reactor. Her crew numbered upwards of 3,000 Sailors, and when the airwing was embarked, it added an additional 2,500 Sailors, making *Reagan* indeed a small city with its everyday needs for electrical power, lighting, heating, drinking water, food, air conditioning, and wastewater treatment. Multiple galleys produced 10,000 meals daily, and the ship included a barbershop, fitness center, closed-circuit television station, and a wide range of other services required to operate and maintain the over 90 aircraft embarked.

Sitting in an overstuffed chair in the well-appointed Flag cabin, drinking coffee, and enjoying fresh blueberry scones, Colt found it strange to think of the *Reagan* as one of the most powerful weapons of destruction in the world. He, Lenny and Special Agent DeSantis had been escorted up to the Flag Cabin by the *Reagan*'s commanding officer, Captain Johrita Solari, where they were introduced to Admiral Carlisle and his chief of staff, Captain Gary Winters. After Captain Solari left the cabin and headed for the ship's bridge, the four men sat in chairs around a low coffee table, while Anna DeSantis remained standing near the cabin's exterior door. As he sipped his coffee from a fine china cup, Colt glanced subtly around the cabin until his eyes rested on a portrait on the opposite bulkhead. It was a large oil painting of Rear Admiral Carlisle in his full dress blue uniform, complete with medals, sword and white gloves. Colt thought of the countless offices he had visited in the Pentagon and couldn't recall a single instance where an officer displayed a portrait of themselves on a wall. Joe Carlisle was indeed a piece of work.

"Mr. Garrett," Carlisle said, "Captain Winters has told me you spent some time in the Navy and retired as a captain. Surface warfare, right? So, you're probably not accustomed to the opulence of an admiral's cabin."

Colt knew immediately that the one-star admiral was letting him know this was *his* ship, and that he simply saw Colt as another retired reserve officer. This wasn't the first time Colt had dealt with an official asserting dominance in a meeting, attempting to control the relationship. He knew the key to dealing with this personality type was to pretend to not understand the insult and then recalibrate the individual.

"You're right about that, Admiral. The last time I served on a carrier, I was a lieutenant and didn't get invited much to the admiral's cabin for coffee and scones. I do appreciate your taking time from your schedule to see me this morning. I actually was surprised we didn't see you when we landed."

Captain Winters caught the admonition imbedded in the undersecretary's comment but wasn't confident his admiral did. Winters considered jumping into the conversation to make an excuse for the admiral's protocol mistake but decided it would be more interesting to watch his boss squirm and put out his own fire.

"Well, I guess I didn't realize what honors were required," said the red-faced admiral. "We don't get many civilian bureaucrats visiting us way out here," he added.

Colt smiled. "No worries, Joe. Say, Lenny, would you ask the ship's captain to lend Rear Admiral Lower Half Carlisle a copy of Naval Tactical Publication 13? I guess us old ship drivers just assume all Naval officers have a copy." Turning back to Admiral Carlisle, Colt explained, "You see, Joe, NTP-13(B) is the Navy's bible for honors, or at least it was way back when I served."

Admiral Carlisle turned a deeper shade of red and quietly cleared his throat. "That won't be necessary. I know the regulations."

"Good, Admiral. Now let's talk about the purpose of my visit."

Later, after Colt and his team left the cabin and headed toward their assigned berthing, Admiral Carlisle and Captain Winters sat back down, and each poured himself another cup of coffee.

"Did you hear what that jerk said to me?" Carlisle snapped. "I'll be damned if I'm going to let that civilian get away with treating me like a junior officer! I'm glad we stuck him and his assistant in that small stateroom!"

Captain Winters thought the undersecretary's dressing down of the admiral was well deserved and actually nicely done. He phrased his response carefully.

"Mr. Garrett did seem a little offended at how we handled his reception. I heard that Vice Admiral Shaffer personally welcomed him aboard the *Blue Ridge* with full honors. Perhaps a graceful way out would be for you to invite him to breakfast tomorrow morning in your cabin. We don't need him calling Shaffer and making trouble. Maybe have his son come, too, so things will be calm and friendly. Just an idea. . ."

Admiral Carlisle was still irritated, but he saw the logic in Winters' suggestion. They could have a nice, friendly, breakfast and then he could figure out how to get rid of Garrett ASAP. Carlisle smiled and said, "Good idea, Gary. Ask him, his assistant, and his son to join me for breakfast tomorrow."

Undersecretary's Stateroom, The Reagan

"I just about died when you put Carlisle in his place," remarked Lenny to Colt. "What an egotistical asshole!"

Lenny had worked closely with Colt Garrett for years and thoroughly enjoyed the rare occurrence when Colt made it clear he wouldn't be bullied by anyone.

"I probably shouldn't have done that," Colt admitted, "but I've never liked that sort of officer. I'm glad Admiral Shaffer gave me a heads-up regarding Carlisle. I'm guessing his chief of staff probably talked him into the breakfast invitation. Adding Dan was a smart move, too."

"When are you going to let him off the hook?" Lenny asked. "We're going to need his cooperation to get this review done."

"You're right, of course." Colt took a deep breath. "Tomorrow, I promise to play nice and pretend today didn't happen. But for now, you better climb down from that bunk because Dan is due any minute and we're going to need some privacy."

When there was a knock on the door a moment later, Lenny opened it. There stood Lieutenant Dan Garrett with a slight scowl on his face. Dan stood 6' 2" and weighed 190 pounds. Although he had a more athletic build than Colt, it was clear the two were father and son.

"Hi, I'm Len Wilson, and I'm guessing you're Lieutenant Garrett. I work for your dad," explained Lenny as he extended his hand. Dan firmly returned the handshake, looking Lenny squarely in the eye as his father had taught him to do more than 20 years ago. "Lieutenant Dan Garrett, sir. Pleased to meet you," Dan replied.

"I think I'll go see if they're serving lunch yet and give you two some time to catch up," said Lenny as he disappeared into the passageway.

"Have a seat, Dan. Thanks for coming by. It's good to see you! How are you doing?"

Dan hesitated, then pulled a metal chair out from the desk and sat down, keeping the stressed look on his face.

"Just fine, Dad — or I was until I saw you step off the Osprey. Why are you even here? And why didn't you let me know you were coming?"

Colt could see Dan was not necessarily happy to see him, and he was suddenly worried this was not going to go well.

"I'm officially here to review our western Pacific operations and assess our interactions with the North Koreans and Chinese. But as an added benefit, I get to see you and meet the people in your squadron. I also was able to visit your mom on this trip when I stopped in Seattle. We had a chance to talk things out a bit, which we needed."

Dan still blamed his father for his parents living on separate coasts and couldn't seem to let it go. He was close to his mother and hated to see her unhappy. At least it was good to hear they had spent some quality time together.

"How's Mom doing?" Dan asked. "I talked to her last week, and she had just gone skiing with friends. She sounded like she had a pretty good time."

"I think she's doing well," replied Colt. "We do miss each other, so it was good to be together. We agreed to speak again after this trip. She even talked about flying to D.C. and possibly staying awhile."

Dan felt unexpectedly relieved and reassured. "That's excellent news, Dad, and it makes me happy to hear it." Then quickly changing the topic, "So, how long are you going to be here on the *Reagan*?"

"Most likely a couple of weeks, but I'll know more in a few days. I did get a chance to see Admiral Shaffer when I came through Tokyo, and he said to say hello to you." Colt poured two cups of coffee, handed one to his son, and continued. "So, tell me, what does your squadron think of Admiral Carlisle?" Colt figured the airwing would have an opinion of the group commander. Since the time of John Paul Jones, Sailors had been freely offering critical observations of their commanding officers.

"I haven't met him," Dan confessed. "But those who have think he's a joke. Seriously! People say he's barely competent in the airplane, and that he's using the Navy and this tour as CTF 70 just to launch a political career and follow in his father's footsteps. He's even got a news crew following him around the ship making a film or something. Sounds like he's just an empty suit."

Colt found it ironic that the crew's unfavorable opinion of Admiral Carlisle mirrored that of the 7th Fleet commander, and Dan suddenly remembered how good it felt to spend time, be honest and level with his father. He was a good man to talk to.

"Well, son, you're going to get the chance to see and decide for yourself, because we've been invited to his cabin for breakfast tomorrow morning."

"But I have a flight during Event One tomorrow morning! We brief at 0700!"

"Not anymore," Colt said. "I talked with your skipper, and asked him to pull you off the flight schedule."

The more relaxed expression on Dan's face suddenly changed back to one of anger.

"Wait — you talked with my skipper and canceled my flight, without asking me first?"

Before Colt could respond, Dan stood, turned, and said, "You know, I have a lot of work to do. I got to get going." He quickly left the stateroom, letting the door slam behind him.

Day Four

Russian Military Intelligence HQ, Khodinka Airfield, Moscow

General Korobov learned that Colton Garrett was to be appointed as acting secretary of defense even before Garrett was notified, but it didn't make the news any better. In fact, things couldn't be worse. Any hope for a shift away from the *O'Kane Doctrine* and its punitive effect on Russian affairs was eliminated entirely with the doctrine's primary architect serving as the acting defense secretary. *True,* thought Korobov, *the appointment is not permanent, but all indications coming from the White House strongly suggest the acting appointment could soon transform into a nomination and inevitably be confirmed by the Senate. Garrett will no doubt replace or reassign those key individuals the former deputy secretary, Travis Webb, had positioned. And what about Travis Webb and that ridiculous photo scandal of his? Why do these Americans pose for politically damaging photographs and then express shock when the photographs become public and threaten their political careers? Truly remarkable! Webb might yet prove useful, though, depending on where he lands. He will probably have to keep his head down until the scandal becomes yesterday's news. An eventual position with a major defense contractor could be the best scenario, given our appetite for American military technology. And what to do about Colton Garrett? We have no leverage on him, and to date, we have been unable to have much influence on him.*

The more consideration the GRU chief gave to the challenges posed by Colton Garrett as defense secretary, the more he became convinced the man must not be allowed to serve in that critical position. The report on his desk indicated Garrett was not currently in Washington, but on an aircraft carrier somewhere in the Pacific. The GRU had recruited and maintained sources of intelligence on several of the American aircraft carriers, and that included the very ship on which Garrett was embarked, USS *Ronald Reagan*. These sources typically were Sailors or Marines motivated by a wide range of personal reasons.

Historically, most U.S. government and military organizations assumed only those who were susceptible to some type of leverage would betray their own country. Security background investigations focused on finding personality flaws, allegiances, political beliefs, and other undisclosed behaviors that might make a typically patriotic person vulnerable to blackmail by a foreign power. But in recent years, it had become evident to U.S. counterintelligence agencies that people would betray their country for the most basic of all reasons: greed. The Walker case of the 1980s, which typified this kind of scenario, would not have been discovered had Warrant Officer John Walker's wife not reported her suspicions to the FBI. But greed is exceptionally difficult to discover through a security background investigation, and almost impossible to detect without full access to an individual's financial transactions — or a phone call from a suspicious spouse.

General Korobov knew he needed to contact his superiors as soon as possible with an approach to prevent Garrett's permanent appointment, a plan that would require approval at the highest level of the Russian government. That would take time to obtain, time he would need to fully develop some options from which he would select the most promising approach. He reached into his drawer for the file on the *Reagan* and reacquainted himself with the list of Russian officers controlling the *Reagan* collection efforts. He smiled when he saw that Colonel Dimitri Petrov was the principal controller, and he proceeded to initiate the clandestine contact protocols necessary to instruct Colonel Petrov to develop several options to eliminate Colton Garrett.

Office of the Supreme Leader, Pyongyang, North Korea

The Supreme Leader sat at his massive desk and nodded as he read the intelligence summary in his hands. He had insisted on personally reading all significant intelligence reports regarding his foe to the south, and today he marveled at the stupidity of an officer sharing vital military secrets with a woman while making love. The Democratic People's Republic of Korea had extensive networks of agents throughout South Korea. One of the most recently placed operatives had discovered that the Americans had unknowingly misplaced several biological warheads many years ago, which the South Koreans now had hidden somewhere. There was a time when the discovery of weapons of mass destruction in South Korea would have caused panic in the north, and immediate operations would have been initiated to locate and seize them. But today, the Supreme Leader saw the newly discovered warheads as a way to further delay the reunification of his country, a precondition imposed by the Americans before sanctions that were strangling his country would be lifted. He began to formulate a strategy. It would start with a communication to the U.S. that North Korea held indisputable proof that South Korea was hiding several American biological warheads, and because of that fact, he could not consider even the smallest reduction of his military forces. The international coalition formed by the Americans to expand their sanctions on his country would collapse when the existence of the warheads in South Korea became public.

The Supreme Leader called his secretary into his office. He instructed the man to schedule an emergency meeting of his military council, to be followed by a statement to the international press. Formal notification to the American president and to the United Nations secretary general would come next, and then his country would be free of the American sanctions forever.

Flag Cabin, USS Ronald Reagan

In over 240 years of defending the United States against its enemies, perhaps the most essential process the U.S. Navy had perfected was how to feed Sailors at sea. And although many would say submariners of the Silent Service ate best, it would be hard to compete with the admiral's galley on a *Nimitz*-class carrier. This morning's meal included a selection of breakfast meats, eggs cooked to order, French toast, and an attractive selection of fruits and pastries. Admiral Carlisle beamed as he watched his grateful guests partake in the sumptuous breakfast.

"We try to make do at sea as it takes the monotony out of a long deployment. More sausage for you, Lieutenant?" asked Admiral Carlisle, turning to face Dan Garrett.

Dan, who had remained quiet and preoccupied through the meal, now pushed back from the table and shook his head. He was sure he had consumed the equivalent of three typical breakfasts. On second thought, maybe losing the morning's flight was worth the meal he had just finished. Perhaps he could forgive his father. Again.

"No, thank you, Admiral," he replied politely. "I couldn't eat another bite."

"How about you, Mr. Undersecretary? There's plenty more if you're interested."

It had been a pleasant albeit quiet morning, with snippets of small talk on assorted subjects of relative unimportance. Now, Lenny watched his boss's face as Colt wiped his mouth with the fine linen napkin, remembering yesterday's promise to smooth things over today with the admiral. Colt had been uncharacteristically quiet during the meal, and Lenny knew his response to the admiral would indicate if things would improve today.

"No, Admiral, I think I've had my fill," Colt answered as he placed his napkin on the table. Lenny glanced over to see if the admiral had caught the double entendre, but Carlisle was already listening to his chief of staff discuss the day's operations plan.

"It looks like we're conducting flight ops in the Sea of Japan today. It might be a good opportunity for you and Mr. Wilson to tour the ship," suggested the admiral. "I'm sure Captain Solari can get you into the catapult and arresting gear spaces, and I know the airwing commander can get you out on the Landing Signal Officer platform. It's exhilirating to stand so close to the aircraft as they land!"

Lenny wondered if the admiral was simply trying to be hospitable, but Colt knew the proposed tour was just a ploy to keep him busy and block him from assessing the carrier group's operations. He and Lenny had limited time, and several hours wandering through the enormous ship would be better spent talking with the admiral's staff regarding interaction with North Korean and Chinese naval forces.

"I appreciate the tour offer, Admiral, but Lenny has prepared an agenda of things I'll need to discuss with your staff."

Lenny took the prompt, opening his briefcase and passing copies of the agenda around the table. Admiral Carlisle took a few minutes to read the three-page document and then loudly slammed his fist on the table.

"What the hell is this, Garrett?" Carlisle demanded. "I don't want my staff wasting valuable time answering your questions. I have a Battle Force to run! My orders from 7th Fleet say nothing about any evaluation of my operations. I won't waste time dealing with this Pentagon bullshit just so you can justify flying halfway around the world to see your kid!" He thought for a moment, then added, "I'm placing a call to Admiral Shaffer to get this crap straightened out!"

Several things simultaneously floated through Dan's mind. *The admiral really is a piece of work*, he mused. *Furthermore, Dad is an old shipmate of Vice Admiral Schaffer, and I'm reasonably sure he wouldn't be conducting this assessment without Shaffer's knowledge and permission. But most importantly, where did this asshole get off calling a me a kid?*

Captain Winters was still wincing from his admiral yelling at the senior DOD official. He, Lenny, and Dan took secret delight as Garrett grinned and very calmly responded, "That will be an interesting phone call, Joe."

The red-faced admiral was about to react to Colt's threatening tone when there was a loud knock at the cabin door. A lieutenant commander had come into the cabin with a gold, braided aiguillette draped on his left shoulder, indicating he served as the admiral's aide.

"What is it, Mike?" sneered Carlisle, clearly irritated at the interruption.

"Admiral, we just received a *PERSONAL FOR* from the president."

Pleased with the prospect of a private communication directly from his commander in chief, Carlisle abruptly ordered, "Good. Hand it over!"

But the aide's face told a different story. "Admiral," he answered haltingly, "the *PERSONAL FOR* is addressed to Mr. Garrett, for his eyes only."

The room went silent as the officer handed Colt a sealed envelope. As the others at the table looked on, Colt opened the envelope with a small silver butter knife from the table and read the message silently to himself.

Dan watched as his father read the note for a second time and then carefully folded the paper and slipped it back into the envelope. He saw a strange but pained look grow on his father's face. "Dad, are you alright? Is everything okay? What is it?"

After another knock on the cabin door, the admiral's admin chief walked in.

"Admiral," said the chief petty officer, "you're going to want to see this. The president has just made an announcement, and all the networks are replaying it." He then crossed the cabin past the dining table where everyone was still seated and turned on the television mounted on the bulkhead. All eyes in the room shifted to the TV as the President of the United States addressed the nation.

"My fellow Americans," he began. "I am sorry to have to report that Monday morning, Secretary of Defense Patrick O'Kane suffered a massive stroke and sadly passed away.

Secretary O'Kane had a long and distinguished career as a fighter pilot, astronaut, senator, and finally as defense secretary. I personally will miss him, and our warmest thoughts and prayers go out to his family and friends. But," he paused briefly, "in our sorrow at the passing of this great man, we cannot allow our grief to distract us from the defense of our nation. Effective immediately, I am appointing current Undersecretary of Defense Colton S. Garrett as acting Secretary of Defense. I will announce my nomination for Secretary O'Kane's permanent successor at a later date. Mr. Garrett has been notified of his appointment, and I look forward to closely working with him as we further develop our defense strategies. May God bless you, and may God bless these United States of America."

Immediately, all pairs of eyes in the room focused on Colt Garrett. The newly appointed cabinet member smiled quietly and looked over at his son. Dan beamed with pride at the thought that the person who taught him everything he knew about being a man was now the secretary of defense and responsible for the most powerful force the world had ever known. The unexpected but auspicious moment was suddenly interrupted when Captain Winters solomnly stood up from his chair to the position of attention, and loudly proclaimed, "Attention on Deck!"

Washington State Route 3, Southbound near Poulsbo

Professor Robert Jordan had led a full and exciting life. He had traveled extensively and lived and worked in many countries. Extremely fit for a man in his early sixties, Jordan took full advantage of living in the Pacific Northwest, where one could sail, fish, waterski, and snow ski all in the same day. But his favorite hobby was rock climbing, a sport that tested his skill, strength, endurance, and daring. It was only on one of the many peaks in the nearby Olympic or Cascade mountains that Jordan could truly test himself and be the person very few knew him to be.

Although this morning's activity was much less adventurous, Professor Robert Jordan thoroughly enjoyed driving his Honda Accord on the highway that ran north and south through Washington State's Kitsap Peninsula. At nearly 20 years old, the silver two-door coupe was surprisingly quick, with its three-liter, V6 engine. And the car seemed to fly this cold, clear morning. Jordan needed to remind himself to keep the car near the speed limit to avoid any uncomfortable conversations with state troopers.

Robert Jordan chaired the computer information security program at Kitsap College and the associated cyber range, which supported its training and testing programs in cybersecurity systems, cyber defense, and cyber technology development. Jordan's programs were particularly attractive to active-duty personnel who were stationed at one of several nearby military installations and were planning to pursue high tech careers after leaving the service. There was no shortage of potential candidates for the program.

State Route 3 was also designated as a Strategic Highway Network corridor under the National Highway System as the main road connecting the many commands of Naval Base Kitsap — the host command for installations located in the cities of Bangor, Bremerton, Jackson Park, Keyport, and Manchester. Naval Base Kitsap also hosted 70 tenant commands, including

Submarine Group Nine and its eight nuclear-powered submarines, as well as the Naval Undersea Warfare Center, the Naval Facilities and Engineering Command, Fleet Logistics Center Puget Sound, a Naval shipyard, a submarine repair facility, and a naval hospital.

A short ferry ride across Puget Sound was Naval Air Station Whidbey Island with its P-8A Poseidons and EA-18G Growlers, and Naval Base Everett, where aircraft carriers and guided-missile destroyers were homeported. That same ferry ride also took passengers to one of the world's meccas of technology, Seattle, hosting the likes of Microsoft, Amazon, Boeing Aerospace, Twitter, and Groupon. Seattle was also home to the University of Washington and its Paul Allen School of Computer Science, a program well-known for its close association with the local tech giants and the source of many notable IT breakthroughs. The dense concentration of military, IT, and defense research installations combined to establish a large and well-qualified pool of potential students for Professor Jordan's information security program.

More importantly, the much-acclaimed technical program provided Robert Jordan with close, personal contact with people who had access to some of the country's most vital defense secrets and technologies, those individuals who might somehow be encouraged to conduct espionage against their country and share its intelligence. That, of course, was essential, because Professor Robert Jordan was actually a Russian spy.

His real name was Dimitri Petrov, and he held the rank of colonel in Russia's GRU. Colonel Petrov was more than a spy. He was a spymaster, controlling a total of eight GRU operatives who were deeply embedded into American life in the Pacific Northwest, all posing as natural-born U.S. citizens. These eight individuals were tasked with developing sources of intelligence within the military and technology communities, and then collecting and forwarding that information to GRU headquarters in Moscow. In addition to Petrov's supervisory responsibilities, he also personally recruited select Americans to provide him with highly classified defense information, and his teaching position gave him unfettered access to prospective recruits. Colonel Petrov chuckled to himself as he passed exit signs for Submarine Base Bangor and Naval Undersea Warfare Center, Keyport, where the Navy tested torpedoes. This, in fact, was Petrov's prime hunting ground, and he was hoping Moscow would provide for more GRU agents to sufficiently cover the targeted area.

The Russian Consulate in Seattle had been closed by the United States in early 2018 in response to what many believed was a chemical weapon attack on a former Russian officer and his daughter in England. The Russians had countered by closing the American Consulate in St. Petersburg and expelling more than 50 U.S. diplomats. While most Americans saw the Seattle Consulate as a place to obtain travel visas and arrange for doing business with Russia, the diplomatic station was also used for many years as a base for Russian intelligence officers posing under diplomatic cover. These *legal* operatives would control vast networks of deep-cover *illegal* operatives, like Colonel Petrov, who in turn, ran their own networks. With the closure of the Seattle Consulate, Petrov lost his local support. He now reported directly to GRU headquarters in Moscow.

The urgent communication from his GRU superior was quite out of the ordinary and was the reason for today's drive south. Personal contact between Petrov and his assigned operatives was considered dangerously risky and was to be avoided at all costs.

Nevertheless, he had been ordered to personally deliver the new mission tasking so that there could be no misunderstanding or confusion.

Petrov pulled his small Honda into a parking lot, got out, and walked to the door of a small coffee shop. He stepped up to the counter and said, "Good morning, Sara," as he looked at her name tag. "Are you ready for my order?" Sara Olson stared at Colonel Petrov for a brief moment, and then returned his smile, saying, "Yes, what can I make for you?"

Neptune's Grounds Café, Bremerton, Washington

Sara let Derwin know she was going to take her break, then grabbed a bottle of water from the cooler and joined Petrov at a table near the restroom. She noticed Petrov silently assessing the risk of sitting relatively near another customer, but Sara quietly assured him, "Not to worry, the Cat Lady is a regular. She's only interested in that poor animal and her crossword puzzles." But the homeless woman wearing an old, tattered coat could sense that she was intruding and abruptly moved two tables away. Neptune's was the only place in town that still tolerated her, and winter was no time to start looking for a new mid-day hang-out.

"I just moved here, and I'm looking for part-time work. Are you hiring?" asked Petrov as he looked intently at Sara and carefully sipped from a steaming cup of coffee.

"I really don't know," Sara replied. "You'll have to ask the assistant manager," and she pointed in Derwin's direction. Petrov stood and walked over to speak with Derwin as Sara quietly stared out the window. Since "part-time" was prearranged code for an emergency meeting, Sara's next task would be to check a series of dead drops for information regarding the meeting's time and place.

Flag Cabin, USS Ronald Reagan

The newly appointed acting secretary of defense, Colton Garrett, was momentarily stunned when Captain Winters called the room to attention. It took a few seconds for him to realize the honor was for him. He looked up and said, "Please, be seated. And thank you, Captain Winters, that was quite unexpected but very much appreciated."

Admiral Carlisle remained standing and offered his hand. "Mr. Secretary, let me be the first to offer my congratulations on your appointment. I imagine you'll be heading back to Washington right away, so let me or my staff know if we can be helpful in any way."

"Thank you, Admiral, I appreciate the offer," Colt replied, knowing Carlisle would gladly help if it meant he'd be rid of the new secretary of defense. "But I'll need to contact the new deputy secretary to understand what's next and exactly when I'll be heading home." The brief message from the president indicated that Undersecretary Steve Holmes would immediately be appointed deputy secretary of defense, and Colt wanted to talk with his friend Steve as soon as possible to get a sense of what had just happened and how they'd be moving forward. In the last few minutes, Colt Garrett had become the second most senior person in the U.S. military; he, therefore, needed to be briefed immediately on current operational force status.

"Sir, can my staff help with that communications set up?" Carlisle asked, still standing.

Ignoring Admiral Carlisle for the moment, Colt turned to Lenny. "Mr. Wilson, effective immediately, you are appointed special assistant to the secretary of defense. You're going to have to cobble together a local support component from ship, airwing, and flag staff. We'll need people with top-secret clearance; you can read them into any required programs."

"Flag staff?" Carlisle interrupted.

Colt put his right hand up, palm facing out. "Excuse me, Joe. I'm speaking now to Mr. Wilson."

Admiral Joe Carlisle was about to protest but thought better of it and closed his mouth when he saw the stern look on Garrett's face. Powerless, he stepped away from the table and sat down in a chair on the far side of the cabin. Garrett continued, "We'll need to build a full communications and admin staff — about 20 people. Work with the ship's commanding officer and Captain Winters here to configure a dedicated and suitable working space for the team. We'll call it the Office of the Secretary of Defense – Reagan Detachment, or OSD Reagan." Colt caught his breath and went on with his orders.

"Right away, I'm going to need a secure video link with Steve Holmes at the Pentagon, and other links ready to go with the joint chiefs and the White House Situation Room. I'll need to talk with the president's chief of staff as soon as you can arrange it." Lenny was getting it all down, writing as fast as possible, with his pen on the white linen tablecloth. He hadn't had a chance to find a notebook or tablet when Garrett started listing tasks.

Dan Garrett sat, watching his father. Since the moment the president had announced the appointment, he had been mesmerized by how quickly the man he'd known his entire life transformed from a polished policy specialist into a confident and competent leader in command. He knew his dad had served in the Navy — in fact, he was present at his retirement ceremony. But that was 15 years ago and long before Dan knew anything about the Navy. Now, he was impressed with the precision and effortlessness with which his father pushed the ineffective admiral aside, and he wondered where this all was heading.

Garrett began writing a series of notes on a paper tablet when he suddenly remembered, "I believe we'll need to make some berthing changes. Joe, you and Captain Winters will have to make arrangements to find other quarters, immediately. I'll have my luggage shifted into the Flag cabin, and Mr. Wilson, you will move into Captain Winters' stateroom."

When Carlisle stood up, it appeared to the others as though he might be experiencing a stroke. "Other quarters?" he bellowed. "Where do you expect me to move?" Without looking up or skipping a beat, Colt hinted wryly, "Well Joe, perhaps you and Captain Winters can take the stateroom that Lenny and I have been sharing."

Admiral Carlisle stared at the new secretary of defense, realizing now that his earlier disrespect of the former undersecretary had not gone unnoticed.

Lenny turned to face Gary Winters. "Captain, any possibility the ship has a secretary of defense flag onboard?"

Captain Winters smiled and replied, "Yes, sir, I bet they do. If not, I'm certain we can get one of the squadron riggers to make one up." Turning to the admiral, Winters asked, "Sir, shall I ask the ship's captain to have it hoisted?"

Before Rear Admiral Lower Half Carlisle could respond, the

new Secretary of Defense looked up from the table and ordered, "Make it so! And one other thing: Have someone tear that ridiculous portrait off the bulkhead and hang a picture of Ronald Reagan in its place. This ship is named for the man!"

Harborside Fountain Park, Bremerton, Washington

Sara Olson walked to the supermarket on the block next to Neptune's Grounds and examined the assortment of business cards and "for sale" notices thumbtacked to the store's crowded community information board near the entrance. She scanned the ads offering piano lessons, lawn maintenance, yoga instruction, and several people seeking roommates, until she found what she was searching for — a small piece of paper offering tennis lessons at $20 per hour. The local phone number printed on the paper ended in the digits "2-5". By subtracting the 2 from the 5, she knew that she was to rendezvous with her GRU control officer precisely at 3:00 pm at the pre-arranged meeting location. She removed the small piece of paper from the board and casually dropped it in the trash bin as she exited the grocery store.

GRU Captain Yelena Denisovna Ivanova, or Sara Olson as her name read on her Social Security card, had been trained in the specialized tradecraft required of a deep-cover Russian operative. She was well aware of the dangers inherent in most face-to-face meetings. After 30 minutes spent watching the reflections in the windows of the downtown stores to make sure she wasn't being followed, Sara walked the few blocks to Bremerton's Harborside Fountain Park. As she crossed the busy street to enter the park, she brushed by a rusty iron lamppost and placed a small white mark on the post with a piece of chalk she held tightly in her right hand, indicating she was not under surveillance. Finally, she walked to the far end of the park, sat on a bench facing the waterfront and plugged in her earphones. Then she waited. The park was adjacent to the terminal, where the state-run ferries deposited vehicles and walk-on passengers before reloading for another trip back across Puget Sound to Seattle. Several children in the park were playing at the base of the water fountain, even though the water had been turned off many months earlier when the warm weather had given way to cooler temperatures. Mothers kept their eyes on their children while talking to one another about the arrival of flu season and plans for the weekend.

A few moments later, Colonel Dimitri Petrov, Sara's GRU controller, sat down on the bench behind and slightly to the left of her and removed a mobile phone from his pocket. He pressed some buttons, waited a few seconds, and said, "Hello, Sara, it's Robert." By looking in the reflection of her own phone, Sara could see the colonel sitting behind her. The green woolen coat and grey herringbone cap he now wore altered his appearance dramatically from when she had last seen him, just a few hours earlier in the cafe. Now, Colonel Petrov watched as the children played in the fountain. "Only in America could one watch children play on fountains in the shape of submarine sails," he commented into his phone.

"Not so strange," replied Sara. "If you consider that the building next to this park is the Puget Sound Naval Museum. Bremerton has been a Navy town since before the Great Patriotic War, and the people who live here are proud of that heritage. But you didn't call this meeting to discuss U.S. Navy history."

"You are right, Sara," said Petrov into his phone, as though he were actually talking to someone via the device. "You will receive your orders in the usual way, but I have been instructed to stress to you personally the significance of this new assignment. Its success is vital to our overall mission, and we have great confidence in your abilities and the abilities of those you control. You will need to ask a great deal of your network, and it likely will prove challenging to get NIKITA and VADIM to do what needs to be done. We are prepared to help motivate them should it be needed, and you should know that if we are successful with this mission, your promotion to the rank of major will be assured."

Sara considered what the colonel had just shared. She was eager to learn the details he had hinted at, and she knew the promised promotion was intended to motivate her as well. She also knew that failure would lead to an equally significant negative consequence.

"I understand the gravity of the mission, and I will not let you down, Robert," she assured her GRU superior as she stood without looking behind her and walked back the way she had come. While instinctively Sara's eyes scanned the landscape for suspicious-looking cars and pedestrians, she was barely aware she was doing it.

NCIS Offices, the Reagan

Afloat Special Agent Kevin Orr quietly sat in the one comfortable chair in the cramped office he had called home for the past two years since reporting aboard the Reagan. As part of a program to provide investigative, counterintelligence, and force protection support to deployed commanders, the NCIS Special

Agent Afloat Program sent agents aboard aircraft carriers and other large ships (e.g., hospital ships, amphibious assault ships). The special agents were individually selected for the independent duty, and the tour gave them first-hand experience with Navy operating forces that would help them throughout their career. A fully credentialed federal law enforcement officer, Kevin was responsible for investigating suspected felony violations. The latest challenge on board was the increased use of Lysergic Acid Diethylamide (LSD), anabolic steroids, and psilocybin mushrooms. The Navy had been using random urinalysis screening since the late 70s to discourage Sailors from using illegal substances. Those who were found to have substances in their system were promptly removed from the service. But since the American Revolution, Sailors had been inventing ways to circumvent Navy policies, and today's Sailors were no exception. LSD, mushrooms, and steroids had now become increasingly popular options with very short half-lives making them challenging to detect. In late 2018, more than two dozen *Reagan* Sailors had faced charges of possession and distribution of a controlled substance, and Kevin Orr knew he was just getting started. This was only one drug ring, and he was certain there were others still in operation.

Afloat special agents also focused their efforts on counterintelligence recruitment activities. Kevin Orr spent the majority of his time conducting threat assessments of each port the carrier visited and then providing a series of threat awareness briefings for the ship's crew. A forward-deployed force was continually susceptible to threats while ships were in-port, primarily in bars and entertainment establishments Sailors would frequent. But an increasing and more direct recruitment tool used by foreign intelligence operatives was the commercial Internet, which crewmembers had access to while in-port and underway. Special Agent Orr knew that the wide range of social media platforms and interactive games available to the Sailors offered unlimited opportunities for foreign intelligence operatives to create relationships that might develop into something more nefarious. He had access to all Internet traffic coming in and out of the ship, but the vast magnitude of electronic signals he picked up made his counterintelligence efforts perfunctory at best.

Across from Kevin Orr, Special Agent Anna DeSantis sat in an exceptionally uncomfortable chair and looked at the wall behind Kevin's desk. There were six framed silhouettes of heads with red question marks on each one. Hanging above the six silhouettes, a sign said, "Kevin's Most Wanted," and beneath the title in a smaller type, the question, "Which One Is You?"

Anna motioned to the wall and asked, "What is the purpose of that?"

"Usually," Kevin explained, "people sitting in that chair are here because they have done something very wrong, or because they are answering questions in a security clearance investigation. In either case, my wall puts them on edge a bit, and I'll take any advantage I can get." Just as Kevin thought he had answered the question pretty well, Anna commented, "Well, I think it's stupid and offensive."

"See? It's even working on you!" Kevin retorted, then smiled to himself. "Okay, what can I do for you, *very* Special Agent DeSantis?"

Anna looked intently across the desk at her fellow agent, knowing she had to get Kevin's full cooperation while retaining direct control of her protection assignment.

"Since Mr. Garrett has been appointed SECDEF," she began, "he has been occupying a permanent Level 1 Protection High-Risk Billet. As you probably know, Army CID has primary responsibility for the secretary of defense. But since Army CID is not here, and we are, and so is Mr. Garrett, this is a Navy mission until or unless the Army relieves us. I've been designated by our headquarters as the personal security advisor for this protective service detail, which from this moment on, will be providing full-time, 24/7 coverage. This is the full meal deal, Kevin, same as what POTUS gets from the Secret Service. I think it's going to be easier while he's on this steel fortress, but there are thousands of people on this floating city, and it's going to be our job to make certain that none of them can harm Garrett."

Kevin looked at Anna with a sly smile. "Gee, thanks, Anna," he responded. "I *really* appreciate your explanation of what Level 1 protection looks like. I must have missed that day at very-special-agent training. Do we get to wear guns and badges and have radios, too? Very cool!"

Anna DeSantis felt her pulse quicken as she considered whether to storm out or throw something. Instead, she abruptly stood and said, "Look, Kevin, I'm just making sure you know what has to happen here. I'm going to rely on your help."

Kevin raised his hands in mock surrender and said, "Okay, okay! Don't get your shoulder holster in a knot. I promise I'll do my job. What do you need from me?"

Anna took a breath, thought for a moment, and sat back down in her chair. "I'm sorry. I didn't mean to imply you don't understand protection operations. To be honest, I'm nervous about being personally responsible for the new secretary of defense, and I don't want to screw it up. I think we need to divide up the work. I'll run the detail and manage the protection schedule, but I need your help selecting master-at-arms Sailors to form our protection team. You know the ship and crew, so you're in the best position to select the detail."

"I can do that. But only if we can outfit them with black suits, dark glasses, and secret decoder rings!"

Anna almost took the bait but decided to play along with the jokester. "That sounds perfect! And trench coats too!"

Both agents had a good laugh. "I'll start working with the ship's executive officer to find the right people," offered Kevin. "It shouldn't be a problem. Anything else I need to do?"

"Just one other thing. Although SECDEF automatically gets Level 1 protection, I think it's a good idea to do a vulnerability assessment to determine the actual level of risk while he's on board. Again, your familiarity with the ship's crew will give us a leg up on creating a shortlist of people who might have an issue with PATRIOT."

Anna stood once more, but this time she smiled, offered her hand, and said, "I appreciate your working with me on this, Kevin. I'm guessing this will only be for a few days, and then PATRIOT will head back to D.C. and I'll go back to Tokyo."

Kevin shook her hand. As he watched Anna leave his office, he thought to himself, *I actually hope it lasts more than a few days.*

Mountain View Apartments, Bremerton, Washington

When she returned to her apartment after meeting with Colonel Petrov, Sara refilled a small plastic bowl with cat food. She had been leaving food out for the old black cat for several months as she wasn't sure where he lived when he wasn't laying on the mat in front of her door. She knew she shouldn't be feeding him, but she enjoyed the company, and his occasional presence made her feel less isolated. Being a deep-cover operative meant she couldn't develop any real or lasting relationships. It was too complicated to compartmentalize one's life and guard private thoughts while trying to share an intimate relationship and space with someone else. The cat, on the other hand, was the perfect companion for her. He didn't ask questions and she could tell him anything.

Sara made herself dinner, poured a glass of merlot, and then turned on her laptop. Moscow's tasking was clear. She was to make contact with her agents on the *Reagan* and work with them to develop several options for eliminating the new secretary of defense. It sounded straightforward enough, except that her agents were not assassins — and far from it. For two years NIKITA and VADIM had provided Sara and her GRU superiors with exceptional information regarding American defense capabilities and operations. Their information was graded by Moscow as highly valuable and reliable, a combination not typically attributed to stolen material. The most important information they provided involved state-of-the-art avionics and weapons systems — information Russia could use to develop competing weapons systems and counter a threat from the U.S. But now, Petrov was asking Sara's agents on the *Reagan* to take an active role in the assassination of one of the most senior members of the American government. It was a role for which they were untrained, and a task which they might be unwilling to accept.

Communicating with agents onboard a U.S. Navy ship at sea

was made possible through the Internet, which was available on most ships. Crew members corresponded regularly with friends and family via email and video conferencing, making multi-month deployments somehow more bearable. Sara knew that the American counterintelligence forces monitored crew members' emails and video calls, so the best way to covertly communicate with NIKITA and VADIM was via the personal messaging tool within an interactive online game. She logged into *Channel Defence*, a first-person World War II game where players assumed roles as either British or German fighter pilots battling one another over the English Channel. On a pre-arranged schedule, Sara would enter into a battle and then look to see if NIKITA or VADIM were online. She would then initiate a private message with one or both of the agents and exchange coded information. Before logging into the game, Sara had previously written out her intended instructions in detail and then laboriously encoded them into a series of words associated with the game. Even if someone monitoring the game were able to hack into her private messages, they would only see words and phrases communicating air-to-air tactics and strategies between game participants.

After launching the game, she searched for a battle in which her *Reagan*-based agents were participating. She was pleased to find them both online and sent them individual invitations to message her privately. As she began to relay her instructions to the two Americans, she wondered how they would react to this new mission, and whether she would need to use the leverage that Petrov had offered.

Seattle Field Office, The Federal Bureau of Investigation

Clay Taylor thoroughly enjoyed the view from his office on Seattle's Third Avenue. It was a panoramic vista of Elliott Bay and Seattle's vast and active waterfront. Regardless of the dreary winter weather, he always looked forward to his daily ritual of grabbing a double tall mocha from the coffee shop across the street and spending the last few minutes of his day watching the busy harbor 30 floors below. He became mesmerized as tug boats, ferry boats, container ships, tour boats, Coast Guard cutters, and even an occasional pleasure craft sailed back and forth before his eyes. As Special Agent in Charge of the FBI's Seattle Field Office, Clay Taylor had ascended as far as he could go in the Bureau, and that was fine with him. A native Washingtonian, Clay was raised in West Seattle and attended Chief Sealth High School, named for a Suquamish and Duwamish tribal head. The city of Seattle was also named for the same chief, but the settlers slightly altered his name to avoid the tribe's belief that if a person's name was mentioned after his death, he would roll in his grave. Clay smiled as he remembered his high school classmates rapidly saying the school's name over and over, thinking they were causing the dead chief to roll in his grave. Cruel, but typical of teenagers.

This evening's magical moment was interrupted by Clay's assistant. "Excuse me, Clay. Greg is here." Clay turned to greet Greg Cassidy, Special Agent in Charge of NCIS's Northwest Field Office, located in Silverdale on the west side of Puget Sound.

"Hi, Greg. Have a seat!"

An impressive figure, Greg Cassidy stood 6' 6" and was an athletic 250 pounds. He and Clay Taylor had been working closely together over the past 18 months in a joint agency counterintelligence surveillance of a suspected Russian illegal operative based in Bremerton. The FBI had primary jurisdiction for counterintelligence operations within the U.S., but since the attacks of 9/11, all Federal law enforcement agencies closely coordinated their efforts to thwart foreign intelligence collection. The Bremerton case was of high interest to NCIS because the Russian agent was targeting Sailors, Marines and military contractors. The surveillance operation had established that the Russian was a GRU officer named Yelena Ivanova who was using the assumed identity of Sara Olson. The GRU agent worked as a barista at a Bremerton coffee shop and had stolen the identity of the real Sara Olson who had died as an infant in Boise, Idaho, 20 years earlier. In addition to gathering evidence of Sara's espionage activities, the primary purpose of the surveillance was to identify her GRU controller, who presumably had responsibility for an entire network of other GRU operatives in the Pacific Northwest. Only by identifying the GRU control officer would the joint FBI/ NCIS team be able to identify and then locate the entire Russian intelligence collection apparatus in the region. Then there were the Americans who may be providing those Russian operatives with highly classified military intelligence, information technology, and valuable intellectual property. Yesterday, the surveillance team had been lucky.

"Clay. I almost fell off my chair when heard that the team observed Sara making contact in the park with someone who appears to be her GRU control officer. It looks like our surveillance team was not detected, and they were able to follow this new guy to Poulsbo. What do we know about him?"

Clay put his coffee down. "His name is Robert Jordan, and he's a professor at the Poulsbo branch of Kitsap College. He runs the computer information security program there. I've got the folks at the Hoover building working now to find out who he really is. Our bugs in the coffee shop caught a bit of the conversation between him and Sara, and the team was even able to catch a majority of their conversation in the park using the new acoustic gear. The names Vadim and Nikita were overheard, and we are assuming these are codenames for other deep-cover GRU operatives, or maybe even for covert assets working on your Navy installations."

"Where do we go from here?" Greg asked. "It's clear Jordan's tasking her with something out of the ordinary. Why else would he risk a personal meet?"

The FBI man stood and walked to his office window. Looking out at the sound, he responded, "I agree that it must be something major to be worth him taking the risk. I'm glad the search warrant includes Sara's laptop and everyone with whom she communicates. The keyboard recording software is working great, and they tell me its undetectable. I think we'll need to have another team just to keep an eye on Professor Jordan, and that's going to take more resources. I've already requested that D.C. provide six more agents, and I've received authorization to place an agent undercover at the college. Operating on a college campus is politically challenging, and getting a warrant to place equipment there is probably a non-starter. We'll try it the old-fashioned way first: Our guy can watch their guy. Our agent can wear a wire and if we get anything close to probable cause, then we can talk to the assistant U.S. attorney to get the electronic surveillance approval."

"I know I can get more resources based on this new development," Greg said. "I'll formally request four more NCIS counterintelligence types to flesh out the team to improve our coverage, particularly if we need to get creative. If Jordan is Sara's control officer, he's probably more experienced and will be much better at spotting surveillance than our young Bremerton barista."

The FBI man walked back across his office and said, "I appreciate the Navy's help, Greg. This time, I think the GRU is up to something unusual, and it could take everything we have to find out what they're planning, and then to prevent it!"

Defense Secretary Cabin, the Reagan

The ship's commanding officer, Captain Solari, had spared no effort arranging for the video conferencing system Colt Garrett had requested to be set up in his cabin. Garrett was sitting at a small conference table looking at a 65 inch, high-definition video monitor showing the new deputy secretary of defense, Steve Holmes, in his Pentagon office, on the other side of the world. Holmes was slightly built, but his 172-pound body was in exceptional shape because of his almost fanatical love of swimming, running, and bicycling. He had an eye for detail and was reputed to be one of the most intelligent analysts in the Pentagon. Garrett was more than pleased that the president had appointed Steve as his deputy.

"How's the weather in the capital, Steve? You look like you're cold!"

"I suspect your chair is a bit warmer than mine, Mr. Secretary."

Colt Garrett smiled at his friend's joke and looked down at his notes. "I've got a few things we need to go over while we have this great video link."

"Okay, I'm all ears, Boss!" answered Steve.

"Well, first, why didn't Harrison appoint Webb as secretary?

They've been grooming him for years, and I've always assumed he'd just slide right in if anything happened to O'Kane."

"Some pictures surfaced of Webb in blackface from years ago, and the press is having a field day with others who've been similarly outed. Seems the president doesn't want anything to distract from getting his budget approved. And I know you think Pat O'Kane when you think "defense secretary," but you better get used to being called that yourself. By the way, Army CID is more than eager to implement their protection detail surrounding you. When are you planning to return, to D.C., sir?"

"You should probably start making the arrangements, Steve," Colt told him. "My new job makes this mission on *Reagan* secondary at best, and I'd like to get working on any departmental changes we have to make. Is there anything on the hot burner that we need to discuss?"

"Funny you should ask. I'm looking right now at a copy of a communique from our friend in Pyongyang to POTUS that came in yesterday. North Korea is claiming to have intelligence that Seoul grabbed some of our bio warheads back during the Bush 41 administration and has them hidden someplace in-country. I know it sounds crazy, but now he's reneging on his pledge to start disarmamant because of this new "threat," as he calls it. At first, we all thought it was just another excuse to delay and get us to lift the sanctions, but some of his information regarding the mysterious warheads is very specific. So, I have the Agency and the Army digging into it. If it's really true we lost some warheads, and South Korea has them, delay in the reunification of the Korean Peninsula could be the least of our concerns."

"Unbelievable! Let me know as soon as you verify the weapons loss. What is State saying?"

"They want to wait until we verify the loss. If it's true, they're not certain the international support for the sanctions will hold up. I have a meeting with the National Security Council later this evening to talk about options. I'll get back to you with their recommendations. Oh, and one more thing, I've deployed a Nightwatch aircraft to Tokyo to support you, and to provide transport home. As defense secretary, you're supposed to have one whenever you travel overseas or are not able to immediately access a DOD facility."

The Air Force maintained four E-4B Mercury "Nightwatch" Airborne Command Post aircraft at Offutt Air Force Base, Nebraska, and operated by the 1st Airborne Command and Control Squadron of the 55th Wing. Called the NAOC (National Alternate Operations Center), these aircraft were also known as *The Doomsday Planes* because, in the event of a nuclear strike or other major attack on the U.S., they could be used to give the National Command Authority, which is the president and the secretary of defense, a means to launch weapons of mass destruction and talk with anyone, anywhere on the planet. The planes were modified Boeing 747-200B jumbo jets and also included a very modest executive suite with two beds. One aircraft was specifically assigned to the secretary of defense for his use.

Colt smiled, thinking how much Lenny Wilson would appreciate having a real bed —finally.

Day Five

Ready Room 4, the Reagan

Colt Garrett and his newly appointed special assistant Lenny Wilson sat in the back row of Ready Room 4, the combination brief room, clubhouse, and coffee shop of Electronic Attack Squadron 132. Its commanding officer, Commander Tom Robinson, had invited Colt and Lenny to stop by this morning to meet the officers in Dan's squadron. The two men had entered the space via the rear door and sat quietly through the squadron's weekly training session. Tom Robinson noticed them when they came in and was surprised at the presence of Special Agent DeSantis standing at the rear of the room. She looked every part the executive protection agent with her dark business suit and the weapon on her waist that was concealed yet slightly noticeable to the trained eye.

Since before World War II, Navy aircraft squadrons were assigned spaces in carriers that were virtually identical to this one. The room was filled with aluminum-framed reclining armchairs with folding tables and storage compartments below. The upholstered seats and chair backs were covered in a bright red vinyl material that resisted coffee spills and perspiration from men and women who had just survived another carrier landing. The chairs were arranged in five rows of seven, with four chairs on one side of a center aisle and three on the other.

Secured to one wall was a coffee station with its rows of ceramic coffee mugs neatly hanging from hooks. Each mug donned the squadron's logo and the callsign of its owner. Most people assumed Navy callsigns reflected the personal and heroic attributes of the officer. It was much more common, however, for callsigns to be "earned" during flight training for some small mishap or error in judgment, either in the air or out on the town, as best exemplified by Vice Admiral Shaffer's callsign TEDDY. There were few MAVERICK or ICE MAN callsigns in the fleet.

Mounted on the back of the door at the rear of the room, the "Greenie Board" documented each pilot's ability to safely execute the supreme test of aviation skill: an arrested gear landing on an aircraft carrier at sea. Every landing was graded by the white-vested Landing Signal Officers (LSOs) who stood on a small platform dangerously close to the plane landing area on the carrier's stern. The grading system intended to encourage pilots to work on improving their skills when conditions were good in order to increase their chances of landing safely when the visibility, weather, seas, and a violently pitching deck combined to challenge even the most skillful pilot.

The LSOs were young pilots who had been specifically trained to help guide a pilot through the final stages of landing on the ship. After each recovery, they would visit the ready room to debrief the pilot on his or her landing and rate their performance using a four-point scale:

A 4.0 grade, called an *Okay*, indicated a perfect landing, or *pass*, and earned the pilot a green square opposite their name on the board, hence, the *Greenie Board*. A 3.0 grade, or *Fair* pass, indicated the pilot needed to make a few minor corrections. A 2.5 grade called a *Bolter* meant the pilot had failed to catch an arresting gear wire and needed to try again. A 2.0 grade was given for a below-average pass, also described as *Safely Ugly*. Further down the scale

98

was a grade of 1.0 for a *Wave-Off*, which was defined in the LSO instruction as "unsettling dynamics, potentially unsafe." The worst possible grade was a 0.0, for a *Cut*, for unsafe conditions inside the wave-off window. It was every pilot's goal to earn a GPA above 3.0, which indicated he or she was professionally safe. When landing on an aircraft carrier, to be safe was a very good thing.

The public acknowledgment of a pilot's skill didn't end with the Greenie Board. At the conclusion of a number of weeks or even months — depending upon how long the carrier had been continually operating at sea — all of the squadrons would gather for Foc's'l Follies, an irreverent celebration with skits and other pranks. At the end of the evening, the aviators with the highest landing grades were recognized, and the most proficient pilot earned the title of *Top Hook*.

Colt glanced around the Ready Room until his eyes rested on a large, rectangular-shaped quilt hanging from the bulkhead. The quilt was covered with hand-embroidered messages from loved ones waiting back home at Whidbey Island. The quilt was there to soften the space and perhaps make it feel more like home. But it simply wasn't home, and as a young man on a long deployment, Colt recalled, he found it more helpful to focus on the mission rather than think about home.

Today's training lecture was led by Lieutenant Katrina Pierce, the NFO usually paired with her good friend and aviator Dan Garrett on this deployment. Katrina, callsign HURRICANE, had also been raised in the Pacific Northwest, graduating with a degree in history from Central Washington University in Ellensburg. An attractive blonde in her early 30s, Katrina was

happily married to Gene Pierce, a 737-captain flying for Alaska
Airlines. Gene had flown C-141 Starlifters for the U.S. Air
Force and now used his skills to fly the C-17 Globemaster one
weekend a month for the Air National Guard when not flying
for Alaska. HURRICANE had earned her callsign not only from
a devastating storm in 2005, but also because of her quick wit,
sarcastic attitude, and bold delivery. Commander Robinson had
assigned her as squadron training officer because she commanded
attention during even the most mundane of training topics.

"This morning's topic is active shooter defense," she began,
"and the reason we are all here today is because not a single one
of you mental giants have taken the mandatory online training
that I assigned two months ago!" Responding fearlessly to the
heckles and jeers from the room, Lieutenant Pierce shouted,
"Knock it off, boys and girls! You had your chance to get this
done on your own time, and now you're going to have to sit
through it, keep quiet, and learn something!"

Katrina began the training, which was based on the
Department of Homeland Security's Run, Hide, Fight model.
The strategy recommended, first, immediately running away from
an active shooting scene and preventing others from entering
the area. Second, if unable to run, it recommended hiding from
the shooter by barricading oneself in a locked room and turning
off all cell phone alarms. Third, if the active shooter persisted
and entered the hiding space and you were with others, you were
advised to all band together, grab anything that could be used as
a weapon, attack the shooter, and not stop until he or she was
completely incapacitated or dead.

"Okay, pretty straightforward," Katrina summarized, "run,
hide, and only in the last resort, fight. Anybody have questions?"

Katrina winced when she saw Dan Garrett's hand go up. Garrett's callsign — JOKER — had been well-earned. "Yes, Lieutenant?"

Dan stood up as the other junior officers snickered in anticipation.

"Well, HURRICANE, I actually think you got it backward."

"Make your point, JOKER!" urged Lieutenant Pierce.

"Well, if some dude with an assault rifle strolls into the barracks blasting people away, I figure I should get him before he gets me. I'd grab a fire extinguisher from the bulkhead and smack him on the head. Makes the active shooter training easier to remember, don't you think? Just Fight!"

"Oh, really, Dan?" remarked Katrina, rolling her eyes as she sat down next to him and punched him on the shoulder.

Listening from the back row, Lenny turned to Colt and teased, "You got a pretty smart boy there, sir. If someone threatens me while on board, I'm following his advice!"

Colt groaned and held his hand to his forehead. Commander Tom Robinson stood and walked purposefully to the front of the room, the noise died down "Good morning, Scorpions! We have a very special guest visiting us this morning, whom I have the distinct pleasure of introducing. Besides being the proud father of our very own Lieutenant Dan Garrett, he is the newly appointed secretary of defense. May I introduce the Honorable Colton Garrett."

The startled aviators and NFOs seated in Ready Room 4 suddenly all came to attention as Colt walked from the back row to the front of the room and stood behind the lectern.

"Please be seated, ladies and gentlemen, and thank you, Skipper Robinson," Colt began. "I asked the skipper if I could

101

stop by and simply thank all of you for the great work you are doing here. I personally know how hard these long deployments can be on both you and your families. This morning I want you to know how proud our country is of you and how deeply we appreciate the risks you take each day to protect our nation and our freedom. I served in this squadron as an intel officer many years ago when we were flying Prowlers, and I have memories from those years that will be with me for the rest of my life. For now, though, I told the skipper I'd take a few questions. But go easy on me; I've only had the job for a few days!"

"Sir, I'm Lieutenant Commander Wasankari. Can you tell me what the DOD is doing to retain pilots? As we're all aware, the airlines are replacing their retiring pilots, and the benefits, time off, and pay are much better than we get, while the risks aren't nearly as high."

Colt considered the aviator's question and then responded, "I can't argue with you, Commander. I resigned my commission when I was about as senior as you are now. We all have to make career decisions that are right for us and for our families. We *are* looking at some innovative approaches to creating new career models, some allowing pilots to remain flying and not necessarily pursue a command path. Other ideas include options for officers to move back and forth between military and commercial flying. But I think the bottom line is that we know the pilot shortage isn't going away, and we can't just keep doing things the same ways we have in the past. Anyone else?"

A young ensign in a pressed khaki uniform stood up. "Sir, I have a question."

Richard Gundersen was a newly minted graduate of the Naval Intelligence Officer School in Dam Neck, Virginia. He held a baccalaureate in political science from Princeton University and had career ambitions to either become a naval attaché in an embassy or find civilian employment with a three-letter agency in D.C. He had frequently communicated to the squadron his preference to be called Richard rather than the more common nickname.

"I find it interesting that you served in the very same billet I now occupy. When you were in this squadron, who did you find to be the most arrogant — Naval aviators or NFOs?"

"Shut up, *Dick!*" shouted a voice from the back. The room erupted in laughter as a volley of pens and baseball caps quickly cascaded upon the young intelligence officer while he tried to protect himself with an aluminum clipboard.

Colt laughed with the rest and noted, "I can see things haven't changed much! But seriously, I think the key to be a good intel officer is understanding that you are here to support these brave aviators who risk their lives every day while you drink coffee in the intel center. You need to earn their respect first, and then they'll be more receptive to hearing how you can support them." The ready room erupted in applause from those in the room wearing flight suits.

"You can sit down now, *Dick*," said Katrina, goading him with an emphasis on his forbidden nickname. She turned to Colt at the front of the room. "Sir, I have a question!"

"Yes, Lieutenant?"

"Sir, can you tell us please if Lieutenant Garrett has been a pain in the ass his entire life?"

Once again, the ready room erupted in laughter, until Commander Robinson decided it was time to wrap things up. Before he did, Colt thought a moment, smiled, and replied, "No, just since earning his wings!" The officers all stood and applauded enthusiastically as Commander Robinson shook Colt's hand and then escorted the secretary of defense and his special assistant back to Flag country.

When they had gone, and the officers in the ready room began to move around, Katrina approached and cornered Dan. "Have you had a chance to talk with your mom? How is she?"

Dan turned to face Katrina. "She's doing great! Still working out every day at her gym. She complained about some lower back pain, but when I said she should see a doctor, she said what she usually does, that doctors are for people who are really sick. She did mention that Dad had stopped by Olympia on his way out here and that she's considering joining him in D.C. at some point. And she made me promise to stop blaming him for their separate living arrangements."

"Your old man doesn't seem too bad — nothing like the hard-ass you've been telling me about."

Dan rinsed out his coffee cup and hung it on a hook above the sink. "Sometimes," he told her, "people surprise you."

Electronic Repair Spaces, the Reagan

Malcolm Simpson liked his job as a civilian system engineering contractor working for Boeing onboard the *Reagan*. A University of Oregon engineering graduate, he once had been awarded a full-ride Army Reserve Officer Training Corps (ROTC) scholarship but was removed from the program during his sophomore year after failing a random urinalysis test. During his administrative discharge hearing, Malcolm tried to explain that his positive test results were caused by his attendance at an Oregon football rally where heavy clouds of thick marijuana smoke had drifted through the crowd. But the military had collected data that indicated one could not fail a urinalysis solely because of exposure to second-hand cannabis smoke. Malcolm was promptly released from the Army ROTC program and prohibited from ever serving in the armed forces of his country. He had even gotten dumped by his girlfriend, a nursing student, when he was discharged.

But it was the loss of his scholarship that was particularly devastating for Malcolm. Since his family was not able to support his college tuition or living expenses in Eugene, he was forced to take a series of low-paying jobs to support himself and cover his expenses. College campus work was difficult to find in the small college town because of the relatively large number of job-seeking students. When Malcolm finally secured a job as a night janitor with the university, he considered himself extremely lucky.

The job wasn't particularly difficult — mostly emptying trash in campus buildings after they had closed for the evening. After a few weeks, Malcolm had determined how to get all his tasks completed within two hours, leaving the remaining two hours of his night shift free for studying, reading, or even streaming a movie. One late evening after emptying trash receptacles in the ROTC building on Agate Street, he passed by Colonel Webster's office at the end of the hall and realized the last time he had been in that room was when he was told that he had lost his scholarship and was being dismissed from the brigade.

Like most building janitors, Malcolm Simpson had master keys that allowed him access to individual classrooms and offices. He also had a curious eye and would occasionally glance around at things on people's desks. Later that evening, he let himself into Colonel Webster's office, where he began looking through the assorted papers on her desk. When he noticed a manila colored folder with the word "Confidential" stamped in red on the cover, his curiosity overcame him, and he opened the folder. Inside, he found reports concerning a recent military exercise that had taken place at Joint Base Lewis McChord. Each of the individual documents was also marked "Confidential" in red in the top and bottom margins. Each paragraph was marked with a red "C" or "U" indicating the paragraph was either confidential (C) or unclassified (U). *If this got into the wrong hands, Colonel Webster would be in big trouble,* Malcolm instinctively thought. But any concern over Colonel Webster, the woman who had taken away his scholarship, gave way to a promising and creative idea. He picked up the folder and searched for a copy machine.

The next morning in his dorm room, Malcolm tucked a photocopy of one of the classified documents and a brief, typed note of his own into a plain envelope addressed to the Russian Consulate in Seattle. Several weeks later, he was contacted by a Russian intelligence officer and a meeting between them was arranged — a meeting that would launch a new chapter in Malcolm's life.

For the next three years, Malcolm funded his education through what he thought of as the Malcolm Simpson Full Scholarship plan. He held on to his job as a janitor at the university, as it provided him with unlimited and unsupervised access to the school's research and technologies department as well as the Army ROTC building. His Russian controllers were more than happy to finance his college career, and there was even enough left over to buy a new car and move out of the dorm. In exchange, he had only to visit the offices of certain professors whose names were on a list provided by the Russians and make photocopies of documents he would find there. Life was good for Malcolm, and he felt important and powerful. *Screw the Army and the Oregon ROTC!* he thought.

After college, the GRU suggested that Malcolm apply for a job as a systems engineer with a company in Seattle. After a series of interviews and background checks, he was hired by Boeing Defense, Space & Security (BDS) in Seattle. It seemed Boeing was not as concerned as the Army regarding a prospective employee's recreational use of marijuana during college. Boeing's web site stated:

> *Defense, Space & Security is one of the Boeing Company's three business units. Its portfolio includes manned and unmanned space and satellite systems, intelligence and security systems, and extensive integration expertise. The business employs a total of about 32,000 worldwide. The world's second-largest defense company, Defense, Space & Security is the only aerospace business offering products and capabilities that allows its customers to meet mission requirements from the seabed to outer space. It serves a diverse customer base, but its portfolio is focused in six key market areas: Commercial Derivatives, Military Rotorcraft, Human Space Exploration, Satellites, Autonomous Systems, and Services.*

Based in Arlington, Virginia, BDS had numerous other offices at Boeing locations throughout the world, including Seattle, its original corporate headquarters. Malcolm appreciated the challenge provided by his work with Boeing, particularly the highly advanced avionics control systems. It was state-of-the-art technology in which the GRU was keenly interested. Malcolm's current assignment was as a direct support system engineer onboard the USS *Ronald Reagan*, where he was responsible for supporting aircraft squadrons when they encountered technical problems beyond their training and experience.

Although Malcolm genuinely liked what he was doing, what he truly lived for was the online game *Channel Defence*. He enjoyed the first-person shooter simulation, and he imagined himself as a fighter pilot over the English Channel. He created the screen name GEOFFREY to honor squadron leader Geoffrey Wellum, the youngest Spitfire pilot to fly in the Battle of Britain, who had died in 2018 at the age of 96.

After breakfast, Malcolm closed his stateroom door, plugged in his gaming computer, and joined an online battle in progress. A few minutes into the game, he received a request from Sara Olson for a private message. He shut down the game and thought to himself, *It looks like it's time for NIKITA to get to work!*

O3 Level Fitness Room, the Reagan

VADIM usually preferred to work out before lunch, but this morning's ship training schedule had gone longer than planned, keeping VADIM from the one activity on the ship that provided a distraction from the daily operational routine. VADIM entered the exercise space and selected the stair climber directly across from the pull-down machine that Ensign Rebecca Clarke was using. Rebecca was a Surface Warfare Officer, or SWO, assigned to the *Reagan's* Fire Control Division. Called "black shoes" or simply "shoes" by the carrier's aviators, SWOs were the Navy's ship drivers, commanding and operating all naval vessels other than submarines or aircraft carriers. Although some large amphibious ships were often commanded by aviators, that was primarily done so that senior aviators could gain deep draft experience prior to commanding one of the nation's eleven aircraft carriers. As the ship's fire control division officer, Ensign Clarke was responsible for the operation and maintenance of the ship's defensive missile and gun weapons systems and their associated radars. She stood watch on the ship's bridge as a Junior Officer of the Deck as well as at a variety of other watch stations in the *Reagan's* combat information center.

Rebecca Clarke had graduated from Cornell University, where she lettered in field hockey. Her bright smile and toned, athletic figure had attracted VADIM's interest ever since Rebecca had first reported aboard. Whenever they passed one another in a passageway, Rebecca's subtle but intoxicating cologne stirred a deep passion in the Sailor's soul. VADIM knew two things: (1) their respective positions in the Navy prohibited a romantic relationship, and (2) the best and least obvious way to appreciate Ensign Clarke's fragrance and physique was to casually show up in the fitness room whenever Rebecca worked out.

Twenty minutes into VADIM's stair climber workout, Rebecca left the fitness room to get ready for a bridge watch. Knowing it would not be cool to follow Rebecca out of the gym, VADIM instead used the time to think through the implications of what Sara had tasked via the *Channel Defence* game: the elimination of the new secretary of defense, Colton Garrett. This was a dramatic escalation of previous GRU requests, one that would be a leap for VADIM to accept. Thus far, GRU tasking had been limited mainly to requests for copies of highly classified documents, then adding that information to other materials obtained by NIKITA, and finally, finding a way to get the entire package safely to Sara Olson and the GRU. The ship's postal facility was the most nonattributable means of delivering classified material, but recently VADIM had needed to find other ways to move the classified material because the postal clerks had started to randomly scan outgoing packages.

What started out as a solution to a bad gambling habit had simply evolved into a whole new addiction and had turned VADIM's life upside down. Initially, weekend flights to Reno and Vegas had provided a welcome relief from shipboard responsibilities while *Reagan* was moored in Bremerton. VADIM's thirst for danger and excitement, which had once been quenched by gambling, was soon satisfied again, this time by casual sex with exotic women. The best part was that these women of every age, shape, color, and race all came without the baggage of a personal commitment. It made for an uncontrollable addiction. Uncontrollable, but not unnoticed. VADIM remembered being first approached by the woman who offered to help pay off excessive gambling debts. Only after accepting several payments from the woman did VADIM fully understand the high price to be paid for agreeing to this. The price, in fact, was treason.

Sara Olson had offered two choices: Either provide the required classified documents or within days an envelope containing high-resolution photographs of VADIM receiving money from Russian consulate staff would be mailed to the local NCIS office. Two choices, but really, no choice at all.

Anything can be rationalized; one needs to survive after all. And who was really harmed by the transfer of technology and intelligence from one global power to another? What difference would it ever make? And with all the money VADIM had saved these last few years, a well-funded retirement wasn't far off — a retirement far more comfortable than 20 years in the Navy would have provided! Perhaps, once VADIM was out of the Navy, the fascinating Ensign Rebecca Clarke might consider a romantic relationship; there were substantial savings in a numbered bank account that could certainly provide for them both. It never hurt to dream.

The timer on the stair climber said it had been an hour since Rebecca had left the fitness center. Taking a few moments longer to think about Rebecca, VADIM clicked the machine's cool-down cycle and started to formulate a plan to carry out Sara's latest and most risky assignment — the assassination of Colton Garrett.

Dan Garrett's Stateroom, the Reagan

Dan Garrett returned to his stateroom to find Katrina Pierce waiting by his door. "Hey, JOKER, what's up? You been watching the lovely Ensign Clarke do her bench presses again? Don't think I haven't seen you stare at her whenever she works out."

Dan unlocked the stateroom door, and both officers walked inside. He pulled out a chair for Katrina and then toweled off after his workout.

"Yes, my dear Navy wife, I do stare at the voluptuous Ensign Clarke at every opportunity I get, just like every other red-blooded man onboard this bird-farm. Don't tell me you're getting jealous?"

Katrina threw a flight boot at the Growler driver snorting,

"Jealous? Of that skinny little black shoe? Please! And stop calling me your Navy wife, young Jedi! My husband makes you look like a pre-pubescent child!" Katrina's husband Gene was indeed a real specimen, competing successfully in Ironman events when not flying for Alaska. Katrina's friendship with Dan had started when they were first paired together at the training squadron at Whidbey Island. It had become a close, trusting, sibling-like relationship, and their frequent adolescent sparring was how they best communicated with one another.

"So, how weird is it for you to have your dad be appointed SECDEF? The squadron and the whole damned ship is going nuts with this. And you were all in the admiral's cabin when your dad found out?"

"Yep, he was handed a P-For from President Harrison, and a few minutes later, we saw it on the news at the same time everyone else did. You should have seen poor Admiral Carlisle's face when Dad kicked him out of the flag cabin and told him to make other arrangements. I thought Carlisle was going to stroke out!" Dan chuckled.

Katrina's mood changed to serious as she intentionally changed the subject. "You really need to talk to your father about test pilot school, Dan, it would only take one phone call from him. It's not as if you're not qualified."

Dan thought for a moment. "Maybe I'll talk to him after the dust settles a bit. This appointment came as a complete surprise to him, and I think my control-freak dad has his hands full right now. He has the entire DOD to run. But speaking of careers, why don't you worry about yourself?"

Katrina had been struggling with a decision to leave the Navy as well. She had aspired to be a pilot all her life, but vision issues prevented her from passing a Class I Flight Physical. Plus, the long deployments were putting stress on her marriage to Gene. Now she was seriously considering leaving the Navy and attending law school.

"I know, I know, I got my own stuff to deal with. I'm pretty sure I'll sign up and take the LSAT in February and see how I do."

"Have you thought about the kind of law you'd want to practice? I picture you as one of those high-priced corporate sharks!"

Katrina smiled at the thought. "I think I'm torn between the fun of suing people and the satisfaction of putting them in jail. Maybe I'll work as a kind of prosecutor for hire, traveling from town to town like the Lone Ranger, with a briefcase instead of a revolver with silver bullets!"

She laughed at the entertaining scenario she had just conjured up and turned to leave the stateroom when she caught Dan checking out his recently pumped biceps in the mirror.

"Uh, Schwarzenegger, have you considered getting a tattoo? Ensign Clarke might like it!"

Dan continued to flex his muscles and retorted, "Who puts a bumper sticker on a Maserati?"

Katrina giggled and headed down the long passageway to her own stateroom, being careful to step over the 20-inch jambs of water-tight hatches along the way. The obstacles were affectionately known as knee-knockers because of the injuries to a Sailor's shins if they failed to lift their legs high enough when passing through. Katrina paused while unlocking her stateroom door. "I've got to find a way to get Secretary Garrett to make that phone call," she reminded herself and went inside.

SECDEF Cabin, the Reagan

Carissa Curtis sat down in the comfortable, overstuffed chair in the spacious cabin that now belonged to the secretary of defense. She was about to meet with his special assistant, Len Wilson, in preparation for an interview with Secretary Garrett. It was ironic how things had worked out. Two days earlier, she was feeling sorry for herself because her editor back in New York had given her an assignment that was more a promotional, public relations piece and less real journalism. Senator Emmett Carlisle had pulled a few strings with her network and gotten Carissa, a seasoned reporter, to fly out to the *Reagan* with a camera crew to interview his son, the carrier group commander. It was unlikely the story would ever run in prime time, but Senator Carlisle was a powerful force in town and couldn't — or wouldn't — be ignored. Carissa was the sacrificial lamb. The camera team had already captured video of the ship and crew to be used for cuts and filler. She had just been waiting to hear when she could actually do the interview and go home. Then the news broke about Colton Garrett being named acting defense secretary. In the 30 minutes it took for her editor to get through to Carissa on the ship, her assignment went from a puff piece on the spoiled son of an aging politician to an exclusive first interview with the newly sworn-in defense secretary. The best part was that he wouldn't have a gaggle of handlers and press professionals there to groom him for the interview. It meant he was more likely to be relaxed, natural, and candid in his responses. Garrett had agreed to the interview just this morning. His only request was that she speak with Len Wilson first to get some background on Garrett and more importantly, to discuss the scope of the position he had just accepted.

As she waited for Wilson to finish a phone call, she thought again about the path that had led her to this meeting. Growing up in Michigan, she had attended Western Michigan University at Kalamazoo, earning a B.A. in French and an M.A. in French and Francophone Studies. After earning a second master's in international education, she spent several years working as a high school French teacher in Winnetka, Illinois. While she enjoyed working with the bright students at New Trier High School, she had an intense dislike for the controlling, overly ambitious administrators, and she began to think about a career change. Her neighbor, who worked for the local CBS affiliate in Chicago, offered to make a phone call on her behalf, and after a series of interviews and video tests, she found herself doing human interest stories on camera. She took to the work and excelled at it immensely. She became known for actually listening to people and eliciting interviews that were both compelling and meaningful. Another chance encounter, this time with an influential network producer, resulted in a move to 30 Rockefeller Plaza in New York as an on-air correspondent for the CBS Evening News. Carissa's listening skills continued to yield effective interviews, and she eventually managed to get herself assigned to the Pentagon beat. She had only been there a week when she found herself flying to an aircraft carrier in the western Pacific Ocean.

Lenny finished his call with the JCS staff and poured himself a cup of coffee from the cart near the cabin door. "Can I offer you a cup?" he asked Carissa as he poured creamer into his mug.

"Yes, please, Mr. Wilson, just black!"

Lenny poured a second cup of coffee and placed it on the table between them as he sat down. "Okay, where would you like to start? And call me Lenny, please."

Carissa reached into her messenger bag and pulled out a small digital voice recorder. "Do you mind if I record our interview?" she asked. "It will help me with my notes and ensure that I get your comments down accurately."

Lenny leaned back and said with a surprised look, "Whoa — I thought you just needed a little background on Secretary Garrett and his new role at Defense!"

"You're right, I do, but the voice recorder helps me put the information into context after we're done. Are you okay with it?"

Lenny wasn't comfortable at all being recorded, but he was even less comfortable sharing his discomfort with a major network reporter. "No problem," he assured her. "I just haven't done too many of these interviews before."

In fact, Lenny Wilson was quite experienced at dealing with the press. He just never liked the fact that every word he said would be on the record.

Carissa pressed the "record" button and began to speak. "This is Carissa Curtis, and I'm onboard the USS *Ronald Reagan* in the western Pacific. I'm sitting here with Mr. Leonard Wilson, special assistant to acting secretary of defense Colton Garrett. Mr. Wilson, do I have your permission to record this interview?"

"Yes, you do."

"Before we talk about Mr. Garrett, can you give me a high-level description of the duties of the defense secretary? I just started working at the Pentagon, and I don't really understand his role."

"We should start with the department's official website, which explains that the mission of the defense department is to provide a lethal joint force to defend the security of our country and sustain American influence abroad. The secretary of defense oversees the department and is its principal defense policymaker and advisor. To understand the department is to recognize that there are two chains of command: administrative and operational. On the administrative side, the service chiefs of the Army, Navy, Air Force and Marines each report to their respective department secretaries, and they in turn, report to the secretary of defense, who reports directly to the president. Operationally, it's even more simple. The operational chain of command runs from the president and the secretary of defense to the commanders of the Unified Combatant Commands, which include the six geographic commands: Africa Command, Central Command, European Command, Indo-Pacific Command, Northern Command and Southern Command; and four functional commands: Cyber Command, Special Operations Command, Strategic Command, and Transportation Command. Each is headed by a four-star officer."

Carissa was furiously taking notes despite the presence of the voice recorder. "Okay," she said when she was done writing for a moment, "I think I understand. Can you continue to track the operational chain from the Commander, Indo-Pacific Command down to Rear Admiral Carlisle for me?"

"Sure. Next below the Indo-Pacific commander is a Navy four-star, the commander of the Pacific Fleet, who is responsible for all Naval forces in the Pacific. Vice Admiral Shaffer is next at 7th Fleet, where he runs just the western Pacific, and finally, Rear Admiral Carlisle, as the carrier group commander in this area.

Carissa asked, "Why do the combatant commanders report to the defense secretary *AND* the president?"

Lenny paused for a moment and explained, "If you looked

at the chain of command org chart, the defense secretary and the president are in a box labeled, National Command Authority or NCA. It takes both of them together to authorize a nuclear strike."

Carissa set her pen down and pressed the stop button on the voice recorder. She looked at Lenny and confessed, "I had no idea of the secretary's scope of responsibility. I thought it was basically similar to the other cabinet members."

"Next to the president of the United States, the U.S. secretary of defense is the most powerful person in the world. It's why the Air Force right now is flying one of their Nightwatch 747 aircraft to Tokyo for his support."

Carissa paused for a few moments to look at her notes, and then asked, "Let's talk about Garrett's Navy background. Why did he join? Was his father in the service?"

"I think his dad worked in a shipyard in Seattle during World War II — the man may have had tuberculous as a boy, and I think he had back problems as well," Lenny began. "Regardless, I think that Colt was the first person in his family to join the military. He was in the Sea Scouts as a kid, and that's when he learned to sail. The Navy was the obvious choice for him."

Carissa looked up from her notes. "What can you tell me about Secretary Garrett as a person? What sort of man is he?"

Without a moment's hesitation, Lenny answered, "First of all, he's one of the smartest people I know. He cares deeply about protecting our country and the people who defend it. He has no political ambitions whatsoever, and despite my advice to the contrary, he seems to enjoy telling elected officials exactly what he thinks. He's loyal to a fault. He loves his family but has trouble telling them. He's firm in his beliefs and doesn't understand why everyone else doesn't see the world as he does. He was more surprised than anyone that the president selected him to succeed Patrick O'Kane, and although I know he'll do an outstanding job as secretary, I'm pretty certain he's privately questioning his suitability for the position. And," he added with a wink, "if you repeat any of that, I'll deny every word."

Carissa looked straight into Lenny's eyes. "You really admire him, don't you?" she asked.

As Lenny stood and walked Carissa to the door, he offered her his hand and said, "I'd do anything Colt Garrett asked of me. No other choice."

Carrier Intelligence Center, the Reagan

An aircraft carrier's intelligence center, or CVIC, is the domain of the ship's senior intelligence officer, and it provides a space for several critical functions to support the carrier's operations. The section of CVIC known as the sensitive compartmented information facility (SCIF), contains the most highly classified intelligence on the ship. Only those with an above top-secret clearance based on an exhaustive background investigation and a polygraph examination are granted access. CVIC also provides storage space for information and intelligence that has been classified as top secret, secret and confidential. Basically, it is a specialized library of highly classified hard copy and digital publications and other media. The ship's intelligence department is divided into different divisions and work centers to manage the workload.

When the airwing is embarked, CVIC also hosts the mission

planning and briefing/debriefing of aircrews. The airwing intelligence officer is responsible for coordinating and overseeing these activities, as well as the intelligence officers attached to each squadron. This team provides briefings for every flight event of the day, covering the missions of each aircraft, communications frequencies, area operating constraints, and, most importantly, any potentially hostile forces in proximity to the battle group. After aircrew land, they first head directly to CVIC to debrief on their completed missions with waiting intelligence officers. In addition to the brief/debrief cycle, CVIC provides space for aircrew to conduct detailed mission planning for upcoming operations.

Reagan's intelligence officer, Commander Jennifer Abrams, had arranged to meet with Lenny and the two NCIS special agents to discuss what they might require from her team in support of the new secretary of defense.

"Thank you, Commander Abrams, for agreeing to sit down and work with us on this," said Lenny. Jen Abrams, seated upright at the end of the table, was focused and ready with pad and pen.

"No problem, sir," she replied. "How can I help?"

Lenny cleared his throat, adjusted himself in his chair, and continued. "I think we should start with the morning intel summary. As you know, the Defense Intelligence Agency reports to the defense secretary and provides a daily summary of all-source intelligence and analysis. It would be great, Jennifer, if you or one of your officers would review these materials for us and then brief the secretary?"

"I think I would give that morning brief myself," she explained, "as I'm the only officer on board who has given briefs at the Pentagon. I'm most familiar with the briefing style and also with the specific elements the secretary would likely be most interested in."

"Okay, sounds good," Lenny continued. "We also need message boards for special access traffic. Can you set up a space for us in CVIC for that purpose? It's probably easier than attempting to create another SCIF somewhere else on the ship."

"You're right about that," Commander Abrams agreed. "Getting one of those facilities certified is a major undertaking with layers of bureaucracy."

Lenny laughed and added, "True, but if we really needed to get one approved, I think I know the person who could authorize it!"

Jen had to remind herself exactly who she was dealing with now. She wasn't accustomed to supporting such a senior government official. She supposed he could authorize his shirt pocket as a SCIF if he wanted to. "Is there anything else I can help you with, sir?"

Lenny motioned to the two NCIS agents who had been patiently waiting for the opportunity to discuss their specific needs.

"Special Agents DeSantis and Orr had a few things they wanted to discuss. Anna?"

"Thank you, Mr. Wilson," DeSantis said. "I'll be heading up the protective service detail for the secretary, effective immediately. Special Agent Orr is about to conduct a vulnerability assessment to determine the likelihood of a threat to the secretary while he's onboard *Reagan*. He's going to need your team's assistance in looking through crewmember service records to develop a shortlist of people who might be worth interviewing."

"What sort of things are you looking for?" Jen asked Kevin.

Kevin paused, then opened a file, and glanced over a set of notes he had prepared for the meeting. "We're interested in anybody who might have an issue with authority or who has a history of violence or disruption. People who have some type of addiction or just seem or act strange or suspicious. Everyone onboard has some type of security clearance, but in most cases, their clearance is based merely on a national agency check for criminal convictions. We're also looking for people with an unmanageable amount of debt or who seem to be spending more money than their military pay could support. These are the kinds of indicators that might point to potential areas of concern. It's just the first step in the vulnerability assessment."

Jen looked over at the list Kevin had prepared. "Okay," she assured him. "I can help with that as well. I'd probably recommend keeping this effort restricted to just a few of us. I could see the crew misinterpreting it and starting to freak out."

Anna DeSantis was pleased. "Good point, Commander. Thanks," she said. Anna reached into her jacket pocket and handed Jen a small gold lapel pin. "I'd like to give you one of these NCIS protective service pins. Only those who are assigned to our detail will wear one so that we can immediately identify who can be trusted. No pin, no unescorted access to the secretary."

Lenny looked around the table and announced, "I think that's all for now. I really appreciate your help, Commander. We'll try not to be too much of a burden."

Jen shook hands with Lenny and the two NCIS agents and escorted them out of CVIC.

Rear Admiral Carlisle's Stateroom, the Reagan

Rear Admiral Joe Carlisle was in a foul mood, and he didn't seem to care who knew it. Just yesterday morning he had been enjoying himself, hosting a pleasant breakfast in his cabin. Suddenly, he and the rest of the world learned that the president had appointed Colt Garrett as secretary of defense. Since the moment Garrett had arrived onboard *Reagan*, Carlisle had done what he could to make certain the former undersecretary knew his place. Although Captain Winters had warned him to show Garrett the respect he deserved, that warning went unheeded, and now Rear Admiral Joe Carlisle was paying the price. When a call to his Senator father did nothing to ease his anxiety, he was reminded that the old man's influence was waning as his health declined. Joe figured that the Washington power brokers could sense the Senator was fading, and as a result, his son now found himself out in the cold in a mess of his own making. Not that he would admit that to Winters or anyone else.

"Well, Captain, now you have really screwed things up. Mr. Garrett has kicked us out of the flag spaces, and I'm now being treated like a common seaman on my own flagship! So . . . what do you propose to do about it?"

Captain Winters knew he was on dangerous ground with his admiral blaming him personally for the current situation. Winters thoroughly enjoyed the way Garrett summarily dismissed the arrogant Carlisle, but the man was still his boss and could easily end his career if he wanted to. He decided to ignore the admiral's admonition and respond instead to his direct question.

"Admiral, I think the best approach is to maintain a low profile for the time being. Garrett will be more than busy learning his new job, and most likely, he will soon be heading back to D.C. anyway. Then things will get back to normal. He doesn't write your fitness report and will probably forget about you and everyone else on this ship the moment he sets foot in the Pentagon."

"Are you telling me to hide in this stateroom until he leaves?"

"No, sir, I just meant that you should lay low and try to avoid confronting him during his remaining time onboard. You can act as if nothing happened between you, and you just want to offer assistance in any way you can."

Captain Winters didn't want his personal opinion of the admiral to prevent him from doing his job as chief of staff. At times, however, he felt as though he was giving advice to his teenage daughter.

"Fine. I'll keep my mouth shut and play nice, but he better not do anything to put this carrier group at risk."

Winters left the stateroom and headed to flag plot to see how the rest of the task force was doing. Walking down the long passageway with the blue deck, he had to wonder what Garrett could possibly do that would ever put the task force at risk?

Headquarters, Republic of Korea Marine Corps, Hwaseong, South Korea

The three-star Korean Marine Corps general looked out his office window at the frozen ground below. He saw children playing with one another in the small nearby park and wondered what their parents might think if they knew he was inside planning for the defense of their nation. When General Cho first learned that North Korea knew about the Americans' lost biological weapons — and knew those weapons were hidden somewhere in the South — he initiated a quiet yet exhaustive investigation into how the information could have been leaked. He could count on two hands the number of people who were aware of the weapons' existence in South Korea, and he had entrusted Colonel Chang to identify the traitor. Chang and his security team had thoroughly interrogated each person, using a variety of techniques from polygraph testing to increased electronic and video surveillance. Chang had even subjected himself to a polygraph test to demonstrate to the general his unrestrained pursuit of the truth, but he passed the test with flying colors, and no significant leads had ever emerged. General Cho knew he needed to do something different to find the leak in his organization. Perhaps a trap or two?

Colonel Chang now stood in the general's office, facing him and waiting for his next order. General Cho walked to his desk, sat down, and adjusted the chair. "Colonel Chang, I think we should accelerate our timeline for moving the American weapons off that island and positioning them closer to our operating forces near Seoul."

Chang couldn't contain a gasp. The general had never shared any specifics before regarding the weapons' current location. Hearing the passing reference to an island, he started guessing which island would be the most likely weapons cache. It would have to be remote and not associated with any major South Korean military facilities, and yet offer impenetrable storage for the very dangerous weapons of mass destruction.

General Cho paused to let Chang process the new information and then opened a file on his desk. "Have a seat, Colonel, and let me share my secret with you."

The nautical chart that General Cho unfolded for Colonel Chang to inspect depicted Jeju Island, located south of the Korean peninsula in Jeju Province. Home to a natural and active volcanic with an extensive system of lava caves, the island had long been a popular tourist destination, with a large portion of its economy relying on both tourism and the economic activity generated by its several military bases.

"Jeju is where my warheads are," he said, pointing to its location on the chart. "I want you to start planning how to covertly move them back to the mainland. Take two days and then brief me on the most promising options. After we select the best approach, we will bring in a few more staff to further develop the operations plan. Tell no other person about this island; you and I are the only people who know what lies hidden there. Our national security rests with your discretion."

Colonel Chang left the general's office and immediately began to weigh some options for safely transporting the weapons. By the end of the day, he had written up four different scenarios using a variety of transport alternatives. Drawing on his vast experience in special operations, Chang then drafted summaries of each option, listing their respective strengths and weaknesses. Finally, late at night, he gathered his materials and planning documents and locked them all in his office safe. He double-checked his office to ensure that everything related to the American warheads was safe and secure, then walked down the four flights of stairs and checked out of the highly secure military facility. He returned the salute of the guard on duty and walked the few city blocks on the now deserted street to his apartment.

Locking the heavy front door behind him, Colonel Chang

went to his bedroom, where he quietly undressed and slipped into his bed next to Kang Ji-woo, who was sound asleep on her side. He moved close behind her and began kissing her neck and stroking the small of her back. Ji-woo stirred, arched her back, and said softly, "Welcome home, my colonel. I am lucky to have such an important man as my lover."

The Blue House, Seoul, Korea

Kim Seong-ho had served as head of state and president of the Republic of Korea for three years and still appreciated the perks of his high office. The most visible of those perks was his office and residence in the Blue House in the capital city of Seoul. The Blue House was actually a group of buildings that had been built on the grounds of the royal garden of the prominent Joseon Dynasty, which ruled South Korea from 1392 to 1910. Consisting of the presidential residence, the state reception house, the press hall, and various secretariat buildings, the entire complex covered more than 62 acres. An important reason President Kim had been elected was because of his promise to pursue normalization of relations with North Korea, which hopefully could lead to the eventual and long-awaited unification of the Korean peninsula. Although Kim was assured the South Korean people supported his peace overtures with the North, he was well aware that several high-ranking military officers didn't share their enthusiasm. When President Kim first heard North Korea's claim that his government had somehow stolen American biological warheads, he initially considered the idea absurd. Surely as president, he would know if his country was in possession of such powerful weapons. He began to have his doubts, though, when the American denial of the reported loss seemed less than absolute. His concern further increased when he considered some of the factions within his military that conceivably could have done exactly what the North had claimed and kept the fact secret — even from him. In recent days he had tasked his security apparatus, the National Intelligence Service, or NIS, to get to the truth regarding the missing weapons.

According to its official publications, the NIS — formerly the Korean Central Intelligence Agency — was divided into three directorates: international affairs, domestic affairs, and North Korean affairs. The NIS had responsibility for the collection, coordination, and distribution of all information regarding the nation's strategy and security. In addition, the NIS led the investigation of crimes affecting national security and enforced provisions of both the Military Secrecy Protection Law and the National Security Law.

NIS Director Pang now stood before the president, prepared to summarize what his investigators had learned thus far. "Good evening, Mr. President," he began. "It appears your hunch that the military may have obtained biological weapons from the Americans was prescient. Our sources within our marine corps tell us there are records dating back to the removal of the American weapons from our country in 1991. They indicate that a number of those warheads might not have made the journey from the weapons storage facilities to the American transport ships. We have now increased our surveillance of military communications in the hope that someone may provide some piece of information that could lead us to the weapons."

President Kim wasn't sure whether to be pleased or troubled with the news. Regardless, the presence of such weapons would undoubtedly derail his plans to reduce tensions with North Korea. Furthermore, when the Americans discovered the truth about their careless mistake, they would lose face with the world and subsequently blame him and South Korea.

"Mr. President," said Director Pang, "What are your instructions should we discover the weapons' location? I am concerned we may not fully understand how broadly this conspiracy may have spread within our own military leadership, and how the leaders might respond if, after all these years, their own president forces them to give up their precious weapons."

President Kim pondered the same point as he paced back and forth in his ornate office. How ironic that an American mistake that occurred so many years earlier might now be the one obstacle preventing the reunification of the Korean peninsula. If only there was a way to make the terrible weapons simply disappear.

Director Pang could see his president struggling with the problem, and for what was not the first time in his life, he thanked his ancestors that he was not the president of South Korea.

President Kim suddenly stood still and turned to Pang. "I need you to keep this information to the absolute minimum number of your staff. Create a codeword level of security for the existence of these weapons and include only people that you would trust with your life because that's exactly what you will be doing. Notify me personally the moment you find the warheads."

Director Pang digested what Kim had just instructed and left the president's office. He headed to NIS headquarters in Naegokdong, in southern Seoul, very much aware he would be spending the night on his office cot.

Day Six

Republic of Korea Joint Chiefs of Staff Headquarters, Seoul, South Korea

Lieutenant General Cho Yeong-su sat patiently in the executive briefing room of the impressive JCS Building in Seoul. He had been attending the daily foreign counterintelligence briefings along with the other service chiefs, even though he was the only three-star officer in the room. The briefings typically lasted 90 minutes and covered a wide variety of counterintelligence issues. Today these were primarily some recent covert cross-border incursions by North Korean operatives. This morning's briefing was led by a young intelligence major who walked the small group of senior military officers through a series of presentation slides.

General Cho was only half-listening as the major described some minor issues until he heard the major say, "We have had a significant increase in North Korean activity on Jeju Island in the last few hours. At least five separate communications events have been intercepted referencing either Jeju or the military facilities located on the island. What makes these intercepts most interesting is their association with the Reconnaissance General Bureau, who have never previously shown any interest in Jeju Island."

The Reconnaissance General Bureau was North Korea's premier foreign intelligence service, overseeing all intelligence collection and covert operations. Organized into several divisions, the RGB was considered the elite of the North Korean

132

intelligence organizations. If they were interested in Jeju Island, it meant something of note was happening there.

General Cho asked, "What is the RGB doing on Jeju Island?"

The young major replied, "That is an interesting question, General Cho. Our military and naval installations are mundane, and the island's industry is primarily focused on tourism. Our analysts are looking into this, and I expect to be able to update you tomorrow with our initial assessment."

The chief of the army staff, who had remained quiet until now, leaned across the conference table. "General Cho," he asked, "are your marines doing something on Jeju Island you would like to share with us?"

General Cho quickly answered, "Sir, I can absolutely state that my marines have no activities on Jeju Island whatsoever. I have never set foot on Jeju, and I am quite certain the only marines that may be there are all on military leave."

At first, Cho found it unsettling that the army chief of staff had asked him such a pointed question. On second thought, he decided the question was intended to underscore the army officer's own high level of authority, nothing more. The briefing continued to describe other counterintelligence activities on the peninsula and then transitioned into a discussion of increased funding for new detection systems.

After the briefing, Admiral Pak Jeong-hun grabbed General Cho's arm and asked, "General, would you walk with me over to the commissary? I need to pick up some oranges before I return to my headquarters."

Cho was surprised at the admiral's request. Although Cho commanded the marine corps, he did technically report to the four-star navy admiral. Not only did he dislike being subservient to another service, but the organizational structure meant he could never receive his fourth star.

"Of course, I will accompany you, Admiral. My wife gave me a list this morning just in case I was able to stop by the commissary."

As the two service chiefs walked down the long corridor, soldiers, sailors, marines, and airmen ceased their conversations and moved aside to make way for the highly decorated officers.

"Tell me, Cho, why do you suppose our cousins at the National Intelligence Service are sniffing around my commands, asking questions about biological weapons? The navy has never had access to these types of weapons. It has always been more of an army concern. Now it seems our president is concerned there may be some truth to the North's claims that we may have gotten our hands on the Americans' warheads as they were being removed from our country."

General Cho kept his face expressionless as he listened to the admiral's comments. He silently realized he now had to conceal the warheads' existence from the NIS agents as well as from the North Korean intelligence operatives.

"Admiral," he suggested, "I suspect the NIS is also looking at army and air force installations for the president's "phantom weapons." They have not sniffed around my marine bases yet, but it is probably only a matter of time."

Secretary of Defense Cabin, the Reagan

Lieutenant Dan Garrett knocked on his father's cabin door and then entered, removing his squadron ball cap and stepping forward to shake hands with Colt.

"Hi, Dan! Take a seat while I finish up with Mr. Wilson," said his dad.

Dan poured himself a cup of coffee and sat down on one of the chairs in the cabin's office area.

"Good morning, Lieutenant Garrett. Flying today?" Lenny asked as he collected all his papers together and prepared to give the father and son some privacy.

"Yes, sir, I'm flying in Event Two. We're going to do a little air combat maneuvering with some Hornets today and practice missile engagement."

"I hope you don't shoot anybody down for real — those F-18s are very expensive!" joked Lenny.

"I hear you, sir. I promise not to splash one!"

Lenny left the cabin, and Colt sat down in a chair opposite his son.

"Is there anything, in particular, you wanted to talk about? I've been pretty consumed with the new job almost since I've been here. I really had hoped to spend more time with you."

"No problem, Dad, I understand," Dan assured his father. "I was wondering if you've spoken to Mom since your appointment as secretary. I'm guessing she's not too pleased."

"We have talked a few times since the president's announcement, and she's actually been pretty supportive. She realizes it means even more of my time will be spent in D.C., but she's seriously considering coming there to join me on a more permanent basis. We're exploring buying a house in Virginia and renting out our Olympia home until my assignment ends."

"When do you think it will end?"

"No idea, except that all political appointments eventually

end, and the secretary job has a reputation for burning through incumbents. Not many have survived as long as Secretary O'Kane. And besides, I'm only the acting secretary until the president appoints a permanent replacement."

"I'm really happy to hear Mom's thinking about moving east and that things are going better between you two," Dan said, smiling. "I did want to speak with you about something else, too. I've been talking with my skipper about my future in the Navy, and I told him I'm thinking about leaving the service and flying for the airlines. I love the flying part of my job, but I'm not looking forward to leaving the cockpit and taking a desk job before my next operational tour. The skipper suggested I apply for Navy Test Pilot School, but he's pretty certain I'd need a waiver because I lack the technical degree. He suggested there might be strings you could pull to give me a leg up."

Colt looked at his son. "Dan, you know that I think it's inappropriate to use a position of power to influence decisions in a person's favor. I don't believe it's right. I really don't see how I can help you with this."

"I understand, Dad," said the young pilot. "That's exactly what I told the skipper you would say. I just figured I'd take a shot."

Colt felt badly that he couldn't do something to help Dan achieve his dream. He realized he had disappointed his son once again.

"How about joining me for a meal on the mess decks?" he offered. "I thought it might be interesting to directly hear what the Sailors are thinking about."

"Sounds fun!" Dan said with a slight smirk. "Let's go hear what Joe Sailor has to say to the secretary of defense!"

Mess Decks, the Reagan

Special Agent DeSantis was not happy. Colt wanted to spend a few hours on the mess decks and be available should any Sailors or Marines want to speak with him. A personal protection agent's worst nightmare.

"But sir! I can't protect you in that environment! The only thing I'll be able to do is react if something happens."

"I understand, Agent DeSantis, and I appreciate your concern. Nevertheless, it's off to breakfast we go."

And with that, the secretary, Lenny Wilson, Dan Garrett, and Special Agent Anna DeSantis headed to the 3rd Deck aft mess decks. The three men joined the long breakfast buffet line while DeSantis vigilantly looked on, watching Colt interact with Sailors and Marines in the chow line and started to fill up his tray. Scrambled eggs, bacon and sausage links, homemade baked goods, and a platter of tropical fruits made for an abundant meal, thanks to the carrier's recent replenishment from a supply ship.

Colt and his entourage selected a vacant table, took their seats, and started to dig in. For a while, it seemed as though they might have the table to themselves until a Sailor sat down opposite the secretary.

"Morning, gentlemen," he said, looking around the table. "I'm Petty Officer Nells Johnson." He was dressed in the green camouflage Navy Working Uniform Type III that was the most recent in a series of attempts to develop a suitable and comfortable working uniform for Sailors at sea.

Colt extended his hand and said, "I'm Colt Garrett. Glad to meet you. What do you do on the *Reagan*, Petty Officer Johnson?"

"I'm an IT, an Information Systems Technician, 3rd class," he replied, his mouth full of eggs and bacon. "I work in the comms spaces processing message traffic and making sure our brass can talk to other brass when they want or need to. Who are you guys, and what do y'all do?" The young Sailor wasn't sure he had ever seen the man named Colt Garrett before, but his name seemed familiar.

"Well, I've just become the secretary of defense, and I'm here to meet some of the crew and get an idea of how our Sailors and Marines are being treated. You know, when I was in the Navy myself years ago, we used to call you guys "radiomen." Did the Navy change the rate name to make it sound more technical?"

"Well, sir, it *is* pretty technical," Petty Officer Johnson replied. "Back when you were in the Navy, the radiomen were probably still using a telegraph key and Morse code! The truth is, the Navy combined the Radioman and Data Processing Technician ratings into the new IT rating. Most of the tools we use now are computers anyway, although we usually specialize in either radio or computer stuff. I even hear they're talking about splitting the rate back to how it was before."

Colt liked how the Sailor wasn't afraid to speak directly to him. Perhaps his idea of mingling with the troops might bear fruit after all. After a few minutes, Petty Officer Johnson was joined at the table by a few other Sailors and two Marines. Lenny and Dan, who had finished their meals at the same time, got up from the table to make more room. At a nearby table, Carissa Curtis and her film crew had positioned themselves to film the secretary's interaction with the crew, unbeknownst to him.

"Who has something they'd like to share about their experience with the Navy or Marines? I can't promise to make things better, but I promise to listen."

"I have something, sir," Petty Officer Johnson said. "The newest Sailors, the E-3s, are getting screwed. When we end our deployment and pull into our home port, if the barracks are full, the undesignated seamen have to live on the ship. This means they have to live where they work. They get a hanging locker and the storage under their rack, and that's it. There's no point in buying anything because they don't have a place to put it. What kind of life is that?"

Colt looked at the Sailor and knew he was justified in his concerns for the junior, unrated Sailors.

"So, if we increased capacity in the barracks, would the junior Sailors feel they were being treated better?"

"Yes, sir. I think so. And one other thing: The Navy makes a big deal about giving us 30 days of leave each year, but the chain of command complains and resists when we ask to take leave. I mean, we earned it, and we have it coming to us, right?"

Slowly, curious men and women began encircling Colt's table, nodding in agreement as Petty Officer Johnson spoke. Carissa whispered to her camera operator, "You are getting this, right?" The operator silently nodded his head without moving the handheld video camera.

Meanwhile, Colt was taking notes on a pad he had brought for this purpose. His breakfast was getting cold, but he remained focused on what the young service people were saying. "Who else?" he asked.

A Marine sergeant aggressively pushed her way forward, causing Agent DeSantis to tense up and take a step closer to the secretary.

"I have a gripe, sir," voiced the Marine, a woman about 22 years old. As Colt turned around clockwise in his seat so he could

139

face the young woman, the growing crowd of onlookers leaned in as well so they could hear her more easily. "When we're not embarked on a ship, we're entitled to a certain housing allowance determined by the cost of apartment rentals where we're based. It can take several months before the extra money shows up in our bank accounts, and during those months, we have to pay the rental fees out of our own pockets. We do eventually get a big reimbursement check, but most of us don't have that kind of money that will cover big expenses like rent, which means we have to apply for short-term loans. And we don't get reimbursed for that bank interest, either. It's a definite hardship and it isn't fair."

The large crowd of Sailors and Marines was now enthusiastically echoing their support for the two enlisted people who had voiced their concerns with Garrett. "Anyone else?"

"Yes, sir, I have a problem with Medical."

Colt switched around to his left and saw the young man in a purple flight deck jersey step forward. Garrett remembered that the Sailors who fueled the aircraft wore purple jerseys and float coats.

"Yes, Petty Officer?"

"Sir, someday, I hope to be a pilot. Right now, I'm finishing up my degree and am planning to apply for officer candidate school." The mess decks erupted momentarily with hoots and jeers, which, just as quickly, subsided. The young man continued, "but I don't dare go to sick call or make an appointment for even a headache because that becomes part of my medical record and could ruin my chances for a commission and flight school. What I'm saying is that people like me aren't getting medical attention because we don't want to jeopardize our careers. Heck, I know the pilots in my squadron go to civilian doctors because they know the flight surgeons will remove them from flight status for even the most minor medical problem."

Colt glanced over to see Dan silently nod his head. The mess decks were suddenly quiet, as everyone present waited for Colt to respond. He knew he had to come up with something to say or else risk losing the small amount of trust he sensed he might have gained. He handed his notes to Lenny and stepped up onto a chair so that he could be seen from any spot in the large room.

"I want to thank all of you for your candor in letting me know what you are experiencing in the service. I'm now going to go back and review my notes and do some thinking, after which I'll have a conversation with the chief of naval operations and the commandant of the Marine Corps to see what can be done to address these issues and make things better for you. You won't see a difference overnight, and I think you already know that. But I'll leave you with this: You patriotic men and women are serving in the most powerful force on the face of the earth. But even the best ships, planes, and tanks aren't worth a damn without the skilled and dedicated people who operate them. I'm here to tell you that the well-being and safety of our Soldiers, Sailors, Airmen, and Marines will become, and will remain, my highest priority as long as I'm secretary of defense. So now, let me close by personally thanking each and every one of you for your dedication and service to our nation!"

As Colt stepped down from the chair, he was both gratified and humbled by the thunderous cheers and applause coming from every corner of the room. Soon he was surrounded by young men and women seeking to shake his hand and take a selfie with the secretary. Fifteen minutes later, Colt, Lenny, and Dan were escorted by Special Agent DeSantis up the ladder back to the 03 level. As the mess decks emptied out, Carissa turned to her cameraman. "I have a feeling," she said, "that we may be seeing this on tomorrow's news."

Kitsap College, Poulsbo, Washington

Colonel Dimitri Petrov rested his eyes as he stretched out on the sofa in his campus office. As a tenured professor at a state college, he practically had a lifetime employment contract. He was virtually untouchable by the college administrators who were forever trying to get faculty to increase their effectiveness or develop and adopt new academic and technical programs. His daily late morning nap was his way of notifying the world that his time was simply that: his time. If he chose to spend an hour resting his eyes while pondering the greater meaning of life, that's what he would do. Today, he was thinking instead of his GRU assignment to eliminate the new American secretary of defense.

When he first received the tasking from Moscow, he found it so hard to believe that he forced himself to decode the transmission twice. What were the odds that he would be facing Colton Garrett again? How many years had it been since Gibralter? More importantly, how could his superiors expect him and his network to execute a high-ranking member of the American cabinet? His agents were selected because they had access to valuable information, and because they had demonstrated their willingness to commit treason against the United States — not because they were murderers. Although they had been extremely effective over the past few years, asking them to actually kill someone seemed completely beyond reason. The mental capacity to coldly plan and carry out a murder required years of specialized training and a high level of skill. And he would know, having been personally responsible for a significant number of executions in the past. Even if the mission were accomplished, it was highly probable the agents responsible for it would be apprehended and interrogated by American security forces. And how long would or could untrained agents withstand professional interrogation before folding and identifying Sara Olson and her handler, Professor Robert Jordan? Perhaps GRU headquarters had already determined his cover would be blown as a result of the operation. Had headquarters concluded that his arrest, trial, and subsequent deportation to Russia were acceptable?

The realization made him sit up from his nap and consider his options. He started writing notes on a pad of paper to get his thoughts organized. First, any attempt on Colton Garretts's life was likely to fail; there were just too many safeguards and security mechanisms in place on an aircraft carrier to make the task easy or feasible. Even if the plan to kill Garrett were to come to fruition, the GRU assets onboard *Reagan* would surely be identified and arrested. At that moment, he made a note to review and update his emergency evacuation plan a.s.a.p. so that in the event of the mission's failure, he could leave America within an hour. He pulled a plain manila folder from the bookshelf behind his desk and was reviewing his current extraction plan when there was a knock on his office door.

"Come in," he said as he quickly returned the papers to the folder on his desk.

"Good morning, Professor Jordan. I'm Vicki Pitzer. The

registrar's office sent me over to talk with you. I know the quarter started two weeks ago, but I wanted to ask you if I could still enroll in your information security program. It's okay with the registrar's office, but they said I'd need your approval and signature."

The registrar's office staff knew better than to enroll students this late into the quarter. Instead of just telling the student they were out of luck, they often passed the buck and gave conditional approval, sending the student — and her problem — to the faculty member to handle. Petrov sighed with exasperation and held out his hand. "Let me see your paperwork."

The woman gave him her college application, transcripts detailing other courses taken, and a short professional biography.

"The reason I didn't get my application submitted on time is that I just transferred to a reserve billet at Submarine Group NINE at Submarine Base Bangor last week."

The deep-cover GRU colonel glanced through the stack of papers he had been handed. "So, you are a CT, a Cryptologic Technician? What branch?"

"I'm an N-brancher. It's a pretty new group — we specialize in network-centric operations. The Navy's unclassified website says that we detect, protect, and respond to threats against Navy networks, external and internal."

"Thank you. I know what a CTN is. We have several in the program here. Where was your last duty station?"

"I worked primarily at Fort Meade in Maryland, occasionally in Norfolk, and at other crypto commands on the east coast. The reason they have me doing security clearance processing at Group NINE is that they don't have a CTN billet."

Professor Jordan continued to look at the young woman's

application. "I see that you studied at Georgetown. Isn't that a bit rare for a petty officer?"

"I suppose," said Vicki. "I did really well in high school, but my family couldn't help with college, so I enlisted in the Navy. I tested well enough to qualify for the CTN rate, and after boot camp, I received orders to A-school at Pensacola. Once I was at Fort Meade, I was accepted into an evening program at Georgetown, and I've been working toward a degree ever since. I had hoped to enroll at the University of Washington when I first moved to Bremerton, but I didn't realize the UW campus is on the other side of Puget Sound. I need to work for at least a year before I can afford to move to Seattle."

Petrov put down the application and signed his name to the registrar's form. "Welcome to the program, Ms. Pitzer. Take this back to the registrar's office, and I'll see you at 8:30 Monday morning in Balford Hall, room 210. I hope you're ready to work hard!"

Vicki Pitzer closed the office door behind her and headed back to the registrar's office. She wasn't too concerned about the hard work ahead of her in the professor's class, because she had already earned a batchelors degree in electrical engineering from Caltech. As proud as she was of that degree, she was most proud of another framed certificate on the wall of her small apartment in Bethesda, Maryland — the one that read, "Honor Graduate, FBI Special Agent Academy, Quantico, Virginia."

Ship's Library, the Reagan

GRU agent VADIM opened the door to the ship's library

and wasn't surprised to find it nearly deserted. Since the Internet was made available to Sailors at sea, the library was one of the loneliest places on the ship. Except for the young Sailor at the front desk, there were only two other people in the small library — one of the ship's chaplains and Malcolm Simpson, GRU agent NIKITA.

VADIM walked over to the desk where Chaplain Mike O'Brian was reading.

"Good morning, Father Mike! Doing some research for Sunday's sermon?"

"Not likely," he chuckled, pointing to the book he was reading, *A History of Satanic Worship in the 20th Century*. The Roman Catholic priest stood up and placed the book on the cart marked "RETURNS."

"I find it helps to research the enemy before I go into battle," he said with a wink, then turned toward the door and left the library. VADIM had discovered that the best way to get some privacy in the library was to comment on what a person was reading and make them feel uncomfortable about it. They typically would respond with a sentence or two and then leave as quickly as possible.

VADIM moved to the front desk and spoke to the young man standing there. "I'm planning to be in here for a while. If you need a break, I'm happy to cover for you. And you can take your time."

The young Sailor was performing library desk duties as a result of failing his last uniform inspection. The executive officer had said working a shift or two in the ship's library might help him improve his attention to detail.

"Thanks!" replied the Sailor as he raced out of the library, letting the door slam behind him.

VADIM walked back over to the table where Malcolm was reading an aviation magazine and said quietly, "So, it appears we have to find a way to get rid of Mr. Garrett, hopefully without either us landing in prison, or worse."

Malcolm scanned the library to ensure that they were alone and then put down his magazine. "You sure know how to clear a room. Yep, I've been thinking a lot about this tasking, and I'm not sure I want to do it."

"I don't think we have a choice. I know they have leverage on me and my family, and I assume they have stuff on you too. I think we're going to have to come up with some options and just hope that Garrett leaves the *Reagan* before our friends ask us to do the deed. You do understand we have no choice?"

Malcolm nodded his head, wearily. "I know, I know, I just don't like it. Taking classified information off the ship is one thing; ending somebody's life is another. Remember, I'm just an engineer. The only killing I've ever done is in our online game over the English Channel."

"Okay, let's use this private time while we can. Have you come up with any ideas?"

Malcolm leaned in and whispered, "The simplest thing would be to push him off the deck at night. I hear he likes to walk on the flight deck in the evenings after flight ops are secured. A quick shove, and that would be that. A 60-foot drop from the flight deck to the water is a pretty nasty fall, particularly if you aren't prepared. I haven't seen him wear a float coat during his walks, and it takes more than a mile to turn this ship around even if someone hears him go overboard. That's a long time for a person to tread water in the middle of the ocean, and that's assuming he survives the fall. The Sailors call it a long drop with a quick stop."

VADIM considered the idea and replied, "I don't think so. That NCIS protection agent never leaves his side. Even if we were able to get close enough to push him off the ship, she would be right there to see us. You're an engineer, what about rigging something in his cabin to electrocute him, say, the clock radio or a light fixture?"

"That might be a possibility. We'd need to gain access to his cabin to check out what's in there, then time to build, test and install some kind of device. I suppose it could be done, and his death would look like an accident, at least for a while."

"A while? What do you mean?"

"Well, if the secretary of defense is electrocuted by something in his cabin, I'm pretty certain the investigation would eventually determine the cause of the death was a modified device."

"I could see that investigation leading right back to you, NIKITA."

"Not necessarily. There are probably hundreds of people on board with the skills to modify a light fixture or radio."

"Okay," said VADIM. "What about the software system you work on, the magic thing?"

"You mean Magic Carpet?

"Yes, tell me more about that."

"Well, basically, Magic Carpet simplifies carrier landings. When pilots are coming in to land, they pay attention to three things. First, they line up with the ship and set up their approach to hook the number three arresting gear wire. Next, they adjust their angle of attack, that's the pitch of the aircraft. The plane needs to be at a certain angle so its tailhook is in position to catch the wire. The third thing they're managing is airspeed. So, as they land, they are continually adjusting the aircraft controls to meet all three objectives simultaneously. Hundreds and hundreds of minor corrections. Magic Carpet is a software program that simplifies the pilot's approach because it flies the plane down a three-degree slope, regardless of the weather or the sea state. The pilot puts the plane in the right angle of attack and line up, and then releases control to the computer. Pretty cool, right?"

VADIM thought for a moment and said, "Maybe there's something we can do with that."

The Flight Deck, the Reagan

After lunch, the deck was secured from flight operations and an area on the stern was configured for pistol qualification. The ship's captain had invited Colt, Lenny, and Special Agent DeSantis to participate in the weapons training. Colt jumped at the chance to fire the pistol he had received as a gift just last week from Vice Admiral Shaffer. The Command Master at Arms, Senior Chief Steadman, was performing range safety officer duties for the pistol qualifications and had set six B-21 silhouette targets at distances of three, seven, and fifteen yards from the firing line. The silhouette targets were segmented into scoring areas based on the approximate lethality of the hit: five points for a fatal wound, and fewer points for less-damaging hits. Sailors were instructed to fire a total of 48 rounds from the three distances in a variety of firing positions. Scoring above 180 points was the minimum qualification score, from 180-203 earned the "marksman" designation, 204-227 earned the "sharpshooter" designation, and those scoring between 228 and the perfect score of 240 were designated as "expert." The Navy pistol qualification course was designed for the two pistols currently being issued, the M9 and the M11, both double-action, semi-automatic firearms chambered in 9mm Parabellum.

Colt, Lenny, and Anna DeSantis observed from behind the safety barrier as Sailors in groups of six received safety instructions and then fired the qualification course. Because the revised course now included drawing the weapon from a holster, firing from a weak hand, and even firing from a kneeling position, extra safety measures were employed to ensure that the qualification exercise was conducted without injury. Those awaiting their turns to shoot watched their shipmates compete with one another for the highest scores. Those skilled enough to qualify as "expert" received marksmanship medals to wear on their dress uniforms.

After all the Sailors had completed the shooting course, Senior Chief Steadman approached the three civilians and offered, "Captain Solari said you would like to attempt the qualification course. Do any of you have experience with pistols?"

Lenny answered first. "I haven't shot a pistol since I was a Midshipman at the Merchant Marine Academy, and that was a long time ago, Senior Chief. I qualified as "marksman" with a government 1911 .45 caliber back then."

"That's pretty good, sir! Those old 1911s were fairly beat up. We used to joke that you could do more damage with that pistol by throwing it at the enemy than shooting it! How about you two?" he asked, turning to Anna and Colt.

Anna DeSantis presented her NCIS credentials and badge. "I'm pretty good with my issued Sig Sauer P229," she said. "It's chambered for .40 caliber, so I borrowed some rounds from

Special Agent Orr." She placed a box of 50 rounds on the table along with her pistol.

Senior Chief Steadman picked up the agent's P229 and looked it over closely. "This is similar to our issued M-11s, but your weapon is clearly in much better condition," he said, smiling as he handed it back to her.

"What about you, sir?" the senior chief asked, turning to face Colt.

"I shot lots as a kid, and I was trained with several weapons as a Naval Intelligence officer. I've carried 1911s, PPKs, Berettas, Sigs, and just about everything in between. Vice Admiral Shaffer gave me this pistol as a gift last week, and I'd like to shoot it on the qualification course."

Colt handed Steadman a blue plastic case embossed with the manufacturer's name —Colt. The senior chief opened the box and picked up the new pistol.

"What do we have here? A Colt 1911 Combat Commander Elite in 9mm, with a special stainless finish. This, sir, is an impressive firearm. May I?"

Colt nodded. The senior chief ejected the empty magazine and pulled back the slide to be sure the weapon was unloaded. Then, he released the slide with a snap, pointed the pistol down range, and squeezed the trigger. The exposed hammer fell on the empty chamber, and the senior chief commented, "About a four-pound trigger pull, and it brakes as smooth as glass. You just can't beat a 1911 trigger. No excuses for accuracy with this beauty, sir!"

"Thanks, Senior Chief. Any problem if I use a single action on the qual course?"

A 1911 pistol could only be fired if a round was loaded in the chamber, and the hammer had previously been cocked back.

Experienced shooters would conceal-carry the pistol in that condition, with the manual thumb safety engaged. This was called "Condition One" or "Cocked and Locked." To shoot, one needed to draw the pistol from a holster, bring the weapon on target, release the manual thumb safety and pull the trigger. Some less experienced shooters found the 1911s to be too complicated and often forgot to release the manual thumb safety before squeezing the trigger. It was one of the reasons why military and police forces had transitioned to double-action pistols.

"No problem, sir. Some of the Recon Marines and SEALS carry 1911s and have qualified on this range. Just don't shoot yourself in the foot!"

Colt, Lenny, and Anna positioned themselves in adjacent lanes, Lenny shooting a Beretta M9, Anna shooting her Sig Sauer P229, and Colt Garrett shooting his 1911 Colt Commander Elite. They fired 12 rounds each at their respective three-yard targets, all scoring a perfect 60 points.

"Not too shabby, lady and gentlemen! It probably will get more interesting as we move the targets back a bit."

The next distance was seven yards. After another 12 rounds, the targets were moved back again to 15 yards, or 45 feet, and the trio shot a final 24 rounds each. The senior chief declared the range as "safe" and walked out to the targets to score each shooter.

Counting the holes in Lenny's target, the senior chief said, "Well, sir, you missed earning sharpshooter by just one point. Pretty nice shooting for a guy who hasn't picked up a pistol in a long time!"

Lenny looked at his target. "Senior Chief, with all due respect, I think this hole is touching the 5-circle. Would a case of soda help to convince you?" he asked with a grin.

The senior chief took another look at the target, and then adjusted the score, saying with a broad smile, "Congratulations, Mr. Wilson, you just scored sharpshooter!"

A large group of Sailors who had stuck around to watch now applauded the result and Lenny took a stately bow. Senior Chief Steadman next scored Anna's target, and said, "Ma'am, you scored a 231 — expert! I can see they do a good job teaching marksmanship at NCIS."

"Thank you, Senior Chief! I carry every day. I need to know I can hit what I'm aiming at."

Finally, Senior Chief Steadman stepped over to Colt's target and counted the holes. He scored the target twice more and turned to Garrett. "Sir, you scored a perfect 240! I think I need to get me one of those shiny toys! Really, sir, exceptional shooting!"

"It's a lot easier when the target's not shooting back," murmered Colt to himself.

Colt knew that operating a weapon while under direct fire was the most demanding thing he had ever had to do. And the experience still haunted him. Meanwhile, Lenny and Anna silently looked at one another and then at the older man as he carefully placed his pistol back into its case. After the three civilians left the firing range, Senior Chief Steadman examined Colt's target again and commented to no one in particular, "I'm glad he was shooting at a paper target and not at me!"

Secure Video Conference Room, the Reagan

The video connection with the White House Situation

Room had been open and thoroughly tested for over an hour to ensure that once the meeting got started, the system would be operational and ready. Seated in the conference room in the *Reagan* were Colt Garrett, Lenny Wilson, and Rear Admiral Joe Carlisle. At the center of the table was a control screen for the video system and two omnidirectional microphones. All three men were turned toward a large, high-definition video monitor, which showed the Situation Room conference table, thousands of miles away. Seated around that table were Deputy Defense Secretary Steve Holmes, CIA Director Michelle Walker, Chairman of the Joint Chiefs of Staff General David Schmidt, Secretary of State Jonathan Unger, and President William C. Harrison. President Harrison initiated the meeting. "Michelle, will you start by bringing us up to date?"

CIA Director Walker positioned a microphone in front of her and began her presentation.

"Gentlemen, over the past several days our intelligence community has been able to confirm with a high degree of confidence that North Korean claims that U.S. biological warheads, which were stolen years ago from our own stockpile in South Korea, are still in South Korea and being held at an undisclosed location. We believe that back in 1991, during Bush 41's term as president, nine warheads containing Anthrax 455, a mutated version of the biologcal agent with the codename, ALPINE LANCER, were somehow illegally removed from an outgoing shipment. At that time, we were removing all biological weapons from the Korean peninsula. We're currently gathering more specific information regarding that theft and who was involved. Now, back to the present: As long as North Korea believes the South is hiding weapons of mass destruction within their borders, we believe they will never agree to reduce their own weapons programs. So, the purpose of today's meeting is to create a strategy to find those weapons, and once we do, develop plans to recover them."

"You mentioned Anthrax 455 is a mutated version of Anthrax. Wasn't *regular* Anthrax bad enough?" the president asked. General Schmidt promptly responded to the question.

"Mr. President, Anthrax 455, or ALPINE LANCER, was developed by the Army to facilitate more effective airborne dispersal of the agent. We destroyed all of those weapons years ago, or at least we thought we did." The president considered the combined destructive capacity of the nine missing warheads and wondered fleetingly if his presidency would someday be defined by the existance of these horrific weapons.

The CIA director continued, "The South Koreans publicly deny that they have our warheads, but they have also requested that we send a delegation to Seoul to discuss the issue. We don't know why they want to talk, but we believe it's worthwhile to hear what they have to say. We do know there are factions within South Korean military leadership that don't support their government's efforts to thaw relations with the North. We've also considered that the weapons may exist in South Korea without President Kim's knowledge. This theft would have occurred almost 30 years ago. It's hard to know how many people might even be aware of the warheads' existence."

The president turned to face General Schmidt. "General, don't we have systems that can remotely detect biological weapons?" he asked.

Before the General could answer, Steve Holmes jumped in.

"Yes, sir, we do have aircraft-deployed systems that can detect the presence of several types of biological agents. It would take hours just to explain the the basics of the underlying science and technology involved. But their use would require that the aircraft overfly most of South Korea. Our lawyers have cautioned us that the use of these systems could be interpreted as an act of war. I don't see how we could use these planes in this situation."

Colt pushed a button on a console to unmute the room's microphone. "Garrett here, sir. We do have an experimental system on one of our geosynchronous birds." He was referring to the DOD's reconnaissance satellites capable of maintaining a stable position over a point on the earth's surface. "Its function is similar to the air-breathing platforms, except we don't have to violate sovereign airspace to use it. Its code name is SISTINE BEACON, and initial testing has been very positive."

The president leaned forward. "Sistine? Like the chapel in the Vatican?"

General Schmidt smiled. "Exactly, Mr. President. You've seen Michelangelo's painting on the ceiling of the Sistine chapel where the hand of God gives life by pointing a single finger, but not actually touching Adam? SISTINE BEACON is like that pointing finger. Imagine a laser-focused beam of light pointing down at the earth. But the problem is that it's an experimental system, and very, very slow. SISTINE BEACON takes a full hour to scan a target area of two square miles, and South Korea encompasses nearly 39,000 square miles. It would take SISTINE BEACON over two years to scan the entire country!"

Garrett offered, "But if we were able to localize the general target area first, the scanning could then be done much more efficiently. The warheads would have to be in some sort of secure facility with military control. The Agency could work with our team at Defense to identify and prioritize target areas, and we could start from there."

Admiral Carlisle leaned toward Lenny and said, "I'm glad I'm not in Billy Harrison's shoes right now. This mess is going to turn out bad, and I don't want to be anywhere near it or him when it does."

Almost in unison, the people in the White House Situation Room looked with disbelief at Admiral Carlisle on the video system, prompting him to take note of the illuminated green light on the table microphone, which indicated it was unmuted, or live. No one spoke for several moments until the president broke the silence. "Well, thank you for your unwavering support, Admiral Carlisle."

Carlisle turned red and glared at the green light on the microphone. Lenny pushed a button to mute the mic and quietly assured the admiral, "It's okay. It's off now."

The president, clearing his throat, said, "Let's move on." He turned to the secretary of state and asked him, "Jon, what are your thoughts regarding sending a delegation to Seoul? What do we have to gain?"

The experienced career diplomat was already prepared with an answer. "I agree with Director Walker, Mr. President. We need to hear what President Kim has to say, and perhaps more importantly, how he says it. I also believe it is key to have the meeting as soon as possible to get a read on the present situation. I recommend we send our new secretary of defense to Seoul. He's just a few hours away, and although he is not a diplomat, that may demonstrate to the South Koreans that we see this as a pressing national security issue, rather than solely as a diplomatic concern."

Colt Garrett wondered if the secretary of state wasn't also trying to distance himself from the problem and for the same reason so eloquently voiced by Admiral Carlisle.

The president breathed deeply. "I like it. Colt, work with Jon to set up your visit. I want you in Seoul by mid-day tomorrow. Meet with President Kim and see what you can learn. Make sure Kim understands that we won't tolerate South Korea keeping our warheads. We're getting them back, one way or another."

After the president had left the Situation Room, Secretary Unger spoke up again. "Colt, we have some work to do. I'll be in touch!" He pushed a button and disconnected the video call.

Gathering up his notes, Colt stood, turned to Admiral Carlisle and remarked with a grin, "You know, Joe, I'm not too sure about a future for you in politics."

Colt and Lenny exited the room together, leaving Carlisle alone to contemplate the damage done by his tactless comment. The now rattled one-star admiral remained seated at the table and put his head in his hands. He knew he was running out of viable career options. He would find himself a laughingstock, he feared. An embarrassment to his family and his reputation. And it was all thanks to that son of a bitch, Colt Garrett. The longer Garrett was on this ship, the bleaker his future looked. He knew he should just make a bold move against Garrett. It was a huge risk, but one he was willing to take.

Headquarters, Republic of Korea Marine Corps, Hwaseong, South Korea

General Cho arrived at his headquarters and headed directly to his office. The speed at which the North Koreans had responded to the information he had strategically planted with Colonel Chang was alarming, telling him that whatever means Chang was using to transmit information was incredibly efficient. Chang had been on his shortlist of those he suspected of leaking information, and now his suspicions were, disturbingly, confirmed.

Now Cho needed more details regarding Chang's activities, as it was critical to know the extent of his conspiracy. He decided to have a team install a full surveillance package in Chang's apartment. A few phone calls later, and he had arranged for not only the equipment installation but also a diversion that would get Chang and his girlfriend out of the apartment to allow for the surveillance equipment to be placed without raising his suspicion.

Later that evening, General Cho was sitting at his desk when his direct phone line rang. "Yes, what is it?"

"Mission complete," the caller said.

Cho smiled and asked, "What are the details?"

"We phoned in a natural gas leak, so the police evacuated the entire city block, including the colonel's girlfriend, who was in the apartment at the time. She called him once she was standing in the street and told him about the gas leak. Our team entered the residence and placed audio and video surveillance equipment in each room, on both the phone line and the WIFI router. We looked for anything out of the ordinary but saw nothing unusual. We tested the equipment from the apartment across the street and made sure everything checked out before we left. The surveillance team is on station, and we can now see and hear everything that takes place in the colonel's residence."

General Cho was pleased with the speed and creativity with which his orders had been carried out. He also had requested the bugging of Chang's office, car, and mobile phone, and was likewise satisfied to hear that those, too, had been carried out.

"Is there anything else you need us to do, General?" asked the caller.

"Just keep me informed if you learn anything."

"Yes, sir. We certainly will."

General Cho hung up the phone and wondered what Chang would have to say for himself when he was ultimately brought in for questioning. Not that what he said would have any bearing on his fate. That was already determined.

The Blue House, Seoul, South Korea

President Kim Seong-ho impatiently waited for the director of the national intelligence service to make his way to the Blue House through Seoul evening traffic. The information Director Pang needed to provide to him could not be entrusted to any form of electronic communication, and even having the conversation in his office was taking a risk. Pang had indicated on the phone he had something of vital importance to discuss, and Kim suspected it had to do with the missing American warheads. He hoped Pang would tell him unequivocally that the weapons were not in his country, and he could return to the normal duties of his office.

The president's secretary announced Director Pang as he entered the office and briskly shook the hand of his president.

"I am afraid I have bad news, Mr. President. The American biological weapons are indeed within our borders, and it appears that Lieutenant General Cho is responsible."

The president sat down and waited while his intelligence chief unfolded a map of South Korea and placed it on his desk.

"We have a high degree of confidence that the warheads in question are on Ulleungdo Island, here," he said, pointing to a small island off the eastern coast of South Korea. Director Pang unfolded a second map, this one depicting the island in much greater detail, and placed it in front of President Kim.

"Tell me what you know about the island, Director."

"Mr. President, it is a small island about 100 kilometers off the eastern coast. Ulleungdo is roughly ten kilometers by ten kilometers and totals approximately 50 kilometers. It has been occupied by many nations in the past. During the Russo-Japanese War of 1904-1905, Japanese forces occupied the island as one of a series of acquisitions intended to fortify their defenses in the area. The islands provided the Japanese with a band of observation towers and wireless transmitting stations that provided an effective early warning network, depending upon visibility. Ulleungdo was of particular importance to Japan because of its position in the Vladivostok shipping lane near the Tsushima Straits."

"As you may recall," Pang continued, "our air force established a radar station on the island just last year, intended to protect our airspace over the East Sea. The deployment of some marines to Ulleungdo was a component of the plan to strengthen border defense. The marines deploy to the island for a few months before being relieved by another company-sized unit. There are barracks there that we built to support the troops, and there are amphibious assault vehicles for the use by rotating troops. Now that we have become aware that there may be American weapons on Ulleungdo, it appears the actual reason General Cho deployed his marines to the island may have been to provide security for those weapons. Our intelligence sources tell us the assigned marines are not aware of what they are guarding. They only know it is an extremely important mission."

The president looked closely at the map, then stood and began pacing the floor.

"So, General Cho is responsible?" asked the president, sadly, needing to hear it again before he could process it fully.

"Yes, sir. Apparently, as a young major, he was in charge of the warheads' shipment within our borders. A careless error in a shipping manifest provided him the opportunity to secretly remove some of the warheads, and he has kept them hidden all these years since."

"How did you discover all this?" Kim inquired. "Do you have a spy in the general's command?"

"Mr. President, I have spies everywhere, including in our own marine corps." Director Pang folded up the two maps and returned them to his briefcase. "What are you going to do now, sir?"

"The new American secretary of defense and his delegation will be arriving in Seoul tomorrow to discuss the matter of the missing warheads. I assume the delegation will include Ambassador Greer and General Boyd. As president, I cannot just tell them we have the weapons and advise them as to where they are hidden. Our enemies within the military would see me as a traitor, and my days as president would surely be numbered. Ideally, the Americans would discover the weapons' location on their own and then make them disappear. In the end, I could not be blamed for turning over something that was not even here."

President Kim began pacing the floor again, barely noticing when Director Pang closed his briefcase and quietly left the president's office. Kim knew that the optimal way out of this situation was simply to have the Americans make it go away. After all, it was their incompetence that created the problem in the first place!

Carrier Intelligence Center (CVIC), the Reagan

Ensign Rebecca Clarke knocked on Commander Abrams' office door. As she entered, she smiled as she greeted the senior officer and asked, "Commander, do you have a moment? I'd like to discuss a personal matter with you."

Jennifer straightened the items on her desk, took a sip from her coffee mug, stood up, and shook Rebecca's hand.

"Sure, Ensign, what can I do for you? Please, have a seat."

Rebecca sat down on the chair next to the desk. "Ma'am, I wanted to get your advice about something. And can we keep this just between us?"

Jen sat down in her chair and said, "Well, Rebecca, I guess that depends. There are some things you might tell me that I have a mandate to report up the chain of command. Can you give me a clue what this is about?" She looked at the young officer and could tell she was deeply troubled.

"This is about a superior officer who has been sexually

harassing me for several weeks. I hoped it would just stop, but it hasn't, and I don't know what to do."

Rebecca's eyes started to tear up, and Jen handed her a tissue. "Why did you come to *me*, Ensign?"

"Well, Commander, I thought you might have experienced this type of thing yourself. And if you have, I thought you might have good advice about how to handle it."

"Okay, Rebecca, I agree this can remain between us at this point. So, tell me the circumstances."

"Well," Rebecca began, "it usually happens in the gym. I go there to work out about the same time every day, before going on watch. This person always seems to be there, positioned directly across from whatever machine I'm on, continually staring at me and my body, finding reasons to walk close by and touch my back or shoulders, always smiling and looking into my eyes. It's just creepy. It is extremely uncomfortable, and even after I purposely shifted to working out after my watch, after a few days, it all started up again."

"Is this officer in your direct chain of command?"

"No, ma'am, we work in different departments. Actually, it's Lieutenant Commander Bryant from Engineering. I never see him except in the gym and occasionally in the wardroom during meals. He has tried several times to sit next to me in there, but now I sit where there is no empty seat next to me."

"Is there any reason he would think that you are interested in him? I mean, even remotely?" Jen knew from personal experience how the most innocent comment or action could be misinterpreted by some men as an invitation or indication of interest.

"No, ma'am, nothing at all," she answered, stiffening slightly at the mere suggestion she may have prompted this behavior. "Like I said, I've hardly said a word to him since I reported aboard. It just feels sort of like a weird obsession."

Jen looked at the young woman and knew exactly why this guy was attracted to her. She was quite pretty, with a great smile and a figure even a polyester uniform designed for males couldn't hide. She had been a collegiate athlete, and it showed. But there was something else. During the occasional steel beach picnics when the flight deck was turned into a beach party, Rebecca had worn clothing that was not really appropriate for a Naval officer on a ship at sea. Even the ship's captain had remarked that the ship's officers needed to maintain a certain degree of military bearing, even at a picnic.

Jen stood and walked around her desk. "I think I understand," she said to Rebecca. "Have you ever spoken to Lieutenant Commander Bryant and told him to knock it off? I mean, in the most direct way?"

Rebecca looked down and replied, "Not really. I've been hoping he would stop. I wasn't sure if I should submit a formal complaint. Frankly, I'm afraid that if I did, I could kiss my career goodbye."

Commander Abrams knew there was some truth to what the ensign was saying. Many organizations still blamed women when they reported being harassed or mistreated. She was also aware of harmful retaliatory actions after women exposed men who had behaved this way toward them.

"How about this," Jen offered. "I'll drop in to the gym before your watch this evening. Perhaps I'll see him in action."

Rebecca stood and hugged the senior officer. "Thank you, ma'am. I didn't know who else to tell, and I appreciate you helping me. I'll see you later, then," she said and headed to her stateroom.

Jen Abrams sat back down at her desk and thought further about what Ensign Clarke had told her. Women had been serving on Navy ships for many years, but some men still saw them as objects, or even as an opportunity for a few moments of affection. Jen was annoyed to hear that this young Naval officer was being abused by this jerk. She was determined to put an end to it.

Day Seven

Officer's Wardroom, the Reagan

Rear Admiral Joseph Carlisle had been eating his meals in the ship's wardroom since losing his cabin to the secretary of defense. He had tried disguising his resentment by telling his staff he preferred to eat in the wardroom as it gave him opportunities to meet informally with ship and airwing officers. At the same time, the ship's supply officer had started noticing a dramatic increase in the number of officers eating in the more casual *dirty shirt* wardroom, where aircrew typically went for meals because they didn't want to deal with the more formal wardroom, and presumably, Admiral Carlisle. The supply officer laughed to himself when it occurred to him that he should ask the admiral to alternate between the two wardrooms just to even out the seating.

Today the admiral was joined only by his chief of staff as the other officers had already managed to find seats at the far end of the wardroom.

"Did you hear about Garrett's "town hall" on the mess decks? What was *that* about, sitting down with a bunch of junior Sailors and Marines, answering their questions and letting them complain about their living conditions? It reminded me of the late 80s when the Navy jumped on the quality movement. Ship captains were directed to hold open forums and let the Sailors tell them how to run the ship. It was a joke then, and it's still a joke now!"

Captain Winters, who had decided not to stoop to the adolescent level of the admiral's comments, replied, "That was a few years before my time, sir. It does seem the Navy goes through phases of social experimentation, usually a few years on the heels of the civilian business community when it attempts something new."

"We've got more than 5,000 people on this ship. Is Garrett planning to talk with every one of them to help him figure out how to do his job? Nobody asked me, but I don't think this is how you run the department of defense!"

That's right, nobody asked you! thought Captain Winters as he reached for the coffee carafe and refilled his cup. After he heard what the one-star admiral had said on the video call with the president, Winters thought it unlikely that anybody would be asking his opinion about anything, ever again. It also occurred to him that he should distance himself from this self-important, self-absorbed admiral who seemed to gain toxicity with each passing day. It would be a difficult tightrope to walk, maneuvering away from the admiral without appearing to be disloyal to him. Perhaps he should ask Lenny Wilson if there was any possibility of an assignment on Garrett's staff at the Pentagon. Who would blame him for leaving Carlisle's staff to accept a position in the new defense secretary's organization? It was something to consider.

"And did you hear about Garrett shooting the pistol qualification course on the fantail? I mean, what's he trying to prove? You'd think the guy was running for office."

"I did hear about that, sir, and they say he scored 100 percent. That's some pretty good shooting. I wonder if that has anything to do with his mysterious intel background."

"No, he probably pressured the senior chief to give him a high score. He seems like the type who'd do that." After a pause, Carlisle said, "Gary, I want you to help me with something."

"Yes, sir?" Winters replied, always suspicious when Carlisle used his first name to start a sentence.

The admiral looked around the wardroom to be completely sure their conversation would be private.

"I want to get Garrett off this ship. That thing during the video call with the president didn't do much for my Navy career, or my post-Navy political aspirations either, and I blame Garrett. Every day that man spends on this ship seems to cause me more problems, and I want to do something about it."

"Just what do you have in mind, Admiral?" asked Winters, mildly entertained while also feeling discomforted by Carlisle's childish and spiteful thought process.

"I don't know. Perhaps he could 'accidentally' slip and fall," Carlisle suggested, using air quotes for emphasis. "Ships are dangerous places, and accidents happen all the time."

Winters couldn't believe Admiral Carlisle was actually serious.

"True," Captain Winters said, then continued dryly, "Maybe you could challenge him to meet you on the flight deck at high noon. What do you think, Admiral, pistols or boarding cutlasses? Maybe cutlasses would be the better choice, given his skill with that pistol!"

But when Captain Winters looked at the admiral, he could see the man wasn't at all amused by his archaic scenario. He felt a cold chill and took another sip from his coffee cup.

"I'm kidding, of course!" declared the admiral, thinking twice about appearing too diabolical. "I just want to discredit him before he jeopardizes my career, and I wouldn't miss him if he were off this ship."

The admiral abruptly got up, threw his napkin down, and quickly left the wardroom. It wasn't long before the atmosphere in the wardroom immediately changed, with officers once again joking around and enjoying their meals with their shipmates. Captain Winters finished his coffee and stood to go back to his stateroom. He wasn't all that certain the admiral *was* just joking about causing harm to the defense secretary. He wondered if he ought to do anything about it.

Carrier Intelligence Center (CVIC), the Reagan

Commander Abrams was not looking forward to her meeting with Lieutenant Commander Bryant. She wasn't in his chain of command and had no official role in protecting Ensign Clarke from his unwanted advances. But Jen was a senior female Naval officer, and as such, she felt a responsibility to the other females onboard when they found themselves dealing with unprofessional behavior. In fact, Jen's lack of official standing made her the perfect advocate for Ensign Clarke. Now, she intended to do what she could to keep Gary Bryant from continuing to harass the young woman.

Bryant knocked on Commander Abrams' office door and entered as Jen said, "Have a seat, Gary."

Gary Bryant worked in the ship's engineering department as the main propulsion assistant, responsible for the nuclear reactor that powered everything onboard the *Reagan*. He had graduated from the Naval Academy and served on an *Arleigh Burke*-class guided-missile destroyer out of Rota, Spain, where he earned his SWO qualification. He subsequently attended Nuclear Power School in Goose Creek, South Carolina, where he learned the fundamentals of nuclear propulsion, and then attended a 26-

week prototype training at the same location, where he applied the concepts learned in nuke school while running a full-scale operating plant. He next reported to the USS *Nimitz*, and finally transferred to the *Reagan* for his current assignment. Ever since his days at the Naval Academy, Gary Bryant was known by his fellow officers as a party animal. His bad behavior at Annapolis nearly got him kicked out on several occasions, and it was only his exceptional scholastic performance that convinced the Academy to allow him to graduate, earning a degree in nuclear engineering. Gary Bryant was a very smart man. When he received a curt invitation to report to the commander's office, he sensed it wasn't because he had done something well.

"What can I do for you, Commander Abrams?" Bryant asked.

"This is an unofficial meeting, Gary, and it's off the record. There are concerns that you have possibly been acting inappropriately toward Ensign Rebecca Clarke. Do you know Ensign Clarke?"

Bryant shifted in his chair. "I think so. Isn't she that young thing that works up in combat systems? I think I've seen her around."

"Young thing? Is that how you refer to another Naval officer?" Jen leaned forward in her chair and looked intently at the engineering officer.

"Sorry, Commander, I meant to say, 'young officer.'"

Jen Abrams realized this might turn out to be easier than she first thought.

"Several of the *Reagan's* officers have told me you've been seen leering at Ensign Clarke while working out in the gym."

"Has *she* complained?"

"It's strange that you don't deny it, Mr. Bryant. Should I

assume these observations are accurate?"

Bryant smiled and said, "No, ma'am. I just wondered if Ensign Clarke herself has complained to you. She hasn't said anything to me about bothering her. If it was a problem, why wouldn't she say anything to me?"

"I can't answer that. All I'm saying is that several people have noticed something. Perhaps you should try being more professional toward the women on this ship and avoid any contact with this particular one. I haven't said anything about this to the chief engineer — I wanted to allow you to correct this situation before it became a major problem. Do you catch my drift?"

"Yes, Commander, loud and clear. I have no idea what these people could be talking about, but I'll make certain to steer clear of Ensign Clarke going forward."

After Lieutenant Commander Bryant stood and left Jen's office, she wondered whether she had scared him off, or if her warning would just encourage him to continue his inappropriate behavior, only more discreetly. Regardless, she decided to arrange her personal schedule so that whenever Ensign Clarke was working out, she would be, too.

Headquarters, Republic of Korea Marine Corps (ROKMC), Hwaseong, South Korea

General Cho was impressed with the level of detail in the report describing the surveillance of Colonel Chang's apartment, and with the speed at which it was prepared and provided for his use. According to the report, Chang had arrived at his apartment in the late afternoon to find his girlfriend, Kang Ji-woo, waiting for him with a martini. Chang and Ji-woo enjoyed a quiet evening together, the surveillance team recording it all as the marine colonel described to the young woman what had happened to him that day. She skillfully asked probing questions that led Chang to provide her with a shocking amount of classified information. The surveillance report also included details of the couple's intimate activities, but there was no further breach of security during the remainder of the surveillance period. After midnight, once Chang was sound asleep, the team observed as Ji-woo quietly climbed out of bed and carefully removed a piece of clothing from her closet and placed it in a dry-cleaning bag. The seasoned surveillance team considered the incident odd and provided detailed notes regarding the event.

In the morning, said the report, after Colonel Chang had left for work and Ji-woo had gone for her morning run, the surveillance team entered the apartment. They carefully examined, photographed, and cataloged the contents of the dry-cleaning bag and placed a tracking device inside one of the bag's seams before replacing it and exiting the apartment. After Ji-woo returned from her run, she showered and dressed for work, grabbing the dry-cleaning bag on her way out the door.

With a street surveillance team in tow, Ji-woo's first stop was at a small dry-cleaning shop about three blocks from Chang's apartment building. Mr. Yi's Alterations and Dry Cleaning had been the neighborhood's sole dry-cleaning establishment for over 20 years, with Mr. Yi still performing a majority of the work. Ji-woo was observed dropping her dry-cleaning bag off at the shop and then continuing on her way to work at Sacred Heart Hospital as a respiratory therapist. The surveillance report ended with the recommendation that additional surveillance assets should be assigned to Ji-woo and the dry-cleaning shop. Complete background investigations were also recommended for both Kang Ji-woo and Mr. Yi.

General Cho placed the report on his desk and thought through the situation. Several things had now become clear. First, the source of his intelligence leak clearly was Colonel Chang's nightly conversation with his young girlfriend, who was likely a North Korean intelligence agent. Second, although Colonel Chang should never have been telling his girlfriend anything about the work he does, it was Chang's girlfriend who appeared to be the true conspirator, and not Chang himself. While troubling, of course, it was still somewhat a relief to General Cho that he wasn't so far off the mark when it came to trusting others. The dry-cleaning shop was probably being used as a communications relay for the agent. Either Mr. Yi was her North Korean controller, or he was — knowingly or otherwise — passing information along to another unidentified person. At least now, Cho knew how to stop the flow of information.

The question remained, what if anything would be gained by further surveillance of the young woman and her dry-cleaning contact? The longer Cho ran the surveillance, the more likely Director Pang and his counterintelligence thugs would become aware of the operation. If the fact that one of Cho's marines had been compromised by a North Korean agent was to become known by the Korean General Staff, Cho's career would be over, at a minimum. Cho decided there could not be any further surveillance of Colonel Chang or his young companion. He decided to immediately terminate the surveillance operation and have the technicians reassigned to other duties. They would be briefed to forget about the operation and destroy the notes and materials developed during the surveillance.

With that resolved, Cho returned to the nagging subject of how to deal with Colonel Chang himself. Although Chang's role appeared to be only that of the unwitting fool, there also was the possibility that the colonel had a much more calculated and profound role. He decided to have Chang meet him at one of the several locations in the city used for covert meetings. Perhaps a few hours with some of Cho's enthusiastic interrogators might motivate the colonel to provide additional insight into the North Korean penetration of Cho's organization.

General Cho finally turned his thoughts to tomorrow's visit by the new American secretary of defense. *Why would President Kim invite the Americans to visit now?* he wondered. Kim had already denied any knowledge of the missing warheads. Perhaps it was just an excuse for the president to meet Secretary Garrett and form a first-hand impression. Cho knew that Admiral Pak would be at the meeting. Cho made a mental note to have lunch with the admiral afterward.

Ready Room 4, the Reagan

Lieutenants Dan Garrett and Katrina Pierce— dressed in their flight suits — were seated in the front row of the Scorpion's ready room. The squadron duty officer selected a channel on the video monitor that was mounted on the bulkhead, changing the picture on the screen to a camera shot of a young Naval intelligence officer.

"Good morning, ladies and gentlemen," the handsome officer

said, "I'm Ensign Parker Smith, welcome to the Event 2 brief. Let's go upstairs first for the weather."

The picture changed again, this time to show a meteorology officer in front of a weather map of the region. The Navy's meteorology and oceanography officers supported Naval strategy and tactics by integrating the sciences of oceanography, meteorology, mapping, charting, and geodesy with Naval operations. Onboard an aircraft carrier, they were affectionately known as "Weather Guessers."

After the weather specialist had provided the aircrews with his prediction for the next few hours, he signed off, saying, "Have a safe flight! Back to you in CVIC." The screen shifted back to Parker Smith who began to brief the aircrew on the airspace in which they would be operating, including any restricted airspace and associated radio frequencies for which to request access. The airspace briefing was followed by a threat briefing, which showed the locations of any potentially hostile ships, submarines, and aircraft currently in the area. Next was an overview of the friendly naval and commercial ships and aircraft within a few hundred miles of the carrier. Parker went on to describe each squadron's participation in the event, listing the numbers and types of aircraft, the planned mission, the area of operation, and assigned radio control frequencies. Throughout the presentation, aircrew in each squadron ready room took notes, and asked clarifying questions of the briefer.

Before concluding the briefing, Parker added, "One last thing, ladies and gentlemen: We have a lost item here that's currently available to the highest bidder." The camera view then shifted to a flight helmet with "VFA-67" displayed on the crown and "CHEMO" painted on the side.

Within a minute, Parker reported, "I see we have an offer from Ready Room 7! Are there any others? No? That's a pity! Lieutenant CHEMO Wilkins, you can come to CVIC and claim your helmet. And don't forget to bring the five bucks! Okay, that's all for the Event 2 brief. Have a safe flight!"

Dan Garrett turned to Katrina Pierce with a wide grin. "Wouldn't want to be CHEMO right now!" he chuckled.

"That's the third time this cruise he's done that!" Katrina laughed. "You'd think he'd learn! You ready to dress?"

The two officers left the ready room and walked across the passageway to a smaller room where squadron aircrew stored their flight gear and began the time-honored ritual of suiting up for their flight. Directly over their dark green flight suits they put on G-suits, or "speed pants," which inflated during very high-speed maneuvers to prevent blood from draining from a pilot's brain and causing a loss of consciousness. Next was the integrated harness and survival vest with an inflatable life jacket. An oxygen mask and flight helmet came last, along with a pair of fire-proof gloves. After dressing, the two officers made a last trip to the head and then made their way to the flight deck to inspect their aircraft.

Onboard a CMV-22B Osprey from the Reagan to Osan Air Base, South Korea

The large aircraft lifted straight into the air and then moved forward and upward as it transitioned to conventional flight. Although Colt Garrett felt this trip to Seoul was the most important mission of his career thus far, he wasn't certain he would be successful, or even what success, in this case, would look like. POTUS had tasked him to meet with South Korean President Kim to hear what Kim had to say regarding the missing U.S. warheads, but the South Koreans had already denied any knowledge of the weapons and were unlikely to provide additional information, so what might be gained by this visit?

When Colt had sought guidance from Secretary of State Jon Unger about protocols and expectations when in Seoul, Unger had given him wise advice. "Your job is to develop a relationship with President Kim, or at least start one in the short time you will be meeting with him. He'll be assessing you as a person and asking himself if you can be trusted. You cannot fake sincerity. Don't lie, and never say anything without considering its impact. It's okay to take a moment and think before you speak. Make certain the others in your party pay close attention to Kim as well as his staff; nonverbal communication can be most revealing. After you leave Seoul, we'll talk again to get your perspectives and anything else you may have learned or have questions about." The experienced diplomat had tried to give Colt a crash course in foreign diplomacy, and Colt hoped it would be enough.

For the diplomatic mission, Colt decided he would take Lenny, the *Reagan's* senior intelligence officer, Commander Jen Abrams, and the two NCIS special agents, Anna DeSantis and Kevin Orr. Actually, it was DeSantis who had insisted the protection detail accompany him on his mission to Seoul. Colt wanted Jen along because of her intel background and her in-depth knowledge of Western Pacific politics. Abrams also possessed a working knowledge of the Korean language, a skill that could prove useful during the meeting with the South Koreans.

Colt looked at Jen now, sitting directly across from him in the

Osprey. She was impeccably dressed in her service dress blues, with three gold stripes and a gold star on each sleeve and three rows of ribbons on the left side of her uniform jacket. While reading an issue of *Proceedings*, a magazine published by the U.S. Naval Institute, Jen looked up and caught Colt looking at her. She smiled warmly at him and let their eyes meet for several moments more than would be typical. Purposely shifting his gaze to a section of the aircraft fuselage, Colt wondered if Abrams was flirting with him. During their flight from Seattle to Tokyo, she had shown no real interest. Perhaps now that he was the secretary of defense, he had more potential in her eyes. Was she the type of woman who would pursue him to advance her career?

Anna DeSantis shifted in her seat as the aircraft banked to the left, adjusting herself so her concealed pistol wouldn't dig as much into her side. The pistol was a continual reminder of her role as an NCIS special agent, and also of her responsibility for the personal safety of the secretary of defense. Garrett had initially declined Anna's suggestion that she and Kevin Orr accompany him, fearing that it might be seen as an insult to the South Koreans. Anna had insisted, however, telling him that because he was such a critical element of the National Command Authority, he was required to have his personal protection detail with him at all times. Ultimately, he agreed. Anna had also contacted the Army CID command in Seoul, and the Army had agreed to provide the remainder of the personal protection detail once the Osprey landed at Osan Air Base.

Kevin Orr sat next to Anna, thinking about his threat vulnerability assessment and its progress to date. He and Commander Abrams had been developing a list of those on board the *Reagan* who might be a danger to Secretary Garrett.

Abrams had proved very accommodating in providing Kevin with access to military service records and the background investigation results he needed for his research. At this point, he had a list of 27 crew members he intended to interview, and he hoped to have them completed over the next few days. Nobody really stood out as a serious threat, but nevertheless, Kevin wanted to meet each individual to draw his own conclusions. Next on his to-do list would be a review of all the civilian contractors onboard, to determine if any of them met his threat criteria. Commander Abrams would be getting those records from the contractors' respective employers, a task that undoubtedly would be extremely challenging. Once that review was completed, Special Agent Orr would be able to complete his report and submit it to Anna.

Kevin looked to his right at his NCIS colleague sitting next to him. Although she certainly had her own way of doing things, *Very* Special Agent Anna DeSantis had become an unexpected pleasure to work with. Over the past few days, they had spent quite a bit of time together as they looked through personnel records and planned for the protection detail. As an excuse to spend more time with her, Kevin had given Anna a private tour of the *Reagan*, showing her some of the more interesting places and spaces he had discovered since first reporting aboard. He was pretty certain she wasn't dating anybody, and he, of course, was single. Kevin liked to think it was because the crew saw him as *the Law*, but more likely it was because he was a fairly shy guy — except when he was around Anna. He was fully aware that he might be falling for his captivating co-worker, and he wondered whether she, too, might be interested.

The Flight Deck, the Reagan

The EA-18G Growler was the most advanced airborne electronic attack platform in the world. Manufactured by Boeing, it was the only electronic attack aircraft currently in production. A variant of the combat-proven F/A-18F Super Hornet, the Growler provided tactical electronic jamming and protection to U.S. military forces and their allies all around the world. At over 60 feet in length and with a wingspan of 44 feet, the Growler could generate 44,000 pounds of thrust from its two General Electric F414-GE-400 engines and reach a speed of 1,000 miles per hour or more. Operated by two crew members, a pilot in the forward seat and an electronic warfare officer in the rear, the airplane could provide an electronic envelope of protection for the carrier's attack aircraft, and it could also protect itself, against other aircraft with the AMRAAM medium-range missile or ground-based missile systems with the HARM anti-radiation missile. But the Growler's primary purpose did not involve the use of missile systems. Instead, it used its signals receiver and multiple electronic signals jamming pods to counter enemy radar sensors.

After an in-depth visual check of the aircraft, Dan and Katrina climbed up into the cockpit of the airplane to go through a series of flight readiness checklists. Dan then started up both of the powerful engines, closed the canopy, and followed the flight deck crew's instructions to position the aircraft on one of the ship's steam catapults. He positioned the Growler's front landing gear into the catapult mechanism, and a massive jet blast deflection barrier was raised behind the aircraft. Dan advanced the throttles fully forward, turned to salute the launching officer, and then pressed his head back against the headrest. Moments later, the Growler was accelerating down the bow of the ship and, after only two seconds, was airborne.

"Looks like we're going flying rather than swimming today!" Dan commented into the plane's intercom.

"Thanks for not killing me again, JOKER!" replied Katrina, as Dan raised the plane's landing gear and kept climbing away from the carrier. The Growler continued to accelerate until it reached 500 knots and climbed above 10,000 feet before Dan started to level off.

"Thanks for noticing, HURRICANE! It's heart-warming to know you appreciate my exceptional aviator skills that are keeping you safe from harm and making it possible for you to survive so that one day you can put innocent people in jail!"

"Amazing that you can fit that big head of yours into a flight helmet, JOKER! How about doing me a favor and come left to 275 whenever it suits you so that we can rendezvous with our two playmates? I'll check in with the *Hawkeye*."

A moment after Katrina gave Dan the new heading, he rolled the Growler into a tight left turn to initiate the intercept.

"Coming left to 275, HURRICANE!" Dan grunted as he fought the G-forces that were pressing him into his ejection seat.

Today's "playmates" were two F/A-18E Super Hornets that were tasked with finding the Growler and then simulating a missile shoot down of the aircraft. The Growler's task was to avoid being detected. In addition, an E-2D Advanced Hawkeye with a 24-foot APY-9 rotodome radar affixed to its fuselage was tasked with providing initial control of the exercise and then going silent once the exercise commenced.

When the two Super Hornets began the intercept, Katrina

flipped a switch on her control panel and announced, "Master Rad on!" indicating she had energized the ALQ-99 pod to jam the Super Hornets' radars. Four attempts later and the Super Hornets remained unable to obtain radar lock-on of the Growler. After the E-2D controller announced "FINEX, FINEX" over the radio frequency, one of the F/A-18 pilots radioed, "Hey, JOKER, how about turning that damn machine off and letting us practice shooting your butt out of the sky? Or are you worried that your piloting skills aren't up to our standard without the help of HURRICANE?"

While the Super Hornet pilot was still transmitting, Dan had banked his Growler into a sharp right turn and rapidly descended on the pair of fighters.

"Let's keep the music off for a sec, HURRICANE," said Dan into the intercom as he pushed the Growler into afterburner, injecting additional fuel into the jet pipes downstream of the turbine engines and making the Growler go supersonic. Five seconds later, Dan keyed the radio and proclaimed, "I got tone!" indicating he had locked-up the fighters on his fire control radar. And then, "Fox Two, Fox Two!" as he simulated the firing of two air-to-air missiles.

The E-2D controller keyed his mic. "Splash two Hornets! Let's call it a day and head back to the boat."

Dan maneuvered the Growler into the landing pattern and lined-up the aircraft for final approach to the carrier. "I just engaged Magic Carpet," he said to Katrina, "Now the computer has the ball!"

Dan considered the use of the Magic Carpet landing system to be a bit like cheating — Navy pilots prided themselves on their keen ability to manually "fly the ball" and land an aircraft on a violently pitching flight deck. He understood that the system was intended to make landings safer and allow combat pilots to focus on the assigned mission rather than on landing their aircraft. But his own preference was not to rely on a computer to do his job.

Katrina found the entire issue ironic. "Let me get this straight, JOKER," she said, somewhat mockingly. "The whole purpose of this aircraft is to use *our* computers to fool an *enemy's* computers, and yet you think it's cheating if we use yet *another* computer to land on the carrier? That's priceless!"

"Well, yes," Dan replied as the Growler slammed onto the deck and snagged the number three-wire. He pulled the throttles back, raised the tailhook, and then taxied to the spot on the deck as directed by a Sailor wearing a yellow jersey.

Dan and Katrina put their ejection seats in a safe condition, disengaged a variety of attachments and electronic connections and then climbed down from the aircraft. Opening the hatch on the way to CVIC for debriefing, Dan boasted playfully, "Well, HURRICANE, I brought you back safely again, *and* simulated the splashdown of two Hornets!"

Katrina removed her helmet and turned to Dan. "Congratulations, JOKER! Just three more *simulated* kills, and you'll be a *simulated* ace!"

U.S. Embassy, Seoul, Korea

Colt Garrett was met by an impressive welcoming committee as he walked through the main entrance of the U.S. Embassy in downtown Seoul. First to greet him was Ambassador Aaron Greer, a retired four-star Navy admiral with a wealth of experience in the Pacific Theater. Unlike many of his fellow ambassadors, Greer was appointed as ambassador for his in-depth experience in the region, rather than as a reward in exchange for a political favor or campaign contribution. Ambassador Greer hadn't let his new role as diplomat change his military bearing or the firm handshake he had developed after nearly four decades of service to his country.

"Welcome to South Korea, Mr. Secretary, and congratulations on your appointment! Secretary Unger has told me he's extremely pleased to be working with you and your DOD team on this issue. Is this your first time in Seoul?"

Colt returned the ambassador's handshake and replied, "Thank you, Ambassador! I did visit Seoul many years ago but didn't have much time to see anything other than the inside of a command center."

Colt was pretty certain that Greer would have ordered an exhaustive review of his history with the Navy, department of defense, and any tourist travel, making the ambassador's question simply an icebreaker to make him feel at ease.

"Mr. Secretary, may I present General Leon Boyd, Commander of U.S. Forces Korea."

Leon Boyd was a West Point graduate and proudly wore the uniform of an Army four-star general with the requisite rows of impressive ribbons and qualification badges on his uniform jacket.

"Welcome, Mr. Secretary. USFK stands ready to assist you in any way possible."

Colt shook the general's hand. "Thank you, General!" he said. "I hope to get the chance to meet with your command staff and perhaps a few troops before I fly back to the *Reagan*."

Ambassador Greer stepped forward again. "Mr. Secretary,

I'd like to present Dennis O'Keefe, the agency's man in Seoul."
Dennis O'Keefe had been the CIA's station chief for three years,
coordinating all U.S. intelligence activities in South Korea.

"Welcome to Seoul, Mr. Secretary," O'Keefe said. "Thank you
for getting here so quickly. I have a secure room all set up and
waiting so that we can prepare for this afternoon's meeting with
President Kim and his staff."

Another man, dressed in a dark blue suit, stood next to Dennis
O'Keefe and offered his hand. "Mr. Secretary, I'm Special Agent
Glenn Carpenter from Army CID. I'm the supervisory agent
responsible for your protection detail. I have a team of three
other CID agents with me, and we'll be supporting your NCIS
protection agents during your stay here in Seoul."

Colt looked at the serious and well-fit man. "Weren't you with
Secretary O'Kane when he died?" He asked. "That must have
been difficult for you and your team."

Carpenter's eyes softened, and he said, "Yes, sir. Secretary
O'Kane was a fine man and a real American hero. He was never
quite the same after losing his wife, so somehow it felt right that
he passed on while visiting her grave."

Colt placed his hand on the agent's shoulder. "I liked him, too.
He was a good man, and he left large shoes to fill. I hope to do
the job half as well as he did. Will you be coming with us back to
the *Reagan?*"

"No, sir, unless you want or need us to. Deputy Secretary
Holmes has us flying back to Tokyo to wait for you there with the
Nightwatch aircraft. He said NCIS would handle the protection
responsibilities while you're onboard *Reagan*. Do you know when
you'll be leaving for D.C.?"

"Not yet. I guess that depends upon how things go today."

Ambassador Greer motioned toward the door. "And now, Secretary Garrett, please follow Mr. O'Keefe to our secure conference room. I believe we have some refreshments waiting there for us."

Anna DeSantis had been standing back while the group of senior officials introduced one another. She now stepped forward to talk with Special Agent Carpenter.

"I'm Anna DeSantis, NCIS. I heard you say you're Glenn Carpenter. I hope CID isn't too bent that the Navy has been providing the detail for the defense secretary for a few days?"

"Actually, I was relieved to find out you were with Mr. Garrett when his appointment was announced. There was no way we could have had a team ready for his protection detail that quickly out here in the Pacific. We'll just work with you while PATRIOT's in Seoul, and we'll assume responsibility when you bring him to Tokyo in a few days."

The Blue House, Seoul, Korea

The State Room in the Blue House was the most spectacular location in which to hold a summit between the governments of the United States and South Korea. The room had at least four times the amount of space needed to hold the 20-foot, boat-shaped conference table, which was constructed of beautifully finished cherry wood and included four chairs on each side.

Colt was seated on one side of the table, with CIA Station Chief Dennis O'Keefe on his left, Ambassador Greer on his right, and General Boyd next to the ambassador. Directly across from Colt sat President Kim, and across the table from the CIA chief sat Director Pang of the South Korea's NIS. Across from Ambassador Greer was General Lee, the Minister of National Defense, and across from General Boyd sat Admiral Pak, the South Korean Chief of Naval Operations. Lined up behind the conference table were more than two dozen senior advisors and staff members representing both nations, Lenny Wilson and Commander Abrams among them. President Kim brought the meeting to order.

"Good day, gentlemen," he began, in near-perfect English. "And a special welcome to Mr. Colton Garrett, the new American secretary of defense. Our two nations have joined forces for many decades to protect the Republic of Korea. We are honored by your visit today, and I ask that you convey my expression of friendship and gratitude to President Harrison. My staff tells me you have visited our country previously?"

"Yes, Mr. President. Many years ago, I participated in an exercise known as ULCHI FOCUS LENS, and I worked in both Chinhae and Seoul. You have a beautiful country which I would like to see at some point. Perhaps one day my schedule will allow me to visit as a tourist rather than as a representative of the United States."

The South Korean president smiled and said, "Ah, yes! I would welcome such a visit! I do hope you will give me the honor of serving as your guide someday should you find your way back to our shores. But today we have other pressing matters to talk about. Both our countries and the entire world, for that matter, are closely watching how we resolve this important and delicate issue. I have invited your delegation to meet with us face-to-face so that you can see with your own eyes that we are most sincere when we unequivocally state that the biological warheads which your government claims were stolen during transport through our country many years ago are not in the possession of this government. Additionally, you have my solemn promise that our government does not control these weapons and quite frankly, wishes they simply did not exist, wherever they might be. I believe that North Korea's claim of the existence of these weapons is actually an excuse to avoid the reunification of the peninsula and the normalization of relations between the Korean people. As you know, the normalization of relations is our highest priority. I am as distressed about this issue as I am sure President Harrison is."

Colt noticed President Kim had chosen his words and meanings carefully. He silently wished that the South Korean leaders weren't quite so proficient with the English language. Using a translator had definite advantages, including the inherent delay the service required, a delay that usually bought a few extra moments in which to consider what had been said and develop a suitable and intelligent response. Colt was glad he had tasked his staff to take detailed notes so that the meeting could be reviewed in detail after they had returned to the *Reagan*.

"Thank you, Mr. President. As Secretary Unger has previously shared with me, South Korea maintains that the missing warheads are not in your country. It is important to add that the U.S. is not asserting that they are."

President Kim appeared surprised and then doubtful as he looked at Ambassador Greer, who remained silent. The Americans had agreed that only Garrett would speak for the delegation unless the secretary addressed a specific question to someone on the team.

"You could have saved yourselves a long journey had your

country shared that perspective with us days ago," President Kim commented.

Colt Garrett looked directly into President Kim's eyes. "Mr. President," he stated, "to be perfectly clear, we don't know where the weapons are, but we do know who stole them. Mr. O'Keefe, please share with President Kim our information regarding the theft of our warheads."

The CIA chief of station began a high-level briefing of then-Major Cho's responsibility for the warheads' transport and eventual theft. He provided copies of the weapon manifests showing the accounting error, and he detailed Cho's role in the incident. When finished, O'Keefe looked to Colt to indicate that the CIA's part of the meeting had now concluded.

President Kim hesitated a moment, then spoke. "This appears to be only circumstantial evidence of General Cho's involvement. There is no information that indicates he has the weapons or that he is aware of their location."

Colt paused for several moments and then responded. "You are correct, Mr. President, but I'm not here to accuse or arrest General Cho nor place him on trial. I'm here to make it crystal clear that the United States will not tolerate the purposeful theft and continued withholding of these warheads. President Harrison has personally asked me to convey that message to you, and to make certain that everyone — and I mean everyone — understands the seriousness of this issue and its significance to my country. I am not a diplomat, Mr. President, and I am not even certain how long I will *have* this job. But I do need you to help me find these warheads before something catastrophic happens."

Once again, President Kim hesitated before speaking, "I agree with you, Secretary Garrett," he said. "You are not a diplomat. But I strongly disagree with your assessment of your career prospects. You may tell President Harrison that I understand the American position completely. The problem is that we do not know where your warheads are, and continued accusations will not resolve the matter."

President Kim rose from his chair and walked around the table, shaking the hands of the four Americans. When he grasped Colt's outstretched hand, he said, "I have enjoyed meeting you, Mr. Secretary. I was sincere in my offer to act as your guide should you return to my country."

Kim accepted a small package handed to him by one of his aides, then presented it to Colt. "Please accept this small token of the friendship between my country and yours. It is a copy of my favorite guidebook of South Korea. You will forgive the actions of a doting father; my oldest son is the book's author."

Colt accepted the book and thanked President Kim, adding, "I had hoped we would be leaving today with something else more critical."

"I have already given you everything I can," President Kim replied, and then he turned and exited the room.

Osan Air Base, South Korea

The VIP lounge of the Air Mobility Command terminal at Osan Air Base was typically occupied by senior officers waiting for a flight to another duty station or perhaps a leave destination. This afternoon, the secretary of defense and his party were waiting for an Osprey to be refueled for their return flight to the *Reagan*. While sipping on a cup of coffee and snacking on a bag of stale chips she purchased from a vending machine, Commander Jen Abrams was speaking with the NCIS agents. Not far from them, Colt Garrett was sitting with Lenny Wilson near a large window, looking out at the activity on the runway. They watched as two F-16C Fighting Falcons from Osan's 36th Fighter Squadron accelerated down the runway and ascended into the evening sky. Colt thought the Falcon was one of the most beautiful airplanes in the U.S. inventory — even if it was an Air Force platform. To him, the Falcon just seemed to reflect the perfect balance of design and performance.

"I just don't get it," said Lenny, looking glumly into his paper coffee cup, "Why can't the Air Force make a decent cup of coffee?" He poured his half-empty cup into a trash bin.

Colt sighed, "I thought you were talking about the meeting in the Blue House. What do you think Kim meant by his comment that his government does not control the weapons and wishes they did not exist?"

Lenny looked up from his notes. "I really don't know," he answered. "Maybe he was reflecting on the jam he's in. I mean, those warheads were stolen when he was only about 20 years old. Presidents come and go. It wouldn't surprise me if the South Korean military has them hidden and are keeping the fact from him."

Colt was still pondering the meeting. "And did you see the look on Kim's face when the CIA chief of station told them about General Cho's involvement? I had a definite feeling they already knew or somehow suspected it. Regardless, they seemed quite surprised that *we* knew."

"Maybe you're reading more into it than is there, sir. They've got to be sweating this problem — big time. They are well aware that our relationship is dramatically one-sided, and they clearly want this to go away. I sure wouldn't want to be General Cho right now. I have a feeling the ROK marines might be finding themselves under some serious pressure."

"OK, maybe I am overthinking — I'll concede that. But it's been a very long day, and this diplomacy stuff is not my skill set. Maybe I'm just tired." Colt leaned back into his chair and closed his eyes.

There was something odd about the meeting with Kim, and he couldn't put his finger on it. It was nagging at him, but experience told him it was useless to keep thinking about it when he was this exhausted, and particularly when he had a headache. His migraines had started again after he was appointed secretary, and his recent lack of sleep and changes in his diet were enough to trigger a bad one. He had suffered from migraine headaches since childhood, but fortunately, the accompanying pain and nausea had decreased over the years. Now he just wanted to close his eyes and get some rest, but he still had to endure the long flight back to the *Reagan*.

Watching his friend, Lenny could tell Colt was having another headache. The man was working pretty hard and really wasn't taking care of himself. Lenny left the VIP lounge in search of some aspirin.

Secretary of Defense Cabin, the Reagan

Rear Admiral Carlisle wandered slowly through his former cabin spaces and realized how badly he missed the luxury and privacy of the spacious suite. Garrett had made some changes: The furniture was rearranged, and most of the mementos depicting the admiral's career were removed, perhaps discarded. Just two weeks ago, this aircraft carrier was his flagship and he was in command of the most powerful force in the Pacific Ocean. Now he was a minor player in a major event involving his country. All thanks to Colton Garrett.

Carlisle stepped into the sleeping quarters of the suite and carefully surveyed the room. Garrett had added no personal items except for a few items of clothing in the closet and a well-worn copy of Tom Clancy's *The Hunt for Red October* next to a small clock radio on the nightstand. Carlisle looked into the head and then went out into the office area. He was about to leave altogether when the cabin door suddenly opened and in walked Special Agent DeSantis, followed by Secretary Garrett. Both Garrett and DeSantis were surprised to find the admiral in the cabin.

"Good evening, Admiral. Are you lost?" Colt inquired, standing just inside the door.

Carlisle seemed to gather his thoughts for a moment. "No, sir. I haven't seen my briefcase in a while and thought I may have left it in my closet — I mean *your* closet. Sorry to have bothered you, sir."

He briskly walked to the cabin door and let himself out.

"Well, that was strange!" Colt said to himself out loud as he poured himself a glass of water from the faucet and sat down to remove his shoes.

"Good night, sir," Anna said, then headed for her stateroom.

A few moments later, Colt heard a knock at his cabin door. Wishing he could ignore it, he got up from his chair, crossed the cabin, and opened his door to find Commander Jen Abrams standing there.

"What can I do for you, Jen? Weren't we going to debrief our meeting with the South Koreans tomorrow morning?"

"I wanted to ask you something, sir. I'll only take a minute, but first, I need to use your head." A few minutes later, Jen came back into the cabin's office area and joined Colt at the small conference table.

"I really don't understand that Seoul meeting at all," she said. "Why would they ask us to come, and then not tell us anything? It doesn't make any sense, sir!" Colt was exhausted and not in the mood for this or any other discussion.

"I agree with you," he responded, his head throbbing. "But I need to think about it further, and right now, I have a splitting headache and I need some sleep. I do want to hear your thoughts, so let's continue this tomorrow. Stop by in the morning for coffee and we'll talk more."

After Jen left his cabin, Colt headed back into his bedroom, changed out of his clothes, and fell into his bed. *Jen is right*, he thought. *Something doesn't make sense.* And he quickly drifted off.

Day Eight

Headquarters, Republic of Korea Marine Corps, Hwaseong, South Korea

The South Korean Marine Corps historically operated with a great degree of autonomy, an autonomy that was about to come to a sudden and dramatic end. Yesterday's meeting with the American delegation had caused high-level concern throughout both the South Korean government and the military. The South Korean officials had not anticipated that the Americans could so quickly and accurately have identified the individual responsible for the theft of the warheads. It was additionally distressing that the Americans knew that the guilty party was the commandant of the marines, the very man who now sat across the desk from Admiral Pak.

President Kim and Minister of Defense General Lee had made it clear that they held the navy directly responsible for what General Cho and his marines had done. This morning's meeting between Pak and Cho was the first step in a plan to realign the marines back into the navy chain of command.

"General Cho," Admiral Pak began, "the Americans believe you are the individual responsible for the theft of their warheads, and they also believe our government knows their whereabouts. Do you acknowledge you removed the warheads during their transport many years ago and now have them hidden somewhere?"

General Cho had been sitting silently, listening to Pak's

accusations. He finally said, "Admiral Pak, the Americans have either orchestrated an elaborate plan to discredit me and our country, or they simply have botched their own investigation. In either case, I can unequivocally assure you that I neither stole the biological warheads nor am I aware of their whereabouts. I continue to believe this is some sort of scheme that was hatched in the North to not only halt the reunification talks but also to cause us to further mistrust one another."

Pak suddenly realized that General Cho had no idea President Kim already knew Cho had stolen and hidden the weapons and that he was now guarding them with his own troops. Admiral Pak also knew that his own chances for possible promotion to Minister of National Defense were dependent upon his ability to artfully and effectively resolve the missing warheads issue and remove General Cho from power.

"That is an interesting response, General," the admiral commented. "You should know that if I discover you are lying to me regarding your involvement in this affair, the damage you will bring upon yourself and the entire marine corps will be devastating."

The admiral stood and walked toward the door, turning back to leave the general with one final point. "You see," he said, "the truth has an uncanny way of surfacing. When it does, I hope it aligns with your statements." The admiral left the general's office and closed the door behind him.

General Cho remained seated at his desk and proceeded to think through the situation he was in. First, no one other than he and a few of his trusted marines knew the location of the biological weapons. The admiral had to be bluffing. The Americans were much more likely to be concerned about the reunification talks than about the location of a few old warheads. Second, with Colonel Chang's reckless sharing of classified information with the North Korean agent he was sleeping with, any relocation of the warheads would now have to be delayed until other world events caused the Americans to become distracted. Any unusual movement of South Korean forces could be detected by the Americans. Third, he would continue to deny any involvement with the warheads' theft. There was no proof at all that he actually removed them. He decided instead to accelerate his interrogation of Colonel Chang to discover the extent of the North Korean penetration of his forces.

SECDEF Cabin, the Reagan

Colt Garrett looked at his reflection in the mirror above the sink as he moved the electric shaver over his face. Like most men performing the daily ritual, he approached the task in the same way each morning, shaving each portion of his weathered face in the same sequence he had used since becoming old enough to grow a beard. He noticed his ever-receding hairline and the growing amount of gray in his thinning hair, wondering to himself, *Where have all the years gone? Am I turning into my father?* But when he looked closer into the mirror, he saw a man staring back who had lived a good life, made a few mistakes along the way, and hopefully had learned from them. He hung his robe on the hook behind the door and stepped into the shower stall.

The "Hollywood Shower" that Colt was enjoying this morning, with its endless flow of water, was typically forbidden on a Navy ship at sea because it could consume more than 60 gallons of fresh water. A standard "Navy Shower" used only three gallons of water: a brief wet down, soap, and then a final spray to rinse the soap away. If *Reagan's* 5,000 crew members each took a daily "Hollywood Shower," more than 300,000 gallons of fresh water would be wasted every day.

For some reason, Colt seemed to do his best thinking in the shower. This particular morning he was fixated on yesterday's meeting in Seoul with President Kim, and he recalled Kim's statement that the government did not control the stolen warheads and wished they did not exist. Lenny thought Colt was seeing things that weren't there, and maybe it was just the headache he was experiencing at the time, but it still gnawed at him. *Okay*, he thought, *let's walk through this one more time. If the South Korean government doesn't control the warheads, was President Kim implying that another entity, perhaps the military or some subset of the military,* does *control the weapons without government knowledge? If General Cho was the last person to see the warheads all those years ago, perhaps he was doing this on his own. And if indeed the South Koreans had discovered that Cho had hidden the weapons without government knowledge, they wouldn't just throw Cho under the bus like that — would they?*

Colt turned off the water and toweled off before leaving the shower stall. He stood still for a few more minutes, continuing his thought process. *If Kim knew the stolen weapons were secretly hidden in his country, of course he would wish they weren't there!* And then, with a jolt, it came to him. *Was Kim saying he wishes the Americans would go and find the warheads and just remove them* as if they were never there? *But to remove the warheads, the U.S. would have to know their precise location, which at this point is the missing piece of the puzzle.*

Colt started to dress for the day — khaki slacks, light blue button-down shirt, brown oxford shoes — his default choice for business casual attire when he didn't want to put too much thought into it. While tying his shoes, Colt let his mind wander to another thing President Kim had said at the end of yesterday's meeting: "I've given you everything I can." *What did he mean by that? Kim denied the weapons are in South Korea and had abruptly ended the meeting, but he had given me nothing . . . except for that tour book.*

Colt quickly crossed the cabin to the table where he had placed his gift from President Kim. It was a small, pretty standard, paperback book titled *A Westerner's Guide to South Korea.* Picking it up, Colt noticed that a tiny section of one page had been folded over in the middle of the book. He sat down on the edge of a chair and opened the book to the folded page. It marked the beginning of a chapter on Ulleungdo Island.

O3 Level Fitness Room, the Reagan

Although Jen Abrams hoped that her warning to Lieutenant Commander Bryant was sufficient to end his harassment of Rebecca Clarke, she decided the only sure way to protect the young woman was to be in the gym whenever Rebecca worked out. The two female officers had agreed to meet before breakfast and get in a workout together before the day began.

When Jen entered the gym, she saw that Rebecca had already arrived and was working on her pectoral and anterior deltoid muscles with the Machine Fly. Watching her perform the seated exercise prompted Jen to reflect on her own physical condition. She was fifteen years older than the attractive, young ensign, and gravity had started taking its toll. Jen thought it was unfair that men's looks seemed to improve with age, while women waged a never-ending battle to reverse the effects of time. Despite her nightly ritual of costly creams and special serums — all intended to halt the effects of aging — Jen still saw a middle-aged woman in the mirror, looking back at her with sad eyes and a worsening complexion.

Jen seated herself on the Lat Pull/Low Row machine to work on her back, which had recently begun bothering her. She blamed the pain on having to sit most of the day at a desk while reading message traffic, and she had considered ordering a standing desk to help with the problem. While resting between sets, Jen looked over and saw that Rebecca had also taken a break.

"How have you been, Rebecca?" asked Jen.

"Great, Commander. Hey, I really appreciated your talking with me the other day. I just wanted to thank you again for that."

"Any more issues since then?"

"No, ma'am." Rebecca paused to look around the gym before going on, "Since we talked, I've had no issues at all. Did you speak with him?"

Jen looked around to ensure that nobody was within earshot and paying attention to the two women.

"I did have a conversation with him about you. I said I'd been approached by a few others who had observed him harassing you on several occasions. Although I didn't demand a confession, I made it clear that this kind of behavior would put his career in jeopardy, and that if he continued, I would file an official complaint. I'm fairly certain you won't be bothered by him anymore."

Rebecca was obviously relieved. She let out a sigh and said, "Thank you, Commander! You honestly don't know how grateful I am for your help." Rebecca stood up and walked over to the seated bench press machine, while Jen finished her third set and then shifted to the Fly Machine vacated by Rebecca. Jen added twenty more pounds of resistance and began a three-set exercise. She enjoyed helping the young woman and thought perhaps she had made a new friend on board — something she hadn't anticipated.

Defense Secretary Cabin, the Reagan

Lenny came into his boss's cabin to find the secretary seated at the conference table looking at the guidebook he had been given yesterday by President Kim.

"What can I do for you, sir?" he asked as he pulled up a chair for himself.

"Lenny, I think I might have an idea of where those stolen warheads are. So, I want to walk through my reasoning with you to see if you can poke any holes in my theory."

"I'm all ears," Wilson responded, clearly curious to hear Colt's idea.

Colt proceeded to explain how he had arrived at his hypothesis that the warheads could be hidden on Ulleungdo Island. He added that he was considering tasking the SISTINE BEACON system to search the island before the rest of South Korea.

"Well, what do you think?" he asked Lenny.

"I'm not sure, sir, it seems weak to me. You're assuming that President Kim actually wants us to find the warheads. You're also assuming he purposely gave you a tour book containing a clue to the warheads' location, and which has led you to conclude the warheads are on the remote island of Ulleungdo. If we had any kind of corroborating intelligence, that would be one thing. But to base the entire hypothesis on a single, tiny fold in a paperback book, is a stretch, in my opinion."

"I know," Colt agreed, "but my gut is telling me we have something here. It's the only thing I can come up with that explains yesterday's meeting in Seoul and some of the weird things Kim said."

Colt could tell by the look on Lenny's face that he wasn't convinced. He reminded himself that Lenny's background was policy and politics rather than intelligence analysis. Colt hadn't assumed anything. He felt he had logically worked the problem and had developed a plausible explanation. He was just going to have to trust his own interpretation of the events to drive the next steps.

"Lenny, I appreciate your candid feedback. Your view makes you the perfect person to write this up as a brief for Steve Holmes and our team at the Pentagon. For right now, I've been asked by Commander Robinson to come to Ready Room 4 and watch a holiday video some of the families made for the squadron. Get a conference call set up with Steve and the team for noon, our time, to see what they think. That should give you enough time to put the brief together and get it to Steve so they can be prepared for the call."

Lenny left his boss looking at the tour book as he made his way to the new defense secretary operations room. He just wasn't sure about Colt's Ulleungdo Island theory, and he was concerned that Steve Holmes and the other senior DOD executives would be similarly skeptical. He knew that the Ulleungdo Island idea was a very long shot, and the right political move would be to continue the search as planned. He was certain about one thing, however. Once Colt Garrett became convinced about something, there were few people who could change his mind.

Ready Room 4, the Reagan

The holiday season is a difficult time for those deployed at sea. On the one hand, you're thinking of those at home and how they miss you. On the other hand, you're being reminded of what you are missing.

Colt Garrett sat in the front row of Ready Room 4, watching the squadron's holiday video as it played on the large screen secured to the room's forward bulkhead. Produced by the skipper's wife, the video included several short video clips submitted by squadron family members and friends back home on Whidbey Island. Even though access to the Internet provides Sailors with plenty of opportunities to video chat with their families, the holiday video is a decades-long Navy tradition, and traditions were important when people were separated from their families at Christmas. The annual video productions started many years ago with simple clips of family and friends in front of a decorated Christmas tree, but in recent years the videos have evolved into a major competition between families to see who can create the most unusual or hilarious message. This year's edition started with a shot of Katrina Pierce's husband Gene in his woodworking shop, ripping a long pine plank on his table saw. An accomplished woodworker, Gene prided himself on following safety precautions, and so the entire ready room was shocked to watch him slip and run his right hand directly into the blade of the 10-inch saw. Katrina screamed as endless spurts of blood coated the table saw and the shop floor with red, while Gene stumbled and fell against the wall. Just then, the camera zoomed into a closeup of Gene's face as he smiled and said, "Just kidding, HURRICANE! I love you! Merry Christmas!" The ready room exploded with laughter as Katrina attempted to regain her composure.

"Wow, that was impressive, Katrina!" Dan Garrett teased. "You must want to kill him!"

Once Katrina had caught her breath again, she answered, "Oh, he's already dead. He just doesn't know it yet."

The next video was of three young women performing a karaoke version of Taylor Swift's, *Shake It Off*, singing the same song in numerous bars around Oak Harbor, Whidbey Island's main town. The women were dating three of the squadron's NFOs. In each scene, they changed their clothes into skimpier and more provocative attire. The ready room once again roared as the women danced and flirted with the men in the bars, with the clear intent of making certain their boyfriends in the squadron knew what they were missing this holiday season.

Colt turned to the skipper and chuckled, "Hey, Commander, good luck keeping those men focused on flying!"

Commander Tom Robinson replied, "It's already difficult enough! It's a good thing we'll be standing down from flight ops this week. It'll let people take a bit of a break and think about home."

While Colt thought it unlikely that there would be a break from operations, he decided that news could wait until he knew more.

The next video was of a young woman who was obviously very pregnant. Her message for her deployed husband was simple.

"David, I miss you, and so does our baby. Come home to us soon!"

The holiday video continued with a series of ordinary, heartfelt "we miss you" messages, although they were anything *but* ordinary to the Sailors they were meant for. The next video was recorded in a location very familiar to Colt and Dan — their living room in Olympia. On the sofa sat Colt's wife, Linda, his daughter, Alexandra, and Alexandra's husband, Kyle, who was holding their cat, Uncle Rico.

Linda Garrett smiled and said, "Dan and Colt, we love you, and we miss you! We wish we could be with you this Christmas. And congratulations, Colt, on your appointment as secretary of defense! We know you'll do an amazing job."

"And Danny, don't worry," Alexandra Garrett added. "I'm recording all your favorite chick flicks, so you will have hours and hours of romantic comedies to watch when you return!"

Several items were hurled at Dan as his squadron mates howled at his expense. Suddenly, Uncle Rico decided he had had enough and tore his way clear from Kyle's grip, scratching both Alexandra and Kyle in the process. The unplanned scene ended with the Garrett family scattering and leaving the living room.

The final family video was of a young woman holding a cute little toddler on her lap wearing pigtails with pink ribbons. "Hi, Rick," the young mom said. "Heather has a question for you."

The camera zoomed in close to little Heather, who asked sweetly, "Daddy, do you still remember me?"

Lieutenant Commander Rick Becker's eyes teared up as a chorus of voices went, "Aww," causing the mood in the room to come down considerably. The squadron duty officer turned off the display screen, and the lights in the Ready Room were turned back on.

Commander Robinson stood and commented, "That's what happens with these videos. Sometimes they make us feel better, and sometimes they make us feel worse. But today, we have something else very special to do. Mr. Secretary," he said, facing Colt. "Would you join me up here, please?"

Taken a bit by surprise, Colt stood to join Commander Robinson at the front of the Ready Room.

"Sir," Robinson began, "we're very proud to know that a fellow Scorpion is leading the DOD, but we're also a bit embarrassed that you seem to be out of uniform. Dan, can you help me out?"

Dan Garrett rose and stepped forward and proudly handed his father a Navy issue brown leather flight jacket. Colt noticed a leather nameplate had been sewn on the front, with a gold embossed Surface Warfare Officer insignia. Under it were the words, "Colton Garrett, SECDEF."

Commander Robinson continued, "Sir, while it is a bit unusual for a Black Shoe to have a flight jacket, we figured there is only one person who would dare complain, and he's probably too busy being president to worry about Navy uniform regulations!"

The officers in the ready room stood up in unison and applauded as Dan helped Colt put the jacket on.

"Thank you, Commander!" Colt said. "I really appreciate this! Now, if I could just get a ride in one of your Growlers!"

Commander Robinson looked at Dan Garrett standing next to his father, and an idea began to form in his mind. He'd need to check with the Air Wing Commander, but the chance to get the secretary of defense a hop in a Growler was too good an opportunity to pass up.

Secure Video Conference Room, the Reagan

The secretary of defense and his special assistant sat at a conference table as Anna DeSantis stood in her spot by the door. They waited for the secure video link with the Pentagon to sync. The display screen momentarily flashed and then revealed the faces of Deputy Secretary of Defense Steve Holmes, JCS Chairman General David Schmidt, and CIA Director Michelle Walker.

Steve Holmes spoke first. "Good morning, Mr. Secretary. Can you hear us okay?"

"Yes, Steve, five-by-five. So, what did you think of the brief that Lenny sent you earlier this morning?"

Steve Holmes looked at his colleagues in the room with him and then into the video camera. "To be honest, Mr. Secretary, it seems like a long shot to us. Both the CIA and JCS agree that your scenario is based on too many assumptions. Also, it isn't supported by any other intelligence we have. We agree that President Kim's comments were cryptic, and the tour book with one page folded down was interesting. But the thinking here in the building and at Langley as well is that we should continue with the prioritized search of mainland South Korea with SISTINE BEACON we started yesterday unless we get something more solid. We do not believe that shifting SISTINE BEACON to Ulleungdo is the best course of action, and frankly, we're afraid it would be a waste of time and effort."

CIA Director Michelle Walker continued, "Mr. Secretary, my team strongly supports continuing the SISTINE BEACON search of the prioritized locations list we have developed with the Joint Staff. We've even run the decision through our system analytics, and the result is in agreement with our conclusion. We don't believe we should shift the search to the island at this time. I have our country people looking into Ulleungdo and what the South Koreans have been doing there. So far, it all looks pretty benign."

Colt could tell how the wind was blowing. The smart money was on working the problem in an ordered manner and not on chasing wild guesses.

"General," he said to the JCS chairman, "you've been quiet so far. What do you think?"

The highly decorated general looked down at his notes and then into the video camera.

"Mr. Secretary," he said, "I have to admit I'm in complete agreement with what's been said here. The DIA agrees with the CIA and the Joint Staff that the smartest move is to keep SISTINE BEACON searching the peninsula unless we get hard evidence to the contrary. If we get some other strong indication that we're going about the search in the wrong way, we'll shift our efforts. I understand that you personally feel strongly about Ulleungdo, but it's been my experience that the experts should be allowed to make these types of decisions."

This was the first time since being appointed secretary that Colt questioned whether he was suited to the challenge of the job. Perhaps these three were all correct. Even Lenny didn't buy his Ulleungdo Island theory. Colt had to agree it was thin and that conventional wisdom favored the more measured approach of a systematic search of South Korea. And yet . . .

"I want to be very clear on this," Colt said. "You are strongly advising that SISTINE BEACON continue its search as currently tasked unless something changes. Do I have that correct?"

The three senior government officials simultaneously nodded and said, "Yes."

Colt made a few notes on the pad of paper before him, then looking back into the camera, he continued. "General, you say the experts should be allowed to make these types of decisions. In my experience, the experts make recommendations, but commanders make the decisions. Are we clear, General?"

The four-star general was immediately reminded of when he was reprimanded by an upperclassman as a new cadet at West Point. He straightened his back and looked squarely into the camera. "Crystal clear, Mr. Secretary."

Colt referred once more to the notes in front of him. "Ulleungdo Island is only 28 square miles," he stated. "SISTINE BEACON could completely search the island in fewer than 15 hours. I understand that you three disagree, and I've made a note to that effect for the record. I've decided to shift the tasking. If I'm wrong, you will all be covered. General Schmidt, have the Joint Staff issue the appropriate orders, and inform me the moment Ulleungdo is being searched."

General Schmidt opened his mouth to say something, but instead answered, "Yes, sir!"

"Director Walker," Colt continued, "thank you very much for the CIA's assessment and recommendation, but this is a Defense decision. I'm asking the Agency to stand up a team to gather everything you can on Ulleungdo Island, and I mean everything. I assume you have the resources to do that, Michelle?"

"Yes, Mr. Secretary. Of course. And will you inform the president of the new tasking?"

"I will. Steve, hang on for a moment when we're done; I'd like to cover a few more things with you."

The general and the CIA director promptly exited the Pentagon conference room and walked down the long corridor together.

"Well, that was interesting," commented Director Walker. "I can see he isn't afraid to make a decision!"

The chairman of the Joint Chiefs of Staff stopped walking and turned to Director Walker. "I think we know who's running the department of defense. I hope he knows what he's doing!"

Back in the Pentagon conference room, Steve Holmes again looked directly into the video camera.

"Are you going to chew me out for not supporting your idea, Mr. Secretary?"

Colt Garrett smiled at his old friend. "Not at all, Steve. I asked for your honest opinion, and that's what you gave me. But have a gut feeling about that island, and I need to confirm it, one way or the other. If I'm wrong, and we waste the SISTINE BEACON time, the president may appoint you as secretary, effective tomorrow!"

Steve Holmes ended the video call and thought to himself, *I hope not.*

Undisclosed Safehouse, Seoul, South Korea

Colonel Chang was thinking back to his childhood. He and his friends would meet on Saturday afternoons to play cowboys and Indians, mimicking the American westerns they liked to watch on his uncle's television set. It didn't matter then on which side you played, although being an Indian meant you could tie up any cowboys that were captured during the game. In those days, the boys used small pieces of twine to secure their captives. They were much easier to break than the firm leather straps which now bound his hands behind his back.

Worse than being bound, was the fact that his hands were also tied to a hook and rope that were threaded through a pully secured to the room's ceiling. As the rope had been tightened, it lifted him several feet off the floor, swinging him back and forth like a limp rag doll on a string. The pain he had initially felt in his shoulders as he was lifted off the floor hours earlier had ceased, replaced by the brutal and relentless beating being inflicted on him by two of General Cho's associates. He suspected they were former ROK marines, dismissed from the service for some serious, violent offense, but he couldn't identify them, though, due to the black hoods that covered their heads. The steel rods they were using to strike Chang's torso, legs, and genitals had broken countless bones and torn his flesh. He wondered if he would die before the actual interrogation began. He started to hope he would.

Just as the colonel felt he was about to lose consciousness, a door opened at the end of the darkroom. General Cho entered and pulled up a chair. He looked at Chang bound tightly and swinging slowly from the ceiling and he saw blood dripping from the man's battered body onto the cement floor.

"So, Chang, what can you tell me about the young woman who shares your bed in exchange for our state secrets? She must be extremely skilled to be able to convince a man of your dedication and patriotism to dishonor himself and turn traitor against his country — and our beloved marine corps."

Chang lifted his bloody head slightly and looked at the general with his one eye that would open.

"General, believe me," he uttered weakly, blood trickling from his lips. "I had no idea. I thought she loved me."

General Cho looked back at the beaten man with disgust. "Why would a pretty, young woman such as Kang Ji-woo take you into her bed? Did you really believe your colonel's uniform would blind a woman to your age and appearance? You are a fool and a traitor, and I have no use for either!"

Colonel Chang suddenly realized the general had arranged his beating as a punishment rather than as an interrogation. His exciting love affair with Ji-woo had been nothing more than a ruse to get information from him. Now, most likely, he would never leave this room alive.

He was still thinking of Ji-woo as a heavy steel rod came down and crushed his skull.

Forward on the Flight Deck, the Reagan

As the massive aircraft carrier plowed its way through the icy cold sea, its flight deck raised and fell in rhythm with the ocean swell. No matter the size of the ship, every vessel that sailed felt the effect of the waves. Colt and his son Dan stood at the forward edge of the flight deck, directly over where the ship's bow was cutting through the water, while the ever-present Anna DeSantis stood a few paces back, watching over the secretary.

"Did I ever tell you about the time I was on the *Eisenhower* in the Mediterranean in the 80s?" Colt asked Dan. "We were steaming at max speed to the eastern Med to support the evacuation of one of our embassies, and *Ike* was the only ship that could get there in time."

Dan Garrett had heard the story more times than he could count, but he enjoyed watching his father retell it because he always seemed to be re-energized by the vivid memory from his days in the Navy, so many years ago.

"I think I remember something about it, Dad. Wasn't it about how fast the ship was going?"

Colt exclaimed, "Yes! That's right! I was standing right about here with the admiral, and we were going so fast that we could lean forward and not fall over. We spread our arms out wide, and our flight jackets became our wings. The admiral leaned so far forward, I was afraid he was going to go right over the bow and down into the sea!"

Colt extended his arms and started to lean forward, but Dan grabbed him just as he seemed to lose his footing. "Let's not tempt fate, okay?" Dan offered.

"I guess we were going faster than we are now," Colt laughed.

"Or maybe you weighed a little less!" Dan teased.

Colt glanced around and walked over to a young Sailor who was wearing a sound-powered headset and microphone.

"Sailor, are you the lookout? Are you talking with the bridge right now?"

"Yes, sir," the lookout said. "What can I do for you, sir?"

Colt leaned close to the Sailor and said, "Tell them this."

The Navigation Bridge, the Reagan

Captain Johrita Solari was enjoying her tour as commanding officer of one of America's eleven nuclear-powered aircraft carriers. The path that led her to the chair she now occupied began over 20 years earlier at Annapolis. One of the very first women to attend the Naval Academy, Johrita had learned how to successfully navigate what previously had been a man's world. Her bachelor's degree in electrical engineering from the academy, followed by a master's in operations research at the Naval War College in Newport, provided a solid foundation for a series of challenging assignments and eventually, her command of an E-2C Hawkeye squadron. Her selection for deep-draft command and eventual command of this ship marked her as one of the Navy's very best, and certain for promotion to rear admiral.

And what a ship this was: The *Reagan* could go wherever and whenever Captain Solari desired, with unlimited range. Powered by *two* Westinghouse A4W nuclear reactors with *four* steam turbine engines driving *four* shafts connected to *four* bronze propellers, the *Reagan* could easily steam at more than the published 30 knots. 260,000 shaft horsepower was available to the captain at a moment's notice.

Hearing some commotion, Captain Solari looked forward through the bridge windows and noticed a growing number of Sailors gathering at the ship's bow. She asked the officer of the deck to find out what was going on. What looked like almost 50 people had assembled at the bow, and she was becoming concerned that someone had been injured.

The officer of the deck soon reported, "Captain, apparently the secretary of defense is down there, bending forward and leaning into the wind. He says he used to do it when he was a junior officer."

Captain Solari looked back down at the crowd on the bow and smiled. Since the day Secretary Garrett had come aboard, the ship's routine had somehow changed. His impromptu visit to the mess decks and later his weapons qualification participation demonstrated that he enjoyed interacting with the crew, something Solari didn't expect from such a senior DOD official. On the other hand, Admiral Carlisle clearly was not pleased with the arrangement. After all, he had been booted from the prestigious flag cabin. For days, Carlisle had been wandering the ship like a lost dog in search of a place to lick his wounds until Garrett would finally leave for D.C.

"And Captain, you're not going to believe this, but the bow lookout says that Secretary Garrett wants you to increase the ship's speed. He wants to see if he can lean further into the wind!"

Captain Solari stared back at her officer of the deck, and then belted out a laugh so loud the bridge team thought she had hurt herself. "Well, mister, I guess you better do what he asked. I'm just thankful he doesn't want to go water skiing!"

With that, Captain Solari climbed down from her chair. "If anybody needs me," she said, "I'll be on the bow trying to see how far *I* can lean into the wind!"

Schriever Air Force Base, Colorado Springs, Colorado

Master Sergeant Margaret Pulrang stared at the monitor as it tracked the progress of SISTINE BEACON scanning a remote island off the coast of South Korea for the specific signature of a biological weapon. Master Sergeant Pulrang had served for more than 20 years in the Air Force and loved her work at the 50th Space Wing, which was responsible for the operation of more than 180 Department of Defense satellites. There was continued speculation that the 50th would be absorbed into the new Space Force. In fact, some of her fellow airmen were already wearing different versions of a Space Force patch on their civilian clothes. Air Force, Space Force, or wherever the 50th Space Wing ended up, Master Sergeant Pulrang wanted more than anything else to keep working on her favorite program, SISTINE BEACON.

The revised tasking had the system searching a small island in the Sea of Japan named Ulleungdo. Margaret suspected this was just another routine test of the system's capabilities. She had just refilled her coffee cup and returned to her workstation when her monitor suddenly began flashing the message, *SUSPECTED CONTACT*. Margaret pushed the coffee cup aside and typed in a series of codes to intensify the search in the contact area so the system could more precisely determine the location of the device. When she was certain of the contact's accuracy and location, Margaret pressed four digits on her desk phone and announced, "Watch Officer, this is Sergeant Pulrang. SISTINE BEACON has a confirmed contact. I'm forwarding you the report as we speak."

Secure Video Conference Room, the Reagan

Colt was out of breath from his unplanned sprint from the ship's bow to the video conference room. Anna had told him that Steve Holmes was waiting to speak with him and had good news. He had just sat down when Lenny appeared at the conference room door dressed in work-out gear. Lenny explained when he saw the surprised look on Colt's face, "I was working out when I heard Steve was waiting for us, and I didn't have time to change."

Colt turned on the conference system and said, "No problem,

Lenny! It's just that I had no idea you ever worked out!"

Steve Holmes appeared on the video screen and announced, "You were right, boss! SISTINE BEACON has detected a significant signature on Ulleungdo Island that approximates what we'd expect from nine Anthrax warheads. The warheads appear to be located in an old weapons magazine that the Japanese built when they occupied the island in the 40s. The location is not very isolated. I gather that the population has grown dramatically through the years since the island started becoming a tourist destination. What was once a secluded spot is now the middle of a city. Michelle Walker has redirected her CIA team to gather everything we will need to develop recovery options. I've asked the Joint Staff to have recommendations ready for us first thing tomorrow morning, your time. I think it's going to be a late night for some people!"

Colt slammed his fist on the table and shouted, "Outstanding! Have you told the president yet?"

"I just briefed him, Mr. Secretary, and he asked me to pass his congratulations on to you. Looks like you get to keep your job for a while! And when you have the opportunity, General Schmidt would like to speak with you. He feels he might have been a bit disrespectful and wants to apologize."

"Just tell him to forget about it, Steve — I already have. Let's focus all our efforts on getting those damn warheads back!"

Day Nine

Secure Video Conference Room, the Reagan

Steve Holmes looked tired, and Colt was anything but surprised. Steve had most likely not slept in a day or two, and sleep was also something that wasn't likely to happen for anyone else, at least not for the next two days.

The secretary of defense and his special assistant Lenny Wilson were seated at the same table as the day before, in front of the large video screen on which they could see and communicate with Colt's deputy, Steve Holmes, and General Schmidt, the chairman of the Joint Chiefs of Staff. "Well, gentlemen, what are we looking at?" asked Colt.

General Schmidt began, "Sir, before we start, I'd like to apologize to you for my comments at yesterday's meeting. I hadn't considered your background as an analyst, and on reflection, I was acting as if I was responding to questions from oversight staff, instead of the secretary of defense. Your assessment of President Kim's conversation and actions was spot on, and we're only in the position of developing warhead recovery options because you pressed forward."

"Thank you, General," Colt replied. "I sincerely appreciate that. Let's schedule some time together after I return to D.C. — I'd like to get to know you better and to get your perspective on defense force realignment and the president's defense appropriation. But now, I'm eager to hear about your plans to recover those biological weapons."

General Schmidt looked relieved after hearing Colt's comments, and he was glad he wouldn't need to submit the resignation he had prepared hours earlier and was now in his vest pocket.

"Mr. Secretary," the general began, "we've developed four alternatives for your consideration. With your approval, I'll walk you through each one, listing positives and negatives."

Colt nodded his head and reached for his pen and notepad.

"Go ahead, General."

"Option one is simply to do nothing. The advantages and disadvantages are obvious. There is no risk whatsoever, but it means the weapons remain out of our control. We realize option one isn't really viable, but we feel we should keep it on the table as we consider the other actions."

Colt was familiar with military plans including the option of not taking any action at all. It was a prudent practice that reminded decision-makers that the lack of action was sometimes the best alternative.

"Thank you, General. Please proceed."

"Sir, option two is a Tomahawk cruise missile strike on the munitions magazine where the warheads are being stored. In this option, the biological agent would be incinerated. The primary advantages of option two are that no U.S. forces are in danger, and it has a relatively high degree of mission success. The primary disadvantage of option two is the likelihood of collateral damage to nearby buildings and to South Korean nationals."

"By damage to South Korean nationals, do you mean injury and death?" Lenny Wilson asked.

"Yes, Mr. Wilson, I most certainly mean death." General Schmidt glanced at Steve Holmes and then continued.

"Option three is an insertion of a special operations team with Explosive Ordnance Demolition (EOD) specialists, possibly by small boat, to covertly gain access to the munitions magazine and then incinerate the warheads with conventional explosives before the team's extraction. We like this option because it limits damage to just the munitions magazine itself. Disadvantages are the increased risk to our people on the ground, plus we'd lose the ability to deny our involvement — a big hole in the ground is a hard thing to explain. We'd also likely run the risk of severly injuring South Koreans in the process."

"And that leaves us with option number four," said Colt.

"Yes, sir, option four. This scenario has us inserting a special operations/EOD team via parachute and have them gain access to and custody of the warheads, render them safe and then remove them from the island. Option four definitely puts our people at risk, but if executed successfully, it would allow us to not only plausibly deny our involvement in the warheads removal but ultimately, the fact that they were ever stolen in the first place."

"How would our people get the warheads off of the island? Those things must weigh a ton." Lenny was sensing that option four would be the preferred plan, but he wanted to be sure it was feasible.

General Schmidt responded. "The insertion team would use either boats or helicopters to remove the weapons and then get them back to us. If Secretary Garrett selects option four as our primary scenario, the planners and operators would work through the details of the plan and apprise the secretary before seeking final approval."

"I understand that, General," Colt interjected, "but you must have some preliminary thoughts regarding the actual removal process. The plan's success hinges on that central element."

"Mr. Secretary," Steve Holmes said, "I'd like to let the planners continue to flesh this out and then get back to us with their conclusion. We'd just be guessing at this point if we try to be any more specific."

"Is that it for now?" Colt asked.

"I'm concerned about one other matter," Steve added. "I understand that Admiral Carlisle has a news team onboard *Reagan* at this moment. No matter what we eventually decide to do, the *Reagan* will be involved. We'll have to take the news team's presence into account if we expect to plausibly deny our involvement."

"Good point, Mr. Holmes," General Schmidt responded. I'll make certain the operations security plan includes a cover story to explain any *Reagan* operations associated with the weapons recovery."

"Okay," Colt agreed. "Go ahead with further development of option four. Let me know when I can hear more details, and what the force package will look like. After we finish this call, I'll contact the president to get his approval to execute the operation. Nice work, gentlemen. Thank you."

After pushing the button on the control panel to end the call, Colt turned to Lenny, "Lenny, contact the White House to schedule a call with the president. And let Commander Robinson know I'll meet him in my cabin in ten minutes."

Defense Secretary Cabin, the Reagan

Commander Tom Robinson felt slightly intimidated in the cabin of the United States secretary of defense. This wasn't something he was accustomed to doing. Raised in the small town of Kalispell, Montana, Tom preferred to remain out of the spotlight and had developed a reputation as a quiet and highly competent professional Naval officer.

He had requested the meeting with Secretary Garrett for two reasons, and he decided to get right to the point.

"Sir, you mentioned you wanted to get a hop in a Growler. I spoke with CAG and he's on board."

CAG was short for Commander Air Group, and as a title was a holdover from decades before. The current title was Commander Air Wing, but the old acronym CAG had remained in common use.

"That would be great, Skipper! What do you need from me?"

"Well, we'd like you to see a flight surgeon for a medical checkup, just to rule out any problems and to be sure there are no surprises. Dr. Beehler, the airwing doc, can arrange that at your convenience. After that, we'll want to schedule an aerospace physiology briefing to go over hypoxia, the Valsalva maneuver, G-LOC, the Growler's emergency egress system, and our ejection seat. I know you flew in the Prowler, but that was some time ago, so we want to be absolutely certain you are safe. Finally, after the systems briefs, we'll get you fitted for flight gear, helmet, and an O2 mask."

"I'm guessing I'll need a larger flight suit than the one I wore as a young lieutenant," Colt confessed with a wry smile. "I hate getting old."

"No comment, Mr. Secretary. I'm pretty certain I couldn't fit into my old flight suit either. I do remember watching an admiral climb out of a Prowler years ago and how shocked I was when I saw he had been sitting on an inflatable donut during the flight! I specifically remember laughing about that in the ready room. But now, every time I fly, I wish I had one of those pillows!"

"Okay, Tom, when are you thinking of taking me up?" Colt asked, eager to fly in a tactical jet again.

"You'll need a driver to take you up, and the younger Mr. Garrett happens to be my best pilot. I've already talked with him, and he's all in. CAG is planning an air show in a few days during a steel beach party, and each of the squadrons is flying a section to demonstrate their capabilities. We'll have your flight as part of the show."

"Commander, you'll be hearing about this in a few hours, but the steel beach party will likely be postponed. I'm asking you to keep this to yourself until you get it from your chain of command, but a covert operation is in the planning stages that might involve *Reagan* and her airwing."

"Roger that, sir. Understood."

Tom Robinson turned to go, and then remembered the second reason he wanted to talk with the secretary.

"Sir, I have something else I'd like to discuss with you. This is more personal, so I wonder if we could take off the rank for a few minutes?"

Colt was intrigued by the Naval officer's request. He motioned to the chairs nearby, and the two men sat down. "Of course," he assured Tom. "What's this all about?"

"It's about your son, sir."

"My son? What is it? Is he okay?"

"Oh, yes, sir, he's in perfect health! Back a few minutes ago, when I said he's my best pilot, I wasn't just making that up. The kid's got a natural talent for the air, with the brains to match. He and I have been talking about his future in the Navy, but I'm afraid he may decide to submit his resignation if he doesn't get selected for test pilot school. I think it would be a mistake for him and a missed opportunity, and I wonder if you'd be willing to step in."

Colt let out a long sigh and stood up. "Can I get you a cup of coffee, Tom?" He poured two cups and sat back down at the table with Tom.

"Dan's already spoken to me about test pilot school," Colt said. "I'll tell you exactly what I told him. I will not use this position of trust for personal gain or that of my family. Dan could have studied harder in college and been accepted into an engineering program, but studying wasn't his priority at the time. I think the smells of alcohol, gasoline, and perfume combined to keep his mind from his books. We all make decisions in life, and they have impact. I suspect the technical degree required for test pilot selection is there for a reason. It's a technical job and he simply hasn't met the requirements."

"But you and I both know that most of the requirements for military program selection exist solely to create barriers. The uncorrected vision requirement for pilots is the best example. How many senior pilots have you noticed wearing glasses? Are you telling me it's okay for *old* pilots to have bad vision? Hell, if not for that vision requirement, I would have been trained as a pilot rather than as a back-seater!"

The squadron commander paused for a moment, then tried another tack.

"I'm just asking you to consider how important this is to Dan and realize that you are in the perfect position to help him. You may not be secretary of defense for very long, but you're going to be Dan's father for the rest of your life."

Colt saw the conviction on Tom's face. He was pleased the Navy had rewarded this fine man with the command of a squadron — especially a squadron in which his son was serving.

"Thank you for your input and perspective, Tom. I appreciate your efforts on behalf of one of your officers, and I'll give your comments additional consideration, but as I said, I'm not certain there's anything I can do."

"Thank you, Mr. Secretary. Thank you for listening."

Ship's Library, the Reagan

VADIM and Malcolm were sharing a table in the *Reagan*'s library after breakfast. Several books and periodicals dealing with Chinese history were spread out in front of VADIM, while Malcolm was glancing through a gaming magazine. Looking casually around the room, Malcolm verified they were the only people in the library, other than the young Sailor at the front desk at the other end of the large room.

"Were you able to check out Garrett's cabin?" Malcolm asked. "Anything useful?"

Malcolm was anxious to start working on the plan to assassinate Colton Garratt, as the GRU had ordered. It still had to be approved by Sara back in Bremerton, and then he needed enough time to prepare the selected device.

"I was able to spend a few minutes in his cabin," VADIM answered. "I looked in the bedroom, and there is a clock radio, but I think we have a problem. The flag cabin is unlike any other space on the ship in that most of the fixtures and appliances are not Navy standard issue and were probably purchased specifically for the cabin. Our plan assumed we could temporarily replace an appliance with another while you made the necessary mods to it, but a similar clock radio does not exist onboard. I just don't see how we could remove the clock from the cabin without Garrett noticing it was gone. I think you need to come up with another plan."

"Me?" Malcolm snapped back. "Don't expect me to do it all!"

Malcolm had noticed over the past few months that VADIM had become less interested in the operation, and perhaps was even getting cold feet. He knew it was going to take both of them to pull off the elimination of the secretary of defense.

"Get a grip! I'll do my part! In fact, I overheard CAG say that Garrett will be flying in a Growler in an air show later this week. How much time would you need to mess with the Magic Carpet landing system?"

VADIM had been intrigued with using the landing system for this operation ever since Malcolm had first mentioned it as an option several days earlier. Not wanting to attract attention by directly asking questions about the system, VADIM instead found mountains of information regarding Magic Carpet on the Internet. A newspaper article published in 2015 described the new Magic Carpet system in the Navy's F-35C. The carrier version of the Joint Strike Fighter, the F-35C and its Magic Carpet system simplified the task of landing an aircraft on a carrier. The Navy was now in the process of working with Boeing to back-fit the

Super Hornets and Growlers with the software necessary to give the more traditional airframes the same automatic landing system installed in the stealthy F-35C. All of the *Reagan's* Super Hornets and Growlers had received the software update during the past year, and now pilots were required to use the system on each approach. As the Navy had projected, the software had reduced pilot training time and had even minimized maintenance costs. As an additional benefit of the reduced number of flights, the Navy was anticipating a lessening of public resentment toward the noise created by pilots practicing landings near populated areas in the United States.

Malcolm thought for a moment before answering VADIM's question. "I'd need about 20 minutes with the plane's landing control module to upload the software changes, but the problem isn't just how much time I'll need. I'll need to know which exact aircraft Garrett will be flying. The Scorpions have five planes, and one of them is always in maintenance. I'd have only a 25 percent chance of guessing the right airplane."

"Couldn't you just make the software modification to all four airplanes?" VADIM asked.

"I could, but after Garrett's plane crashed, they would stop flying the remaining aircraft until they determined the cause, and that would lead right back to me."

"So, what we need is a way to ensure that Garrett flies in one particular Growler," VADIM concluded, "and we'd need to know which one it's going to be several hours before the flight."

Malcolm stood and replaced his magazine on the rack. "I think I have an idea."

COLT'S CRISIS

Secretary of Defense Cabin, the Reagan

Television journalist Carissa Curtis had spent the last ten minutes trying to get her digital recorder to work while Secretary of Defense Colton Garrett sat patiently at the table waiting to be interviewed. Garrett didn't mind the delay. It reminded him of sitting in a dentist's chair while the hygienist took x-rays and measured his periodontal pocket depths — activities that significantly reduced the amount of time he actually had to suffer through the teeth cleaning process. Now, every minute that the reporter spent fiddling with her recorder was another minute Colt didn't have to deal with her questions, which he figured would be as much fun as a teeth cleaning appointment.

Colt noticed Carissa was getting increasingly flustered and frustrated with her technical glitch. "Take your time, Ms. Curtis. No need to rush," he said as he watched the clock on the bulkhead count down on his scheduled interview time.

"Oh, well," said Carissa, clearly exasperated. "I'll just have to take very good notes."

Garrett noted the clock once more and reminded her, "Please remember that I have another meeting at noon that I need to take."

Carissa realized not only that she had wasted valuable interview time, but also that Colt Garrett had probably enjoyed watching her do it.

"Well, then let's get started," she said to Garrett, pad and pen in front of her. "I understand that at one time you were in the Navy, Mr. Secretary. Perhaps it would be best if you could give me an overview of your career and then I can ask you a few questions."

"Sure," he said. "I attended Navy Officer Candidate School in Newport. My first duty was in a minesweeper. I fleeted up to serve as executive officer and then submitted a change of designator request to become a special intelligence officer."

"What prompted you to do that? Didn't you like the minesweeper duty?"

"I really did like that tour. A 172-foot wooden ship is a great place to learn seamanship and, more importantly, leadership. I guess I was looking for a role that had a broader perspective and impact. After intel school in Denver, I was assigned to a squadron at Whidbey Island. I got myself qualified to fly in the squadron aircraft, and we made two deployments to the Mediterranean during that tour."

Carissa furiously wrote everything she could catch on her pad, then stopped for a moment. "So, when did you leave the squadron?"

"That was in the fall of 1986. My wife and I were married in November, and I reported to FOSIF Rota, Spain, just two weeks later."

"FOSIF?"

"Sorry. Fleet Ocean Surveillance Information Facility. The Navy maintained several of these intelligence centers throughout the world. Rota's particular responsibility was the Mediterranean and its Atlantic approaches, the Black Sea, and the Red Sea. We were also responsible for Southern Europe, North Africa, and the Middle East. If it walked, drove, flew, floated, or sank, we tracked it. The best part was that we were an intelligence fusion center, which meant we gathered all sources of intelligence and then synthesized the information into a cohesive picture. I loved the work."

"And yet at the end of that three-year tour, you abruptly submitted your resignation from the Navy and requested a reserve commission, this time as a surface officer again. Can you tell me why?"

Colt was surprised the young reporter had somehow managed to excavate the details of his service record, and he wondered how much else she knew.

"There really was no one reason. First, the Cold War was over, so I figured the Navy would be downsizing soon, and I wanted to make the transition to a civilian career before everyone else figured it out. Plus, our daughter Alexandra had just been born, and I wanted to be more of a full-time dad."

Carissa paused for a moment to check her notes and then looked up. "Forgive me, Mr. Secretary, but it doesn't really track. You had an outstanding future in the Navy. You were an early selection for lieutenant commander and you were awarded a Navy Cross. The Navy Cross is the country's second-highest decoration, awarded for valor in combat. The U.S. wasn't even at war in 1989."

"Actually, the Cold War was just ending at that time," Colt responded. "The Berlin Wall fell in November, and the Warsaw Pack wasn't dissolved until 1991."

"Okay, let's move on to the Navy Cross. The citation in your service record is mostly redacted. What can you tell me about that?"

"That's highly classified, Ms. Curtis. And now, unless you have specific questions on another topic, I need to get going."

Carissa noticed the frustration in Garrett's tone, jotted down a comment in her notes, took a quick breath, and regrouped. "Why are you still on the *Reagan*?" she asked. "I understand that as undersecretary, you were in the Pacific conducting a defense policy review, but I would think your appointment as acting secretary would require you to immediately return to Washington. What is it that's keeping you here?"

Colt had anticipated this question, so he had worked with the White House communications office to prepare a response.

"I assume you've been following the news regarding the claims of missing biological weapons in South Korea. It's been widely covered by the press."

"Yes, I'm aware of the Anthrax issue," she said. "I understand the South Koreans have denied that our weapons are in their country."

"That's true. President Kim had requested that the U.S. send a diplomatic delegation to Seoul to discuss the issue. President Harrison and Secretary of State Unger decided to take advantage of my presence in the region and asked me to lead the delegation. We met with President Kim two days ago."

Carissa was surprised to hear that Garrett had led a delegation to Seoul. The fact had not been released to the press, so she was eager to conclude the interview so she could file it as an exclusive story with her network. But before she left, she needed to be certain that Garrett fully understood not only that he had provided her with new information but also that she fully intended to report it and name him as her source.

"I'd like to be clear, Mr. Secretary. You just told me, on the record, that you were in Seoul two days ago meeting with the South Korean president about the missing warheads. What was discussed in that meeting?"

Colt stood up from the conference table and led the reporter to the cabin door.

"I think I'll leave it up to Secretary Unger and the State Department to answer that question, Ms. Curtis." Looking at the clock once more, Colt said, "I see our time is up. Thank you for an enjoyable interview."

Colt opened the door, and Carissa took a few steps before racing down the passageway to draft and submit her story.

Neptune's Grounds Café, Bremerton, Washington

Sara watched the customers in the coffee shop as they talked with one another while sipping the drinks she had just prepared. Thinking back on her GRU training in Russia for this assignment in America, the workers who frequented the café didn't appear to be exploited or ill-treated as her instructors had claimed they would be. Instead, they seemed reasonably well paid, and for the most part, they seemed to enjoy their work and the comfortable lifestyle it allowed them. She listened in as they discussed upcoming vacations to exotic locations, or their plans to buy a new car or even a home. They talked about their families and friends and they appeared to thoroughly enjoy their lives, planning for the future with hope and optimism. Although her trainers had stressed the fact that Americans were simply deluded into a state of compliance and acceptance, Sara's own observations since coming to the states had convinced her that the American system was actually much better than the Russian system. At times she allowed herself to daydream about how her life might have been different had she been born in Bremerton, Washington.

Sara had received the draft plan from NIKITA and VADIM to eliminate the American secretary of defense and had passed it on to her controller, Colonel Petrov. The plan itself seemed overly complex as it depended upon a number of different steps to be implemented. She suspected the plan was drafted because it provided a reasonable degree of deniability and distance for her operatives onboard the *Reagan* — not that she could blame them. The prospect of being arrested for the execution of an American cabinet member would certainly influence the amount of risk the operatives might be willing to assume. Just because the GRU considered VADIM and NIKITA to be expendable didn't mean the operatives themselves felt the same way.

Sara had obtained details on the Magic Carpet system from GRU Moscow, and from the file, it appeared the method selected to execute Garrett was at least plausible. NIKITA and VADIM were extremely lucky he was planning to fly in the aircraft. They even had enough advanced notice of the flight to allow them to make the necessary software modifications. She was concerned the two inexperienced operatives had underestimated the ability of the American counterintelligence forces to quickly determine the cause of the accident. She also felt they were naive enough to think they could survive the resulting investigation. How long would they be able to endure relentless questioning by experienced interrogators while not revealing Sara's own role in the entire operation?

"Excuse me, Sara. Could I get a refill of hot water for my teabag?"

Sara realized the homeless man, "Mr. Trench," had been standing in front of her all the while she was contemplating her GRU mission. She smiled at him pleasantly as she filled his paper cup with hot water.

Kitsap College, Poulsbo, Washington

Vicki Pitzer had just installed the last listening device in Colonel Petrov's office when she heard footsteps coming from out in the hallway. She quickly sat down in the chair opposite the professor's desk and had just opened her backpack when Petrov entered his office through the unlocked door. He was surprised to see anyone sitting in his office, and he showed it. The college had implemented a new policy months earlier requiring faculty to keep their office doors unlocked during working hours — a nod to creating a more open and inclusive environment.

"What are you doing in my office?" he asked guardedly.

"Hi, Professor Jordan," said Vicki as she continued to remove her laptop from her backpack. "I'm here for our conference."

Petrov sat down at his desktop computer and opened the calendar application. "Our conference is scheduled for 1:00 pm *tomorrow* afternoon," he said, slightly annoyed. "You're off by a day."

Vicki looked embarrassed and began to put her laptop into her backpack.

"I'm so sorry, professor! I thought we were meeting today. But I don't suppose you have time to talk about my paper now?"

The deep-cover Russian agent replied, "Not today, Ms. Pitzer. I have some lecture notes to prepare. Please just come back tomorrow, as we had previously scheduled."

Vicki smiled and left him sitting alone in his office.

That was a bit odd, thought Petrov. He carefully scanned his office and checked to confirm that a few key items he intentionally left in specific locations had not been moved. Then, satisfied that the ditzy student had simply been confused about her conference day, he returned to thinking about the communication he had just received from Sara. The plan drafted by the *Reagan* operatives sounded intelligent but overly complex. He would have preferred a more direct and less complicated option. In his earlier days, when he was tasked by Moscow to eliminate someone, his usual approach was to simply place the barrel of a .22 caliber pistol against the temple of the target and pull the trigger. He would immediately drop the pistol, calmly walk away, and dispose of the pair of gloves he was wearing. It was difficult to prove guilt without a witness, motive or any physical evidence.

In contrast, the convoluted, draft plan depended on NIKITA's ability to sufficiently alter the system software that would render the aircraft out of control and ultimately result in the destruction of the plane and its crew. *Too many things could go wrong, and probably would*, Petrov thought to himself. Regardless, it was his duty to forward the plan to GRU headquarters for their consideration, where he anticipated it would be either rejected or dramatically modified.

Petrov decided he would probably need to make use of his personal escape plan. He would, therefore, need to begin putting the plan's essential elements into place immediately. By the time Moscow approved the final method to eliminate Garrett, he would need to be ready to go at a moment's notice.

Turning back to his desktop computer, the man known as Professor Robert Jordan initiated an Internet search for local aircraft charters. This would set in motion the first leg of his escape from America and his subsequent journey back home to Russia.

Carrier Intelligence Center (CVIC), the Reagan

After dinner, Colt and Lenny headed to CVIC with Special Agent Anna DeSantis in tow. Earlier in the day, Colt had been advised that the Joint Staff had provided the warhead recovery operational plan to the ship's airwing, and a high-level briefing had been scheduled to provide senior officers with the roles and responsibilities the *Reagan*'s aircraft would fulfill during the operation. Now, Colt, Lenny, and Anna entered the secure spaces, and those present rose from their chairs when someone announced, "Attention on Deck!"

"Thank you, ladies and gentlemen," Colt said, reaching for a chair. "Please take your seats. Go ahead, Commander Robinson."

The Scorpion squadron commanding officer stepped forward. "Good evening, Mr. Secretary, Admiral Carlisle, Chief of Staff, and CAG. I've been assigned as mission commander for Operation SPELLBIND. This briefing is classified Top Secret." Commander Robinson directed everyone's attention to the video screen where his briefing slides were beginning.

"SPELLBIND is an operation intended to provide electronic warfare support for an even more highly classified U.S. Special Operations Command mission taking place in theater. The cover story for SPELLBIND, however, is a simulated, war-at-sea exercise against Chinese naval forces in the Sea of Japan. As far as every person in the battlegroup who is not in this room is concerned, that *is* Operation SPELLBIND. Are there any questions before I proceed?"

Admiral Carlisle was the first to speak up, "Yes, Commander. Exactly what is SOCOM doing in this area, and why is this the first time I'm hearing about it?"

"Sir, the JCS tasking order was very clear on this point," replied Commander Robinson. "Only those with the need to know have been read into the specifics of the SOCOM operation. If you are first hearing about it now, Admiral, it means your name was not on that list."

Admiral Carlisle was about to take it further when he felt his chief of staff grabbing his left thigh under the table. Instead, he said simply, "Please continue."

"Thank you, sir. The airwing's responsibilities during SPELLBIND will be to provide an electromagnetic blanket over Ulleungdo Island, which is a small South Korean island off the eastern coast of the Korean peninsula. We will shut down the entire electromagnetic spectrum, radars, and communications for about an hour after midnight, allowing the "snake eaters" to execute their mission."

The commander next displayed a slide that showed Ulleungdo Island in great detail, as he provided a summary of the island's features, population centers, and most importantly, their sources of electronic emissions. "I'd now ask Lieutenant Pierce to brief you on our mission package and it's tasking. Pierce, you're up!"

Katrina picked up the computer remote and continued where her squadron skipper had left off. "The next slide lists the mission package. Two Growlers with the jamming mission, two Hornets providing barrier combat air patrol duties, and a Hawkeye for early warning. Five total aircraft with spares ready and briefed." Katrina continued the detailed mission briefing and then concluded by saying, "Any questions?"

"Are you saying we're going to send my aircraft up to actively jam South Korean communications and radar systems?" Carlisle asked defiantly. "What about their reactions?"

"Admiral," Katrina said, "we anticipate no reaction from the South Koreans. They have very few military forces on Ulleungdo Island, and power outages are common. Any complaints can be managed by providing our cover story and apologizing for our mistake in not notifying South Korea before the exercise."

"I'm not buying it, Lieutenant," Carlisle challenged her again. "I've worked with the South Korean military for the past two years, and there will be hell to pay if we jam their systems. I'm going to task my intel staff to take another look at this before we move forward."

"Actually, Admiral, the lieutenant is correct," came a voice from the back of the room. "The South Koreans will not react, and the cover story will hold."

Admiral Carlisle turned around to see who had contradicted him like that. His gaze fell on a lieutenant commander standing in the rear who had been observing the briefing.

"Who the hell are you," he bellowed, "and why are you in this briefing?"

The young officer took a few steps forward and replied, "I'm Lieutenant Commander Jason Baker, a reserve intel officer on my annual two weeks active duty. As I just said, the lieutenant is correct, and I'm confident the South Korean military will not react."

The room was silent for a moment until Admiral Carlisle argued, "I don't really think I need a weekend warrior to tell me my business. How about you go find someplace to be useful and let the professionals do the thinking?"

The admiral turned back around. "Okay, I think we're through here," he said. "I need to know a lot more before I agree to support this mission!"

Colt Garrett said, "Hold on there, Joe. This briefing *isn't* over yet."

Garrett turned to the back of the room to face the reserve officer. "Mr. Baker, you sound very sure of yourself. I find myself wondering what you do in your day job, that is, when you're not performing your Navy Reserve duties?"

"Mr. Secretary, I usually spend my time at Langley, where I run the CIA's Indochina desk. This part of the world has been my daily focus for over a decade, and in fact, I assisted Lieutenant Pierce with today's analysis and presentation. You have my word her assessment is accurate and reflects the intelligence communities' best thinking — with all due respect to Admiral Carlisle."

Joe Carlisle remained looking toward the front of the room, thinking to himself, *Crap.*

"Thank you for helping us out and for serving your country as a citizen-sailor," said the defense secretary. "I seem to recall that presidents Kennedy, Johnson, Nixon, and Ford were also Navy Reservists. You are in very good company, Commander Baker."

As the men and women in the room murmured their agreement with what Garrett had just said, Commander Robinson stood up. "That concludes this portion of the briefing. I'd like to ask the aircrew to remain for a bit so we can go over mission tactics."

With that, the officers in the room began to either leave CVIC or move closer to the front for the tactics briefing. Colt spotted Admiral Carlisle as he started to exit the room. "Joe," he said, "I wonder if you could drop by my cabin for a few minutes?"

Seattle Field Office, The Federal Bureau of Investigation

FBI Special Agent in Charge Clay Taylor read the surveillance report carefully, then placed it on the desk in front of him. It was getting late in the day, but looking on the bright side, he was pretty sure his commute home would be a breeze, as most of the Seattle traffic would have subsided when he eventually left his office. He removed his glasses, sat back in his chair, and said, "Okay, I've read it. Now give me your take on what this all means."

Clay's NCIS counterpart, Greg Cassidy, took a deep breath. "It looks like we have identified a very senior GRU officer operating a network, or more likely a number of networks, in the Pacific Northwest. He's here illegally, posing as Kitsap College professor Dr. Robert Jordan, but he's really Colonel Dimitri Petrov of the Russian GRU. He appears to be directly controlled by the GRU in Moscow with at least five junior GRU officers in this geographic area reporting to him and working their respective networks of agents. Our file on Petrov is remarkably complete. Prior to coming to the U.S., we have him active in both Canada and Latin America, and personally responsible for several assassinations in Venezuela. He's a very dangerous dude, Clay. And although most of the espionage activity here appears to be targeted against our research and software engineering industry base, at least one of the networks is definitely focused on Navy afloat units, the *Reagan* in particular."

Cassidy opened a folder and placed a photograph on the FBI agent's desk. "Our friend Sara Olson in Bremerton happens to be one of Petrov's GRU officers, and she has at least one and possibly two agents onboard the *Reagan*. She communicates with them via messages embedded in an online game called *Channel Defence*, and defence *is* spelled with a C. We believe a person with the screen name of *Geoffrey* is one of Sara Olson's agents." Cassidy pulled out a transcript of messages between Sara and Geoffrey and handed it to Clay.

"Looking back through the game's message logs, it appears that Sara requests items and asks Geoffrey to deliver. Our analysts think these are tasking requests, probably for specific information. It's impossible to determine what she's asking him to do because they appear to be using a one-time pad technique, using pre-determined words or phrases."

"Does the name *Geoffrey* mean anything?"

"The only aviation reference we could find is to a British pilot during World War Two. Some guy named Geoffrey Wellum."

Clay got up from his desk and walked to his window where he could look down at the busy harbor below. The ferry to Bremerton was just leaving Coleman Dock, packed full of cars and pedestrians heading home from work.

"I have a call scheduled with FBI headquarters tomorrow morning to talk about this," Clay said to Greg. "They've already agreed to provide anything we need. Anything else I need to know before I speak with them?"

"Just one thing more," Greg said. "We discovered that Colonel Petrov has been searching on the Web lately for charter flights to Vancouver, Canada. It may be nothing, but a charter flight sounds like a pretty high-profile way to leave the country. I mean, he could just take a ferry to Seattle and then drive a few hours north to Vancouver. Or he could drive to Port Angeles and take a ferry to Victoria B.C. and then catch another ferry to Vancouver. Anyway, we'll continue to watch this and let you know of any developments."

As the FBI agent started to pack up his briefcase, he asked, "Who do you have on the *Reagan*? Someone dependable, I hope?"

Greg smiled with confidence and replied, "All our agents are dependable, Clay. But to answer your question, we do have a good guy on the *Reagan*. Kevin Orr is very squared away. I'll reach out to him and get him working on finding out who *Geoffrey* is."

Defense Secretary Cabin, the Reagan

Rear Admiral Carlisle knocked on the door of his former cabin and entered to find the defense secretary seated at what had been the admiral's former desk. He started to take a seat when Colt Garrett stopped him. "Admiral," he ordered, "please remain standing, and at attention, if you don't mind."

The one-star admiral glared at Colt, then straightened his back and placed his hands at his sides.

"Admiral, this is going to be a one-way conversation. I'll do the talking, and your responses will be limited to 'Yes, sir,' 'No, sir,' 'Aye aye, sir,' 'No excuse, sir,' and 'I'll find out, sir.' Do you understand?"

"Yes, sir!"

"Since I've arrived onboard, you've made it clear that you do not respect civilian authority, which as you know is in direct conflict with the oath both of us have taken numerous times in our respective careers — an oath that requires us to defend the Constitution of the United States. What is your response to that, Admiral?"

"No excuse, sir."

"That is correct, you have no excuse. I get that you don't respect me, and I don't really give a damn. But you *will* respect the office I hold, and that of our president. If you want to remain in command of this battle group, you will recalibrate your attitude, Admiral, and I mean immediately. Do you read me?"

"Yes, sir."

Colt Garrett got up from his chair, stepped around his desk, and stood directly in front of Carlisle. "Admiral, you will leave this cabin a changed man. You will immediately issue orders that this battle group will fully support Operation SPELLBIND."

"Aye aye, sir."

Colt walked back to his desk and poured himself a glass of water. After taking a long sip, he looked back at the visibly perturbed admiral. "This meeting is over," he said. "If I get any indication you aren't following my direct orders, you will find yourself leaving this ship with your tail between your legs and a fitness report that will end your career forever. Your next tour of duty will be as assistant barracks officer at Naval Air Station, Lemoore. You are dismissed!"

Stunned and seething, Admiral Carlisle left the cabin and stormed down the passageway to his stateroom. He was now convinced more than ever that he must get rid of Colt Garrett, and the sooner, the better.

Day Ten

The Flight Deck, the Reagan

It was after midnight when Dan cycled the flight controls, then pushed the Growler's throttles fully forward and waited for the sudden but reassuring kick from the bow catapult, propelling the jet forward and into the air. He raised the gear and reduced the flaps as the plane climbed to reach the rendezvous altitude. Seated directly behind him, electronic warfare officer Katrina Pierce checked in with the Hawkeye controller while Dan scanned for the other Growler that had launched a few seconds earlier. He keyed his intercom and asked, "HURRICANE, do you have the XO yet?"

Katrina scanned the moonless sky looking for the other Growler. "He's about ten degrees above us at eleven o'clock, and we just got directed to go to Texaco to top off our fuel." Texaco was Navy slang for a Super Hornet that was equipped with an auxiliary tanking module to provide airborne refueling for the airwing's planes. The Navy was experimenting with drones to assume the tanker mission, but control issues had delayed the program.

The XO, the squadron's executive officer, Commander Fred Armstrong, was flying the other Growler, with Commander Tom Robinson as his electronic warfare officer in the back seat. Dan held a position on the XO's starboard — or right — wing and watched as the more experienced pilot expertly eased his aircraft's refueling probe into the tanker's trailing fuel basket. After receiving several thousand pounds of JP-5, the standard Navy jet fuel, the XO disconnected from the tanker and swapped positions with Dan. Airborne refueling was a critical skill for Naval aviators to master. If they had any trouble getting aboard the carrier after a mission, the ability to refuel in the air could mean the difference between having another chance to land or having to eject at sea.

Dan eased the Growler forward and then made contact with the tanker's refueling basket. "Check sweet, taking gas," said Dan into the radio. Katrina used the tanking time to perform inflight configurations of the Growler's jamming systems to ensure that they would be ready when she turned them on. After topping off his fuel tanks, Dan backed off the throttles and eased the jet into position on the XO's starboard wing. The two Growlers departed the tanker pattern to also allow the two Super Hornets to refuel. Once the refueling was all complete, the Growlers and Super Hornets proceeded to their assigned stations to await the signal to commence the mission.

USS Hawaii (SSN 776), Vicinity of Ulleungdo Island

The four Navy SEALs sat quietly in the Mk-11 Seal Delivery Vehicle (SDV) as the pilot and navigator (also Navy SEALs) conducted a series of tests using checklists to ensure that the submersible was ready to detach from the *Hawaii*. A *Virginia*-class fast attack submarine, Hawaii had a crew of over 130 and was the first commissioned vessel of its name. The Mk-11 SDV was a recent improvement over the earlier Mk-8 version, providing increased range and improved navigation, communication, and an added electro-optical periscope. The Mk-11's electrical motors were powered by lithium-ion batteries and could propel the small submersible at more than five knots. All in all, it was considered an effortless way to travel compared to swimming while carrying weapons, ammunition, and heavy equipment.

The four special operators riding as passengers were members of a squad from SEAL Team THREE based in Coronado. The pilot and navigator were from SEAL Delivery Vehicle Team ONE stationed in Pearl Harbor. All six SEALs had endured over two years of brutal training to become members of one of the most elite fighting organizations in the world. The SEALs had been trained to operate in all environments — sea, air, and land — for which they are named. Proficient combat swimmers and parachutists, SEALs could operate efficiently and effectively in any region of the world.

Rather than breathe compressed air from SCUBA tanks, on this mission the SEALs used rebreathers, which were closed-circuit mixed gas systems that recycled the diver's expelled breath while filtering for carbon dioxide and adding another gas. Because rebreathers didn't emit the air bubbles associated with more traditional SCUBA equipment, they were much preferred for covert missions. Instead of wearing the more commonly used wet suits which allow some water to enter the suit and then become heated by the diver's body, the SEALs used the much warmer dry suits that didn't allow any water to touch the diver. The men wore insulating undergarments, which enabled them to retain body heat.

When the last systems check was completed, the SDV pilot contacted the *Hawaii* to request permission to launch and commence the next phase of the mission: to find and disable the underwater telecommunications cable that connected Ulleungdo

Island to the Korean mainland.

U.S. Marine Corps Air Station Iwakuni, Japan

Two huge Boeing CH-47G Chinook helicopters were positioned in a remote corner of Marine Corps Air Station Iwakuni after being wheeled out of a large aircraft hangar. The two U.S. Army Chinooks were identical to the other aircraft in the squadron, except they had now been painted to look exactly like South Korean Army helicopters, including tail numbers and squadron insignia. The transformation was remarkably successful; the twin-rotor aircraft didn't look like any other helicopters in the sky, and their Korean markings made the deception complete. The large Boeing Chinooks were basically lifting machines, capable of carrying up to 33 fully equipped combat troops or 20,000 pounds of cargo. A design that first flew in the early 1980s, the Chinooks could fly at over 175 miles per hour with an unrefueled range of more than 400 miles.

In the lead aircraft, eight men who were dressed in the uniform of the South Korean Marines sat with their backs against the helicopter's fuselage as the machine rapidly ascended and headed for the target drop zone. All team members checked and then double-checked their gear as well as that of the Sailor to their left. A low altitude parachute jump on a dark night didn't leave much room for error. A simple miscalculation or equipment failure could mean injury — or worse.

Master Chief Special Warfare Operator and squad leader Jim Farrell tugged on his parachute harness and then checked the safety on his 5.56 mm K1A submachine gun, ensuring that the weapon was ready for the jump. He wasn't particularly familiar with the weapon used by the ROK Marines, but like all SEALs, Jim Farrell was a small-arms expert. He scanned the other members of his team to be sure they were checking their gear, paying particular attention to the two attachments sitting across from him. One Sailor, EOD Technician First Class Michael Buckley, was assigned because of his skill in safely handling biological weapons. The second team attachment was Cryptologic Technician - Interpretive Second Class George Telemann, who could verbally communicate with any South Koreans they might encounter. The Master Chief then looked at the SEAL sitting next to him, Petty Officer Doug Kim, and thought it ironic that Kim's grandfather had emigrated to the U.S. from Seoul, yet Doug couldn't speak a word of Korean.

When the first warning light illuminated, the eight operators stood up and shuffled their way to the rear of the helicopter, where the jumpmaster waited for them. After they checked one another for a final time, the jumpmaster opened the rear loading ramp, significantly lowering the cabin temperature.

On the jumpmaster's command, they walked down the ramp and stepped silently into the dark and frigid night. After closing the ramp, the jumpmaster then asked the pilot to radio the command center that the SEALs had been dropped. The two Chinooks rendezvoused with a KC-130 Hercules tanker to refuel again before going on to the next phase of the operation.

Dive Boat "Sea Plunder" west of Ulleungdo Island

Ted Purcell had owned and operated his SCUBA dive

company for more than ten years. His primary customers were people vacationing on Ulleungdo Island, hoping to earn initial or advanced SCUBA certification during their stay. Interestingly, he learned that the Korean and Japanese diving students preferred to take lessons from an American. He figured it was because of all the old TV shows about American divers.

The 35-foot dive boat slowly made its way to Ted's favorite dive location as his students finished getting into their wetsuits for the upcoming night dive class. To qualify for advanced certification, the students were required to perform a total of five specific dives. Two dives were mandatory — a navigation dive and another dive in waters between 18-39 meters deep. Then, students could each select three additional dives from a variety of options. When the six students had originally asked to dive after midnight, Ted figured it must be some sort of millennial thing. He could never figure out the minds of young people.

Ted liked the dive site on the western side of Ulleungdo Island because that one single location could be used for wreck diving, night diving, and boat diving. As he approached the area, he eased the throttles to neutral, coasted over the GPS position on his navigation screen, and shifted the engines into reverse. He had already assigned one of his more experienced students to be stationed on the boat's bow with a small anchor in hand, ready to drop the anchor when Ted indicated.

"Let go!" Ted shouted as the small dive boat backed down. Once the anchor cable had been paid out, and the anchor had grabbed the bottom, Ted increased the reverse thrust to ensure the anchor was set and then he shut down the engines.

"Okay, folks," Ted began, his voice accompanied by the rhythmic lapping of the water against the sides of the boat. "Let's

get started with our dive briefs and then get into the water!"
Soon, Ted and his six student divers were reviewing the logistics
of the dive, the depth of the water, the length of time they'd be
diving, and emergency procedures. After that, they each paired
off with a buddy and helped one another into their cumbersome
SCUBA equipment and gear.

When ready to go, and under Ted's watchful supervision,
each buddy team shuffled to the boat's swim platform on the
stern, stepped off into the dark water below, and then surface
swam to the buoy that marked the anchor line. Ted nodded as
each pair of buddies raised their buoyancy compensator relief
valves above their heads, pressed the valves, and then descended
feet first beneath the surface. After the third team disappeared,
Ted released the air from his own buoyancy compensator and
followed his students below.

Once he was underwater, Ted could see the three pairs of
divers slowly moving further and further down while holding
onto the anchor line, as the escaping bubbles from their SCUBA
regulators obscured everything else around them. As instructed,
the student divers waited on the ocean bottom next to the anchor
until Ted had completed his descent, after which he led them
on a short tour of the immediate area. He checked the dive
compass on his wrist and then slowly finned due north, using his
underwater light to point out animal and plant life he thought
would be of interest to his students.

Ted typically let beginning divers remain at this depth for only
ten minutes, so they would be able to make a second dive on this
trip without experiencing decompression sickness. When it was
almost time to begin their ascent, Ted thought he saw something
moving, perhaps less than 30 feet from the divers. He signaled

for the group to stop, pointing his light in the direction of the unidentified motion to see if he could figure out what it was. He had at first thought it was another diver, but there were none of the telltale SCUBA bubbles coming from that direction. He lingered for several seconds more in hopes of spotting it again — whatever it was — until his dive computer let him know it was time to get the group moving forward. Ted decided what he saw must have been a sea lion or some other sea creature who had lost its way. He signaled to the group to start heading back to the anchor line to safely begin the slow ascent back up to the dive boat.

U.S. Navy SEAL Team THREE, Charlie Squad in the Vicinity of Ulleungdo Island

The four Navy SEALs lay motionless on the ocean bottom, waiting for the civilian divers to move on. CHARLIE ONE, Senior Chief Chris Rawlings, slowly lifted his head in time to watch the seven recreational divers head back to their anchor line and then slowly ascend toward the surface. Only when he was certain the SEALS hadn't been spotted, he touched each man to signal "okay" so they could continue their search for the underwater cable. After several more minutes of searching, the lead diver stopped, rested on the bottom, and turned to face CHARLIE ONE. He flashed his light twice to indicate he had located the telecommunications cable.

Senior Chief Rawlings finned over and stopped next to the half-buried cable. He turned to CHARLIE THREE, who handed him a small metal device about six inches in length which he attached to the cable. After Rawlings had pressed several buttons on the small screen on the side of the device, he led the other SEALS back to the waiting submersible and its two operators. Climbing inside, Rawlings signaled two thumbs up to the SDV navigator who then pressed a series of buttons on his control screen, informing mission command that the device had been placed on the cable and the timer activated. The hard part over, Rawlings slowed his breathing and tried not to be distracted by how cold he was, while his team waited for the command signal to remove the device and return to the warmth and comfort of the *Hawaii*.

Sadong Beach, Ulleungdo Island, South Korea

Four teenagers sat huddled close together in the sand, trying to create some warmth and comfort for themselves on the dark and deserted beach as they passed around the last bottle of Soju. A product of Korea, Soju was one of the world's most widely consumed alcoholic beverages, the favorite of many because of the sweet taste of the sugar that was added during the distillation process. On this particular night, Soju was the favorite of the four teenagers simply because it was the only alcohol available in their parents' rental cottages. At 53 percent alcohol by volume, the six stolen bottles had done serious damage to the young men's judgment and perception, adding to their shock at seeing a group of what appeared to be military parachutists land on the beach just yards away from their huddle.

Meanwhile, Master Chief Jim Farrell pulled his two control toggles and expertly flared his rectangular parachute as he landed gently on the beach. Watching the rest of the SEALS land, he noticed a small group of boys huddled on the far end of the beach, no more than 20 feet from where Petty Officer Doug Kim was about to land. Doug executed his landing, quickly gathered his chute, and then function-checked his weapon. He looked up to see the group of wide-eyed boys staring at him and then remembered he was wearing the uniform of a Korean marine. He considered saying nothing until the interpreter could be brought forward but then suddenly remembered something from his youth that he thought might work now. He stared at the boys, pointed his submachine gun at them, and angrily shouted a short phrase in Korean. The boys looked at one another, dropped the last bottle of Soju into the sand, and frantically sprinted back to the road toward their parents' softly lit cottages.

Master Chief Farrell stepped up to the young SEAL. "Hey, Doug," he whispered. "I thought you didn't speak Korean."

"I don't. But when I was a kid, my grandfather always tried to teach me Korean, and he would use lines from American movies, and say them in Korean."

The battle-hardened SEAL asked, "So what did you say to those kids? They took off like hell!"

"I just pointed my weapon at them and said, 'Go ahead! Make my day!'"

ROK Marine Transportation Lot, Ulleungdo Island

ALPHA SQUAD was spread out and hidden in the dense vegetation near the transportation lot's main gate. Although intelligence had indicated the installation was unguarded at night and only secured by a locked, chain link gate, Master Chief Farrell was taking no chances. "There are old SEALS and bold SEALS," as the saying goes, "but there are very few old *and* bold SEALS." After checking the compound with his night-vision goggles and listening for any sounds of human activity, Farrell silently motioned to two SEALs to cut the gate's padlock. He waited while they opened the gate, then led ALPHA SQUAD into the fenced compound.

The SEALs quickly moved to the three closest trucks, Korean versions of the M35 6X6 Deuce and a half truck used for decades by the U.S. military. The KM-250, manufactured by Kia, was identical to the American version of the vehicle, and even used a similar toggle switch in place of a keyed ignition to start the massive engine — or at least that's what the intelligence report had said. Instead, the SEALs found the Korean trucks were equipped with traditional ignition switches — and they didn't have the keys.

"Doug," Farrell whispered, "hotwire those three trucks." SEAL training had included a wide variety of skills that would be useful in carrying out special operations, including the technique of starting up a vehicle without the benefit of an ignition key. Within a few minutes, all three trucks were running and warming up. The squad of SEALs quickly climbed into them and drove out of the compound into the night. Riding in the lead truck, Master Chief Farrell turned on a red light to illuminate the map on his lap. Checking his GPS receiver to verify his position, he pressed a few keys on his satellite transceiver to indicate the team was heading to the weapons magazine where the stolen American warheads were stored.

10,000 feet AGL, Southwest of Ulleungdo Island

Dan Garrett was monitoring the Growler's flight systems when he heard Katrina say, "Okay, JOKER, master rad is on." She pressed the appropriate buttons on the system's display to activate the radar and communications jamming pods, at which point all surface and air search radars on Ulleungdo Island ceased to function, and all military and civilian radios became useless.

"Is the skipper making music as well?" asked Dan.

"That he is, and it looks like both Growlers' systems are fully operational."

Dan wondered what the radar operators and the civilians on the island who were still awake must be thinking as their electronic systems stopped functioning. He knew the Hawkeye was watching the skies to ensure that the Growlers were notified of any aircraft entering the airspace. Nobody wanted to be responsible for an aircraft mishap caused by the signal jamming.

"We've done *our* part," Katrina said, sounding relieved. "Now, let's hope the snake-eaters have taken care of the cable-based comms." Both Growler crews had been briefed on the SEAL mission to temporarily sever the island's submarine telecommunications cable. Katrina was grateful that she was doing her part at 10,000 feet above the Sea of Japan rather than on the cold ocean floor below. "Hey JOKER!" Katrina said into the intercom. "My feet are getting cold — how about cranking up the cabin heat?" Dan had been focused on flying the pre-determined racetrack orbit to maintain optimal alignment between the Growler's jamming antennas and their assigned targets. "Anything to make you happy, HURRICANE. As Glenn

260

Fry best put it, the heat is on!"

When they finally had a break from all the activity, Katrina decided to take advantage of their time alone to ask Dan about test pilot school. "Have you made any progress convincing your father to help you? It's hard to say how much longer he'll be on board."

Dan sighed, "Not really. Commander Robinson told me he spoke with my dad, but that he didn't get anywhere with him. I'll probably just submit the application anyway and take my chances that the selection board will have heard of my exceptional airmanship skills and give me a slot in the program regardless of my degree. If they don't, I've decided to just tender my resignation from the Navy and start planning a career flying a bus in the sky."

Katrina didn't respond; she felt there was nothing she could say. She, too, was making plans to leave the Navy, but she believed Dan was someone who belonged in a high-performance aircraft in the service of his country. She decided that if she had an opportunity, she would try to talk with Dan's father. It probably wouldn't make much of a difference, but she had to try.

ROK Joint Command Center, Seoul, South Korea

"What do you mean, Ulleungdo Island is down?" The South Korean Air Force colonel stood up from his comfortable leather chair and briskly walked over to the Air Sector Defense section of the large command center. He had been on watch for the past eight hours and was looking forward to going home and getting some sleep. The twelve hours on/twelve hours off watch schedule was brutal, but in just one more day, he would have four days off to enjoy and spend time with his wife.

"Colonel, I mean that *every* radar on the island is down. The screens just show interference noise, and there is nothing we can do to get the picture back!"

The colonel looked at each radar display to confirm what the young staff sergeant had just reported. "Have you reset the system and checked the data feed? It does not make sense that all our radars are down simultaneously."

"Yes, sir, I checked everything, including the system reset. The communications center has attempted to contact Ulleungdo Island with no success. It looks like some sort of active jamming. Even landline communications are down."

"Landline comms cannot be jammed! What the hell is going on?"

ROK Marine Corps Weapons Magazine Annex, Ulleungdo Island

Two young Korean marines were seated at a small table inside the weapons magazine annex, playing cards to pass the time. At three o'clock in the morning, they were playing Mighty, a game invented by Korean students in the 1970s and still popular on both sides of the Korean border. At regular intervals during their four-hour security watch, the two marines would take turns walking down the long corridor to the main gate, checking in with the sentry, and then returning back to the table next to the magazine's large vault door. The duty was boring, but experience had taught the two young men that this was preferable to other tasks that might bring them to the attention of the company's first sergeant, a man with a low threshold for error who took immense pleasure in finding creative ways to punish those who didn't meet his standards. On one occasion, for example, he had made one of the company's marines clean the parade grounds with a leaf blower — during a hurricane.

"Lance Corporal, I believe it is your turn to deal," stated the private, a young man who had been in the marines less than a year.

"Thank you, Private, I believe you are correct," agreed the more experienced marine as all the lights in the corridor abruptly went dark. He felt for the telephone on the desk and lifted the handset to his ear. "The phone is dead, too," said the lance corporal. "Grab the flashlight from the gear bag, and we will walk to the gate to see what is happening." Suddenly, a loud explosion rocked the entire enclosed space as a bright flash of light momentarily blinded the two marines. Both felt their heads crack before losing consciousness.

When they awoke, the two young South Korean marines found themselves sitting on the floor of the weapons magazine, their hands zip-tied behind their backs, their feet zip-tied together, and their backs propped against the wall facing the large vault door. The private opened his mouth to speak, but the lance corporal whispered, "Say nothing!" The surreal site before them appeared to be a team of ROK marines wearing special camouflage uniforms and black balaclavas hiding their faces, silently removing several large and obviously heavy containers from behind the vault's doors which had been blown open with some type of explosive charges. Hushed phrases in Korean were being spoken, but the acoustics of the vault and corridor made the words unintelligible.

The men were removing the last of the heavy containers when one pulled his black hood off to speak into a radio. Although the two marines couldn't make out what he was saying, they could clearly see he was Korean. As the mysterious warriors were about to leave the vault, one leaned down close to the lance corporal and whispered, "You are lucky this was only a training exercise. If this was for real, you would be dead! Be well, my brother!" The hooded man then cut the zip ties on both of the marines and ran out of the corridor toward the main gate. The two dazed guards looked at one another and then slowly stood up, thankful to be alive.

"We should follow them, but not too closely," said the lance corporal. The two marines carefully walked through the darkened corridor to the main gate, where they saw several ROK Marine trucks leaving the compound. Next to the gate and tied to the chain-link fence was the gate sentry, who had also been gagged. After freeing their fellow marine, the three ran down the road to find a working telephone.

Sadong-ri Community Hospital, Ulleungdo Island

When the hospital lost electrical power in the early morning hours, the only person who noticed was the elderly guard sitting in the small security shelter near the hospital's entrance. Power outages were common on the island, and since the hospital had reduced its services to only out-patient care during normal business hours, the hospital no longer made use of its emergency generator. About an hour after the power went out, the guard heard the sound of approaching helicopters and was amazed to see two large twin-rotor military helicopters land on the hospital's helipad, which had been constructed to provide airlift services from the hospital to the mainland for island residents requiring advanced or emergency medical care. Heavily armed men then stepped out of the aircraft and established a perimeter around the helicopters as the blades continued to turn. Soon, several military trucks arrived at the helipad and parked close to the aircraft. The guard left his position in the security shelter and approached the scene of all the activity when a soldier in a camouflage uniform and a black hood over his face stepped forward and extended his hand. Speaking Korean, he said, "Please excuse our noisy machines, Grandfather, as we are conducting a military exercise. We will be gone in just a few minutes."

The security guard stood motionless, watching the soldiers carry large boxes up the loading ramp and into the fuselage of one helicopter, and then gather their equipment and weapons and board the other aircraft. The helicopters' blades began spinning faster and faster until both machines lifted into the air and disappeared into the night sky. The guard removed his notebook from his jacket and wrote down the words he saw on the sides of both helicopters: **REPUBLIC OF KOREA ARMY.**

U.S. Marine Corps Air Station Iwakuni, Japan

As the two Chinook helicopters touched down, a group of people wearing civilian clothes waited nearby. Jim Farrell and his team of SEALs descended the leading Chinook's ramp and walked over to meet the team and their trucks.

"I'm Master Chief Farrell. Which one of you is Ms. Becker?"

A woman in a dark business suit extended her hand. "I'm Judith Becker, and it's good to meet you, Master Chief. I understand you have some items I can take off your hands."

"Yes, ma'am. First, though, can you show me your identification?"

Dr. Judith Becker handed the battle-tested SEAL her credentials, which identified her as an employee of the Centers for Disease Control and Protection (CDC) Global Response Team. Master Chief Farrell handed the credentials back to the infectious disease specialist and said, "Looks good, Doc. Just being careful."

"Being careful is critical in this business. So, how would you like to conduct the weapons transfer?"

"As soon as your team can unload these and check them out, we'll count them together before you sign the custody document. We wouldn't want to make any mistakes!"

Ms. Becker smiled. "Good point, Master Chief," she agreed. "Oh, there's some beer for you and your team in the back of that Suburban, after you complete decontamination."

Primary Flight Control (Pri-Fly), the Reagan

Dawn was just breaking to the east as Colt Garrett searched the sky above and behind the massive aircraft carrier while it turned into the wind in preparation for aircraft recovery. He stood on an open-air platform known as Vulture's Row, affectionately named because it was here that both crew and visitors could gather to watch the launch and recovery of the ship's aircraft.

Unable to see any sign of the approaching planes, Colt stepped forward into Pri-Fly, a small room located seven stories above the flight deck, where a group of Sailors tracked every aircraft, both on the flight deck and in the air. Their primary responsibility was to ensure that all aircraft would take off and land safely.

Colt was met by two officers wearing yellow flight deck jerseys that had, respectively, "Air Boss" and "Mini Boss" stenciled on their chests. The two senior aviators both held the rank of commander and were more correctly known as the air officer and assistant air officer, responsible for control of all aircraft operations within five miles of the carrier.

"Good morning, Mr. Secretary! You're up early today!" the air boss cheerfully greeted Colt.

"Good morning, Commander! I thought I'd watch the recovery from here if you don't mind. I don't want to be a distraction."

"No problem, sir, happy you're here," the air boss said. "Can I show you around our little perch in the sky?" He went on to explain the sequence of events that led to a successful, arrested gear landing on a carrier.

"Because each type of aircraft acts differently when it hits the deck, we first need to know what type of plane is in the landing pattern. Our aft spotter is well trained to identify inbound planes, even in low visibility or during night ops. Next, that information is relayed to the arresting gear crew below decks who configure the arresting gear engines for that specific plane. At about three-quarters of a mile out, direct control of the approaching aircraft is assumed by the landing signal officer — or Paddles, as we call him — who is communicating directly with the pilot and providing recommendations for speed, line-up, and attitude. If everything goes right, the aircraft catches a wire with its tailhook, and it comes to a complete stop. Easy!"

Colt looked back at the ship's stern at the small group of officers dressed in flight suits, white float coats, and sunglasses, standing on a platform near the edge of the flight deck.

"I'm pretty certain that 'easy' has nothing to do with it," Colt stated. "I want you all to know how proud your nation is of the job you are doing here, and how honored I am to shake your hands." The secretary of defense greeted each Sailor in Pri-Fly until the boss announced, "Okay, people, it looks like we have some customers coming this morning. Let's get back to work and bring them safely aboard."

Colt remained in Pri-Fly as several Super Hornets landed, then heard the aft spotter call, "Growler in the slot!" The mini boss handed Colt a pair of binoculars. "Your son just called the ball, sir. These will make it easier to watch his approach and landing."

For the first time, Colt watched as Dan attempt an arrested gear landing. Although, as a junior officer, Colt had spent hours watching landing events, it was altogether a different experience watching his son perform what most believe is the most difficult maneuver in aviation. He could see that the Growler's three wheels and tailhook were down and ready for landing as the plane continued down the glideslope while Dan made minor control adjustments. The plane then forcefully slammed onto the deck, caught a wire, and within two seconds, came to an abrupt stop. The air boss placed his hand on Colt's shoulder and remarked, "Like I said, sir, *easy!*"

As Colt tried to absorb the fact that he had just witnessed his son make a perfect arrested gear landing, the mini boss came over to him. "Mr. Secretary," he said. "There's a call for you," and passed him a handset. Colt listened for a minute or two and finally said, "Thanks, Lenny." Giving the handset back to the mini boss, Colt turned to the air boss and said, "If you will excuse me, Commander, I need to return to my cabin to place a call to the president."

After Colt had left Pri-Fly, the air boss shook his head and thought, *That's the first time anyone has ever said that to me!* Suddenly, the aft spotter announced, "Rhino in the slot!" as the air boss picked up his binoculars and slid into his padded chair.

NCIS Offices, the Reagan

Anna DeSantis looked over the shoulder of Special Agent Kevin Orr as he manipulated the game controller connected to his workstation. Since the field office had tasked the local agents with finding out the identity of Geoffrey, Kevin had been playing the online game nonstop. Anna suspected her colleague's enthusiastic dedication had little to do with identifying the suspected spy. Kevin had expended a few days getting approval from NCIS to load the game onto his issued computer. Now, it seemed to Anna that Kevin was focused more on earning game points and less on finding the agent.

"Will you tell me again why you think you need to continue playing this stupid game?" she asked him.

Kevin shot down the last enemy plane and put the game controller on the table. "Listen, Anna, like I've told you before, I need to earn my way up the player's list until I can request a one-on-one fight against the mysterious Geoffrey. Once he agrees to play me, we can start an online chat, and then I may be able to gather enough information that may lead us to who he really is. Seems pretty straight forward to me!"

Anna smiled as Kevin started another game. She was about to head back to her stateroom when something on his screen caught her eye. "Your screen name is Iron Lotus? What does that mean?"

"You know, from Blades of Glory, the 2007 classic? Come on, Will Ferrell and Jon Heder? Don't tell me you haven't seen it?"

Anna shook her head. "Okay, I won't tell you I haven't seen it," and she left the office and closed the door. Kevin chuckled and thought, *Philistine!*

When Kevin finished the game, he was pleased that he had finally achieved top 20 status, and his screen name now appeared as number 19 on the game's leader board. He crafted a message to *Geoffrey,* challenging him (or her) to a battle and pressed the "send" key. Now he just had to wait.

Russian Military Intelligence HQ, Khodinka Airfield, Moscow

General Korobov had spent the last 24 hours reviewing Colonel Petrov's proposed idea to assassinate the American secretary of defense, Colton Garrett. GRU covert assets within the American department of defense and various other intelligence agencies had confirmed Moscow's assessment that the president of the United States may be leaning toward making Garrett's acting appointment a permanent one, which Moscow considered unacceptable. They wanted him removed before he could damage Russia's plans to increase its global influence.

The success of Petrov's plan seemed overly dependent on the

skills and reliability of the civilian avionics technician onboard the *Reagan*. An asset whose role thus far had been limited to providing classified information to Russia, the man was clearly an opportunist seeking to add to his bank account, for no purpose other than improving his lifestyle. There simply was no way to determine if he was capable of completing the tasks indicated in the plan, and therefore, no real way to predict the likelihood of mission success. General Korobov had not survived decades of political intrigue and the associated political purges to risk his career — and potentially his life — on an unknown chance of success. Should the plan fail, he needed to have an alternative, and he looked around for another file on his desk.

Could Agent VADIM, who is also onboard Reagan, *provide the necessary solution if the primary plan isn't successful?* Korobov wondered. He found the file, opened it to review VADIM's background, training, and psychological profile, making notes on a pad of paper as specific items caught his interest. Traditionally, espionage agents were motivated by a variety of human considerations, including patriotism, revenge, fear, lust, and the desire for money. Blackmail had also been a successful tool for many years, but the liberalization of the west in recent years had made the threat of exposing a person's secrets less effective. Blackmail didn't work if the target didn't care if others learned about his or her personal lifestyle or social activities. The file revealed that VADIM did indeed have several indiscretions as well as personal attachments that could be used as leverage. Everyone had their vulnerability, and General Korobov came to the conclusion that he had discovered VADIM's. He began to write a series of instructions for Colonel Petrov that would create a viable, fail-safe alternative should his primary plan not succeed.

After processing the message for transmission to the deep-cover agent, Korobov imagined the high esteem in which he would be held should his plan become successful. He decided to contact his mistress, Ulyana, who worked in the Ministry of Finance, to plan a short trip to Korobov's personal dacha on the Black Sea to celebrate his anticipated victory.

Neptune's Grounds Café, Bremerton, Washington

Sitting in a booth in the back of the coffee shop, Sara warmed her hands on the large ceramic mug filled with steaming hot coffee. By now, the morning's customers had mostly passed through on their way to work at the shipyard and Naval base, allowing Sara to take her morning break. She was still feeling uneasy with the plan to take direct action against Colton Garrett, and it bothered her. She certainly had no feelings for or about him, and her thorough training had prepared her for this moment. But after sending out the execution message to the agents on board the *Reagan*, she felt an uneasy sense of guilt at the thought of her involvement in the death of another human being. She realized that her reaction was possibly triggered by the growing feelings of loneliness and discontentment she had experienced in recent weeks. Not being able to share an unguarded thought or moment with another person made her feel increasingly isolated, and she had started questioning her broader role in the world.

Sara was lost in her thoughts when the homeless man, whom she called Mr. Trench, sat down across from her in the booth, bringing his own cup of hot water with him.

"Good morning, Sara," he said quietly. "Do you mind if I join you?" As always, the middle-aged man was wearing his threadbare trench coat and underneath it a faded and worn blue chambray shirt. He dipped his well-used teabag into his fresh cup of hot water.

"It's not fair," Sara replied, smiling warmly and looking at his face for possibly the first time. "You know my name, but I don't know yours!"

"Well, let's fix that," he responded. "My name's Sean, glad to meet you."

"And I'm very pleased to meet you!" Sara said. She could see over Sean's shoulder that Derwin was glaring at her. He clearly didn't like Sara befriending the homeless customers. She ignored the glares and looked back at the disheveled man sitting across from her in the booth.

"Is there something I can do for you, Sean?" she asked gently. Sean leaned slightly across the table toward Sara.

"I watch people all day long," he said. "It's what I do. I like to watch their daily routines, coming and going. And I like to think, with some people anyway, that I can actually get to 'know' them, just by looking at them and watching them for a while. But after watching you for as long as I have, I can't get a clear picture of who you are, other than sensing you are not a happy person. I've often wondered to myself, *What could be troubling this young woman?*"

Sara was startled. Not only had she never realized that Mr. Trench was watching her, but here he was, speaking to her articulately and with compassion, and it felt good. It was filling an emptiness in her. She couldn't remember that last time anyone had asked her a personal question or shown any concern about her at all.

"I guess I'm just realizing that I don't like my job very much

— or my life for that matter — and I just don't see a way out. I guess we sometimes find ourselves in situations we never would have planned." Sara was embarrassed when she remembered that she was talking to someone who probably hadn't planned to become homeless. "Enough of my self-pity. What's your story, Sean?"

Sean took a sip from his cup of tea and thought for a long moment before speaking. "I'm nothing special," he said. "I served for 20 years as a Marine. When I got out, my marriage fell apart." He pulled his sleeve back on one arm to reveal a faded tattoo of a globe and anchor, with the words "Semper Fi" written beneath. "Once a Marine, always a Marine, right? That's why I live in Bremerton, for easy access to the Navy hospital, plus I like being around service people. I understand them."

"What did you do in the Marines?" Sara asked.

"I usually tell people I was a cook, just to avoid questions, but I was actually a scout sniper."

Surprised again, Sara looked at Sean's clear but tired grey eyes. She knew exactly what a Marine scout sniper was, as well as the intensive training and skills he had to have.

"I apologize for asking, but how did you end up . . ." and her voice trailed off.

"How did I end up homeless? That's okay, it's a reasonable question. After I split from my wife, I wandered around a bit, trying to get my head straight. It had been a really traumatic time for me. First, to experience so many combat tours, and then to lose my family. I never really got it together after that. Eventually, I decided I just like watching people, and that's what I do. My half of my retirement pay keeps me fed, and I can move around and be wherever I want."

Sara looked at him, wistfully. "I wish I could go wherever I want, be whatever I want to be. You know, a new start."

"What's stopping you?"

Hearing Derwin call her name, Sara stood up and turned to head back to the counter. "Sara, what's stopping you?" Sean repeated.

Sara turned back and smiled at him. "You wouldn't believe me if I told you." She adjusted her apron and headed back to work.

The Blue House, Seoul, Korea

President Kim Seong-Ho quickly concluded his cabinet meeting upon being notified that NIS Director Pang had just requested an urgent meeting with him. The visit by the American delegation had been the last time he had seen Pang. Remembering the subject of that meeting, he wondered whether the Americans had been smart enough to follow his subtle clue in the guidebook regarding the whereabouts of the missing biological warheads.

"Sit down, Director, what is the news?"

"Sir, it appears that last night our marines conducted an unannounced assault on the weapons magazine on Ulleungdo Island. Parachute landings, stolen trucks, a breached magazine vault, and disappearing helicopters. Other than a few bruised egos, there appear to be no casualties."

"An unannounced assault? But why? What are the joint chiefs saying?"

"That's the strange part, sir. They deny any part in or awareness of an exercise. They say the island was electronically jammed and even our landline communications with the mainland

...re somehow interrupted."

"What is General Cho saying?" President Kim asked. "Perhaps he used a training exercise to disguise his removal of the American warheads that have been stored there. You had predicted it was only a matter of time before he would attempt to move them yet again."

"Yes," Pang replied. "But Cho also is denying any involvement — quite strongly in fact. I suppose it makes sense. Why would he admit it, even if it was his operation?"

President Kim's assistant suddenly knocked and entered the room. He had a concerned expression on his face.

"Yes, what is it?" asked the impatient leader, clearly annoyed with the interruption.

"President Kim, the president of the United States is on the special line for you!"

President Kim took a few moments to gather himself before pressing the speaker button on his desk phone. "An unexpected pleasure, President Harrison! I trust that you are well. What can I do for you?"

"President Kim, I owe you an apology," said President Harrison. "I've just received confirmation that the biological American warheads that we thought your country had stolen were actually destroyed in one of our incineration facilities, simply an accounting error. As we speak, our state department is delivering the same information to the United Nations and to the news media. Please accept my most profound apologies and that of my country for this temporary confusion."

President Kim stared at his intelligence chief momentarily, breathed a sigh of relief, and then spoke into the phone. "Mr. President, I understand your concern, and I thank you for your graciousness. Please be assured that the relations between our two nations could not be better. We are friends, are we not? Now, is there anything else I can do for you today?"

"Yes, President Kim. On another subject, it would be good if you would announce that your marines conducted a no-notice exercise last night and that it demonstrated the complete combat readiness of South Korean forces."

Director Pang smiled knowingly at his president and silently nodded his head. "Of course, President Harrison, that is a splendid idea, and I would be pleased to make such an announcement," said President Kim. "It was indeed most successful and I thank you for the suggestion!"

After the call with the American president, Kim rang and asked his assistant to come into his office.

"Please get me Admiral Pak on the phone immediately!'

Headquarters, Republic of Korea Marine Corps, Hwaseong, South Korea

For the first time in his life, General Cho was experiencing pure, unmitigated fear. He stepped out of his private elevator and rushed through his outer office, not noticing the three men in dark suits among the several officers in his large waiting room. Everyone stood in unison as the three-star marine general glared, entered his private office, and slammed the door behind him. Initial reports had made little sense. South Korean parachutists had evidently and inexplicably landed on Ulleungdo Island during the night, stealing several trucks and then driving to a helipad where they were picked up by Korean Army helicopters. Other ports indicated that the island had been completely cut off from the mainland, and even the redundant communications circuits carried by a submarine cable was temporarily inoperative. Cho's attempts at contacting his marine forces on the island had been unsuccessful, and, what was most concerning, he had been unable to communicate with the special troops responsible for safeguarding his stolen biological warheads in the island's weapons magazine.

General Cho had long subscribed to the adage that when attempting to determine the cause of an event, it is best to assume the most obvious. In this case, he believed it was obvious that the North Koreans had used the information gained through Colonel Chang's treasonous relationship and had simply taken the warheads while disguised as South Korean forces. Despite his anger at his loss, he grudgingly admired his adversaries for coming up with such an audacious but well-executed operation.

As he stood there in his office, Cho's assistant announced that Admiral Pak, the chief of naval operations, was holding for him on the phone. He wondered what the old man would have to say. He sat down at his desk, picked up the phone, and greeted him. "General Cho, here. What can I do for you, Admiral?"

"It appears you have had a setback, Cho," said Admiral Pak.

"What are you talking about? What have you heard?"

"What I have heard is that the warheads you stole many years ago are no longer in your possession but are now back in the hands of the Americans, who apparently visited Ulleungdo Island last night and took them."

General Cho skipped a breath, then asked, "The Americans did this? They came into our country and removed my weapons from Ulleungdo? How do you know this, Admiral? How will Kim respond?" Pacing back and forth, General Cho was unable to quell his anger as he considered the arrogance of the Americans who dared to violate South Korea's sovereignty.

"Neither America's actions, nor our nation's potential response to them, are your concern, Cho. You have a decision to make, and you must make it immediately."

The fact that Admiral Pak had omitted the general's rank when addressing him was not lost on Cho as he sat back down at his desk and spoke quietly into the phone. "What decision are you referring to, Admiral?"

Admiral Pak perused the notes he had prepared for this moment. "Cho, we are well aware of your involvement in the torture and death of Colonel Chang. Your accomplices in his savage murder have been most cooperative. It is *you* who has dishonored our nation through the theft of the warheads, and it is *you* who must bear the burden of the mistake you yourself made. You have two choices, and two choices only."

Cho sat silently for a few moments. He could hear his heart pounding in his chest. "Go on, Admiral."

"Two minutes from now, if you choose the first option, several well-armed operatives of our security service will enter your private office and place you under arrest for the brutal torture and murder of Colonel Chang. You will resist arrest violently, and during the struggle for one of the operatives' weapons, you will be killed accidentally. The subsequent investigation will reveal your role in the murder of Colonel Chang, and the motive given will be your irrational desire for his beautiful, young female companion. The public will find the sordid details disgusting and the press will have a field day. You will be posthumously reduced in rank to private, and your pension will be revoked. Your

...ation will be destroyed and you will long be remembered for the worthless old fool that you are."

General Cho sighed and rested his head in his hand. "And what is my second option, Admiral?"

"Your second option begins with the opening of the top drawer in your desk."

Cho slowly and dispassionately opened the drawer and removed its sole contents: a letter from his personal physician, and a 9mm pistol.

"The letter, written to you by your physician, states that you have been diagnosed with an inoperative brain tumor and have just a few weeks to live. If you choose this option, you will pick up the pistol, place the barrel in your mouth, and fire a single round into your brain. You will be honored with a state funeral, you will be posthumously promoted to the rank of full general, and your wife will receive your four-star insignia and its full associated pension. Your memory and reputation will be preserved and honored by a grateful nation."

The general quietly read his physician's letter. He examined the pistol and noted the single round in the magazine. "You say I have two choices, Admiral, but it appears you have left me with no choice at all."

"You are correct, Cho," said the Admiral, with a complete lack of sympathy in his voice. "The British have a name for a situation such as this. They call it Hobson's Choice. I rather like the concept."

A few moments later, General Cho's assistant and the roomful of waiting visitors were startled by the sudden, deafening sound of a single gunshot coming from the general's private office. While the others in the room scattered noisily in different directions, the three men in dark suits sat quietly and gazed out the window.

Kitsap College, Poulsbo, Washington

Colonel Dimitri Petrov quite appreciated the green tranquility of the remote college campus, where his mind could wander as he walked each day to and from the parking lot and his office. Sara's reaction to his ordering the assassination of Colton Garrett had surprised him, and it was still on his mind. It wouldn't be the first time in his career that an operative showed reluctance when ordered to kill someone who was considered an enemy. But typically, after some time had passed, the operative would learn how to compartmentalize the violent act and rationalize their role in the murder. But Sara's reaction was different somehow, and Petrov feared it may negatively affect her performance. He might be held responsible if he hadn't warned Moscow ahead of time. He entered his campus building and made a mental note to communicate his concern about Sara to his GRU superiors in his next report.

Colonel Petrov also was surprised to learn that his operations plan had been modified by Moscow to include a backup option for assassinating Garrett in the event the primary plan failed. Using VADIM to personally kill Garrett —*if* the flight mishap didn't — demonstrated how ardently Moscow wanted him eliminated. And the backup option included instructions for VADIM to also eliminate NIKITA to tie up any loose ends. Clearly, Moscow was ready to expend any resources necessary to optimize mission success.

More than ever before, Petrov also believed he, too, was now considered expendable. Because his escape plan depended on air travel to Vancouver, Canada, he decided to proceed with the necessary arrangements now. He also decided he needed to extract Sara from America as well, as Moscow wouldn't want there to be any other loose ends left behind. He opened his notebook, reached for his cell phone, and called the number for Best Jets, an air charter company based in Seattle.

"Best Jets, Charlene speaking! How can I help you?"

"Hello, Charlene. I am anticipating a quick business trip from Bremerton to Vancouver, B.C., in the next few days," he told the perky receptionist. "Can I schedule a charter flight with your company on short notice?"

"Yes, sir, no problem. We're based at Boeing Field, and we typically have two to four aircraft available for short hops like that. If you can give me just twelve hours' notice, I can have you covered. Can I start with your name, please?"

"Robert Jordan. And I may have an associate going as well, but they'll be booking separately."

"Understood. I just need a bit more information so we can get you in the system. Makes it way easier and quicker when you call back to schedule your flight. What credit card will you be using?"

Flight Deck, the Reagan

Dan Garrett was having difficulty keeping pace as his father, and Lenny Wilson ever-so-slowly jogged a circular route on the flight deck from bow to stern and back again. Dan couldn't call it running. It was all he could do to avoid breaking into a brisk walk. It wasn't the first time in his life Dan was glad he inherited his athletic ability from his mother. "Hey, Dad? Lenny? Could we speed it up just a little? I'm having trouble with this pace — I didn't think it was possible to run this slowly."

Lenny let out a laugh and just narrowly avoided tripping over a tie-down chain securing a Super Hornet to the deck. "Careful, Dan," he cautioned him, "remember, you're talking to the second most powerful man in the world. He doesn't need to run fast, he just needs to be able to talk on the phone while he's doing it!"

"I don't feel like the second most powerful man in the world," Colt said between gasps for air. "I feel like I need oxygen." In fact, it was Colt's idea to break up the workday with a group run on the flight deck before eating lunch — a habit he had formed years earlier as a junior officer. Watching the clouds stretch toward the horizon as the ship plowed through the ocean swell was a spectacular sight, and the combination of sea air, aviation fuel, and fresh paint evoked fond memories of places and people from long ago.

Anna DeSantis jogged next to Dan Garrett and smiled at the good-natured banter among the three men, who were clearly fond of one another despite their never-ending jabs and insults. Anna's profession had provided her with years of exposure to the interaction among men. She was fascinated by how they could say harsh words to one another yet share deep-rooted feelings of trust and admiration. Anna turned to Dan and yelled, "Hey, Lieutenant! First one to the bow buys lunch," as she rocketed ahead. Dan shifted down two gears and tore after her.

"Well, there goes my protection detail," said Colt as he slowed to a gradual stop and used their departure as an excuse to take a break.

Lenny stopped as well, placed his hands on his hips, and arched his back. "Sir," he reassured his boss while trying to catch his breath. "I don't think you need to be concerned about your safety!" He motioned to Colt to turn around and look behind them. There stood a few dozen Sailors and Marines who also had joined the group run. Some of them wore green shirts displaying the graphic of a running horse and the words, "Colt's Herd."

Hangar Deck, the Reagan

Malcolm Simpson needed to determine as soon as possible which of the Growlers Colton Garrett would be flying in during the next day's air show. Two of the squadron's five EA-18Gs were down for maintenance, which meant one of the three remaining aircraft would require the Magic Carpet software modification. But which one? Malcolm walked over to talk with Warrant Officer Steve Wilkes, who managed the squadron's maintenance activities. Although Lieutenant Commander Rick Becker was the squadron's maintenance department head, it was Steve Wilkes who ran the day-to-day operations of what was the squadron's largest and most important department.

"What's up, Warrant?" Malcolm said to get the warrant officer's attention.

Steve Wilkes looked up at Malcolm from the piles of papers on his desk. "I'm pretty busy right now, Malcolm. 502 and 504 are hard down, and I have to get two birds ready to go for tomorrow's air show. What do you need?"

The experienced warrant officer was professionally insulted by the Navy's ongoing practice of having civilian technical specialists onboard during a deployment. Although the technology in his aircraft indeed required their expertise, he didn't like being dependent upon people who weren't under his direct control or didn't wear the uniform he did.

"I need to know which plane Secretary Garrett is flying in tomorrow. The company wants me to double-check all of its systems to make certain they are good to go. Nobody wants the bad press if something should go wrong."

Steve Wilkes put his pen down, stood, and stepped around his desk to face the tech rep.

"If something should go wrong? Mr. Simpson, it is your job and mine to ensure that *every* airplane in this squadron is in perfect flying condition each and every time we let our aviators climb into the cockpit, so *nothing* goes wrong. I don't care if it's the most junior nugget pilot on his first cruise, or the goddamned United States Secretary of Defense! Do you read me, Mr. Simpson?"

Malcolm took a step back from the thoroughly vexed warrant officer and said apologetically, "Sorry, Warrant, I'm just doing what I was told."

Steve Wilkes glared for a moment at the cowering Malcolm, then his face softened, and he placed his hand on Malcolm's shoulder. "Sorry, Malcolm. I take this job very seriously. Lives are always at stake."

Malcolm walked back along the maintenance line thinking to himself, *You've got* that *right, asshole! Lives* are *at stake!*" He started to open the hatch to leave the hangar deck when some movement caught his eye. When he looked up, he saw a Sailor up on a ladder next to Growler 505. The young man was meticulously painting a name under the aft cockpit canopy. It said, "Colton Garrett, SECDEF." Malcolm smiled as he went through the hatch and decided he should arrange a meeting with VADIM right away.

Ship's Library, the Reagan

VADIM was already sitting in the library when Malcolm arrived for their meeting. As usual, the library was vacant except for the clerk at the desk.

"I have good news," Malcolm announced. "I found out which plane Garrett will be flying in tomorrow, and I've already prepared the modified code for upload." He then waited for what he was sure would be enthusiastic praise from VADIM.

Instead, VADIM looked across the table at the unkempt man with intense disapproval, ignoring what he had just said. "Malcolm, when are you going to clean up your act? Lose some weight and put on a clean shirt now and then. You're so gross! Take some pride in yourself!"

Caught off guard, Malcolm took a deep breath and didn't look up as he responded, "Y'know what, you just worry about yourself! I'm not in *your* Navy, and I *don't* have to put up with your insulting bullshit! Seems to me I'm doing all the work and taking all the risks on this operation, developing the code, and uploading it to the plane's system. Up to now, all you've had to do is take the classified material — that I copy for you — off this ship! You are basically a courier and nothing more. You can sit there in your starched khaki uniform and that stupid hat and act superior to me, but we both know who Moscow is counting on to get this thing done."

VADIM was about to respond when the library door opened, and Chaplain O'Brien came in. After the chaplain spent a few minutes talking with the clerk and then signing some forms, he left the library. VADIM leaned across the desk and spoke in a half-whisper.

"Calm down, Malcolm! I know we couldn't get this done without you, and I also know that Moscow has placed a great deal of trust in you. I'm really pleased and impressed that you have been able to identify Garrett's plane, and I have every confidence in your ability to upload the software discreetly without being detected. Please — forgive my comments regarding your appearance. I was out of line. These last few days with Garrett onboard have been a huge distraction. Things will get back to normal after tomorrow."

Malcolm smiled tentatively at VADIM. "Okay, then. I'll need to spend a few hours on it this evening, and I'll let you know as soon as the upload is complete. Where will you be around 20:00 hours?"

"I'll be having a cup of tea in the main wardroom. If you are successful, just drop by and get a scoop of ice cream."

VADIM walked back to the air traffic control center to watch the last recovery of the day. Sitting in a large chair watching the jets descend the glideslope, VADIM thought back to what Malcolm had just said regarding Moscow's respect for his skills. What would Malcolm have to say if he knew about VADIM's assignment in the event he failed in his part of the mission?

NCIS Offices, the Reagan

Anna DeSantis and Kevin Orr had been working most of the day. They were still trying to determine who Geoffrey was, and

Kevin felt they were getting close. He had played three online games against his mystery opponent, and the two had started to develop a casual albeit limited relationship, if such a thing was even possible via game chats.

"So, what do we actually have at this point, Kevin?" Anna inquired.

"Geoffrey is definitely a male, and I'm getting the feeling he might be a civilian. He likes to talk trash about the military as if he isn't part of the organization. He says no one in the Navy has his level of technical expertise, plus he doesn't like officers very much."

"You just described most of the Sailors on this ship! Anything else makes you think he's a civilian?" asked Anna.

"He mentioned something about taking a long vacation after this deployment. Sailors don't go on vacations; they take leave."

Considering Kevin's reasoning, Anna said, "Let's consider that as we move forward, but I think we still need to assume Geoffrey is in the military and we haven't made any progress developing a suspect list."

Someone knocked on the door, and Kevin opened it, surprised to see Chaplain Mike O'Brien standing there.

"Father Mike, come in! What can I do for you?"

"Good evening, Kevin. I hope I'm not interrupting any important crime-solving?"

"Not at all," Kevin assured him. "What's up?"

The Roman Catholic priest had been a cop with the San Francisco Police Department for 20 years when his wife died unexpectedly of liver cancer. He felt lost with no direction for the future until he considered the priesthood. He liked serving his community as a police officer. The priesthood became another way for him to keep serving people.

"I hesitate to bring this to you, Kevin, but the cop in me just can't let it go."

Anna looked at Kevin as he explained, "Father Mike used to be a police inspector in San Francisco before he became a priest."

"An inspector?"

"Oh, that's just what San Francisco calls detectives," the priest said. "You know, like Inspector Callahan in the Dirty Harry movies?"

"Okay, Father, what do you have for me?" asked Kevin.

"You know that the Chaplain's office is responsible for the ship's library, so I visit there with some frequency. On several occasions recently, I've noticed a particular individual spending a lot of time in there, it just seems strange to me, and I've also seen him talking with some pretty senior officers." The priest spent the next few minutes describing his observations to the two NCIS agents and then left the office to prepare his Sunday sermon.

"What do you make of that?" Anna asked after he was gone. "And what do you know about Malcolm Simpson?"

"Not too much," Kevin said. "He's a civilian avionics tech rep who's been on board for the entire deployment. But I have no idea why he would be spending time in the library or talking with officers."

"Well," replied Anna, "right now we need to focus trying to identify Geoffrey. See if you can get your new online friend to give you his age or any other biographical information that might help us narrow our search. Where is he from, where did he go to school, when did he join the service . . . anything would be helpful. If I get a chance, I'll have another talk with Father O'Brien, but I think he's probably reliving his days as an *inspector!*"

Day Eleven

Seattle Field Office, The Federal Bureau of Investigation

"You did what?!?" Clay Taylor shouted at Special Agent Sean Thomas, who was standing in front of his desk.

"I said that I approached Sara Olson at the coffee shop and asked what was troubling her," Sean responded. "She started to open up and then she asked about me. I talked about my service in the Marines, and I followed with my cover story about my divorce and being homeless. She doesn't see me as anything other than another bum on the street, but I can tell you she's questioning her place in the world and wishing for a different life."

"But you told her your real name, Sean! Why did you do that?"

"I suppose it was because I wanted her to trust me, and I needed to keep my story as truthful as possible," Sean answered. "We know the Russians train their operatives how to detect when someone's lying; I just went with my gut."

NCIS Special Agent in Charge Greg Cassidy had been sitting quietly during Clay's questioning of the FBI agent, but now he asked, "Sean, are you saying we might have an opportunity to get Sara to talk and potentially turn her to work against the Russians?"

Sean considered what the NCIS agent had asked. "I definitely think she wants out of the business, but I don't think we could double her. I think we should offer her a choice between facing a trial for espionage or full cooperation with us and a whole new life."

Clay got up from his desk and started pacing the floor. "I'll need to think about this, and then I'll find out what Washington has to say about it. For now, Sean, go back to simply being the poor homeless guy and don't initiate any further direct contact with Sara without my specific approval. Got it?"

Defense Secretary Cabin, the Reagan

"So, Lieutenant Pierce, do those speed pants come in a larger size?" asked Lenny Wilson as he watched his boss struggle to zip up the anti-G garment around his waist and legs. When airborne, the garment was connected to the airplane's pneumatic system and became inflated during high-speed maneuvers to keep the blood in a pilot's body from draining from his brain.

Colt glared at Lenny. "I'd like to see *you* try to fit into this thing! And don't you have anything more important to do than to watch me while I dress for the flight?"

Lenny moved towards the cabin door and apologized. "Sorry boss, I guess I could review those appropriation recommendations again. See you later and have a great flight!"

After Lenny left the cabin, Katrina continued to assist the secretary with his flight gear, including his torso harness, inflatable life preserver, survival vest, and leg restraint straps. Colt looked at his impressive reflection in the mirror and asked, "Did you ever think you'd get me into all this flight gear in time for the brief?"

Katrina Pierce didn't know what to say and just smiled. "Sir, the airshow flight briefing is scheduled for Ready Room 4 at 0900

292

sharp, but I'm pretty sure they won't start until you get there!"

"I suppose that's true! And thanks for helping me get dressed. I'm really looking forward to this, especially flying with Dan!"

Katrina was about to say something and then changed her mind. Colt saw the look on her face and asked, "Was there something else, Lieutenant?"

"Yes, sir, there is. I know you are aware that Dan very much wants to go to test pilot school after his squadron tour, but I also know you feel strongly about not using your influence to help him get into the program. I understand that for you, this is an integrity issue, and I totally admire you for standing by your principles. On the other hand, Dan is your son, and he really deserves your help. I'd hate him to lose this opportunity. He works so hard and is so good at what he does! I was thinking there must be a way to help Dan get into that school and still keep your integrity intact."

Colt was moved by the impassioned young officer standing before him with tears in her eyes. "You really care about him, don't you? Enough to scold the secretary of defense?"

Katrina wiped the tears from her face. "I love Dan like a brother," she said, "and I trust him almost every day with my life. I'd do anything for him."

"Dan's very lucky to have you as a friend, and I promise you I'll think about what you've said. Now I'll ask you to excuse me; I need to take care of a few quick things before the flight briefing."

Katrina left the cabin and started back to Ready Room 4. She was glad she had said her piece with Secretary Garrett, but she wouldn't bet five cents it would make a difference.

Rear Admiral Joe Carlisle's Stateroom, the Reagan

"Admiral, do you still think it's a good idea to give this interview so soon after the weapons recovery mission?" asked Chief of Staff Captain Gary Winters as the admiral stood in front of the mirror and carefully combed his hair. "We did a good job using the cover story of a training flight, but still a lot of people onboard and elsewhere know what really happened. Doing an interview with a major network's reporter could lead to questions you'd rather not be faced with."

"I appreciate your concern, Captain, but I cannot pass up this opportunity to speak directly with the American people about my views and achievements. I want them to consider me for elected office someday. I'm more than capable of avoiding any reference to the special mission and using this time to instead talk about my qualifications for the House or Senate. I assure you I won't talk about the mission."

Captain Winters still knew the interview was a bad move, but he had now done all he could to warn his boss of the potential pitfalls. Soon, he heard a knock on the door of the stateroom, and the admiral say, "Enter." Carissa Curtis, her cameraman Randy Hansen, and all their packed-up equipment came inside the stateroom.

"I figured we could sit at this table for the interview," the admiral suggested as Carissa and Randy got all their gear in order and cables connected. "Would that work, Ms. Curtis?"

Carissa looked up and scanned the small room. "Yes, Admiral," she replied. "That would be fine. Randy, will the angles work for you?"

"Yep, I can make it work. Admiral Carlisle, would you mind

clipping this microphone to your shirt? I'll get a soundcheck and soon we can get started."

Randy helped the admiral with the microphone and then had him say a few phrases to make certain the sound system was working well.

"Admiral, I thought I'd start by asking you a few questions about your background, your education, and your Navy career," said Carissa. "Then, we'll move to your plans for the future and wrap it up with a few comments regarding the carrier groups' current operations. How does that sound?"

The admiral quickly glanced at his chief of staff. "Carissa, I think we'd best stay away from any discussion of current ops, as some are highly classified and well beyond the scope and purpose of this interview."

Carissa nodded in agreement. "I understand, Admiral. May I ask about your views regarding the DOD and any thoughts you might have regarding the need for improvement?"

Captain Winters tried to catch the attention of the admiral, but Carlisle went ahead and answered, "Sure, no problem there," as he checked his reflection in the mirror one last time.

"Just one thing before we start, Admiral. I need you to sign this release form, indicating your permission for our network to use the interview's audio and video for our broadcast. Without your release, we can't use the interview. It's just routine."

Once again, Captain Winters attempted to intervene, but Carlisle eagerly signed the release form with no further discussion. Carissa placed the form into her portfolio and said, "Okay, Randy. Let's start!"

Carissa began the interview by leading the admiral through a summary of his childhood years and his experience as the son of an influential senator. Although careful not to claim the birthright to succeed Senator Carlisle, he did imply that he possessed some of the same characteristics as his famous father. "The Senator and I have long held similar views regarding a wide range of domestic and world issues. I feel as though I have been his apprentice for decades."

"Do you think you will run for office after you retire from the Navy? I realize that may be some years away, but there has been speculation by some in Washington that you may pursue a second career in politics. Any plans in the works you can share with us?"

The admiral shifted in his chair. "No, I'm not making any plans right now. I have a job to do running this carrier group, and if I ever do give serious thought to my future in politics, it will be after I retire."

Captain Winters thought the interview was going surprisingly well. The admiral was staying clear of any discussion of the special mission and other current military operations. Winters poured himself a cup of coffee and began thinking about his next task of the day when he heard Carissa pose her next question. "Admiral, you must be very honored that the acting secretary of defense is onboard your flagship. What is your impression of Colton Garrett?"

Captain Winters thought through the numerous ways Admiral Carlisle could gracefully answer the question, but when he saw the look on the admiral's face, he sensed the interview was about to take a turn for the worse.

"I think he's a fine person. A pleasant enough guy and he has a background in the Navy. He does like to get involved with matters on the operational side, which we find are always better left to the military."

Carissa looked down at her notes to avoid letting the admiral see the shock on her face. "What do you mean when you say he likes to get involved? I mean, isn't he automatically involved? He is after all the secretary of defense. Isn't that his job?"

"Not necessarily," said the admiral. "The DOD is a large organization, and we all have roles to play. The civilians determine policy, and those of us in uniform carry out that policy. Mr. Garrett is a smart man and a good man, but he doesn't really have the training or experience to be directing operations. He should be in Washington getting Congress to fund our programs rather than out here interfering in military operations."

Shaking his head, Captain Winters decided at that moment not to stop the train wreck he was witnessing. He was reminded of the old Spanish expression, "The fish dies by its mouth," and he sat in amazement, watching the admiral destroy his naval career.

Carissa paused for a moment before asking, "Is it your view, Admiral, that the military should not be subject to civilian control?"

Admiral Carlisle replied, authoritatively and by looking directly into the camera. "Certainly not civilian control," he said.

A few minutes later, Carissa concluded the interview by thanking the admiral and then quickly ushered Randy and his unpacked camera, sound, and lighting equipment out of the stateroom.

After they left, Admiral Carlisle turned to Captain Winters and said, "That went quite well, I think. I didn't say a word about the special mission, and I believe I made clear my qualifications for elected office and my views regarding the defense department."

Captain Winters gathered his notes and nodded, "No question about it, sir."

NCIS Offices, the Reagan

Kevin Orr and Anna DeSantis had been working non-stop, trying to discover the identity of the Russian agent using the screen name Geoffrey. Kevin had convinced Anna that they should focus on contractors first because they represented such a small percentage of those onboard. Over the past 24 hours, the two NCIS Special Agents had compiled a suspect list of five contractors who matched the search criteria they had selected for age, gender, and time onboard the *Reagan.*

"I'm satisfied that these five are our most likely candidates for Geoffrey," Anna said as she looked over Kevin's shoulder. "How do you think we should move forward?"

Kevin leaned back in his chair and rubbed the back of his neck. "This guy really interests me. I've been looking at his background, and so far, he's the only one on our list who might have a problem with the department of defense. And this is the same contractor that Father Mike said has been hanging around the library."

Anna moved closer to Kevin, placed her hands on his shoulders, and started massaging his neck. It wasn't the first time she had done it, and he did seem to like it. She enjoyed touching and being close to him — that much she knew. Kevin closed his eyes and breathed in the subtle scent of her natural fragrance.

"Tell me about him, Kevin."

It took him a moment to refocus on the job at hand. "His name is Malcolm Simpson and he's a Boeing Tech Rep. He's been on board for six months, but the interesting part is he was kicked out of the Army ROTC program at the University of Oregon for failing a drug test. It appears Mr. Simpson was smoking cannabis while he was in Eugene. He wasn't on my radar before because this info wasn't in the files his employer provided to Commander Abrams. But when I decided to run a criminal and military records search on our five suspects, that's when it popped up."

While Anna continued massaging Kevin's neck, she said, "Weird that it wasn't in the employer's file, since that's pretty basic stuff that would usually have turned up during a background investigation. Malcolm might be Geoffrey. I think I'll send a formal message request to the security manager at Boeing Defense to see if they have anything more on this guy."

Anna moved around the desk and sat in the chair facing Kevin. She picked up Malcolm Simpson's file, looking at each document and photograph in the folder. "He's a software engineer here to support the Super Hornet and Growler avionics systems. He seems to be one of their best. He's single, lives with his mother in Seattle when he's not deployed on a ship, and spends all his free time playing computer games and flying remote-control airplanes. He reads sci-fi novels and collects comic books. No wonder he's single! Remind me not to date *that* guy."

"Well, what kind of guy do you like to date?"

Anna blushed and straightened her shirt. "I don't think I'm into dating anyone right now."

"Why not?" Kevin pressed. "Don't you want to find Mr. Right someday?"

"Well," she said coyly, "I've been starting to wonder if maybe I've already found him." With that, she smiled demurely, got up from her chair, and left the NCIS office.

Kevin stared at the closed door, wondering if he had heard her correctly. His feelings for Anna had been shifting and intensifying over the past several days, but he hadn't imagined she might feel the same. All he knew was that he liked being around her, and he sure didn't mind those neck rubs.

Kevin looked back at the file on his desk. "So, Mr. Malcolm Simpson," he said, looking at a file photo, "Are you also our man, Geoffrey? And if so, why are you spending so much time in the library?"

Anna wandered back to her stateroom, thinking about Kevin and what she had just said to him. She certainly hadn't planned to reveal her feelings and thought she had probably just said too much. She knew that in a few days, Colt Garrett would be leaving the *Reagan* and she would most likely be leaving with him to go back to Tokyo and, presumably, her next assignment. She definitely liked Kevin, though, and wished she had more time to get to know him. *Life's not fair*, she thought to herself as she sank into a chair and drafted a message to the Boeing Defense security manager.

The Flight Deck, the Reagan

The Steel Beach party was in full swing. Three stages featuring rock, country, and hip-hop music competed for fans on the massive 1,100-foot-long flight deck. At over three football fields long, the flight deck provided plenty of space for the crew to find and enjoy the entertainment of their choice. Making the mood even lighter were the two cold beers rationed per crewmember, while the ship's master-at-arms force watched closely to make sure no one over-indulged.

At noon, the three bands stopped playing and started to break down their equipment, while the rest of the crew moved to the ship's port side in anticipation of the air show.

Joe Carlisle's chief of staff, Captain Gary Winters, had decided to approach Lenny Wilson with his concerns about the admiral's questionable statements during his TV interview. When he found Lenny in the crowd, he stood next to him and said, "Mr. Wilson, if you've never seen an air show before, you're in for a real treat!"

Lenny responded enthusiastically, "I've seen the Blue Angels a few times at Pensacola, and also the Air Force Thunderbirds at Joint Base Andrews. You probably can't get better than that!"

"Those pilots are sure amazing, and they're some of the best pilots in the service," said Captain Winters. "But nothing beats watching operational units show off the skills they use every day. Most people don't realize the Blue Angels and Thunderbirds are pilots that recently served in regular Navy and Air Force squadrons, and the maneuvers you see them execute are the same that all military pilots can perform — the formations are just tighter."

Watching the sky with a pair of binoculars he had borrowed from the bridge, Lenny continued to scan for airplanes. "I'm looking forward to it," he said, "and of course, the chance to see Secretary Garrett and his son fly will be very cool!"

Captain Winters glanced around and asked, "Would you mind if we talked business while we're waiting for the show to start, off the record?"

Lenny lowered his binoculars and looked directly at Gary. "What can I do for you, Captain?"

Captain Winters checked again to see that no one could be overhearing them. "Earlier today, Admiral Carlisle gave a television interview, and he made some statements that I'm afraid will not reflect well on him, the Navy, or the department of defense."

Lenny looked at the concern on the Naval officer's face. "Okay, spill it, Captain."

"Admiral Carlisle said he didn't think civilians should ever have operational responsibility over the military and its functions. He also made what might be construed as some derogatory remarks about Secretary Garrett. I thought you should know."

As Lenny raised the binoculars back up to his eyes, he asked, "I assume he signed a release before they taped the interview? Ms. Curtis had me sign one when she interviewed me."

"Yes, sir. The admiral signed a release. In fact, I saw Ms. Curtis and her cameraman on the bow taping her comments for her newscast, and I'm pretty certain she has already transmitted the interview back to her network in New York."

"That's very unfortunate. It appears your admiral may have tripped over his own sword, big time. But I do appreciate your giving me a heads up. I'll let the Pentagon know about the interview so they can be ready with a response." Lenny paused and then said with a grin, "Speaking of the Pentagon, Captain Winters, do you have any interest in a tour on Secretary Garrett's staff? I understand that colonels and captains are typically relegated to making coffee in the building, but perhaps we can find something more career-enhancing for you."

Captain Winters was taken aback for a moment, but kept his voice calm as he answered, "I'd definitely like to hear more about the opportunities on Secretary Garrett's staff, but first I think you better cover your ears as these two Super Hornets start making their approach."

In less than a minute, two dual-seat F/A-18Fs were rapidly

approaching from the stern just above the level of the flight deck, less than 100 feet above the water's surface. As the two planes passed by where Lenny and Captain Winters were standing, they saw the aircrew waving before rocketing straight into the air. The ship's crew jumped and cheered wildly at being so close to the noise and power of the high-performance jet aircraft.

Next, a single-seat Super Hornet approached the ship with its landing gear and tailhook down, flying as slowly as possible. As the jet came abreast of the ship, another Super Hornet flew past in the same direction but at full military power to demonstrate the dramatic difference in flight speeds. The Sailors and Marines watching the airshow grabbed their chests and covered their ears as the second Super Hornet went supersonic and broke the sound barrier with a loud boom.

A voice from the loudspeaker then directed the crowd's attention to the next squadron in the show as two E-2D Hawkeye turboprop aircraft approached, rotating their massive circular radar rotodomes as they flew by the ship. An SH-60S Seahawk helicopter flying low next to the ship was the next flight demonstration, in which a crewman could be seen dropping into the water and climbing into an inflatable raft to simulate a downed airman. A second Seahawk then swooped down low, and a rescue swimmer jumped off and into the water to assist the simulated victim. He first helped the victim get out of the raft, then hooked a large yellow rescue collar under the man's arms and watched as the Seahawk hoisted the man into the helicopter.

Next up was another F/A-18E squadron, with each of the two aircraft dropping bombs on the water. The crew on the flight deck watched as the bombs hit the water, followed by flashes of light, and finally, the delayed sound of the bombs exploding. The announcer then directed the crew's attention to the starboard side, as two CMV-22B Ospreys approached the ship, one hovering in place like a helicopter while the other flew past at near top speed.

Lenny and Captain Winters looked eagerly to the stern of the massive aircraft carrier as two Growlers approached at 800 feet in a right echelon formation. The entire crew on the flight deck cheered loudly when the control tower announced that the lead Growler was being flown by Lieutenant Dan Garrett, and his father, Secretary of Defense Colton Garrett, was in the NFO seat. The two airplanes flew parallel to the ship and then in sequence banked 90 degrees left across the ship's bow, bleeding off speed and altitude in a maneuver known by Naval aviators as *the break*. They climbed into the air and joined the other airshow aircraft circling the carrier as the flight deck was cleared and prepared for aircraft recovery.

Colt Garrett removed his oxygen mask and keyed his intercom, saying, "This has to be the coolest thing I have ever done! Thanks for the ride, son — you're a hell of a pilot!"

Dan Garrett smiled to himself, feeling a bit embarrassed that his father's opinion still meant so much to him. "Thanks, Dad! But I still need to get us safely aboard, so hold your applause for a few more minutes and get your O2 mask back on! I'm sure Skipper Robinson is pacing in Ready 4 right now, worried that I might screw up and kill us both!"

Colt didn't doubt that Dan's squadron commander was uneasy about the secretary of defense flying in one of his planes, but he believed it when Commander Robinson said Dan was one of the best pilots in his squadron. "Your skipper has a pretty high opinion of your skills as a pilot. In fact, he's been pushing me pretty hard to help you get into test pilot school."

"Dad, c'mon, let's drop that for now. I get your position. It wasn't fair of me to ask for your help, and I'm sorry the skipper brought it up. Right now, I need to get us aboard that bird farm. Lock your harness, and I'll start the landing checklist."

Colt watched out the canopy as aircraft after aircraft entered the pattern and began the descent to the carrier. The Ospreys recovered first, followed by the Hawkeyes and the Super Hornets. Dan banked the Growler left and descended to 600 feet on the downwind leg, running parallel with the carrier's course and about a mile away. He had completed his landing checklist and reported he was abeam of the carrier with wheels and tailhook down, descending at 250 feet per minute. He banked left again and descended further to 450 feet above the water's surface, then continued left one last time to intercept the glideslope for final approach to the carrier. Three-quarters of a mile from the ship, Dan saw the glideslope lens and "called the ball," informing the tower of his side number, squadron, aircraft type, the amount of fuel remaining, and that he had visually acquired the ship's Fresnel lens landing system. He skillfully made countless minor adjustments with his control stick, rudder pedals, and throttles to maintain the Growler's alignment with the landing zone, while simultaneously maintaining the correct airspeed and angle of attack.

But then, everything went terribly wrong.

As Dan pulled back on the stick to raise the nose of the aircraft, the Growler's nose went down instead. He increased the back pressure on the stick, but the plane continued descending even more.

What the hell? thought Dan. *This is nuts!* He then immediately aborted the landing, releasing the pressure on the stick, and allowing the plane's automatic systems to level the aircraft. He keyed the radio microphone and calmly stated, "Sierra Three Foxtrot, this is Growler 505. I'm declaring an emergency due to erratic flight control systems. Request safe altitude hold and get the squadron rep on the line. Expedite!"

Dan attempted to ease the stick back again, but each time he did, the plane's nose dropped. Trying everything, he pushed the stick forward, and instead of dropping the nose, it rose up. He suddenly realized that the stick input that controlled the elevators on the plane's tail was reversed! He experimented with the other controls and was relieved to verify only the elevator function seemed to be reversed.

"Dan! What's going on?" Colt had known enough to remain quiet while his son was fighting to regain control of the airplane, but once Dan had achieved level flight, Colt couldn't help but ask what was happening.

"My control of the elevators is reversed! Back is down and forward is up! And I'm also getting some other warning indications. I'm getting errors for the refueling probe and the emergency egress system. I'm going to need some help getting this broken bird fixed before we can land."

Primary Flight Control (Pri-Fly), the Reagan

"Get all the other planes aboard now, and then let's work the problem, people," said the air boss to the Pri-Fly team in their perch high above the flight deck. "And get Commander Robinson up here, NOW!"

Tom Robinson had already started racing up the ladders to

Pri-Fly when he heard, "Commander Robinson, your immediate presence is requested in Pri-Fly!" over the ship's 1MC. He rushed into Pri-Fly.

"What do we have, boss?"

The air boss was watching as the last of the other planes had landed. "It looks like you've got a broken bird, Tom," he said, his voice showing concern. "Lieutenant Garrett is reporting reversed elevator controls. It's a miracle he didn't slam 505 onto the ramp. How he recovered in time is beyond me!"

Commander Robinson could feel the tension in Pri-Fly, as the entire team stood motionless, staring at him. "Let's get Boeing on the line ASAP!!!"

Carrier Intelligence Center (CVIC), the Reagan

The officers seated around the conference room table were talking in hushed tones but stood in unison when Captain Rami Chavez, callsign *RAMBO*, walked in with Lenny Wilson. As air wing commander, Captain Chavez was operationally responsible for all of the aircraft squadrons onboard the *Reagan*. The position was informally referred to as "CAG," with a nod to the older title, commander air group.

"Seats, people!" said Captain Chavez. "Where are we?"

Commander Robinson opened a file and began describing the situation. "The experts at Boeing believe 505 is experiencing a control system software malfunction. The elevator input signals are reversed, which means when the pilot pulls back on the stick, the airplane dives, and vice versa. They have attempted to replicate the malfunction without success, and don't believe it can be fixed in the air."

The door to the conference room opened again as Special Agent DeSantis came in and took a seat at the table.

"Ms. DeSantis," said Captain Chavez, "isn't this situation outside of your area of expertise? Why don't you go wait in the passageway while we try to get this aircraft under control?"

Anna could tell that all eyes in the room were on her. "The secretary of defense is on that aircraft, and I am the one person on this ship who is *directly* responsible for his safety. I plan to stay exactly where I am, Captain, and I will participate in any decision-making regarding the secretary's well-being."

Captain Chavez glanced over at Lenny Wilson, took a breath, and addressed Anna again. "My apologies," he said. "I obviously didn't think that through, Special Agent DeSantis. *Of course,* you may remain here and offer any assistance that you can." He cleared his throat and continued. "Okay, folks," he said, mildly flushed, "We have an airplane with two people on board and not only are we running out of time, it's also running out of fuel. Tom, do we know what's up with the refueling probe?"

"Lieutenant Garrett is reporting errors with the refueling systems and also the ejection system. We can't get him more gas, we're too far for him to make it to the beach, and they can't eject. Our only option is to take him aboard."

"What does Boeing say about the refueling and egress failures? Are they related to the control problem?" CAG asked Tom.

"That's the weird part," Robinson replied. "Boeing says no way are these two problems related — they're entirely different systems!"

"Have you considered sabotage, Captain?" DeSantis quietly asked. "I mean, is it possible that someone might purposely have damaged the aircraft in an attempt to assassinate Secretary Garrett?" As Anna looked around the table, she could tell from the silence and blank expressions that sabotage had not been considered.

Captain Chavez broke the silence. "Perhaps that's one explanation, and I would ask you to pursue that line of investigation with our contacts at Boeing. Right now, our priority remains getting that damaged plane safely aboard."

"We've discussed using the barrier to stop the plane," Commander Robinson said. "But we're all in agreement that Lieutenant Garrett should first attempt an arrested gear landing. He has enough gas for two shots at the deck, and if he can't get aboard, we'll have to take him in the barrier."

"It's a lot to ask of any pilot, Tom, let alone a young one, to land a plane with reversed controls on a heaving deck. Are you confident this is our best option?" asked CAG.

Commander Robinson pushed his chair back from the table and stood up. "Yes, sir, I do. Lieutenant Garratt's a good stick. And right now, we're wasting time and gas talking about it. Let's get 'em aboard!"

As the meeting ended and the officers all began to scatter, Lenny Wilson approached Anna and motioned her aside. "That was a shocking theory! If you really think someone sabotaged the aircraft, you better get on the phone right away with Boeing to figure out how it might have been done, and who could have done it."

"Yes, sir. I have a meeting already scheduled with them for fifteen minutes from now. I'll let you know what I find out."

COLT'S CRISIS

10,000 feet above USS Ronald Reagan

"Yes, skipper. I agree it's our best option," Dan said into his mic.

"You've been well-trained to handle emergencies, JOKER," Tom reminded him. "Although you've never simulated this particular malfunction, we both know you have the skills to get this aircraft safely aboard."

"Roger that, sir. Let me get a few things lined up here first, and I'll start my approach."

Dan reviewed his landing checklist one more time, making certain nothing was being overlooked, and nothing else was malfunctioning. "Hey, Dad. I wish Katrina was sitting back there right now instead of you."

"You're not the only one!" Colt laughed nervously.

"No, I meant I really wish I wasn't putting you at risk. You're more than just my father now. You're important to our country. And also, Katrina gets flight pay, and you don't."

As Dan carefully worked his way through the landing checklist, Colt had a few moments to think. *Who knows if we're going to get out of this?* he wondered. *I've faced danger before, and I've lived a good and complete life. But Dan is too young to die!* he thought, silently praying his son would survive the flight. He wished he had been a better husband to Linda. He made a promise to work harder to fix their marriage if he somehow walked away from this landing. And he would spend more time with their daughter, Alexandra, too.

"Actually, Dan, I'm glad I'm here with you. I am so proud of you right now. And no matter how this turns out, we're together. But son, like your skipper said, I know you can do this. I have absolute confidence in you."

Colt thought he heard Dan keying his microphone to respond until the radio began to squawk. "Growler 505, this is Sierra Three Foxtrot. You are cleared to land! Good luck, JOKER!"

Dan eased the Growler to his left and began his final descent to the carrier, intercepting the glideslope and lining up for landing. When he spotted the Fresnel lens that would guide him to the ship, he keyed his mic and reported, "505 Growler Ball, 7.0!"

Landing Signal Officer Platform, the Reagan

Standing firmly on the landing signal officer platform near the ship's stern, Katrina was in the only spot on earth she would want to be right now. While Dan was attempting to bring his crippled plane aboard the *Reagan*, the air wing's most experienced LSO, Lieutenant Commander Rob Burnett, was giving power and line-up corrections to him via a radio handset. And Katrina was watching every second.

"Roger Ball, 505, the deck is steady, winds are slightly starboard, you're on glideslope, you're on speed," coached Rob Burnett, who could only imagine the difficulty Dan was experiencing while flying a plane with inversed elevator controls. Under the most ideal conditions, pilots were always challenged when landing on an aircraft carrier. And this situation was far from ideal. Burnett noticed Growler 505 was starting to drop a bit below the glideslope and said calmly into the mic, "Don't settle, easy with it."

Standing on the LSO platform, Burnett watched the Growler climb as Dan increased power, but then noticed the plane lose altitude again. "Power back on, a little left rudder, POWER!"

Now below the glideslope, as Growler 505 continued to descend, once more Dan increased power at the last moment but Growler 505 gained too much altitude, causing its tailhook to miss an arresting gear wire as the aircraft slammed down and continued down the flight deck. Dan immediately increased power to full military, pushed the control stick forward, and the aircraft climbed back into the sky.

"Bolter, Bolter, Bolter!" shouted the LSO as Growler 505 continued to climb into the air and to prepare for its second attempt at the deck.

"Well, that didn't go very well," said Dan to his father as he brought the plane back around and called the ball once more. "I've got enough fuel for one more pass before they rig the barrier."

The barrier or barricade was made of strong, industrial-grade nylon straps that grabbed an aircraft to stop its forward motion. In emergencies, a barricade was stretched across the flight deck to stop an aircraft and to ensure the safety of the pilot and flight deck crew.

This time, Dan made fewer flight control adjustments as Growler 505 gradually descended down the glideslope toward the carrier. The LSO made just a few comments to Dan as he closely watched the plane approach the ship. The crew of USS *Ronald Reagan* watched Growler 505 descend the glideslope on monitors throughout the ship. They stood in silence, motionless, each praying in the way that felt the most comforting, the most reassuring.

Dan slammed the throttles forward as the Growler crossed the ship's stern and Burnett watched as the plane flew by the LSO Platform and caught the Number 2 wire with its tailhook.

Dan kept the throttles fully forward until a flight deck crewman indicated he had safely hooked a wire. Dan pulled the throttles back, raised the tailhook, and taxied out of the landing area.

Rob Burnett placed his handset back into its holder, wiped the sweat from his brow, and turned to face Katrina. "Not the best *landing* I've ever seen, but hands down, that was the best *flying* I've ever seen!"

Holding back her tears, Katrina breathed a deep sigh of relief and silently gave thanks before hurrying off the LSO platform to find Dan.

The Flight Deck, the Reagan

Dan shut the engines down and sat for a few moments longer than usual, collecting himself and calming his nerves before opening the canopy above his head. In no time, technicians were scrambling up the sides of the fuselage to assist the shaken pilot and passenger out of their ejection seats. Climbing down the ladder, Colt saw Anna DeSantis waiting next to the plane with several of the ship's security team alongside her, all armed with pistols and semiautomatic rifles.

"What's with the security detail?" Colt asked Anna.

"Sir, glad to have you safely on board! I'm afraid, we suspect the airplane's malfunctioning may have been an attempt on your life, and we're not taking any chances. Now, let's get you back to your cabin."

"Do you mean this wasn't an accident? Someone was trying to kill us? Do we know who?"

"We're just starting to piece it together, sir," Anna said over the flight deck noise. "We've learned the GRU has one or more assets onboard the *Reagan*. We thought they were being tasked with espionage, but now it appears they might have made an attempt on your life. I can give you more details later, but right now, I need to get you to your cabin!"

As Anna grabbed the secretary by the arm and the security team rushed him inside the carrier's superstructure, Colt thought to himself, *The GRU? Could Petrov be involved with this?*

Squadron maintenance technicians waisted no time to inspect the aircraft to see if they could identify what had caused the system failures, until Kevin Orr arrived and loudly announced, "Everyone step back! This plane is now a Federal crime scene, and nobody touches it without my permission! I need 505 moved down to the hangar deck and secured. Now!"

03 Level Catwalk, the Reagan

Malcolm and VADIM stood apart from the crowd and watched the commotion surrounding Growler 505 as the ship's security detail rushed a bewildered and visibly unnerved Colt Garrett to his private cabin.

"Malcolm," whispered VADIM, "what do you think went wrong? I thought you said there was no way they could have safely landed that plane." VADIM knew it was only a matter of time before the NCIS agents and the Boeing engineers determined that the Magic Carpet system was at least partially to blame for the near disaster. If the Navy discovered that the software had been altered, Garrett's security detail would be increased, and Malcolm would be on a very short list of suspects. VADIM also suspected that Malcolm wouldn't stand up to the inevitable NCIS interrogation.

Malcolm turned his back on the activity on the flight deck, faced the sea and tightly grasped the steel lifeline. "I did exactly what I said I would do, and you agreed with the plan," he said vehemently to VADIM. "It's not my fault that the pilot was able to successfully recover from the system failures and bring that plane aboard. There's not another pilot in the air wing that could have done what he did. Moscow can't blame me!"

VADIM turned to face Malcolm and touched his shoulder. "I'm sure you're right. I'll make certain that Moscow understands you did everything you could. I suspect they'll start working on a plan to get you off the Reagan as soon as possible."

Malcolm released his grip on the lifeline and turned to face VADIM. "Thanks for having my back, and for being a friend," he whispered. "I can't wait for this to be over." Malcolm turned and started to walk away with his head down and his hands in his pockets.

VADIM watched him shuffle along the catwalk and open the hatch to return to his stateroom. VADIM thought, *I'm pretty sure you won't have to wait too long,* as the topside loudspeaker blared, "Now, secure from flight ops!"

Day Twelve

Russian Military Intelligence HQ, Khodinka Airfield, Moscow, the Russian Federation

Colonel General Igor Korobov read through the intelligence reports with increasing concern, as it became more and more clear that the GRU's attempt to assassinate the American secretary of defense had failed. Although he knew better than to consider it a sure thing, he had hoped things would go better than they did so his problem with Colton Garrett could have been solved by the time he read the morning intel reports. His long weekend with the lovely Ulyana had sufficiently distracted him from worrying about the mission on board the *Reagan*, but now that he was back, he faced a difficult decision: Should he execute his fail-safe plan to assassinate Garrett, or should he accept the unfortunate setback and move on? Well, he knew that taking direct action against a senior American official could be a career-ending move, but the general also knew that the goals of a Garrett-led, American defense department would be unacceptable to the Russian government.

Annoyed with an interruption, Korobov pressed the red flashing button on his telephone and grumbled, "Yes, what is it?"

"Colonel General, Director Orlov is holding for you on line three."

Gregory Orlov served as Director of the Russian Federation's Federal Security Service, one of the agencies that survived after the breakup of the Soviet-era KGB. Orlov reported directly to the Russian President, and from his headquarters in the Lubyanka Building in Moscow, he managed a vast agency responsible for internal security. His call now was certainly not a surprise.

Korobov took a deep breath and sat up in his chair as he lifted the phone to his ear. "Good morning, Orlov. I trust you are well. What can I do for you?"

"Colonel General, I understand your operation to eliminate the new American secretary of defense was not successful. How unfortunate for you! I was speaking with our president a few moments ago, and he continues to be concerned that Mr. Garrett will be nothing but an impediment to our interests. He expressed great disappointment upon hearing of your failure. He made me pledge to him that I would contact you immediately and offer any assistance you may require."

General Korobov carefully considered his response. "Thank you, Director. I very much appreciate your offer of assistance. At this moment, I am in the process of initiating the next phase of the plan, which I am confident is fail-proof. I will definitely contact you should there be a resource I require that you can provide."

When their brief conversation ended, the GRU chief considered the purpose of the call from Director Orlov. Clearly, Orlov wanted him to know how quickly the news of the failed assassination attempt had traveled, and that the Russian president was now even more closely monitoring the situation. Korobov saw that he had no choice but to carry out his back-up plan. He called his assistant into his office so he could dictate the order for Colonel Petrov and his agents on board the *Reagan*.

VADIM'S Stateroom, the Reagan

VADIM stared at Colonel Petrov's now decrypted message, and after reading it three times, was forced to acknowledge it was a direct, two-part tasking from Moscow. First, VADIM was to carry out the assassination of Colton Garrett within the next twelve hours, and immediately afterward, permanently silence NIKITA or Malcolm Simpson. The methods used for the two executions were left up to VADIM, but the order itself could not have been clearer: Both Colton Garrett and Malcolm Simpson were to be dead before the sun went down. According to Petrov's message, if VADIM did not comply, VADIM's "closest relative" would "meet with an excruciating death."

VADIM thought back to the very beginning, years earlier, when money had been unusually tight due to a bad gambling problem and the excessive losses that were the result. VADIM's biggest mistake was accepting money from Sara, the barista in Bremerton, who turned out to be a Russian operative and who later threatened to expose VADIM unless specific services were provided. As time went on, additional assignments and payments had come along, while new rationalizations had helped to justify the increasingly risky activities. VADIM could never have anticipated or believed that those slightly dangerous but mildly exhilarating acts of espionage and betrayal would lead to brutal demands that could very likely end in VADIM's capture, incarceration, and possible death.

Murdering someone was a world apart from the initial assignments VADIM had found it so easy to go along with. But now, there was even the added complication of a nearly impossible time frame that directly and violently threatened the

319

life of VADIM's mother. It was one thing to consider refusing Petrov's order and to suffer being exposed as a Russian spy, but quite another to be sentencing your innocent and kind mother to an unthinkable and painful demise.

VADIM was trying to think of ways out of this when the phone rang. "Yes?" A short pause followed, then a quick "I'll be right there!" Glancing at the stateroom clock before heading out the door, VADIM knew time was soon going to run out — for someone.

Defense Secretary Cabin, the Reagan

Carissa Curtis had been waiting by the door for over an hour when Colt Garrett finally returned to his cabin for their interview. She had desperately wanted to talk with him after yesterday's incident in the air, but Garrett's schedule had been consumed by meetings onboard and calls with Washington until early this morning.

Colt opened the cabin door and invited Carissa and her cameraman inside, then briefly excused himself to go into his bedroom and change into a suit and tie for the interview. After dressing, he opened his safe and removed the 1911 pistol which had been a gift from Admiral Shaffer a few days earlier, checking to be sure that a round was chambered. He engaged the slide lock and inserted the pistol into a holster on his waist, behind his right hip.

Several conversations with Anna and the directors of the FBI and NCIS in Washington finally convinced Colt that he indeed might have been the intended target of an assassination attempt.

He was also stunned to learn that there were likely two or more Russian military intelligence operatives onboard the *Reagan* undercover as civilian contractors, and that the NCIS agents on the ship had already been working for several days to identify them.

This wasn't the first time Colt had found himself tangling with Russian intelligence, but he never expected them to have penetrated the *Reagan*. He had long distrusted the Navy's history of hiring civilian contractors to work onboard ships during deployments, and now he decided to ask the secretary of the Navy to reevaluate the practice.

And there was one more conclusion Colt arrived at: He needed to somehow be able to defend himself should there be another attempt on his life. He had a personal history with Dimitri Petrov that went back many years, and now, both the FBI and NCIS suspected Petrov had directed the assignation attempt. If Petrov was indeed involved, Colt assumed the Russian operative would try again, and this time, Colt was going to be prepared. The *Reagan's* captain had vigorously opposed Colt's decision to arm himself, but at this point, there was little she could say to dissuade him. Captain Solari did brief her department heads, though, in the event someone saw Secretary Garrett with his pistol and asked questions.

"Mr. Secretary," Carissa asked Colt when he returned from his bedroom, "how are you feeling after your close call yesterday during the air show? And what did you think of your son's performance as a pilot?"

"I feel much better now that I've had a shower and a few hour's rest," Colt said. "That was a pretty stressful experience, one I hope I'll never have to repeat. Regarding my son's performance as a pilot, I've always known Dan was an exceptional aviator and that he's had the best training in the world. But I also believe that most if not all of the air wing's pilots could have done what Dan did. And that is not meant to minimize Dan's exceptional skills, but to underscore how excellent our training programs are."

"But Mr. Secretary, the entire ship is buzzing regarding the exceptional airmanship that Dan displayed. Don't tell me you're not proud of him!"

"Of course, I am! Speaking as a father, I couldn't be *more* proud!"

"Okay, sir, I'll leave it at that. Now, what can you tell us about the cause of the aircraft's malfunction? What if anything have you learned about what and why it happened?"

"Well, all I can tell you right now is that the mishap is the subject of an ongoing investigation. It's going to take some time to sort out exactly what happened, whether or not it was an intentional, malicious act, and how to prevent it from happening again. We do suspect this is an isolated incident, and that's why there has been no decision as of yet to ground all the Navy's Growlers."

"Intentional act? Is there anything that would suggest the mishap may have been an attempt on your life? It's certainly a bit suspect that the one and only aircraft that had problems yesterday was the one that you were in."

"I suspect that it was just a coincidence, but again, I really can't comment any further on the incident or the investigation at this point. I'm afraid we'll all have to wait for the experts to find the answer."

"Mr. Secretary, there are rumors that some of the *Reagan's* aircraft may have been involved in recent activities involving South Korea. The White House just released a statement saying those missing biological warheads from back in 1991 were not stolen — something about an inventory error. You previously mentioned that you traveled to Seoul just a few days ago to talk with the South Koreans about those same weapons, which were still missing at the time. Were you or this ship involved in any way with the resolution of that issue?"

"I'll have to refer you to the White House for any comments regarding South Korea or the warheads. Personally, I'm pleased to know the weapons were not stolen so we can now move forward with our negotiations with North Korea and, hopefully, the reunification of the peninsula. I spoke with Secretary of State Unger yesterday, and he's very optimistic that real progress can be made this year."

"Let's shift now, Mr. Secretary, to your immediate future, if we may. When are you planning to return to Washington, and do you think the president will nominate you to permanently succeed the late Secretary O'Kane?"

"Len Wilson and I will be leaving the *Reagan* tomorrow. We'll be flying to Tokyo, where we plan to catch a plane back to D.C. and the Pentagon. Regarding a permanent nomination as secretary of defense, again, I'm afraid you'll have to ask the president," Colt added with a slight grin.

"And with that, we thank you, Mr. Secretary, for talking with us. Travel safely, and we hope to catch up with you soon in Washington. I'm Carissa Curtis, on the USS *Ronald Reagan* in the western Pacific Ocean." Carissa then turned around to her cameraman. "That's it," she said.

As the cameraman collected his equipment, Carissa removed Colt's microphone. "I do hope you have a great flight home. And now, I'm off to find that son of yours to get some footage of him in front of his plane. He is quite the hero right now to a lot of people, and it will be great to have a feel-good story for a change to share on the evening news."

Suddenly, an inspired thought occurred to Colt. As he got up from his chair and started walking Carissa to the door, he said, "I wonder if I could ask a small favor of you."

Carissa stopped walking and looked up at Colt. "That depends on the favor," she answered.

NCIS Offices, the Reagan

Anna and Kevin had been working almost non-stop since the aircraft incident, trying to determine whether it was an accident or an intentional act. Despite talking with every expert Boeing provided, including the embarked tech rep Malcolm Simpson, the investigation had thus far revealed nothing. The software responsible for the Growler's flight systems was clearly different from the version provided by Boeing for comparison, but the company's experts couldn't agree regarding the possibility of sabotage.

Now, sitting together in their shared office, Anna turned to Kevin with another idea. "You know, the control systems lead at Boeing seemed a little ill at ease when you asked if he thought someone could have remotely accessed the software and modified the code, but there were several others with him during that video call. I wonder if he would be any more candid if we talked with him alone, without any others on the call with us?"

Kevin rubbed his eyes and took a sip from his coffee cup. "You never know. It can't hurt. Let's give it a shot."

Anna entered a series of numbers into her laptop, and within a few seconds, the image of the Boeing software engineer appeared on her screen. "Hey, Jessie, its NCIS agents Anna DeSantis and Kevin Orr from the *Reagan*. Sorry to bother you again, but we have a few more questions we want to ask you. Do you have a few minutes you can talk with us?"

Jessie Hughes adjusted the video camera on his workstation. "Sure," he said. "The *Reagan's* mishap is a top priority of ours right now."

Kevin asked the first question. "Jessie, I'd like to go back to something I asked you about earlier. I noticed a weird look on your face when I asked you if the software could possibly have been modified remotely. Do you remember that?"

Jessie stood up from his desk and closed his office door. "As a matter of fact," he said, lowering his voice, "when you asked me that question, I did think of something we hadn't discussed. That software was modified in a highly-skilled, very specific way. Without getting into too much detail right now, we're fairly certain that the code was not damaged in a random way. We believe it was deliberately altered."

Kevin sighed. "I know Jessie, we already covered that . . ."

"Let me finish," Jessie interrupted. "There's no way that code can be altered remotely because it's specifically designed to prevent that very thing. There are several people on board the *Reagan* who we know have the technical ability to make those modifications. Let me ask you a question: Have either of you ever written software code? Even just in a college course?"

"Sure," said Anna. "I've done some programming in Java, Python, and C++. Why?"

Jessie removed his glasses and used his necktie to clean the lenses. "Did you learn in your classes that there are several ways to write a program that all provide the exact same results? Stuff like how to use loops and other techniques? What I'm getting at here is that I've seen this particular style of coding before. I recognize it, in fact."

"Do you mean you may know who modified the code on that aircraft?" asked Kevin as he and Anna looked at each other wide-eyed.

"I *do* know who modified the code," Jessie answered. "It was Malcolm Simpson."

The Flight Deck, the Reagan

The wind had been gusting steadily, but just as Carissa Curtis and her cameraman completed their set-up for the interview, it died down just enough to allow the microphones to work properly. Lieutenant Dan Garrett, dressed in a green flight suit and brown flight boots, stood in front of Growler 501 as Carissa began the interview.

"I'm on board USS *Ronald Reagan* with Navy Lieutenant Dan Garrett, a pilot assigned to Electronic Attack Squadron 132, the Scorpions. It was Lieutenant Garrett who skillfully landed a critically malfunctioning plane yesterday, saving not only himself and his aircraft, but also the life of his father, who happens to be the new, acting secretary of defense, Colton Garrett. Dan, is this the plane that you flew and landed yesterday?"

"No," Dan answered. "That plane is down below on the hangar deck, cordoned off for an accident investigation, but this is exactly the same model of aircraft, an EA-18G Growler."

"Dan, can you explain to us what happened during the flight?" Carissa asked.

"Well, I had just completed my pre-landing checklist and was on the final glideslope, or path to the carrier, when I lost elevator control."

"Can you explain what that means to those of us who aren't pilots?"

"Sure. Loss of elevator control means I couldn't safely adjust the airplane's landing angle, or how it's positioned in the air."

Dan used his hands to mimic a plane flying through the air.

"When I pulled back on the control stick, instead of angling up like it's supposed to, the airplane's nose went down. And when I pushed the stick forward, the plane climbed. In other words, the controls were reversed," said Dan.

"I would imagine that made landing the plane extremely challenging, and yet you brought it aboard safely!"

"Yes, and thank you, but before you give me too much credit, remember there were many other people responsible for that successful landing. Lots of people *on* the ship, and even some experts back home at Boeing. We're all trained for these types of emergencies. I'm just happy now that everything turned out fine."

"As I mentioned, your father was in the back seat for the flight. Did having him with you during an emergency make it even more stressful for you?"

Dan thought for a moment. "I would definitely have been more comfortable having HURRICANE, I mean Lieutenant Pierce, my NFO, back there. We've trained together for these emergencies, and we've been flying together for a few years. But to directly answer your question, I think having my dad with me probably helped to keep me calm."

"Lieutenant Garrett, I understand you are coming up for orders. Where do you see yourself heading for your next assignment?"

Dan was surprised by the question and paused for a moment to think about his answer. "I hope to attend test pilot school, but I don't have the required engineering degree. So, I'm just waiting to see where the Navy's going to send me."

Carissa turned to face the camera. "Well, if you ask me or anyone else on this ship, we'd say Lieutenant Garrett has definitely the right stuff to be a great test pilot. This is Carissa Curtis on board USS *Ronald Reagan* in the western Pacific."

The Brig, the Reagan

"I am Kevin Orr, a special agent of the U.S. Navy Criminal Investigations Service. I am investigating the alleged offenses of the attempted murder of the United States Secretary of Defense, the Honorable Colton Garrett, and Navy Lieutenant Daniel Garrett, of which you are suspected. I advise you that under the Fifth Amendment to the Constitution, you have the right to remain silent, that is, to say nothing at all. Any statements you make, oral or written, may be used as evidence against you in a trial or in other judicial or administrative proceedings. You have the right to consult with a lawyer and to have a lawyer present during this interview. You may obtain a civilian lawyer of your own choosing, at your own expense. If you cannot afford a lawyer and want one, one will be appointed for you by civilian authorities before any questioning begins. You may request a lawyer at any time during this interview. If you do decide to answer questions, you may stop the questioning at any time. Do you understand your rights?"

Malcolm Simpson was sitting on a cold metal chair in the *Reagan*'s brig, a secure facility onboard the carrier designed to hold people who had been charged with committing a crime. The small jail included two isolation cells plus a large bunkroom that could sleep eight prisoners. The brig was currently empty, except for Anna DeSantis, Kevin Orr, Malcolm, and Commander Steve Lingenbrink, the Navy Judge Advocate General, or JAG, attorney, assigned to the admiral's staff. The senior JAG officer's jobs were to provide guidance regarding rules of engagement and to assist any Sailor or Marine who might run afoul of local law enforcement during a foreign port visit. He had been summoned to the brig now to serve as defense counsel should Malcolm request his services, and ensure that the interrogation of the civilian was done according to the law.

Malcolm crossed his arms over his chest. "This is bullshit," he said. "You have no authority over me. I'm a civilian, and besides, I didn't do anything wrong."

"Actually, Malcolm, both Special Agent DeSantis and I are fully credentialed federal law enforcement officers, with authority to investigate any felony that impacts the United States Navy. So, let me ask you again: Do you understand your rights?"

"Yes, I understand them."

Kevin looked at Steve Lingenbrink, who nodded and made a note on his pad.

"Malcolm," Kevin continued, "do you want a lawyer?

Commander Lingenbrink is the admiral's JAG officer, and he can represent you. After we pull into port, you can then request a civilian lawyer if you wish."

Malcolm looked across the table directly at the commander and said, "You mean, you'll work for me, and you can't share anything I tell you?"

"That's correct, Mr. Simpson," said Commander Lingenbrink. "I'd be representing you, and the attorney-client privilege applies to whatever you tell me."

Malcolm said, "Okay, then, you can be my lawyer."

Kevin Orr continued on. "Are you willing to answer questions, Malcolm? I mean, you have nothing to hide, correct?"

Commander Lingenbrink rested his hand on Malcolm's shoulder and said, "Hold it, Mr. Simpson. You are not required to answer any questions, and that decision can have no impact on a finding of your innocence or guilt. In my opinion, you should not answer any questions or make any statement."

Looking at the two NCIS agents sitting at the table, Malcolm was certain he was smarter than they were. "It's okay, Commander," he said. "I'll answer their questions. I just want to get this over with so I can get back to doing my job. And I *don't* have anything to hide."

Kevin thought, *Well, okay then!* He produced a document from his briefcase and asked Malcolm to indicate with his signature that he was waiving his right to remain silent and had retained legal counsel. Commander Lingenbrink witnessed the signing, and the questioning began.

Kevin opened his briefcase again and removed a large, thick file folder which he placed on the table. "Before we ask any questions, I'd like to share with you what we have so far." As he handed each document to Malcolm, he briefly explained what it was. "First, this is a sworn statement from Mr. Jessie Hughes of Boeing Defense, saying first, that he is familiar with and recognizes your software coding techniques, and second, that he believes you are the person who altered the control system software in Growler 505. Attached are examples of your coding techniques from your training at Boeing, as well as a sample of the altered code in Growler 505. Next is a warrant to search your stateroom and your workspaces, including both of your personal computers. This is a screenshot of your computer showing your screen name as Geoffrey, along with some in-game coded messaging between you and someone named VADIM, whom we are quite certain is also on this ship. This is a photocopy of a series of in-game communications between yourself and two persons who are not on this ship. They have been identified by the FBI as military intelligence officers of the Russian Federation. This is an affidavit that describes surveillance video evidence that we have of you making modifications to equipment onboard Growler 505. This set of documents details your personal bank accounts, showing balances totaling more than two million dollars, against an annual salary of $110,000. Malcolm, all this combined evidence will be used to charge you with several counts of espionage as well as the attempted murder of Colton and Daniel Garrett."

Malcolm sat silently as Kevin went through each document and set each one in front of him on the table.

"Oh, and one other thing. Last night we partially broke another in-game communication from VADIM to the Russian Federation blaming you for the failed attempt on Secretary Garrett's life. Malcom, it seems that you are quickly running out of friends."

Malcolm silently looked through each document on the table and then looked at Commander Lingenbrink.

"How about this, Malcolm?" asked Kevin. "We'll give you and your lawyer a few minutes to consider your situation," and the two NCIS agents left the brig and waited in the passageway to give Commander Lingenbrink and his new client some privacy.

Thirty minutes later, Commander Lingenbrink walked out of the brig. "Mr. Simpson has a question he would like to ask." Anna and Kevin followed the JAG lawyer back into the brig to find Malcolm seated at the table. The software engineer looked up at Kevin and asked, "Perhaps it's time to discuss a deal?"

Kevin looked at the software engineer and said, "All of this evidence points directly at you, Malcolm. What could you possibly have that would be of any interest or value? Espionage and attempted murder are capital offenses. At the very least, I'd say you're going to be making little rocks out of big rocks at Leavenworth Federal Penitentiary."

"Hold on!" exclaimed Malcolm. "You don't seriously think I did this on my own? I've been removing classified material from the ship for months. How do you think I did that without a courier card?"

Anna looked at Kevin, and in unison, they said, "Defense Courier Service." Anna pressed a series of numbers on the phone. "Master Chief, this is Special Agent DeSantis. I need you to tell me who on this ship has a courier card." As she waited, a bad feeling began to grow in the pit of her stomach as she recalled seeing a certain officer carrying a black courier satchel on several occasions. Anna listened to the phone as she carefully wrote down a list of five names on the tablet in front of her, underlining the last name. While turning the pad so that Kevin could see the list, Anna spoke to Malcolm. "Tell us why you have been meeting in the ship's library with Commander Abrams. Father O'Brian told me he has seen you talking with her. What have you two been discussing?"

"I'm not saying another word unless there's a deal on the table. Commander, I'm done talking." Malcolm pushed his chair back and started to stand up when Kevin grabbed him, forcefully twisted his arms behind him, and handcuffed him. "You're not done until I say you're done, you weasel! Malcolm Simpson, I'm placing you under arrest for the attempted murder of Colton Garrett and Daniel Garrett and for committing espionage against the United States of America."

Steve Lingenbrink intervened. "Take it easy with my client, Special Agent Orr," he warned Kevin.

An angry Malcolm Simpson shouted at Kevin. "Me and VADIM were just following orders! She's the one you really want, if you're not already too late."

Anna looked at Kevin as the blood drained from her face. *The meetings with Malcolm in the library, the ability to remove documents in a courier satchel, and easy access to the most classified information in the ship. And Malcolm just referred to VADIM as a woman.*

"Oh, my God! Kevin, it all fits. VADIM is Commander Jennifer Abrams, and she may be going after Garrett again!"

SECDEF Cabin, the Reagan

"Doesn't it hurt when you lean back in your chair?" Lenny

asked, referring to the stainless-steel pistol in the holster on Colt's belt.

"You get used to it. Besides, don't you think it makes me look like James Bond?" Colt pretended to admire his reflection in the mirror for a second, then sat down at his desk.

"Word on the street is that Admiral Carlisle really did it this time when he was giving that TV interview," Lenny commented. "It's made most of the papers and it even came up in the White House press briefing this morning. What do you think he's looking at as far as fallout goes?"

Colt looked up from his desk, shaking his head. "All I know is that you can say a lot of different things to the press and still recover. But saying the military shouldn't be subject to civilian authority is not one of them. I doubt the president liked hearing that. I spoke with the secretary of the Navy a few hours ago, and let's just put it this way: I don't think our friend Joe will be adding any more stars to his collar. In fact, once Admiral Shaffer flies aboard tomorrow afternoon, Admiral Carlisle's remaining time as task force commander can be counted in hours."

In the narrow passageway outside the secretary's cabin, Commander Jen Abrams had just approached and greeted the security guard stationed at the door. Pointing to her NCIS protective service pin on her uniform for the guard to clear her, she knocked on the stateroom door and entered, locking the door behind her.

"What can I do for you, Commander?" Colt asked somewhat impatiently, as he stood to greet her.

"I hate to bother you, sir," she said, "but Captain Solari said you that are now carrying a personal sidearm, and we have to record the serial number in our weapons log. Navy regulations." She motioned to the aluminum clipboard in her left hand.

Colt removed the pistol from its holster and made sure the thumb safety was engaged before handing it to Jen.

"Careful, Jen," he cautioned her, "it's loaded with a round in the chamber."

"Thank you, Mr. Secretary," she said, dropping the clipboard. Taking the pistol in both hands and pointing it directly at the two men, she instructed, "I must ask you and Mr. Wilson to step over to the bulkhead."

Colt and Lenny were stunned by Jen's abrupt switch from a trustworthy senior officer to an unsuspected adversary, yet they were smart enough to go along with her, do what she said, and stay calm. They both moved slowly toward the bulkhead, where they stood side-by-side, facing her. She had always seemed uptight and creepy to Lenny and unapproachable and nervous to Colt. This could explain a lot, they were both thinking to themselves.

"Jen," Colt said, "is there a problem? Have we done something to offend you that we're not aware of?"

"Yes, Mr. Secretary, there is a very big problem," she answered, her voice lowered but irritated. "You were supposed to be dead by now. You should have gone down in that plane, but you didn't. Now they want me to take care of it."

"You had something to do with that?" Lenny asked, dumbfounded. "Why? Why would you do that?"

"Well, to save my own ass, for starters," she replied, shifting the aim of her outstretched and shaking arms back and forth between the two men.

"What are you talking about, Jen?" Colt asked with a purposely calming edge to his voice. "Who's threatening you? What kind of trouble are you in?"

"I've been working for the Russians for years," she revealed, her voice wavering, "giving them names, dates, classified information, making copies of documents, that sort of thing."

"You said you were responsible for the Growler mishap, and you're standing here with a gun in your hands," said Lenny, pointing out the obvious.

"You don't understand! Now they're threatening my family, and Mr. Garrett needs to die. I have no choice!"

Lenny was about to ask another question, just to keep Jen talking, when she blurted out, "I'm sorry," pointed the pistol at Colt and pulled the trigger.

Colt instinctively ducked to his right, but the pistol didn't fire. Instead, in the absence of a loud shot, Jen looked down at the pistol and frantically tried to find and disable the safety. As she struggled to figure out the pistol's older design, Lenny spotted a ten-pound fire extinguisher just two feet away. In one swift motion, he grabbed it off the bulkhead, raised it in the air, and lowered it, forcefully striking Jen's forehead.

As Jen fell to the floor, Anna DeSantis crashed through the cabin door, her service pistol drawn. She saw the two men standing over a bleeding and unconscious Commander Jen Abrams. "She's a Russian agent," Anna said. And then to Lenny, "You hit her with a fire extinguisher? Where did you get that stupid idea?"

Lenny shrugged his shoulders and said, "Navy training!"

Sick Bay, the Reagan

Commander Jennifer Abrams lay unconscious in a bed inside the ship's intensive care unit, carefully guarded by NCIS Special Agent Kevin Orr, and tended to by the ship's senior medical officer and several nurses and corpsmen. After treating her head wound and monitoring her vital signs, the medical staff had decided to wait until she regained consciousness before making the decision whether or not to medevac her to Tokyo, where she could receive more thorough medical care.

Despite her debilitating injury, Jen's left wrist was handcuffed to her bed frame while an IV line ran into her right arm. Kevin quickly went to the foot of her bed when he noticed Jen moving her head from side to side. She began moaning in faint, jerky sounds, finally groaning, "I feel like shit! What happened? Where am I right now?" Kevin picked up the phone and dialed a number. "She's awake."

The medical staff had been working on Jen for a few minutes when Anna DeSantis and Commander Lingenbrink arrived in ICU and took seats in the chairs next to where Kevin was sitting.

"She's been awake and talking with the docs for about 10 or 15 minutes," Kevin told them. "I've let the doc know that we need to get a statement from Commander Abrams as soon as they say it's okay. I think that's going to happen any minute now."

"Special Agent Orr," said Commander Smith, the senior physician on board, "you can have ten minutes now, but no more."

Kevin read the scripted Article 31 rights notification to Jen, after which she agreed to waive legal counsel and answer questions. Speaking slowly and in just a few words at a time, she provided a very basic summary of her involvement with Russian intelligence and the money they were paying her for her years of espionage. She described her gambling addiction and how debt had motivated her to use her courier credentials to remove classified materials from the ship and pass them on to a Russian intelligence operative in Bremerton. Jen described her conspiracy with Malcolm to crash Growler 505, and she said she had agreed to personally murder Secretary Garrett and Malcolm Simpson only after the Russians had threatened to torture and kill her mother. She said she felt trapped in a corner, with no real choice.

After giving Kevin her mother's phone number and address in Seattle, Jen drifted back into semi-consciousness. "I think that's enough for today," said Commander Smith.

Anna and Commander Lingenbrink left the ICU and headed to the forward wardroom for coffee, leaving Kevin to continue guarding the prisoner.

"What's next for her?" asked the Navy JAG officer, once they had filled their cups and sat down at a small table. "Seems like a pretty solid case."

Anna looked up from her coffee and nodded in agreement. "It does to me too, Commander, but it's way above my paygrade. While I didn't know about the threat to her mother, that certainly doesn't excuse a lengthy history of espionage *and* the attempted murder of several people. In the near term, I understand they're going to medevac her to Tokyo this evening. But down the road, the DOD, the Justice Department, and every three-letter agency in D.C. will have strong opinions regarding her fate. Hers are among the most serious offenses a service member can commit."

"At least you successfully eliminated the Russian operation

onboard the *Reagan,*" Lingenbrink said. "But you do have to wonder," he added, "if they had agents operating on *this* ship, what might that say about the rest of the fleet?"

Defense Secretary Cabin, the Reagan

Colt Garrett awakened from a short "combat nap" by the knock on his cabin door. Colt got up from his sofa and opened the door to see his son standing there.

"I'm not sure I should let you in," he said to Dan dryly. The last time someone came through that door, they tried to kill me."

"Very funny. But seriously, Dad, maybe next time, think twice before giving your pistol to a Russian agent."

"Oh. Good point, son. I'll try to remember that. So, what have I done to deserve an impromptu afternoon visit?"

"Well, I just wanted to stop by and say my goodbyes. I'm scheduled to fly early tomorrow morning, and before that, I have some division officer stuff to do, so I thought I'd come over now if you have a minute. It was really good to see you and spend some time together. We even managed to have a little life-threatening adventure, so now you have another story to embellish! And congratulations again on the appointment as acting SECDEF. I think the president made a great choice, Dad. Are you going to see mom on your way back to D.C.?"

"I'm working on that. I'd very much like to. Lenny and I will be meeting a Nightwatch in Tokyo. I'm hoping I can talk the aircraft commander into a short stop in Seattle. I want you to know I've enjoyed this time with you too, Dan. The best part has been seeing how great you're doing." Colt reached out and wrapped his arms around his son, who stood several inches taller.

"Goodbye, Son. I love you. Be safe!"

"I will, Dad, I promise. And you be safe, too. I love you!

When the younger Mr. Garrett left the cabin, his father couldn't have been prouder.

Day Thirteen

The White House, Washington D.C.

President William C. Harrison made it a point to watch the nightly television news broadcasts as they helped to keep him in touch with the public — something he felt strongly that every politician should do. Last night was no exception and, as often was the case, he began the next day talking with his chief of staff about what he had seen the night before on TV.

"Eric, did you catch last night's news?" he asked. "Garrett made a pretty good showing, and that son of his belongs on a recruiting poster."

Not only had Eric Painter already reviewed each of the major networks' evening newscasts, but he held in his hands typed, detailed summaries of each of the leading stories in the event POTUS wanted to follow up on any of them.

"Yes, Mr. President, I think Colt did a fine job. I think he always does. He is consistently articulate, informed, and unflappable. Perhaps most important, he can make difficult decisions, and the Joint Chiefs are very impressed with his leadership during the Korean incident, which they are now referring to as *Colt's Crisis*. I'm curious to know if you are any closer to making a decision," he said, referring to his boss's still unresolved nomination for secretary of defense.

"As a matter of fact, I am, Eric," said the president. "Let's move forward and officially nominate Garrett. I like how he handled that mess in Korea, and the press like him. After he gets back from the Pacific, I'll make the announcement. He'll have to step down temporarily while he goes through the Senate confirmation process, so I'll appoint Steve Holmes as acting SECDEF until Colt's confirmed."

The well-prepared chief of staff stepped forward and handed the president two folders. "I've gone ahead and prepared both press releases for your review, sir."

Harrison opened the folders and smiled as he signed the two documents. "Good guess, Mr. Painter."

Eric Painter pretended to ignore the president's compliment and continued on with their dialogue. "I have a suggestion about *Lieutenant* Garrett, sir. He is considered quite the hero right now, and the Navy is planning to award him with another Distinguished Flying Cross for saving that aircraft a few days ago. Why don't we fly him back here, and you personally present the award to him in the Oval Office? The optics would be beautiful: You pin on the medal while his father — the newest member of your cabinet — beams with pride. What do you think?"

"I think this idea didn't just occur to you. I'll see what the communications team thinks about it. Is there anything else?"

"Well, yes," Eric replied. "You heard Lieutenant Garrett's comment on TV that he'd like to be assigned to test pilot school. I would think that's something we could make happen. You could announce it when you present the medal, and even comment that the late Secretary O'Kane had attended the same program!"

The president walked over to the South-facing windows and admired the well-manicured gardens outside. "I like that, Eric. Okay, draft a message to Colt Garrett and let him know I will be formally nominating him soon after he returns from the Pacific. And let Steve Holmes know right away about his acting

343

appointment. Get the secretary of the Navy on the phone so Lieutenant Garrett can get his dream job. Did I miss anything?"

"No, I think that's everything, sir. Thank you, sir."

Commanding Officer's Stateroom, VAQ-132 Scorpions, the Reagan

"Enter!" said Commander Tom Robinson when he heard the knock on his stateroom door. Lieutenant Dan Garrett opened the door and stepped inside.

"You wanted to see me, sir?"

"Take a seat, Dan."

The senior naval officer sat behind his desk and looked at the young aviator. "Dan, I wanted you to know that I've recommended you for your second Distinguished Flying Cross, and both Captain Chavez and Captain Solari have endorsed it. That was one fine display of airmanship, and I'm proud to have you serving in this squadron."

Dan was touched by the skipper's sincerity. "Thank you, sir, I really appreciate that. Receiving a DFC is a huge honor, but we both know I was just trying to save my ass, and my dad's."

"But that doesn't detract at all from how you performed. You're an exceptional aviator. And it appears I'm not the only one who thinks so. Take a look at this."

The skipper handed Dan a naval message and gave him a minute to realize, and absorb what it was. Dan took his time reading the words, but finally raised his eyes and looked blankly at his commanding officer.

Guessing correctly that it would help if Dan heard it

spoken out loud: Tom began, "It's message from the Chief of Naval Operations, inviting you to submit an application package for Navy Test Pilot School. You'll receive a waiver from the requirement for an engineering degree. The next selection board meets in May, and if you're selected, you'll receive orders for four months of training in the T-6 and T-28 before reporting to Pax River for the year-long program. After that, you can expect to serve a three-year tour as a test pilot." Tom stopped and took a breath before extending his hand. "Congratulations, Dan! You deserve this!"

Dan Garrett silently read the message again and then handed the document back to Commander Robinson. "Sir, what do you think happened? Did *you* have anything to do with this?"

"Dan, if you think a squadron C.O. has that kind of juice, you must know something I don't know. But I did hear some back-channel gouge that somebody in a big white house in Washington D.C. *may* have seen your news interview with Carissa Curtis, and that same person *may* have suggested to SECNAV that he'd like to see your name on the selection list. If you ask me, I'd say you need to thank Ms. Curtis!"

"Thanks, skipper! I'll track her down right now," Dan yelled as he ran through the skipper's door into the passageway in pursuit of the TV reporter.

Sprinting down the long corridor, still in a daze, Dan suddenly and clumsily collided with Ensign Rebecca Clarke, causing both of them to tumble to the deck. Helping her to her feet, an embarrassed Dan apologized, "That was all my fault. I'm so sorry! Are you okay?" Rebecca brushed her hair back and then looked up to find the tall, good-looking pilot everyone on the ship had been talking about. "Hey, you're that guy!" she said. "You're the one who landed Growler 505 yesterday! I heard Captain Solari on the bridge saying it was the best piece of airmanship she had ever seen. And wait — I saw you on the news, too! Everybody is talking about you!" Rebecca gushed.

It took Dan a moment to believe his good luck. This was the striking young ensign he had been admiring from afar since she first reported onboard the *Reagan*. He wanted desperately to talk with her, but he needed to find Carissa to thank her for what she had done for his career.

"Why, thanks, Ensign Clarke," said Dan, reading her name badge. "Do you have a first name?"

"It's Rebecca, Rebecca Clarke," she said, offering her hand. "I work in combat systems. And you're an aviator in VAQ-132?"

"That's right, and my name's Dan. You have no idea how much I'd like to talk more, but I have to go find someone. When do you get off watch?"

"I have a bridge watch until 20:00. How about meeting up in the gym at 21:00?"

As Rebecca turned to head down the passageway, Dan closely watched her for a moment, thinking *Awesome!*

Defense Secretary Cabin, the Reagan

"It appears I'll be replaced as acting secretary after we get back to Washington," said Colt as he unemotionally handed the president's written message to Lenny Wilson. "It was fun while it lasted?" he added, purposely making it sound like a question.

Lenny quickly read the message, then looked up at Colt. "I think you've missed the point, sir. The president says he plans to nominate you as *permanent* secretary, and that during your confirmation process, Steve Holmes will assume the acting role. Congratulations, sir! Well-deserved!"

"Thanks, Lenny. I see this as the president's acknowledgment of the good work *we've* done out here. You've been a big part of it, every step of the way. I want you to know how much I appreciate all your help and counsel."

"I'm proud to be on the team, sir," Lenny replied, as he gathered some documents on the table.

"Are you all packed up, Lenny? Admiral Shaffer has just landed, and as soon as I get a chance to see him, we'll be boarding that Osprey and heading to Tokyo. We're going home!"

"I hear you, sir! And I just need to check on a couple of things with the staff before we leave." Lenny opened the cabin door, and standing there waiting were Anna DeSantis and Kevin Orr.

"Come in!" said Colt. "Please, have a seat!"

The two NCIS special agents sat on the sofa facing Colt Garrett's desk. "Mr. Secretary," Anna said, "I understand you'll be leaving soon and flying back to Tokyo, but I need to remain here and help Special Agent Orr with Commander Abram's charging documents. I'll contact the special agent in charge there to let him know you are coming. When you arrive at Yokota Air Force Base, Army CID officers will be responsible for your security and protection. I do want to say, sir, that it's been an honor leading your protection detail."

"Thank you, Special Agent DeSantis. And I want to thank both you and Special Agent Orr for the work you've done while I've been here. I hope it hasn't been too hard on the two of you, having to spend so much time together?"

Colt Garrett had an uncharacteristic twinkle in his eye, which made the two young agents squirm uncomfortably on the sofa. Colt continued. "I do have an interesting offer for both of you to consider. I've been talking with the secretaries of the Army and the Navy about initiating an inter-departmental exchange program, in which NCIS and CID agents spend tours working in each other's agencies. We suspect that both agencies could learn a great deal from each other. I'm wondering if you two might be interested in participating in a pilot program that would involve you in my protection detail on a longer-term basis?"

Kevin glanced quickly at Anna. "Uh, Mr. Secretary, I think we'd be incredibly *honored* to work on your detail! We both have a lot we can learn, and a lot we can bring to this opportunity."

Colt stood up and beamed. "Outstanding! You'll receive orders in a few days to initiate the transfer. And believe me, I'll feel better knowing you two will have my back." Both agents shook Colt's hand, waved goodbye, and left the cabin. As they walked together down the passageway, Anna said, "Do you think you can handle reporting to me, Kevin? I mean, I *am* senior to you!"

Kevin smiled. "In your dreams, *very* Special Agent DeSantis!"

Before Colt could get back to his desk to tie up some last-minute loose ends, the 7th Fleet Commander suddenly showed up in his doorway. "Good morning, Mr. Secretary! May I enter?"

"Admiral Shaffer! You made it! Please come in!"

"First, my old friend, let me congratulate you on being appointed as acting defense secretary! The last time we spoke on the *Blueridge,* you were a mere undersecretary! And did I just hear a rumor that the president has decided to make it permanent?"

Colt laughed. "You must be well-connected! Is that why you flew out here this morning, to suck up to the new SECDEF?"

But the three-star admiral's expression changed as he sat down on the sofa. "Not entirely, Colt. I brought my deputy commander out here with me to relieve Joe Carlisle of the task force. His recent interview has caused quite a stir in Washington, and I've lost confidence in his ability to command. I'm relieving him for cause, and his Navy career is over. In fact, I'll be letting him know right after we're done here. Unfortunately for you, I'm also ordering him to fly off the ship with you today — sorry about that."

Having heard nothing that was much of a surprise, Colt said, "I suppose he'll start his working on his run for Congress. I suspect we haven't seen the last of him."

Vulture's Row, the Reagan

Dan Garrett opened the Pri-Fly door and stepped out onto Vulture's Row, where he found Carissa Curtis watching the flight deck crew prepare his dad's Osprey for launching. Sailors in purple-colored float coats were refueling the aircraft, while others were performing various tasks to prepare the plane for its flight to Tokyo.

"Carissa! There you are! I've been looking all over the ship for you!" said Dan as he went over to join her at the railing.

"I just love standing here and watching all the activity on the flight deck," said Carissa. "It's amazing how everyone knows exactly what to do; it's like an expertly choreographed ballet."

"True. It really is something, although I don't think about it much anymore," Dan replied. "The reason I was looking for you was to thank you for asking me in the interview about my plans for after this tour. Apparently, somebody important saw that broadcast, and I've just been advised that if I apply for test pilot school, I'll most likely be accepted. I really have you to thank for that."

Carissa faced Dan: "I'm happy for you! But I have to tell you that the idea to ask you that question actually came from the other Mr. Garrett."

"My dad suggested you ask me about my next tour? When did he do *that*?"

"After my interview with him. I think he wanted to find an indirect way to help you without using his high-profile position. He's really a wonderful man, and he really cares about you."

Dan said, "Thanks for letting me know, Carissa. I think I need to find the skipper right away," and he turned and left Vulture's Row.

The Flight Deck, the Reagan

Colt and Lenny stepped out from flight deck control and headed to the waiting Osprey finding eight Sailors standing in two rows of four at attention. Lenny stepped aside, and Colt walked through the two ranks of Sailors. The ship's bell rang eight times and the topside loudspeaker proclaimed "DEFENSE, DEPARTING" as the boatswain piped the side and the last 32 measures of Sousa's "Stars and Stripes Forever" played over the ship's loudspeaker, formally honoring the United States Secretary of Defense.

Colt continued up the Osprey's ramp, stepped inside, finding his assigned seat on the left, between Lenny Wilson and a stoic

Admiral Carlisle. Colt began getting himself comfortable for the flight when he heard footsteps running up the ramp. When he glanced toward the ramp, Colt was surprised to see his son standing there.

"The skipper said I could ride back to Tokyo with you!" Dan said, beaming and filled with pride and excitement.

"Oh, Dan! That's great! Welcome aboard!" Turning to Admiral Carlisle, Colt said, "Joe, would you mind scooting down a seat so I can sit next to my son?"

As the Osprey lifted off the flight deck and started its transition to conventional flight, its copilot and four passengers were startled by the unexpected sound of a gun being fired every five seconds. The Osprey's pilot smiled and said into her intercom, "Don't worry, gentlemen, that's just the *Reagan* firing a 19-gun salute honoring the Secretary of Defense!"

Yokota Air Force Base, Japan

Lieutenant General Mathew Williams stood at attention as the Navy Osprey taxied to a full stop at the Air Mobility Command passenger terminal. As Commander, U.S. Forces Japan, the three-star general had waited to officially greet the secretary of defense to Yokota Air Force Base. He rendered a crisp salute as Colt Garrett stepped down the Osprey's ramp, accompanied by three other people, one in a business suit, one in a green flight suit, and another in the uniform of a Navy Rear Admiral.

"Welcome to Yokota, Mr. Secretary," said General Williams as they shook hands.

"Thank you, General, very pleased to be here, although I

believe Mr. Wilson and I will be heading soon to Washington. May I introduce Rear Admiral Carlisle and my son, Lieutenant Garrett?"

General Williams shook the two Naval officers' hands and said, "Mr. Secretary, may I present Chief Warrant Officer and Supervisory Special Agent Glenn Carpenter? He and his Army CID team will now be providing your personal protection."

"Nice seeing you again, Special Agent Carpenter," said Colt with a smile as he shook Carpenter's hand. "I'll try not to give you too much trouble."

"And Mr. Secretary, this is Colonel Jim Taylor, who is the mission commander of the E-4B over there. He and his crew will be flying you back to Washington in a few minutes."

Colt turned to look at the large Boeing 747-200 derivative, also known as Nightwatch. He quietly said to Lenny, "It looks like you'll be able to sleep in a bed on the way home!" Colt turned back to Jim Taylor. "Colonel, I'll need a phone link as soon as we board, and I may be needing to make a brief stopover in Seattle. I'll know after I make that phone call. Is that going to be possible?"

"No problem, sir. On Nightwatch, you can talk with anyone in the world. And my flight plan has us stopping to refuel at Joint Base Lewis McChord, an hour south of Seattle. We could stop for as long as you need. Would that work, sir?"

"That will work perfectly, Colonel. Just one more request." Colt handed the colonel a small plastic case. "I'd like to bring this pistol back to D.C. with me. Is there any problem with that?" When Colonel Taylor saw the distressed look on General Williams' face, an idea occurred to him. "Sir," he said to Colt, "it's against Air Force regs to transport a personal firearm. However, if you were to give me a written note stating the Secretary of Defense is authorized to transport the firearm, then I think we'd be okay!"

Colonel noticed a look of relief on General William's face as Lenny produced a pad of yellow paper and quickly penned a note for the secretary's signature. Colt handed the signed note to Colonel Taylor and said, "I think we're going to get along very well, Colonel!"

Dan walked with his father across the tarmac toward the huge Nightwatch aircraft and paused at the bottom of the plane's stairwell. "Dad, I think this is as far as I can go. I just wanted to say thanks. I have a good chance of getting into test pilot school, and I suspect you have something to do with that. So, I just want you to know I really appreciate it — and you."

Colt grasped his son's extended hand and then pulled him into a hug —a genuine, loving embrace between a proud father and a grateful son.

Day Fourteen

Bus 23, Incheon, South Korea

Kang Ji-woo sat quietly on the city bus going from Incheon to Wolmi Island, where she would take the next step in her escape from South Korea. The train ride from Seoul to Incheon had been uneventful, although the crowds made it difficult to determine if she was under surveillance. After arriving in Incheon, Ji-woo spent a few hours pretending to shop in the busy port city, looking in store windows in an attempt to spot anyone following her. She eventually arrived at the Incheon bus station and boarded bus 23 for the short ride to Wolmi Island.

She had received an urgent message in the dry cleaning bag from Mr. Yi that she must leave Seoul immediately and return to North Korea. The original plan was for her to depart the city in two days, but then she received a second communication instructing her to leave a day earlier, citing the arrest and interrogation of Colonel Chang as the reason for the accelerated schedule. Ji-woo was surprised at her sadness upon hearing of Chang's torture. Although he was the target of her intelligence operation, she had developed a fondness for the man whose bed she had shared for the past several months. She certainly didn't wish him any harm.

The small island she was heading toward was not much more than an attraction for local fishermen, allowing them to either fish from the bank or — for those who could afford it — hire a fishing charter into Kyonggi Bay. And Ji-woo certainly could afford it, with the equivalent of $100,000 U.S. in Korean won tucked into her small rolling suitcase. The money had been hidden in Colonel Chang's apartment behind a sofa and under the floorboards, but she had moved it and a variety of passports when she thought she detected surveillance over the weekend.

Wolmi Island, South Korea

As she had been instructed to, Ji-woo got off the bus from Incheon and walked to Cultural Street, where she found a small marina with several piers of fishing boats for hire. Walking down the pier marked #3, she pulled her suitcase along the wooden planks until she came to a small trawler with the name *Seonchang-3* painted on the bow.

"Hello? Is anyone here?" she called from the pier. The sun had just set, and the small boat appeared dark, with no lights showing.

"Yes, I'm coming," said an older man dressed in dark woolen trousers and a green cotton jacket. "What can I do for you, miss?"

Ji-woo smiled and said, "I need to hire you to take me out into the bay to meet my father's yacht. He would have come into the harbor, but certain misunderstandings with the local police prevent him from docking at Wolmi at this time. You will be well paid for your service."

She opened her wallet and handed the old captain a small stack of bills, which he immediately stuffed into his jacket pocket. Looking around briefly, the captain asked, "Where exactly are you to meet your father's yacht?"

Ji-woo passed the captain a small piece of paper and said, "My father said to give these coordinates to you, and that you could enter them into your navigation system. Can you do that?"

He peered at the series of numbers on the piece of paper and said, "Yes, this is only about an hour's ride into the bay. Can I help you with your bag?"

Ji-woo picked up the bag and said, "No, thank you, I can manage quite well."

Kyonggi Bay, South Korea

Once loaded, the small fishing trawler's diesel engine propelled it slowly out into the bay, as the captain followed a course shown as a bright green line on his navigation screen. Ji-woo breathed a sigh of relief as the boat cleared the harbor's breakwater and headed out into the darkness. She was pleased with her first undercover mission, and despite the misfortune that befell poor Colonel Chang, Ji-woo was proud of what she had accomplished. She looked forward to her return to Pyongyang and to her next assignment.

An hour later, still deep in her thoughts of returning to North Korea, Ji-woo was surprised when the boat's captain said, "I believe we are here, but I don't see any yacht!" Ji-woo opened the wheelhouse door and looked to the east. She removed a small LED flashlight from her coat pocket, turned on the power switch, and pointed the light toward the horizon. The captain watched with interest as the young woman sent a series of long and short flashes of light into the night. He was even more surprised when someone flashed a light back in response.

"What's going on?" he asked. "Are you signaling your father?"

She returned the flashlight to her pocket, saying, "Yes, Father is very careful and a bit dramatic. A small boat will arrive shortly to take me to his yacht."

Within a few minutes, Ji-woo and the boat's captain could hear the sound of an outboard motor when a black, inflatable rubber boat appeared. As the small boat gently bumped the fishing boat's starboard side, two men dressed in black stepped aboard the fishing trawler while two others remained seated in the rubber boat.

One of the men nodded to Ji-woo as she handed him her suitcase. She turned to the fishing boat captain. "Thank you for your trouble. Please accept this as a token of my appreciation. Please do not mention taking me out here to anyone."

She handed the small man a good-sized stack of currency before climbing down into the inflatable boat, which immediately sped away and into the darkness. The mystified trawler captain returned to his wheelhouse and shifted the engine into gear as he conned his boat back to the marina.

The four men in the inflatable boat remained silent during the trip out to sea, and that was fine with Ji-woo, who was relieved she didn't have to make conversation. The boat suddenly stopped as one of the men turned on a flashlight and began sending the same set of flashes to the east that Ji-woo had used to communicate with the inflatable boat. She was surprised when a submarine's periscope first appeared just ahead of the boat, and then as the sub continued to surface until its decks were just awash. The inflatable boat approached the submarine, and Ji-woo was quickly boosted up its wet sides, into a group of crewmen who hustled her through an open hatch in the sail and then down a steep ladder into the submarine's pressure hull. She started to speak to a man who appeared to be the sub's captain, but he motioned her to be silent while his crew stowed the inflatable and prepared the submarine to dive.

Ji-woo satisfied herself for a short while by watching the preparations for diving beneath the sea. Having seen enough, she stepped over to the small table in the submarine's cramped control room to help herself to a cup of tea. Finally, retiring to a small chair, Ji-woo was joined by a distinguished-looking man in an expensive suit.

"Good evening Kang Ji-woo," said the man. "I am sorry to give you bad news, but you will not be going back to Pyongyang any time soon. I am Director Pang of South Korea's National Intelligence Service, and you and I are about to get acquainted. Welcome aboard the *Hong Beomdo*, the newest submarine in South Korea's Navy!"

A shocked Ji-woo watched as two well-built sailors moved forward and grabbed her suitcase. She glanced around the submarine's cramped control room to see the captain and his South Korean crew smiling at her. How could this be happening?

South Korea's intelligence chief sat down next to Ji-woo, took a sip from his teacup, and continued. "You are no doubt surprised to find yourself as my guest tonight. You have been under surveillance for some time and, in fact, even the bundles of currency in your suitcase have small electronic devices inserted in them so we merely had to follow the money to track your whereabouts. Once we intercepted the order you received to rendezvous with one of North Korea's submarines, we simply sent you another message instructing you to leave a day earlier, and this time, we sent one of our submarines instead. I suspect that tomorrow night, your friends will arrive at this precise location with anticipation to meet you, but they will be surprised to find our naval forces waiting for them instead. All in all, it is a rather elegant plan, do you not agree?"

Russian Military Intelligence HQ, Khodinka Airfield, Moscow, the Russian Federation

"Director Orlov, what a pleasure to hear from you, and twice within one week! I hope you continue to have good health?" General Korobov knew when his assistant said Director Orlov was on the line, that the Kremlin was aware of his second failed attempt to assassinate the American secretary of defense. He also knew that Orlov might be using the incident to affect a power shift within the intelligence community.

"General Korobov, my health is as good as it was when we last spoke, but how kind of you to ask. I am calling to offer my condolences to you regarding the challenges you are experiencing in the western Pacific. If you recall, I had hoped that you would accept my offer of assistance. Now that your second attempt to eliminate Colton Garrett has gone nowhere, our president has asked me to lead an effort that utilizes all of our resources to produce a more positive outcome to the challenges created by this enemy of Russia."

Korobov knew Orlov would try to use the Garrett incident against the GRU. He was astounded, however, at Orlov's audacity in assuming control of the entire operation and positioning himself in a more powerful role. And now that the Russian president had apparently endorsed Orlov's move to consolidate power, Korobov felt he needed to be exceptionally careful with what he said next.

"Of course, the GRU is most willing to participate in any endeavor to remove Mr. Garrett," said Korobov, "and I believe I have the asset already in place and prepared to make another attempt, should that be the desired course of action."

The telephone line went silent, until Director Orlov said, "You say you have another operative in a position to remove Colton Garrett? Who might that be, General?"

General Korobov pushed his chair back, lifted his highly polished boots onto his desk, and simply smiled. "I believe you are about to be impressed, Director!"

FBI Safe House, 222 Fort Hill Road, Bainbridge Island, Washington

FBI Special Agent in Charge Clay Taylor was an avid World War II history buff, and that had definitely influenced his decision to lease the old brick residence and turn it into an FBI safe house. Situated on the south end of Bainbridge Island and across the street from Fort Ward, the safe house existed under the plausible cover story that it was a vacation rental for tourists. Neighbors had occasionally noticed guests staying there for several days, and then weeks would go by without any visitors at all. It seemed to the surrounding homeowners that the owners of the old house, who were rumored to be software millionaires from Seattle, didn't really care if it got rented out or not. Besides, it always seemed to be unavailable when anyone tried to book a reservation. Most just assumed the property had been acquired for investment purposes.

In the late 1930s, the U.S. Navy discovered that Fort Ward was an exceptional location to intercept communications from the

Far East. They took over the fort from the Army and developed *Station S* as a listening post, manned 24 hours a day, seven days a week. Large antennas were erected on the former military parade ground, which, as Clay Taylor noted with amusement, was now a city park. But Clay knew that the most interesting fact about the fort was that on December 7, 1941, the Navy facility intercepted a message from Japan about breaking off negotiations with the United States, and they forwarded the message to Washington. Unfortunately, administrative errors prevented the message from getting into the right hands until after the Japanese had already attacked Pearl Harbor.

Clay walked into what had once been a small bedroom in the house and looked through a large, one-way mirror into the adjoining room, where an espionage suspect, Sara Olson, was seated at a table and handcuffed to a steel ring bolted to the table's center. The alleged Russian GRU officer appeared to be reasonably calm, given what she had just experienced.

A few hours earlier, Sara had been walking on a dimly lit side street in Bremerton on her way home to her apartment, when she found herself being forcefully shoved into a delivery van by people whose faces she could not see, then blindfolded, bound, and gagged. After riding for several hours in the back of the van, including crossing a bridge of some type, the van stopped, and she was roughly pulled out of the vehicle and led inside a building, into the room where she now was securely restrained. The woman who removed the gag and blindfold had said nothing, despite Sara's continued and desperate pleading to be set free. She was given food and water, and she was allowed to use the bathroom, but only under the close observation of two guards.

Since being forced into the van, Sara had tried to determine the identity of her abductors. *If they are Americans,* she thought, *why did they not take me to a federal detention facility?* She continued to wonder why she had been taken at all when the door to her interrogation room opened and to reveal the familiar face of Sean, the homeless man from the café she had previously dubbed "Mr. Trench." Sean came in and sat down in the chair across the table from her.

"Good evening, Sara. Or do you prefer Captain Yelena Denisovna Ivanova of Russian Military Intelligence?"

"What?" she responded emphatically. "I have no idea what you're talking about!"

"I'm Special Agent Sean Thomas, with the United States Federal Bureau of Investigation," he continued, "and of course, we have met before." He offered his credentials: a black leather wallet with an FBI identification card and the famous FBI shield. Sara glared at the man whom she had seen almost daily at the café in Bremerton. His appearance was dramatically different now. His beard was gone, and his worn, smelly clothes were replaced with a crisply pressed white shirt, maroon necktie, and a navy blue wool suit.

"I apologize for the deception," he said, "but considering your own, we're even. Is it okay if I call you Sara? It's easier for me to pronounce than your Russian name."

"What? My Russian name? What in the world are you even talking about? I'm Sara Olson, the barista in Bremerton. You and I *have* talked before, but you must have me mixed up with someone else!"

The experienced counterintelligence agent began placing a series of documents in front of Sara detailing the espionage case the FBI had long been developing on her and her activities. Nine hours of denial later, when Special Agent Thomas had left the room to take a break, Sara decided to attempt another tactic. She looked over her shoulder and spoke directly to the large mirror on the opposite wall. "Yes, I am Yelena Denisovna Ivanova, and I formally request that you contact the Russian consulate in San Francisco and inform them I am being held here against my will."

The cheers coming from Sean and his colleagues, who were gathered in the adjacent, sound-proof observation room, signaled that the interrogation had achieved a major objective with Sara's admission of her real identity. *It's time to move to the next phase*, Sean thought to himself as he returned to the interrogation room. He explained to Sara that because she was in the country illegally, the FBI had no obligation to notify the Russian consulate of her predicament. "In fact," he added, "I suspect that if your consulate became aware that you were in our custody, they would first, disallow your existence and then, if we eventually released you, they would send you back to Russia to be interrogated and likely severely punished — or worse. You would certainly never be trusted again."

Sara looked down at her hands and asked quietly, "What are my options?"

"Well, that's where I actually have some good news for you, Sara. I've been authorized to offer you a new life. A new name, new city, new job, and a new identity. A whole new start. You would have to agree to spend at least a year cooperating with the FBI and other agencies, revealing everything you can about the Russians' selection, recruitment, training, tradecraft, communications, and security protocols. In short, everything you know. You also would have to agree to several behavioral evaluations and multiple polygraphs, but once we believed we had everything you could tell us, we would relocate you to somewhere safe, where you would be unknown and could start your life over."

"Why am I being offered this opportunity?" Sara asked.

"Because we have closely observed you for several months, and we believe you're worth the risk. Based on the most recent conversation you and I had at the café, we decided to give you a chance at another life, if you're willing to fully cooperate." As Sean continued to try convincing Sara that she didn't have another option, Clay had meals brought in for them. Finally, Sara agreed to his terms. "But there is a problem," she said. "I will never really be safe as long as the GRU thinks I'm still alive. They will never give up until they are sure I am dead."

Sean gathered up the national security agreements Sara had just signed. "Yes, we know that, and we're working on it."

Still sitting in the observation room next door, Clay Taylor picked up his cell phone and called his deputy at the Seattle Field Office. "Juan, this is Clay. Don't you know someone in the coroner's office? We're going to need a female cadaver right away!"

Bremerton National Airport, Bremerton, Washington

GRU Colonel Dimitri Petrov was careful to keep his small sedan under the posted speed limit so as not to be stopped by the police as he took Washington State Route 3 to the airport. Just twelve hours earlier, he had contacted the small air charter company in Seattle to request a flight from Bremerton to Vancouver, Canada. There, he intended to change identities and then board a commercial flight to Mexico City, where he could easily disappear.

After the second attempt to assassinate Colton Garrett had failed, Petrov feared it would only be a matter of time before the Americans discovered his role in the operation and his true identity. He executed his escape plan, which included sending a message to Sara to meet him today at the Bremerton National Airport to leave the country with him. He wasn't surprised when Sara didn't respond to his note. He assumed she had already gone to ground and was no longer in a position to communicate.

Petrov took a left turn off Route 3 and arrived at Bremerton's airport to find a parking space for his Honda right next to the small passenger terminal. He grabbed his backpack from the passenger seat, locked the car, and walked the short distance to the terminal, where he was greeted inside by a young man wearing a white shirt with the four stripes of an airline pilot.

"Mr. Jordan? I'm Nate Peterson, and I'll be flying you to Vancouver today. Is that all the luggage you have?"

"It's *Professor* Jordan, and yes, I have only this backpack. I'm just staying overnight and then meeting a colleague to drive back to Seattle together. Has my associate, Ms. Olson, arrived yet?"

The young airline captain answered, "Not yet, but that's not a problem. This is your charter, so we're flexible. I can wait for an hour, and then I'd just have to call the office for approval to delay any longer. But right now, I need to go visit air operations to check the weather."

As the pilot walked away, Colonel Petrov sat down in one of the worn, vinyl chairs in the small waiting area. He was growing concerned at Sara's absence, and he started to wonder if American counterintelligence was already on his trail. After a casual glance around the sleepy passenger terminal and through the dirty windows at the quiet parking lot outside, Petrov saw no evidence of unusual activity, so he opened his small paperback novel to start a new chapter.

Petrov looked up when the terminal door opened to two deputies from the Kitsap County Sheriff's Department. Scanning the passenger terminal, they went over and sat down in the terminal's small coffee shop at the end of the room. Soon, they were joined by another officer, this time a tall man, wearing the blue uniform of the Washington State Patrol. Petrov watched as the trooper scanned the room, just as the deputies had, before sitting down with them in the coffee shop.

"Professor Jordan, have you heard from Ms. Olson yet?" his charter pilot came over and asked him. "I'm just wondering if I should contact the company about delaying the flight."

Petrov looked at his watch and then at the group of law enforcement officers drinking coffee. "It appears that Ms. Olson will not be joining me today," he said. "In fact, I'm ready to depart as soon as we can."

"Great. Just let me check your passport and get you through security screening, and we can be on our way."

The pilot led Petrov through a hallway to a TSA checkpoint, where he placed his passenger's backpack on the conveyor belt that led into an x-ray machine. The metal detector sounded an alarm as Petrov tried to walk through. The TSA officer motioned Petrov over to the side and said, "Sorry, sir, I'll need to wand you."

The officer proceeded to pass a security wand over Petrov's body, and it, too, beeped several times.

"Sir, do I have your permission to pat you down?" the TSA

officer inquired.

"Do I have a choice?" Petrov asked with slight annoyance.

The TSA officer thoroughly patted down Petrov's body. "Thank you, sir! You should be good to go now."

Petrov picked up his backpack and walked through the terminal doorway that opened onto the tarmac toward the waiting business jet, where his young pilot stood on the ground next to the plane's boarding stairs.

"Sorry about that, Professor Jordan. They make us go through that same process all the time. Okay, just follow me."

The pilot led Petrov up the stairs of the small eight-seater, then stepped aside at the plane's door to allow his passenger to enter the cabin. Typical in many planes of this size, the cabin had four single passenger seats on each side of a narrow center aisle. Petrov tossed his backpack onto one of the second-row seats, sank happily into the seat opposite it, and reached into his back pocket for his paperback. He had waited a long time for this moment. He savored the idea of having his own flight and his own space. *No one I have to make conversation with*, he thought with relish.

He was curious, therefore, when he looked out the window a few minutes later to see three men walking across the tarmac toward his plane. His bewilderment turned to mild apprehension as the men approached the stairs to the plane and began to climb them. *They must be mechanics,* he thought. *The charter company would never add passengers onto a privately chartered flight. They must be boarding to speak with the pilot.* But rather than turning left into the cockpit to confer with the pilot, the three men turned right into the passenger cabin.

"This is a private charter, gentlemen," Petrov said, loudly and authoritatively. You must be on the wrong plane." But despite his efforts to dissuade them, the men continued making their way into the seating area of the cabin. Two of them seated themselves in the two first-row seats, and the other, after moving Petrov's backpack out of the way, took the seat across the aisle from him. None of them had said a word.

Petrov saw that he was both surrounded and outnumbered, and he had a sudden realization that these men might not have boarded his plane by mistake. "Hey, Nate!" he called to the pilot, "What the hell's going on? I paid for a private chartered flight!"

But when the pilot didn't respond or appear, Petrov knew something was wrong. With an instant sense of discomfort, he glanced quickly around the cabin, hoping he might be able to spot an easy way to get off the plane to flee. But the only exit was the one the men had just entered through. *Whoever they are*, he thought, *they cannot stop me if I decide I want to get off the plane. This is still my charter.* But as he considered standing up from his seat, a fourth man stepped inside the cabin.

This time, the man was familiar—very familiar, in fact. The last time Petrov had seen him was during a gun battle on the border between Spain and Gibraltar decades ago. The man was much older, now, but seemed to be in good health despite having just survived two failed assassination attempts. This was the man who was supposed to be dead by now.

"Hello, Colonel Petrov," said Colt Garrett. "I apologize, as it appears I may be interrupting your travel plans."

"Secretary Garrett," Petrov replied, as though nothing were wrong. "This is, indeed, an honor. Congratulations on your new appointment! Come, find a seat so we can catch up. It has been a long time, hasn't it?"

Colt stood where he was, slightly amused by Petrov's disingenuous pleasantries. "I'm afraid I haven't got time to chat as I have some travel plans of my own," he said, gesturing toward the U.S. Army Blackhawk helicopter that was being fueled out on the tarmac. "But first, you and I have some business to discuss. You know why I'm here, do you not?"

"I believe I do," said Petrov, as the entire picture became clear to him. He suddenly knew exactly what Colt Garrett was there to do. "I am sure you are aware that I was ordered by Moscow to eliminate you to prevent your harsh, anti-Russian policies from hurting my country. It was a great disappointment for us that our attempts did not succeed." Petrov paused for a moment to let his last statement sink in. "So, what is next for me now, Garrett? A dramatic arrest at the airport? A lengthy and pointless interrogation with pictures splashed across the newspaper? Must we really go through all that when we both know these incidents involving intelligence officers always just end in an exchange of prisoners?"

"Not this time, Dimitri. There will be no typical prisoner exchange or media interviews, not with everything we now know of your history of deceit, espionage, and murder. And with your recent attempt on my son's life, you crossed a line. You belong to us now. As we speak, your Honda is being driven to Port Angeles, where it will be parked across the street from the ferry terminal. In the back seat is the dead body of Sara Olson with a bullet in her chest and a pistol beside her with your fingerprints on it. Security cameras will show that a man closely fitting your description exited your car and boarded the ferry bound for Victoria, Canada. The same man, carrying your travel documents, will pass through Canadian immigration and customs control, then never be seen again. To the rest of the world, you will no longer exist."

"You bastard!" Petrov seethed. "You had Sara killed?" He attempted to get up, but the men surrounding him suddenly stood up and pushed him forcefully back into his seat. "Relax, Colonel," Colt said. "You won't be leaving this plane for several hours. And your next stop will be a facility which we maintain just to interview and hold animals like you. I don't believe you will ever see the sky again, and I certainly doubt you will be missed by anyone."

Colt turned to leave the plane, but Petrov shouted after him, "You can't do this to me, Garrett! You won't get away with this! Who do you think you are??!!"

Colt took a deep breath, turned back to face an enraged Petrov, and said, calmly, "I'm sorry, Dimitri, but I just did . . . oh, yes I will . . . and I know *exactly* who I am."

And with that, Colt Garrett, United States Secretary of Defense, exited the plane, stepped down the stairs, and walked to the waiting Blackhawk.

THE END

About the author

Captain Tom Carroll served thirty years combined active duty and reserve service in the United States Navy, specializing in Special Intelligence and Surface Warfare. He owns an information technology firm in Olympia, Washington, where he lives with his wife.

This book was cleared for public release by the United States Department of Defense's office of prepublication and security review on October 26, 2020.

Made in the USA
Monee, IL
18 August 2021